The Greatest
Russian Stories of
CRIME AND
SUSPENSE

The Greatest
Russian Stories of
CRIME AND
SUSPENSE

EDITED BY

OTTO PENZLER

PEGASUS CRIME

NEW YORK LONDON

THE GREATEST RUSSIAN STORIES OF CRIME AND SUSPENSE

Pegasus Books LLC
80 Broad Street, 5th Floor
New York, NY 10004

First Pegasus Books cloth edition 2010
First Pegasus Books trade paperback edition 2012

Interior design by Maria Fernandez

Library of Congress Cataloging-in-Publication Data is available.

ISBN: 978-1-60598-266-3

10 9 8 7 6 5 4 3 2 1

Distributed by W. W. Norton & Company, Inc.
www.pegasusbooks.us

For Al Silverman
Gentleman, Editor Emeritus,
Respected and Cherished Friend

CONTENTS

OTTO PENZLER

INTRODUCTION

W hen most of us think of Russian literature, we think of the great,
sprawling novels of the nineteenth century by such masters as Leo
Tolstoy and Fyodor Dostoevsky, and the dark hopelessness of the
giants of drama and the short story. We rarely associate Russian literature
with the mystery story as we know it in the West—and we are right not
to do so.

It is appropriate to the point of obviousness to recognize that the
detective story cannot flourish in a non-democratic society. The chief
protagonist in a detective story is a hero: the person who will right the
wrongs perpetrated by a criminal. This is possible only in a society in
which the rule of law matters, and it must matter to all strata of that
society. If a government is corrupt, or dictatorial, its functionaries are, by
definition, primarily focused on their own interests or in those of the
government that employs them. Self-preservation, advancement and
maintenance of the status quo transcends all other desires of politicians,
the police, state militia and military forces in governments in which the
state is superior to the individual.

The very notion of Russian detective fiction is oxymoronic, as it is a
country whose citizens seldom have enjoyed individual freedom.
Sinking from the oppression of the czarist regime to the horrors of the
Communist police state, Russia was in no position to offer fictional

police officers as the heros of mystery stories, as they were more likely than ordinary citizens to be the criminals and persecutors.

Russian crime and suspense fiction is, therefore, inevitably quite different from the Sherlock Holmes, Agatha Christie and Raymond Chandler novels and short stories of England and the United States that leap to mind when we think of mystery fiction. Seldom do Russian stories involve the traditional format of a criminal activity, usually murder, committed by an unknown villain, with a detective—whether an official member of the police department, a private eye, or an amateur sleuth—called in to solve the crime, using observation and deduction.

There is a pervasive darkness to Russian crime stories that rivals the relatively new fiction genre that is often termed *noir.* The attitude of many characters often may be summarized as: Well, what can we do? Dream sequences, ghostly apparitions, supernatural occurrences, illogical choices and unresolved mysteries abound in Russian stories, which are not merely unlike Western detective fiction but are antithetical to its very definition: crimes are abnormal, anti-social actions for which punishment is the just reward and a representative of society will serve it by employing rational methodology to identify and capture criminals.

Psychological elements produce the resolution of such early Russian crime fiction as Dostoevsky's *Crime and Punishment* and Tolstoy's "God Sees the Truth, but Waits." Readers of traditional detective stories may be disappointed to learn that the question must be asked whether a crime has really been committed in such acclaimed works as Ivan Bunin's "The Gentleman from San Francisco" and Boris Sokoloff's "The Crime of Dr. Garine." Supernatural denouements would never pass muster in a novel by Dashiell Hammett or John Dickson Carr, but they are not rare in the stories of Alexander Pushkin and Nikolai Gogol.

In addition to producing very little in the way of classic detective fiction, Russian publishers during the time of the czar did not make translations of English and American mystery writers available to readers. It was only after the Bolshevik Revolution created a new government that the phenomenon of pulp fiction swept across the country. What these thousands of titles lacked in literary style, they made up in adventure and excitement. Much like their American counterparts of the 1920s, these cheaply produced paperbacks featured unrealistic, super-hero crime fighters who fearlessly engaged in combat with enemies of the state. The most frequent villains were fascists and capitalists who were brought to their knees, or to their end, by secret organizations of workers. The equivalent of American "dime novels," these hastily written potboilers sold in the tens of millions until Josef Stalin's Communist Party decided they were too Western, as well as anti-revolutionary. "Papa Joe" believed that the purpose of literature should be to glorify the party and the state, and that singling out individual heroes and their accomplishments was philosophically opposed to that tenet.

After Stalin's death, the Soviet government became somewhat more permissive, allowing native authors to work in the mystery genre while also translating some of the major Western writers, notably Christie, who became a best-seller. There was little similarity between the two schools, however. While Hercule Poirot could catch civil murderers by using his "little gray cells," Soviet protagonists were invariably KGB agents or policemen who battled evil Western capitalists or spies, and their corrupt Soviet pawns, whose major goal was to bring down the state.

Mystery literature has changed a great deal under the "new" Russia. Many English and American authors are routinely translated, and so are books from other Western countries. Among Russian writers, detective novels have flourished, and readers in the former U.S.S.R. have made them their preferred choice of reading matter. In a reader survey taken in 1995, more than 32% of men and 24% of women named "detektivy" as their favorite type of book.

Among contemporary Russian mystery writers, the most successful have been Julian Semyonov, whose more than fifty somewhat uninspired novels about stolid police and KGB agents sold more than 35,000,000 copies; three were translated into English: *Petrovka .38* (1965), *Tass is Authorized to Announce* (1987) and *Seventeen Moments of Spring* (1988). His popularity has been surpassed in more recent years by Victor Dotsenko, whose Rambo-like hero is a veteran of the Afghan wars and battles the mafia; Aleksandra Marinina, described by her publisher as "the Russian Agatha Christie," whose female protagonist, Anastasia Kamenskaya, is the ultimate armchair detective, solving crimes—like Nero Wolfe and the Old Man in the Corner—without leaving her office; Darya Dontsova, who brings an unusual element into a Russian crime novel–humor; and Boris Akunin, a serious writer who has bridged the two worlds of popular and literary fiction, producing a dozen novels in the classic tradition of nineteenth century novels and who has been translated into many languages, including English.

Like most readers, Russians find their escape from the difficulties of everyday life in literature that provides characters with whom they can identify. Since the fall of the Berlin wall and the destruction of the Iron Curtain, the oppression and seemingly random persecution of ordinary people by the Soviet government has been replaced by a criminal power structure heavily comprised of the former Communist Party officials who have merely switched allegiance from one victimizer to another. As ruthless criminal organizations flourished in the 1990s, as they continue to do today, writers gave the decent, hard-working reader a place of comfort. In popular crime novels, as the brutally powerful took advantage of their weaker neighbors, a hero emerged to do combat with those vile forces and emerge triumphant, providing a vicarious victory for the reader. While many of these adventure/crime novels lack literary merit, they have spurred great interest in and support of the mystery genre. Good defeating Evil. This cannot be a bad thing.

The Greatest
Russian Stories of
CRIME AND
SUSPENSE

BORIS AKUNIN

TABLE TALK, 1882

TRANSLATED FROM THE RUSSIAN BY ANTHONY OLCOTT

Grigory Shalvivich Chkhartishvili (1956–) took the pseudonym Boris Akunin as a tribute to Mikhail Bakunin (B.Akunin), the Russian anarchist, and the poet Anna Akhmatova, known as Akuna. Akunin is also the Japanese word for a bad guy. Born in Tbilisi in the Republic of Georgia (then a part of the Soviet Union), his family moved to Moscow in 1958, where he attended the University of Moscow. Although now known worldwide as a writer of distinguished mystery fiction, as well as one of the most widely read authors in Russia (he was named the Russian writer of the year in 2000), he was a magazine editor and is also a linguist, critic, essayist and translator of Japanese. Because he refused to join the Communist Party, he had little success and, turning 40, decided to try writing crime fiction.

In his first novel, *Azazel* (published in English as *The Winter Queen* in 2003), he introduced Erast Fandorin, who has appeared in about a dozen novels. Those which followed his debut and have been translated into English are *Murder on the Leviathan* (2004), *Turkish Gambit* (2005), *The Death of Achilles* (2005), *Special Assignments* (2007), *The State Counsellor* (2008), *She Lover of Death* (2009) and *The Coronation* (2009). Fandorin began his career as a detective in Czarist Russia in 1876 (the year Bakunin died) but the time-frame shifted quickly into the 20th century, so he is now about 50. He is brave, an accomplished kickboxer, and a dignified gentleman all at the same time, to which Akunin ascribes a large part of his popularity. He has also written several contemporary novels about Sister Pelagia, a crime-solving orthodox nun, including *Sister Pelagia and the White Bulldog* (2006), *Sister Pelagia and the Black Monk* (2007) and *Sister Pelagia and the Red Rooster* (2008).

"Table Talk, 1882" was first published in the Russian edition of *Playboy* in 2000; it was first published in English in the February 2004 issue of *Ellery Queen's Mystery Magazine* in a translation by Anthony Olcott.

A fter the coffee and liqueurs, the conversation turned to mystery. Deliberately not looking at her new guest—a collegiate assessor* and the season's most fashionable man—Lidia Nikolaevna Odintsova, hostess of the salon, remarked, "All Moscow is saying Bismarck must have poisoned poor Skobelev. Can it really be that society is to remain ignorant of the truth behind this horrible tragedy?"

The guest to whom Lidia Nikolaevna was treating her regulars today was Erast Petrovich Fandorin. He was maddeningly handsome, cloaked in an aura of mystery, and a bachelor besides. In order to inveigle Erast Petrovich into her salon, the hostess had had to bring off an extremely complex intrigue consisting of many parts—an undertaking at which she was an unsurpassed mistress.

Her sally was addressed to Arkhip Giatsintovich Mustafin, an old friend of the house. A man of fine mind, Mustafin caught Lidia Nikolaevna's intention at the first hint and, casting a sideways glance at the young collegiate assessor from beneath his ruddy and lashless eyelids,

---

* "Collegiate Assessor" was a civil title—one of fourteen that Peter the Great established when he reformed Russia's bureaucracy—indicating a high rank, the threshold at which someone attained life nobility. The equivalent rank in the army was major.

intoned, "Ah, but I've been told our White General* may have been destroyed by a fatal passion."

The others at the table held their breath, as it was rumored that Erast Petrovich, who until quite recently had served in the office of Moscow's Governor-General as an officer for special missions, had had a most direct relation to the investigation into events surrounding the death of the great commander. However, disappointment awaited the guests, for the handsome Fandorin listened politely to Arkhip Giatsin-tovich with an air suggesting that the words had nothing whatever to do with him.

This brought about the one situation that an experienced hostess could not permit—an awkward silence. Lidia Nikolaevna knew immediately what to do. Lowering her eyelids, she came to Mustafin's assistance. "This is so very like the mysterious disappearance of poor Polinka Karakina! Surely you recall that dreadful story, my friend?"

"How could I not?" Arkhip drawled, indicating his gratitude with a quick lift of an eyebrow.

Some of the party nodded as if also remembering, but most of the guests clearly knew nothing about Polinka Karakina. In addition, Mustafin had a reputation as a most exquisite raconteur, such that it would be no penance to hear even a familiar tale from his lips. So here Molly Sapegina, a charming young woman whose husband—such a tragedy—had been killed in Turkestan a year ago, asked with curiosity, "A mysterious disappearance? How interesting!"

Lidia Nikolaevna made as if to accommodate herself to her chair more comfortably, so also letting Mustafin know that she was passing nourishment of the table talk into his capable hands.

"Many of us, of course, still recall old Prince Lev Lvovich

---

* Skobelev: general whose militant pan-Slavic views and predictions of inevitable conflict with Germany got him in trouble with the government in St. Petersburg and resulted in his recall to the capital, where, in 1882, he died of heart failure.

Karakin,"—so Arkhip Giatsintovich began his tale. "He was a man of the old sort, a hero of the Hungarian campaign. He had no taste for the liberal vagaries of our late Tsar, and so retired to his lands outside Moscow, where he lived like a nabob of Hindi. He was fabulously wealthy, of an estate no longer found among the aristocracy of today.

"The prince had two daughters, Polinka and Anyuta. I beg you to note, no Frenchified *Pauline* or English *Annie*. The general held the very strictest of patriotic views. The girls were twins. Face, figure, voice, all were identical. They were not to be confused, however, for right here, on her right cheek, Anyuta had a birthmark. Lev Lvovich's wife had died in childbirth, and the prince did not marry again. He always said that it was a lot of fuss and he had no need—after all, there was no shortage of serving girls. And indeed, he had no shortage of serving girls, even after the emancipation. For, as I said, Lev Lvovich lived the life of a true nabob."

"For shame. Archie! Without vulgarity, if you please," Lidia Nikolaevna remonstrated with a stern smile, although she knew perfectly well that a good story is never hurt by "adding a little pepper," as the English say.

Mustafin pressed his palm to his breast in apology, then continued his tale. "Polinka and Anyuta were far from being horrors, but it would also be difficult to call them great beauties. However, as we all know, a dowry of millions is the best of cosmetics, so that in the season when they debuted, they produced something like a fever epidemic among the eligible bachelors of Moscow. But then the old prince took some sort of offense at our honored Governor-General and withdrew to his piney Sosnovka, never to leave the place again.

"Lev Lvovich was a heavyset fellow, short-winded and red-faced, a man prone to apoplexy, as they say, so there was reason to hope that the princesses' imprisonment would not last long. However, the years went on, Prince Karakin grew ever fatter, flying into ever more thunderous rages, and evinced no intention whatsoever of dying. The suitors waited and waited and in the end quite forgot about the poor prisoners.

"Although it was said to be in the Moscow region, Sosnovka was in fact in the deep forests of Zaraisky district, not only nowhere near the railroad, but a good twenty versts even from the nearest well-traveled road. The wilderness, in a word. To be sure, it was a heavenly place, and excellently established. I have a little village nearby, so that I often called on the prince as a neighbor. The black grouse shooting there is exquisite, but that spring especially the birds seemed to fly right into one's sights— I've never seen the like in all my days. So, in the end, I became a habitué of the house, which is why the entire tale unfolded right before my eyes.

"The old prince had been trying for some time to construct a belvedere in his park, in the Viennese style. He had first hired a famous architect from Moscow, who had drawn up the plans and even started the construction, but then didn't finish it—he could not endure the prince's bullheaded whims and so had departed. To finish the work they summoned an architect of somewhat lower flight, a Frenchman named Renar. Young, and rather handsome. True, he was noticeably lame, but since Lord Byron our young ladies have never counted this as a defect.

"What happened next you can imagine for yourselves. The two maidens had been sitting in the country for a decade now, never once getting out. They both were twenty-eight years old, with absolutely no society of any sort, save for the arrival of the odd fuddy-duddy such as myself, come to hunt. And suddenly—a handsome young man of lively mind, and from Paris at that.

"I have to say that, for all their outward similarity, the two princesses were of totally different temperament and spiritual cast. Anyuta was like Pushkin's Tatyana, prone to lassitude, a touch melancholic, a little pedantic, and, to be blunt, a bit tedious. As for Polinka, she was frolicsome, mischievous, 'simple as a poet's life, sweet as a lover's kiss,' as the poet has it. And she was far less settled into old-maidish ways.

"Renar lived there a bit, had a look around, and, naturally enough, set his cap at Polinka. I watched all this from the sidelines, rejoicing greatly, and of course not once suspecting the incredible way in which this pastoral idyll would end. Polinka besotted by love, the Frenchie giddy with the whiff of millions, and Anyuta smoldering with jealousy, forced to assume the role of vessel of common sense. I confess that I enjoyed watching this comedy at least as much as I did the mating dance of the black grouse. The noble father, of course, continued to be oblivious of all this, because he was arrogant and unable to imagine that a Princess Karakina might feel attracted to some lowly sort of architect.

"It all ended in scandal, of course. One evening Anyuta chanced . . . or perhaps there was nothing chance about it . . . Anyuta glanced into a little house in the garden, found her sister and Renar there in flagrante delicto, and immediately informed their father. Wrathful Lev Lvovich, who escaped apoplexy only by a miracle, wanted to drive the offender from his estate immediately. The Frenchman was able only with the greatest difficulty to plead to be allowed to remain at the estate until the morning, for the forests around Sosnovka were such that a solitary night traveler could well be eaten by wolves. Had I not intervened, the malefactor would have been turned out of the gates dressed in nothing but his frock coat.

"The sobbing Polinka was sent to her bedroom under the eye of her prudent sister, the architect was sent to his room in one of the wings to pack his suitcase, the servants scattered, and the full brunt of the prince's wrath came to be borne precisely by your humble servant. Lev Lvovich raged almost until dawn, wearing me out entirely, so that I scarcely slept that night. Nevertheless, in the morning I saw from the window how the Frenchman was hauled off to the station in a plain flat farm cart. Poor fellow, he kept looking up to the windows, but clearly there was no one waving him farewell, or so his terribly droopy look seemed to say.

"Then marvels began to occur. The princesses did not appear for breakfast. Their bedroom door was locked, and there was no response to knocks. The prince began to boil again, showing signs of an inevitable apoplexy. He gave orders to splinter the door, and devil take the hindmost. Which was done, everyone rushed in, and . . . Good heavens!

Anyuta lay in her bed, as if in deepest sleep, while there was no sign of Polinka whatsoever. She had vanished. She wasn't in the house, she wasn't in the park . . . it was as if she had slipped down through the very earth.

"No matter how hard they tried to wake Anyuta, it was to no avail. The family doctor, who had lived there on the estate, had died not long before, and no new one had yet been hired. Thus they had to send to the district hospital. The government doctor came, one of those long-haired fellows. He poked her, he squeezed her, and then he said she was suffering from a most serious nervous disorder. Leave her lie, and she would awake.

"The carter who had hauled off the Frenchman returned. He was a faithful man, his whole life spent at the estate. He swore to heaven that he had carted Renar right to the station and put him on the train. The young gentle-lady had not been with him. And anyway, how could she have gotten past the gate? The park at Sosnovka was surrounded by a high stone wall, and there was a guard at the gate.

"Anyuta did wake the following day, but there was no getting anything from her. She had lost the ability to speak. All she could do was weep, tremble, and rattle her teeth. After a week she began to speak a little, but she remembered nothing of that night. If she were pressed with questions, she would immediately begin to shudder and convulse. The doctor forbade such questions in the very strictest terms, saying that it endangered her life.

"So Polinka had vanished. The prince lost his mind utterly. He wrote repeatedly to the governor and even to the Tsar himself. He roused the police. He had Renar followed in Moscow—but it was all for naught. The Frenchman labored away, trying to find clients, but to no avail— nobody wanted a quarrel with Karakin. So the poor fellow left for his native Paris. Even so, Lev Lvovich continued to rage. He got it into his head that the villain had killed his beloved Polinka and buried her somewhere. He had the whole park dug up, and the pond drained, killing all his priceless carp. Nothing. A month passed, and the apoplexy finally came. The prince sat down to dinner, gave out a sudden wheeze, and *plop!* Facedown in his soup bowl. And no wonder, really, after suffering so much.

"After that night it wasn't so much that Anyuta was touched in the head as that her character was markedly changed. Even before, she hadn't been noted for any particular gaiety, but now she would scarcely even open her mouth. The slightest sound would set her atremble. I confess, sinner that I am, that I am no great lover of tragedy. I fled from Sosnovka while the prince was still alive. When I came for the funeral, saints above, the estate was changed beyond recognition. The place had become dreadful, as if some raven had folded its black wing over it. I looked about and I remember thinking, *This place is going to be abandoned.* And so it came to be.

"Anyuta, the sole heir, had no desire to live there and so she went away. Not to Moscow, either, or someplace in Europe, but to the very ends of the earth. The estate manager sends her money to Brazil, in Rio de Janeiro. I checked on a globe to find that Rio is absolutely on the other side of the world from Sosnovka. Just think—Brazil! Not a Russian face to be seen anywhere!" Arkhip Giatsintovich ended his strange tale with a sigh.

"Why do you say that? I have an acquaintance in Brazil, a former c-colleague of mine in the Japanese embassy, Karl Ivanovich Veber," Erast Petrovich Fandorin murmured thoughtfully, having listened to the story with interest. The officer for special missions had a soft and pleasant manner of speaking, in no way spoiled by his slight stammer. "Veber is an envoy to the Brazilian emperor D-Don Pedro now. So it's hardly the end of the earth."

"Is that so?" Arkhip Giatsintovich turned animatedly. "So perhaps this mystery might yet be solved? Ah, my dear Erast Petrovich, people say that you have a brilliant analytic mind, that you can crack mysteries of all sorts, like so many walnuts. Now here's a problem for you that doesn't seem to have a logical solution. On the one hand, Polinka Karakina vanished from the estate—that's a fact. On the other hand, there's no way she could have gotten out of the garden, and that's also a fact."

"Yes, yes," several of the ladies started at once, "Mr. Fandorin, Erast Petrovich, we so terribly want to know what really happened there!"

"I'm prepared to make a wager that Erast Petrovich will be able to resolve this paradox quite easily," the hostess Odintsova announced with confidence.

"A wager?" Mustafin inquired immediately. "And what are you willing to wager?"

It must be explained that both Lidia Nikolaevna and Arkhip Giatsintovich were avid gamblers whose passion for making wagers sometimes approached lunacy. The more insightful of the guests glanced at one another, suspicious that this entire interlude, with a tale supposedly recalled solely by chance, had been staged by prior agreement, and that the young official had fallen victim to a clever intrigue.

"I quite like that little Bouchet of yours," Arkhip Giatsintovich said with a slight bow.

"And I your large Caravaggio," the hostess answered him in the same tone of voice.

Mustafin simply rocked his head a bit, as if admiring Odintsova's voracious appetite, but said nothing. Apparently he had no qualms about victory. Or, perhaps, the stakes had already been decided between them in advance.

A bit startled at such swiftness, Erast Petrovich spread his hands. "But I have not visited the site of the event, and I have never seen the p-participants. As I recall, even having all the necessary information, the police were not able to do anything. So what am I to do now? And it's probably been quite some time as well, I imagine."

"Six years this October," came the answer.

"W-well then, you see . . ."

"Dear, wonderful Erast Petrovich," the hostess implored, "don't ruin me utterly. I've already agreed to this extortionist's terms. He'll simply take my Bouchet and be gone! That gentleman has not the slightest drop of chivalry in him!"

"My ancestors were Tartar *murza,* warlords!" Arkhip Giatsintovich confirmed gaily. "We in the Horde keep our chat with the ladies short."

However, chivalry was far from an empty word for Fandorin, apparently. The young man rubbed the bridge of his nose with a finger and muttered, "Well, so that's how it is. . . . Well, Mr. Mustafin, you . . . you didn't chance to notice, did you, what kind of bag the Frenchman had? You did see him leave, you said. So probably there was some large kind of trunk?"

Arkhip Giatsintovich made as if to applaud. "Bravo! He hid the girl in the trunk and carted her off? And Polinka gave the meddlesome sister something nasty to drink, which is why Anyuta collapsed into nervous disorder? Clever. But alas . . . There was no trunk. The Frenchman flew off as light as an eagle. I remember some small suitcases of some sort, some bundles, a couple of hatboxes. No, my good sir, your explanation simply won't wash."

Fandorin thought a bit, then asked, "You are quite sure that the princess could not have won the guards to her side, or perhaps just bribed them?"

"Absolutely. That was the first thing the police checked."

Strangely, at these words the collegiate assessor suddenly became very gloomy and sighed, then said, "Then your tale is much nastier than I had thought." Then, after a long pause, he said, "Tell me, did the prince's house have plumbing?"

"Plumbing? In the countryside?" Molly Sapegina asked in astonishment, then giggled uncertainly, having decided that the handsome official was joking. However, Arkhip Giatsintovich screwed his gold-rimmed monocle into one eye and looked at Fandorin extremely attentively, as if he had only just properly noticed him. "How did you guess that? As it happens, there *was* plumbing at the estate. A year before the events that I have described, the prince had ordered the construction of a pumping station and a boiler room. Lev Lvovich, the princesses, and the guest rooms all had quite proper bathrooms. But what does that have to do with the business at hand?"

"I think that your p-paradox is resolved." Fandorin rocked his head. "The resolution, though, is awfully unpleasant."

"But how? Resolved by what? What happened?" Questions came from all sides.

"I'll tell you in a moment. But first, Lidia Nikolaevna, I would like to give your lackey a certain assignment."

With all present completely entranced, the collegiate assessor then wrote a little note of some sort, handed it to the lackey, and whispered something quietly into the man's ear. The clock on the mantel chimed midnight, but no one had the slightest thought of leaving. All held their breath and waited, but Erast Petrovich was in no hurry to begin this demonstration of his analytic gifts. Bursting with pride at her faultless intuition, which once again had served her well in her choice of a main guest, Lidia Nikolaevna looked at the young man with almost maternal tenderness. This officer of special missions had every chance of becoming a true star of her salon. Which would make Katie Polotskaya and Lily Yepanchina green with envy, to be sure!

"The story you shared with us is not so much mysterious as disgusting," the collegiate assessor finally said with a grimace. "One of the most monstrous crimes of passion about which I have ever had occasion to hear. This is no disappearance. It is a murder, of the very worst, Cain-like sort."

"Are you meaning to say that the gay sister was killed by the melancholy sister?" inquired Sergey Ilyich von Taube, chairman of the Excise Chamber.

"No, I wish to say something quite the opposite—gay Polinka killed melancholy Anyuta. And that is not the most nightmarish aspect."

"I do beg your pardon! How can that be?" Sergey Ilyich asked in astonishment, while Lidia Nikolaevna thought it necessary to note, "And what might be more nightmarish than the murder of one's own sister?"

Fandorin rose and began to pace about the sitting room. "I will try to reconstruct the sequence of events, as I understand them. So, we have two p-princesses, withering with boredom. Life dribbling through their fingertips—indeed, all but dribbled away. Their feminine life, I mean. Idleness. Moldering spiritual powers. Unrealized hopes. Tormenting relations with their high-handed father. And, not least, physiological frustration. They were, after all, young, healthy women. Oops, please forgive me. . . ."

Conscious that he had said something untoward, the collegiate assessor was embarrassed for a moment, but Lidia Nikolaevna let it pass without a reprimand—he looked so appealing with that blush that suddenly had blossomed on his white cheeks.

"I would not even dare to imagine how much there is intertwined in the soul of a young w-woman who might be in such a situation," Fandorin said after a short silence. "And here is something particular besides—right there, always, is your living mirror image, your twin sister. No doubt it would be impossible for there not to be a most intricate mix of love and hatred between them. And suddenly a young handsome man appears. He demonstrates obvious interest in the young princesses. No doubt with ulterior motive, but which of those girls would have thought of that? Of course, an inevitable rivalry springs up between the girls, but the ch-choice is quickly made. Until that moment everything between Anyuta and Polinka was identical, but now they were in quite different worlds. One of them is happy, returned to the land of the living and, at least to all appearances, loved. While the other feels herself rejected, lonely, and thus doubly unhappy. Happy love is egoistical. For Polinka, no doubt, there was nothing other than the passions that had built up through the long years of being locked away. This was the full and real life that she had dreamed about for so many years, the life she had even stopped hoping for. And then it was all shredded in an instant—indeed, precisely at the moment when love had reached its very highest peak."

The ladies all listened spellbound to the empathetic speech of this picture-perfect young man of beauty, all save for Molly Sapegina, who pressed her slender fingers to her décolletage before freezing in that pose.

"Most dreadful of all was that the agent of this tragedy was one's very own sister. We may agree, of course, to understand her as well. To endure such happiness right alongside one's own unhappiness would require a particular cast of the spirit which Anyuta obviously did not possess. So Polinka, who had only just been lounging in the bowers of Paradise, was cast utterly down. There is no beast in this world more dangerous than a woman deprived of her beloved!" Erast Petrovich exclaimed, a tad carried away, and then immediately grew a bit muddled, since this sentiment might offend the fairer half among those present. However, there came no protests—all were greedily waiting for the story to continue, so Fandorin went on more briskly, "So then, under the influence of despair, Polinka had a mad plan, a terrible, monstrous plan, but one that is testament to the enormous power of feeling. Although, I don't know, the plan might have come from Renar. It was the girl who had to put the plan into action, however. . . . That night, while you, Arkhip Giatsintovich, were nodding drowsily and listening to your host pour out his rage, a hellish act was taking place in the bedroom of the princesses. Polinka murdered her sister. I do not know how. Perhaps she smothered her with a pillow, perhaps she poisoned her, but in any event, it occurred without blood, for otherwise there would have remained some trace in the bedroom."

"The investigation considered the possibility of a murder." Mustafin shrugged, having listened to Erast Petrovich with unconcealed scepticism. "However, there arose a rather sensible question—what happened to the body?"

The officer of special missions answered without a moment's hesitation, "That's the nightmarish part. After killing her sister, Polinka dragged her into the bathroom, where she cut her into bits and washed the blood away down the drain. The Frenchman could not have been the one to dismember her—there is no way he could have left his own wing for such a long time without being noticed."

Waiting out a true storm of alarmed exclamations, in which "Impossible!" was the word most often heard, Fandorin said sadly,

"Unfortunately, there is no other possibility. There is no other solution to the p-problem as p-posed. It is better not even to attempt to imagine what went on that night in that bathroom. Polinka would not have had the slightest knowledge of anatomy, nor could she have had any instrument more to the purpose than a pilfered kitchen knife."

"But there's no way she could have put the body parts and bones down the drain, it would have plugged!" Mustafin exclaimed with a heat unlike him.

"No, she could not. The dismembered flesh left the estate in the Frenchman's various suitcases and hatboxes. Tell me, please, were the bedroom windows high off the ground?"

Arkhip Giatsintovich squinted as he tried to recall. "Not especially. The height of a man, perhaps. And the windows looked out on the park, in the direction of the lawn."

"So, the remains were passed through the w-window, then. Judging by the fact that there were no traces left on the window sill, Renar passed some kind of vessel into the room, Anyuta took it into the bathroom, put the body parts in there, and handed these to her accomplice. When this evil ferrying was done, all Polinka had to do was scour out the bathtub and clean the blood from herself. . . ."

Lidia Nikolaevna desperately wanted to win her bet, but in the interests of fairness she could not remain silent. "Erast Petrovich, this all fits together very well, with the exception of one circumstance. If Polinka indeed committed so monstrous an operation, she certainly would have stained her clothing, and blood is not so simple to wash away, especially if one is not a washerwoman."

This note of practicality did not so much puzzle Fandorin as embarrass him. Coughing slightly and looking away, he said quietly, "I im-imagine that before she began dismembering the body, the princess removed her clothing. All of it. . . ."

Some of the ladies gasped, while Molly Sapegina, growing pale, murmured, "Oh, *mon Dieu*. . . ."

Erast Petrovich, it seemed, was frightened that someone might faint, so he hastened to finish, now in a dry tone of scientific detachment. "It is entirely probable that the extended oblivion of the supposed Anyuta was no simulation, but rather was a natural psychological reaction to a terrible tr-trauma."

Everyone suddenly began speaking at once. "But it wasn't Anyuta that disappeared, it was Polinka!" Sergey Ilyich recalled.

"Well, obviously that was just Polinka drawing a mole on her cheek," the more imaginative Lidia Nikolaevna explained impatiently. "That's why everyone thought she was Anyuta!"

Retired court doctor Stupitsyn did not agree. "Impossible! People close to them are able to distinguish twins quite well. The way they act, the nuances of the voice, the expressions of their eyes, after all!"

"And anyway, why was such a switch necessary?" General Liprandi interrupted the court doctor. "Why would Polinka have to pretend that she was Anyuta?"

Erast Petrovich waited until the flood of questions and objections ebbed, and then answered them one by one, "Had Anyuta disappeared, Your Excellency, then suspicion would inevitably have fallen on Polinka, that she had taken her revenge upon her sister, and so the search for traces of the murder would have been more painstaking. That's one thing. Had the besotted girl vanished at the same time as the Frenchman, this would have brought to the forefront the theory that this was a flight, not a crime. That's two. And then, of course, in the guise of Anyuta, at some time in the future she might marry Renar without giving herself away. Apparently that is precisely what happened in faraway Rio de Janeiro. I am certain that Polinka traveled so far from her native land in order to join the object of her affections in peace." The collegiate assessor turned to the court doctor. "Your argument that intimates are able to distinguish twins is entirely reasonable. Note, however, that the Karakins' family doctor, whom it would have been impossible to deceive, had died not long before. And besides, the supposed Anyuta changed most decidedly after that fateful night, precisely as if she had become someone else. In view of the particular circumstances, everyone took that as natural. In fact, this transformation occurred with Polinka, but is it to be wondered at that she lost her former animation and gaiety?"

"And the death of the old prince?" Sergey Ilyich asked. "Wasn't that awfully convenient for the criminal?"

"A most suspicious death," agreed Fandorin. "It is entirely possible that poison may have been involved. There was no autopsy, of course—his sudden demise was attributed to paternal grief and a disposition to apoplexy, but at the same time it is entirely possible that after a night such as that, a trifle like poisoning one's own father would not much bother Polinka. By the way, it would not be too late to conduct an exhumation even now. Poison is preserved a long while in the bone tissue."

"I'll bet that the prince was poisoned," Lidia Nikolaevna said quickly, turning to Arkhip Giatsintovich, who pretended that he had not heard.

"An inventive theory. And clever, too," Mustafin said at length. "However, one must have an exceedingly active imagination to picture Princess Karakina carving up the body of her own sister with a bread knife while dressed in the garb of Eve."

Everyone again began speaking at once, defending both points of view with equal ardor, although the ladies inclined to Fandorin's version of events, while the gentlemen rejected it as improbable. The cause of the argument took no part in the discussion himself, although he listened to the points of both sides with interest.

"Oh, but why are you remaining silent?!" Lidia Nikolaevna called to him, as she pointed at Mustafin. "Clearly, he is arguing against something perfectly obvious simply in order not to give up his stake. Tell him, say something else, that will force him into silence!"

"I am waiting for your Matvey to return," Erast Petrovich replied tersely.

"But where did you send him?"

"To the Governor-General's staff headquarters. The telegraph office there is open around the clock."

"But that's on Tverskoy Boulevard, five minutes' walk from here, and he's been gone more than an hour!" someone wondered.

"Matvey was ordered to wait for the reply," the officer of special missions explained, then again fell silent while Arkhip Giatsintovich held everyone's attention with an expansive explanation of the ways in which Fandorin's theory was completely impossible from the viewpoint of female psychology.

Just at the most effective moment, as Mustafin was holding forth most convincingly about the innate properties of the feminine nature, which is ashamed of nudity and cannot endure the sight of blood, the door quietly opened and the long-awaited Matvey entered. Treading silently, he approached the collegiate assessor and, with a bow, proffered a sheet of paper.

Erast Petrovich turned, read the note, then nodded. The hostess, who had been watching the young man's face attentively, could not endure to wait any longer, and so moved her chair closer to her guest. "Well, what's there?" she whispered.

"I was right," Fandorin answered, also in a whisper.

That instant Odintsova interrupted the lecture. "Enough nonsense, Arkhip Giatsintovich! What do you know of the feminine nature, you who have never even been married! Erast Petrovich has incontrovertible proof!" She took the telegram from the collegiate assessor's hand and passed it around the circle.

Flabbergasted, the guests read the telegram, which consisted of three words:

"Yes. Yes. No."

"And that's it? What is this? Where is it from?" Such were the general questions.

"The telegram was sent from the Russian mission in Br-Brazil," Fandorin explained. "You see the diplomatic stamp there? It is deep night here in Moscow, but in Rio de Janeiro right now the mission is in attendance. I was counting on that when I ordered Matvey to wait for a reply. As for the telegram, I recognize the laconic style of Karl Ivanovich Veber. This is how my message read. Matvey, give me the paper, will you? The one I gave you." Erast Petrovich took the paper from the lackey and read aloud, " 'Karl, old boy, inform me the following soonest: Is Russian subject born Princess Anyuta Karakina now resident in Brazil married? If yes, is her husband lame? And does the princess have a mole on her right cheek? I need all this for a bet. Fandorin.' From the answer to the message it is clear that the pr-princess is married to a lame man, and has no mole on her cheek. Why would she need the mole now? In far-off Brazil there is no need to run to such clever tricks. As you see, ladies and gentlemen, Polinka is alive and well, married to her Renar. The terrible tale has an idyllic ending. By the by, the lack of a mole shows once again that Renar was a witting participant in the murder and knows perfectly well that he is married precisely to Polinka, and not to Anyuta."

"So, I shall give orders to fetch the Caravaggio," Odintsova said to Arkhip Giatsintovich with a victorious smile.

FYODOR DOSTOEVSKY

MURDER
from CRIME AND PUNISHMENT

TRANSLATED BY CONSTANCE GARNETT

One of the greatest crime novels of all time, *Crime and Punishment* was written by Fyodor Mikhailovich Dostoevsky (1821–1881) and published in twelve monthly instalments (January-December, 1866) in the magazine *Russky Vestnik* (*The Russian Messenger*) before its first book publication in a single volume in 1867. It was first published in English translation in London by Vizetelly (1886) and in New York by Crowell (1886).

As a towering literary achievement, its plot is well known. A poor student, Rodion Raskolnikov, breaks into the apartment of an obnoxious old money-lender planning to rob and kill her. When her half-sister chances upon the scene, he murders her, too. He believes he has the right to commit the crimes, as it solves his financial difficulty while ridding the world of a loathsome creature and, besides, as a superior being, he need feel no guilt as he pursues more noble purposes. The German philosopher Friedrich Nietzsche developed his idea of the superman after reading *Crime and Punishment*. Although he has no solid evidence, the police detective Porfiry Petrovich becomes convinced that Raskolnikov committed the murder and, relying on the killer's conscience, finally persuades him to confess.

This excerpt of the murder scene from *Crime and Punishment* is from the Constance Garnett translation, first published in 1914.

FYODOR DOSTOEVSKY

The door was as before opened a tiny crack, and again two sharp and suspicious eyes stared at him out of the darkness. Then Raskolnikov lost his head and nearly made a great mistake.

Fearing the old woman would be frightened by their being alone, and not hoping that the sight of him would disarm her suspicions, he took hold of the door and drew it towards him to prevent the old woman from attempting to shut it again. Seeing this she did not pull the door back, but she did not let go the handle so that he almost dragged her out with it on to the stairs. Seeing that she was standing in the doorway not allowing him to pass, he advanced straight upon her. She stepped back in alarm, tried to say something, but seemed unable to speak and stared with open eyes at him.

"Good evening, Alyona Ivanovna," he began, trying to speak easily, but his voice would not obey him, it broke and shook. "I have come . . . I have brought something . . . but we'd better come in . . . to the light. . . ."

And leaving her, he passed straight into the room uninvited. The old woman ran after him; her tongue was unloosed.

"Good heavens! What is it? Who is it? What do you want?"

"Why, Alyona Ivanovna, you know me . . . Raskolnikov . . . here, I brought you the pledge I promised the other day. . . ." And he held out the pledge.

The old woman glanced for a moment at the pledge, but at once stared in the eyes of her uninvited visitor. She looked intently, maliciously, and mistrustfully. A minute passed; he even fancied something like a sneer in her eyes, as though she had already guessed everything. He felt that he was losing his head, that he was almost frightened, so frightened that if she were to look like that and not say a word for another half-minute, he thought he would have run away from her.

"Why do you look at me as though you did not know me?" he said suddenly, also with malice. "Take it if you like, if not I'll go elsewhere. I am in a hurry."

He had not even thought of saying this, but it was suddenly said of itself. The old woman recovered herself, and her visitor's resolute tone evidently restored her confidence.

"But why, my good sir, all of a minute . . . What is it?" she asked, looking at the pledge.

"The silver cigarette-case; I spoke of it last time, you know."

She held out her hand.

"But how pale you are, to be sure . . . and your hands are trembling too? Have you been bathing, or what?"

"Fever," he answered abruptly. "You can't help getting pale . . . if you've nothing to eat," he added, with difficulty articulating the words.

His strength was failing him again. But his answer sounded like the truth, the old woman took the pledge.

"What is it?" she asked once more, scanning Raskolnikov intently and weighing the pledge in her hand.

"A thing . . . cigarette-case . . . Silver . . . Look at it."

"It does not seem somehow like silver . . . How he has wrapped it up!"

Trying to untie the string and turning to the window, to the light (all her windows were shut, in spite of the stifling heat), she left him altogether for some seconds and stood with her back to him. He unbuttoned his coat and freed the axe from the noose, but did not yet take it out altogether, simply holding it in his right hand under the coat. His hands were fearfully weak, he felt them every moment growing more numb and more wooden. He was afraid he would let the axe slip and fall . . . A sudden giddiness came over him.

"But what has he tied it up like this for?" the old woman cried with vexation and moved towards him.

He had not a minute more to lose. He pulled the axe quite out, swung it with both arms, scarcely conscious of himself, and almost without effort, almost mechanically, brought the blunt side down on her head. He seemed not to use his own strength in this. But as soon as he had once brought the axe down his strength returned to him.

The old woman was as always bareheaded. Her thin, light hair, streaked with grey, thickly smeared with grease, was plaited in a rat's tail and fastened by a broken horn comb which stood out on the nape of her neck. As she was so short the blow fell on the very top of her skull. She cried out, but very faintly, and suddenly sank all of a heap on the floor, raising her hands to her head. In one hand she still held "the pledge." Then he dealt her another and another blow with the blunt side and in the same spot. The blood gushed forth as from an overturned glass, the body fell back. He stepped back, let it fall, and at once bent over her face; she was dead. Her eyes seemed to be starting out of their sockets, the brow and the whole face were drawn and contorted convulsively.

He laid the axe on the ground near the dead body and felt at once in her pocket (trying to avoid the streaming blood)—the same right-hand pocket from which she had taken the key on his last visit. He was in full possession of his faculties, free from confusion or giddiness, but his hands were still trembling. He remembered afterwards that he had been particularly collected and careful, trying all the time not to get smeared with blood . . . He pulled out the keys at once, they were all, as before, in one bunch on a steel ring. He ran at once into the bedroom with them. It was a very small room with a whole shrine of holy images. Against the other wall stood a big bed, very clean and covered with a silk patchwork wadded quilt. Against a third wall was a chest of drawers. Strange to say, so soon as he began to fit the keys into the chest, so soon as he heard their jingling, a convulsive shudder passed over him. He suddenly felt tempted again to give it all up and go away. But that was only for an instant; it was too late to go back. He positively smiled at himself, when suddenly another terrifying idea occurred to his mind. He suddenly fancied that the old woman might be still alive and might recover her senses. Leaving the keys in the chest, he ran back to the body, snatched up the axe, and lifted it once more over the old woman, but did not bring it down. There was no doubt that she was dead. Bending down and examining her again more closely, he saw clearly that the skull was broken and even battered in on one side. He was about to feel it with his finger, but drew back his hand and indeed it was evident without that. Meanwhile there was a perfect pool of blood. All at once he noticed a string on her neck; he tugged at it, but the string was strong and did not snap and, besides, it was soaked with blood. He tried to pull it out from the front of the dress, but something held it and prevented its coming. In his impatience he raised the axe again to cut the string from above on the body, but did not dare, and with difficulty, smearing his hand and the axe in the blood, after two minutes' hurried effort, he cut the string and took it off without touching the body with the axe; he was not mistaken—it was a purse. On the string were two crosses, one of Cyprus wood and one of copper, and an image in silver filigree, and with them a small greasy chamois leather purse with a steel rim and ring. The purse was stuffed very full. Raskolnikov thrust it in his pocket without looking at it, flung the crosses on the old woman's body, and rushed back into the bedroom, this time taking the axe with him.

He was in terrible haste, he snatched the keys, and began trying them again. But he was unsuccessful. They would not fit in the locks. It was not so much that his hands were shaking, but that he kept making mistakes; though he saw for instance that a key was not the right one and would not fit, still he tried to put it in. Suddenly he remembered and realized that the big key with the deep notches, which was hanging there with the small keys, could not possibly belong to the chest of drawers (on his last visit this had struck him) but to some strong-box, and that everything perhaps was hidden in that box. He left the chest of drawers, and at once felt under the bedstead, knowing that old women usually keep boxes under their beds. And so it was; there was a good-sized box under the bed, at least a yard in length, with an arched lid covered with red leather and studded with steel nails. The notched key fitted at once and unlocked it. At the top, under a white sheet, was a coat of red brocade lined with hareskin; under it was a silk dress, then a shawl, and it seemed as though there was nothing below but clothes. The first thing he did was to wipe his blood-stained hands on the red brocade. "It's red, and on red blood will be less noticeable," the thought passed through his mind; then he suddenly came to himself. "Good God, am I going out of my senses?" he thought with terror.

But no sooner did he touch the clothes than a gold watch slipped from under the fur coat. He made haste to turn them all over. There turned out to be various articles made of gold among the clothes—probably all pledges, unredeemed or waiting to be redeemed—bracelets, chains, earrings, pins, and such things. Some were in cases, others simply wrapped in newspaper, carefully and exactly folded and tied round with tape. Without any delay, he began filling up the pockets of his trousers and overcoat without examining or undoing the parcels and cases; but he had not time to take many . . .

He suddenly heard steps in the room where the old woman lay. He stopped short and was still as death. But all was quiet, so it must have been his fancy. All at once he heard distinctly a faint cry, as though someone had uttered a low broken moan. Then again dead silence for a minute or two. He sat squatting on his heels by the box and waited, holding his breath. Suddenly he jumped up, seized the axe, and ran out of the bedroom.

In the middle of the room stood Lizaveta with a big bundle in her arms. She was gazing in stupefaction at her murdered sister, white as a sheet, and seeming not to have the strength to cry out. Seeing him run out of the bedroom, she began faintly quivering all over, like a leaf, a shudder ran down her face; she lifted her hand, opened her mouth, but still did not scream. She began slowly backing away from him into the corner, staring intently, persistently at him, but still uttered no sound, as though she could not get breath to scream. He rushed at her with the axe; her mouth twitched piteously, as one sees babies' mouths, when they begin to be frightened, stare intently at what frightens them, and are on the point of screaming. And this hapless Lizaveta was so simple and had been so thoroughly crushed and scared that she did not even raise a hand to guard her face, though that was the most necessary and natural action at the moment, for the axe was raised over her face. She only put up her empty left hand, but not to her face slowly holding it out before her as though motioning him away. The axe fell with the sharp edge just on the skull and split at one blow all the top of her head. She fell heavily at once, Raskolnikov completely lost his head snatching up her bundle, dropped it again, and ran into the entry.

Fear gained more and more mastery over him, especially after this second, quite unexpected murder. He longed to run away from the place as fast as possible. And if at that moment he had been capable of seeing and reasoning more correctly, if he had been able to realize all the difficulties of his position, the hopelessness, the hideousness, and the absurdity of it, if he could have understood how many obstacles and, perhaps, crimes he had still to overcome or to commit, to get out of that place and to make his way home, it is very possible that he would have flung up everything, and would have gone to give himself up, and not from fear, but from simple horror and loathing of what he had done. The feeling of loathing especially surged up within him and grew stronger every minute. He would not now have gone to the box or even into the room for anything in the world.

But a sort of blankness, even dreaminess, had begun by degrees to take possession of him; at moments he forgot himself, or rather forgot what was of importance and caught at trifles. Glancing, however, into the kitchen and seeing a bucket half full of water on a bench, he bethought him of washing his hands and the axe. His hands were sticky with blood. He dropped the axe with the blade in the water, snatched a piece of soap that lay in a broken saucer on the window, and began washing his hands in the bucket. When they were clean, he took out the axe, washed the blade, and spent a long time, about three minutes, washing the wood where there were spots of blood, rubbing them with soap. Then he wiped it all with some linen that was hanging to dry on a line in the kitchen and then he was a long while attentively examining the axe at the window. There was no trace left on it, only the wood was still damp. He carefully hung the axe in the noose under his coat. Then as far as was possible, in the dim light in the kitchen, he looked over his overcoat his trousers, and his boots. At the first glance there seemed to be nothing but stains on the boots. He wetted the rag and rubbed the boots. But he knew he was not looking thoroughly, that there might be something quite noticeable that he was overlooking. He stood in the middle of the room, lost in thought. Dark agonizing ideas rose in his mind—the idea that he was mad and that at that moment he was incapable of reasoning, of protecting himself, that he ought perhaps to be doing something utterly different from what he was now doing. "Good God!" he muttered, "I must fly, fly," and he rushed into the entry. But here a shock of terror awaited him such as he had never known before.

He stood and gazed and could not believe his eyes: the door, the outer door from the stairs, at which he had not long before waited and rung, was standing unfastened and at least six inches open. No lock, no bolt, all the time, all that time! The old woman had not shut it after him perhaps as a precaution. But, good God! Why, he had seen Lizaveta afterwards! And how could he, how could he have failed to reflect that she must have come in somehow? She could not have come through the wall!

He dashed to the door and fastened the latch.

"But no, the wrong thing again! I must get away, get away . . ." He unfastened the latch, opened the door, and began listening on the staircase.

He listened a long time. Somewhere far away, it might be in the gateway, two voices were loudly and shrilly shouting, quarrelling, and scolding. "What are they about?" He waited patiently. At last all was still, as though suddenly cut off; they had separated. He was meaning to go out, but suddenly, on the floor below, a door was noisily opened and someone began going downstairs humming a tune. "How is it they all make such a noise?" flashed through his mind. Once more he closed the door and waited. At last all was still, not a soul stirring. He was just taking a step towards the stairs when he heard fresh footsteps.

The steps sounded very far off, at the very bottom of the stairs, but he remembered quite clearly and distinctly that from the first sound he began for some reason to suspect that this was someone coming *there,* to the fourth floor, to the old woman. Why? Were the sounds somehow peculiar, significant? The steps were heavy, even, and unhurried. Now *he* had passed the first floor, now he was mounting higher, it was growing more and more distinct! He could hear his heavy breathing. And now the third storey had been reached. Coming here! And it seemed to him all at once that he was turned to stone, that it was like a dream in which one is being pursued, nearly caught and will be killed, and is rooted to the spot and cannot even move one's arms.

At last when the unknown was mounting to the fourth floor, he suddenly started, and succeeded in slipping neatly and quickly back into the flat and closing the door behind him. Then he took the hook and softly, noiselessly, fixed it in the catch. Instinct helped him. When he had done this, he crouched, holding his breath, by the door. The unknown visitor was by now also at the door. They were now standing opposite one another, as he had just before been standing with the old woman, when the door divided them and he was listening.

The visitor panted several times. "He must be a big, fat man," thought Raskolnikov, squeezing the axe in his hand. It seemed like a dream indeed. The visitor took hold of the bell and rang it loudly.

As soon as the tin bell tinkled, Raskolnikov seemed to be aware of something moving in the room. For some seconds he listened quite seriously. The unknown rang again, waited, and suddenly tugged violently and impatiently at the handle of the door. Raskolnikov gazed in horror at the hook shaking in its fastening, and in blank terror expected every minute that the fastening would be pulled out. It certainly did seem possible, so violently was he shaking it. He was tempted to hold the fastening, but *he* might be aware of it. A giddiness came over him again. "I shall fall down!" flashed through his mind, but the unknown began to speak and he recovered himself at once.

"What's up? Are they asleep or murdered? D–damn them!" he bawled in a thick voice. "Hey, Alyona Ivanovna, old witch! Lizaveta

Ivanovna, hey, my beauty! Open the door! Oh, damn them! Are they asleep or what?"

And again, enraged he tugged with all his might a dozen times at the bell. He must certainly be a man of authority and an intimate acquaintance.

At this moment light hurried steps were heard not far off, on the stairs. Someone else was approaching. Raskolnikov had not heard them at first.

"You don't say there's no one at home," the newcomer cried in a cheerful ringing voice, addressing the first visitor who still went on pulling the bell. "Good evening, Koch."

"From his voice he must be quite young," thought Raskolnikov.

"Who the devil can tell? I've almost broken the lock," answered Koch. "But how do you come to know me?"

"Why! The day before yesterday I beat you three times running at billiards at Gambrinus'."

"Oh!"

"So they are not at home? That's queer? It's awfully stupid though. Where could the old woman have gone? I've come on business."

"Yes; and I have business with her, too."

"Well, what can we do? Go back, I suppose. Aie—aie! And I was hoping to get some money!" cried the young man.

"We must give it up, of course, but what did she fix this time for? The old witch fixed the time for me to come herself. It's out of my way. And where the devil she can have got to, I can't make out. She sits here from year's end to year's end, the old hag; her legs are bad and yet here all of a sudden she is out for a walk!"

"Hadn't we better ask the porter?"

"What?"

"Where she's gone and when she'll be back."

"Hm . . . Damn it all! . . . We might ask . . . But you know she never does go anywhere."

And he once more tugged at the door-handle.

"Damn it all. There's nothing to be done, we must go!"

"Stay!" cried the young man suddenly. "Do you see how the door shakes if you pull it?"

"Well?"

"That shows it's not locked, but fastened with the hook! Do you hear how the hook clanks?"

"Well?"

"Why, don't you see? That proves that one of them is at home. If they were all out, they would have locked the door from outside with the key and not with the hook from inside. There, do you hear how the hook is clanking? To fasten the hook on the inside they must be at home, don't you see? So there they are sitting inside and don't open the door!"

"Well! And so they must be!" cried Koch, astonished. "What are they about in there?" And he began furiously shaking the door.

"Stay!" cried the young man again. "Don't pull at it! There must be something wrong . . . Here, you've been ringing and pulling at the door and still they don't open! So either they've both fainted or—"

"What?"

"I tell you what. Let's go and fetch the porter, let him wake them up."

"All right."

Both were going down.

"Stay. You stop here while I run down for the porter."

"What for?"

"Well, you'd better."

"All right."

"I'm studying the law, you see! It's evident, e-vi-dent there's something wrong here!" the young man cried hotly, and he ran downstairs.

Koch remained. Once more he softly touched the bell which gave one tinkle, then gently, as though reflecting and looking about him, began touching the door-handle, pulling it and letting it go to make sure once more that it was only fastened by the hook. Then puffing and panting he bent down and began looking at the keyhole: but the key was in the lock on the inside and so nothing could be seen.

Raskolnikov stood keeping tight hold of the axe. He was in a sort of delirium. He was even making ready to fight when they should come in. While they were knocking and talking together, the idea several times occurred to him to end it all at once and shout to them through the door. Now and then he was tempted to swear at them, to jeer at them, while they could not open the door! "Only make haste!" was the thought that flashed through his mind.

"But what the devil is he about? . . ." Time was passing, one minute, and another—no one came. Koch began to be restless.

"What the devil!" he cried suddenly and in impatience deserting his sentry duty, he too went down, hurrying and thumping with his heavy boots on the stairs. The steps died away.

"Good heavens! What am I to do?"

Raskolnikov unfastened the hook, opened the door—there was no sound. Abruptly, without any thought at all, he went out, closing the door as thoroughly as he could, and went downstairs.

He had gone down three flights when he suddenly heard a loud noise below—where could he go? There was nowhere to hide. He was just going back to the flat.

"Hey there! Catch the brute!"

Somebody dashed out of a flat below, shouting, and rather fell than ran down the stairs, bawling at the top of his voice.

"Mitka! Mitka! Mitka! Mitka! Mitka! Blast him!"

The shout ended in a shriek; the last sounds came from the yard; all was still. But at the same instant several men talking loud and fast began noisily mounting the stairs. There were three or four of them. He distinguished the ringing voice of the young man. "They!"

Filled with despair he went straight to meet them, feeling "come what must!" If they stopped him—all was lost; if they let him pass—all was lost too; they would remember him. They were approaching; they were only a flight from him—and suddenly deliverance! A few steps from him, on the right, there was an empty flat with the door wide open, the flat on the second floor where the painters had been at work, and which, as though for his benefit, they had just left. It was they, no doubt, who had just run down, shouting. The floor had only just been painted, in the middle of the room stood a pail and a broken pot with paint and brushes. In one instant he had whisked in at the open door and hidden behind it, and only in the nick of time; they had already reached the landing. Then they turned and went on up to the fourth floor, talking loudly. He waited, went out on tiptoe, and ran down the stairs.

No one was on the stairs, nor in the gateway. He passed quickly through the gateway and turned to the left in the street.

He knew, he knew perfectly well that at that moment they were at the flat, that they were greatly astonished at finding it unlocked, as the door had just been fastened, that by now they were looking at the bodies, that before another minute had passed they would guess and completely realize that the murderer had just been there, and had succeeded in hiding somewhere, slipping by them and escaping. They would guess most likely that he had been in the empty flat, while they were going upstairs. And meanwhile he dared not quicken his pace much, though the next turning was still nearly a hundred yards away. "Should he slip through some gateway and wait somewhere in an unknown street? No, hopeless! Should he fling away the axe? Should he take a cab? Hopeless, hopeless!"

At last he reached the turning. He turned down it more dead than alive. Here he was half-way to safety, and he understood it; it was less risky because there was a great crowd of people, and he was lost in it like a grain of sand. But all he had suffered had so weakened him that he could scarcely move. Perspiration ran down him in drops, his neck was all wet. "My word, he has been going it!" someone shouted at him when he came out on the canal bank.

He was only dimly conscious of himself now and the farther he went the worse it was. He remembered, however, that on coming out on to the canal bank he was alarmed at finding few people there and so being more conspicuous, and he had thought of turning back. Though he was almost falling from fatigue, he went a long way round so as to get home from quite a different direction.

He was not fully conscious when he passed through the gateway of his house; he was already on the staircase before he recollected the axe. And yet he had a very grave problem before him, to put it back and to escape observation as far as possible in doing so. He was of course incapable of reflecting that it might perhaps be far better not to restore the axe at all, but to drop it later on in somebody's yard. But it all happened fortunately, the door of the porter's room was closed but not locked, so that it seemed most likely that the porter was at home. But he had so completely lost all power of reflection that he walked straight to the door and opened it. If the porter had asked him, "What do you want?" he would perhaps have simply handed him the axe. But again the porter was not at home, and he succeeded in putting the axe back under the bench and even covering it with the chunk of wood as before. He met no one, not a soul, afterwards on the way to his room; the landlady's door was shut. When he was in his room, he flung himself on the sofa just as he was—he did not sleep, but sank into blank forgetfulness. If anyone had come into his room then he would have jumped up at once and screamed. Scraps and shreds of thoughts were simply swarming in his brain, but he could not catch at one, he could not rest on one, in spite of all his efforts . . .

VIL LIPATOV

GENKA PALTSEV—
SON OF DMITRI

Siberia, the place where Vil Lipatov (1927–1979) was born, remained the great love of his life and the background to all his stories. He reveled in the vast expanses of this eastern region of Russia, its rivers and forests, and this stark, cold landscape is so vividly described in his work, beginning with his first novel, *Deep Stream*, and continuing with his 1977 detective novel, *The Stolotov Dossier*, that it almost becomes a character. The son of a much-loved Bolshevik journalist, Lipatov was a true son of the Soviet Union, writing of the evils of individualism, claiming that it not only led to vice but that it was itself a vice.

Lipatov worked in the Soviet Union's film industry, writing several screenplays, including *Ivan I Kolombina* (1975).

The hero of his short story collection, *A Village Detective* (1970), is Fyodor Aniskin, a divisional militia inspector who has been at his post in a small Siberian village for forty years, showing kindness and wisdom as a member of the close-knit community. He shares the traits that made Sherlock Holmes so successful: an acute observational ability, a logical mind and the uncanny skill of reconstructing events as if he had witnessed them first-hand.

"Genka Paltsev—Son of Dmitri" was first published in English in *A Village Detective* (Moscow, Progress Publishers, 1970).

1

Militia inspector Fyodor Aniskin was considered to be the stoutest man in the village. Cherkashin, the manager of the dairy factory, weighed sixteen stone but Aniskin was a head taller and much fatter. Nobody knew exactly how much he weighed for when he was asked Aniskin used to reply, "Why don't you weigh me yourself?" For all his obesity, however, the inspector moved about the village at a brisk pace, especially on cool days. He liked talking to people and hated the dairy manager's guts.

Aniskin had been village militia inspector for goodness knows how long, but nobody remembered what his rank was, because he only wore his uniform once every three years when he went on some particularly important business to the district centre. For this he gave the following reason, "If I wore my uniform every day, I'd have to spend all my wages on buying new ones." In summer he wore wide linen trousers, a grey shirt usually open at the neck showing his hairy chest and size twelve sandals. In rainy weather he wore heavy top boots and in winter felt boots which made his legs look really elephantine.

When Aniskin walked the length of the village on a winter morning the women listened to the snow creaking as he moved from one house to another and said to themselves, "Six o'clock, time to start making the dough." In summer Aniskin rose at half past six and his round of the village was marked by laboured breathing. Between five in the afternoon and eight in the evening Aniskin had his nap, then drank tea out in the garden in summer and in his small kitchen, whose walls were pasted with colour photographs cut from the magazine *Ogonyok,* in winter.

The militia inspector's wife was his very opposite in that she was extremely thin, with a low even voice and slanting eyes. Her name was Glafira. She did not work anywhere and was therefore regarded as a lady of leisure though nobody had ever seen her taking it easy. She always found something to keep her busy. She had a big vegetable plot, kept various animals and poultry, gathered mushrooms, berries and nuts, but for all her efforts the family was never particularly well-off, because they had many children and there was always a son or a daughter to be supported at college. Aniskin wanted all his children to have a good education. All Glafira's babies were big, pink-cheeked and healthy.

In the summer of 196... Aniskin's weight was calculated to be roughly nineteen stone. One stuffy July afternoon, with the time for his nap approaching, Aniskin was strolling leisurely along the village street keeping on the river side and trying to catch cool wafts from the Ob on his hot forehead. The river flowed lazily to the north, cormorants circled above it, and the ferry-boat made its way creakingly to the other side. The river was its usual self, so was the sky, and at the foot of the high bank children were bathing, snorting like horses. When they caught sight of Aniskin's huge bulk on the rise their shouting and screaming grew louder, and the running and splashing became more energetic than ever.

"Sitting in the water all day long, can you imagine it?" said Aniskin. "Can you imagine anything like it?"

He sucked his tooth, produced a handkerchief from his pocket, examined it carefully, thought a little, then moved his legs apart and bent down to pick a bit of brick. After winding his handkerchief round the brick he threw it down to the river edge, shouting to the children, "Wet the handkerchief for me, my head's fit to split!"

The children rushed to get the handkerchief and Aniskin laid his hands on his paunch, inclined his head to one side and began to twiddle his thumbs. His eyes popped out lobster fashion, his neck contracted and very slowly as though somebody was keeping him in place, he turned to the man who stood behind him.

"Well?" he said quietly.

"Here I am," came the equally quiet reply.

The man was about twenty-five. He wore a checked shirt and military-type breeches tucked into high boots and there was a grey cap perched on his head. But his physical appearance presented a striking contrast to his clothes. His pale, sickly face expressed extreme melancholy and the deep-set eyes glowed in the emaciated face with a strange icon-like beauty. His build was even more incongruous. The gaunt, saintly face and thin neck rested on the powerful torso of a wrestler, with enormously broad shoulders and a huge chest. His bare arms rippled with sweat-bathed muscles and the whole was supported by thick short legs. The man's head lived separately from his body; it was as though they belonged to different people. "Look at him," Aniskin thought to himself. "The image of his father Dmitri. Just look at him."

"You're a funny chap, Genka," Aniskin said with an aggrieved sucking of his tooth. "You have an angel's face and a wolf's body."

"That's not my fault, is it?" Genka retorted in a plaintive voice. "I'm not to blame for it, am I?"

"You must be," Aniskin answered reflectively. "If you weren't to blame I wouldn't have to bother with you in such heat."

Twiddling his thumbs on his paunch and emitting occasional smothered grunts, the inspector gazed at the Ob, and his eyes reflected the river, the water molten in the sun, the oarboat, the old poplar on the tall bank, the bend and the children who were clambering up the clayey bank. The first to reach the top was the liveliest and jolliest of them, and he ran up to Aniskin, the wet handkerchief in his hand, shouting ecstatically:

"Here it is, Uncle Aniskin, as wet as can be!"

For another few seconds Aniskin stood motionless, his legs apart, his head lowered. The boy grew quiet and the smile left his face. On wet feet he walked over to the inspector, touched him cautiously on the elbow, lifted his head, and looked Aniskin in the face. Then Aniskin untwined his hands and laid one of them on the boy's shoulder.

"Good for you, Vitaly Pirogov, son of Ivan Pirogov."

Taking the handkerchief from the boy he straightened up and told him sternly:

"Go back to your swimming now, Vitaly. And you knot the handkerchief round the back of my head, Genka. I can't see."

Genka, the chap in the checked shirt and top-boots, knotted the handkerchief round the back of the inspector's head, breathing cautiously and pantingly, and then walked aside and stood quietly, as Aniskin squeezed his eyes tight with pleasure and twitched his shoulders shiveringly. Water streamed from the handkerchief, which had not been wrung out very hard, onto Aniskin's broad nose and down his hairy chest.

"Ooo, that's more like it," Aniskin groaned delightedly.

With the knotted handkerchief on his head, the militia inspector looked like some primeval Oriental deity.

"Why don't you have a swim?" Genka asked.

"You have a swim yourself."

And Aniskin resumed his progress, down the village street moving his legs with elephantine clumsiness, and staring down morosely, obviously lost in some harrowing thoughts, for he was even hunched up tensely though this was not very noticeable with his enormous bulk. He passed Grandfather Krylov, who was sitting on a bench with his stick, with just a twitch of eyebrows for a greeting, did not so much as glance at the windows of the collective-farm office and did not smile at the woman who passed him with buckets full of water. Silent and redoubtable he marched on till he reached the house where he had his office. Stopping beside the wicket and thrusting his hand between the palings to open it from the inside, he asked drearily after a pause:

"Why the hell are you like you are, Genka? Why in God's name?"

It was as quiet as can be at the edge of a village where immediately behind the houses spread a meadow, and a grove of cedars and young birches stretched up the graveyard hill, where a fir wood ran up right to the last house, the trees looking like warriors in Mongol spiked helmets and the mail of their cones glistening yellow.

"Come on inside," Aniskin said. "Come on in."

Once inside his office, a bare darkish room, Aniskin ordered Genka to stand by the door, lowered himself down on a stool and laid his heavy hands with light hairs on the table. He was immobile for several moments, then popped out his eyes in a stern professional manner and breathed out inquiringly:

"Ah?"

"All I want is three days," Genka said. "Till the boat arrives from up the river. Three days."

"You certainly know what's good for you, Genka," Aniskin answered after some consideration. "Sure enough *Proletary* will come on Monday and you can make your get-away on it. Oh yes, you know what's good for you," he repeated and suddenly barked out ferociously, "Sit down! Sit down, you rotten bastard!"

A second stool stood in the corner and Genka made for it. His wild beast's paws trod stealthily, the massive back floated on at a strangely leisurely pace and his head moved along of its own accord, as it were, separately from the torso. All Genka's movements were lithe and flowing and, sitting down, he put his hands on his knees with an elegant gesture, sighed childishly and fixed on Aniskin a devoted gaze shining with affection. The inspector shivered from this gaze as from a cold shower and said sadly:

"You are a bandit, Genka, and no mistake. You crossed the room without a floorboard creaking."

Hungry black cockroaches scurried over the walls of the office in great swarms. Usually Aniskin paid no attention to them, just apologised to his visitors with a smile. But today he looked at the battalions resentfully, squinting his eyes till they were two angry slits, though he was not so much looking at the cockroaches as peering at something inside himself. But whatever it was that he was trying to make out within himself eluded him and he scowled painfully.

"Why don't you tell me what you have gone and done, Genka?" he suddenly asked politely. "But don't lie to me, my boy, please."

"Oh, dear me, Uncle Aniskin," Genka whispered confidingly oozing affection. "When did I ever lie to you?"

"You never did anything else, my dear lad," Aniskin replied kindly.

"That's not true, it's not true at all. Perhaps I did lie to you once or twice about small things, but when it came to big things, I've always told you the truth, because I haven't got it in me to conceal things. That was the way my dear mother brought me into this world. I just can't lie. I'm always like an open book to you."

As Genka Paltsev chanted on, blinking his saintly eyelashes, Aniskin was moving away further and further from him, and soon Genka's litany seemed to be coming to him from a vast distance. A thick netting seemed to curtain Genka's face, the pallor and sickliness left it and it was no longer Genka's head and body living separate lives of their own before him, but Genka's father, Dmitri Paltsev, sitting in the darkish office. He looked at Aniskin with his icon eyes and suddenly the stool heaved under the inspector and the floor sank. The damp rotting smell of a gully was in his nostrils, a big green star hit him in the eye so piercingly that his head began ringing like bells over an empty church, the star-like scar under his left breast began to ache. Enveloped in powder fumes he felt the pressure of a blood stream on his palm that flowed out to meet the star.

"Shut up," Aniskin whispered and made a motion with his hand as though to brush off a cobweb from his face. "Shut up."

For a minute they were both silent. Then Aniskin asked:

"What did you do at the farm, Genka?"

"I lifted a watch from the hairdresser," Genka answered. "A gold one."

"Well?"

"She squealed, Uncle Aniskin," Genka added inaudibly, "so I had to keep her quiet."

"Killed her?"

"Oh, how can you think such a thing about me, Uncle Aniskin! Now, would I go and kill a person over a mere watch? You are always inventing things, Uncle Aniskin, things it makes me shudder to think about to say nothing of repeating them out loud, really, you're being unjust to me . . ."

Genka chanted on, but his voice kept getting lower and the pauses between words longer and he gradually stretched out his legs before him sprawling on his stool. He lowered and lowered his voice until it became a whisper as Aniskin stared at him with immobile meditative eyes. Something was flowing out of them towards Genka, an invisible but tangible force which bound him hand and foot; Aniskin seemed to be looking right through Genka.

"That's enough!" Aniskin finally said. "Now I know everything about you, Genka. I needn't have received a telegram from the district station ordering me to arrest a dangerous criminal. See, I've found out everything from your own words, not from the telegram."

Genka was now lying rather than sitting on the stool, his muscly arms had slipped from his knees, the thick legs looked boneless and his Slav nose sharpened. Then he opened his mouth gasping fish-like.

"When did the telegram come?"

"Day before yesterday. . . . I never thought you were such a fool."

Aniskin made a grimace of distaste, sucked his tooth and rose from his stool with the resolute air of one who has been meaning to do something for a long time but somehow could not get round to it. Once risen, Aniskin walked over to the Russian stove, took off a box of insecticide from a shelf and sprinkled the front ledge with it.

"The hairdresser lived for two more hours," he said in a smothered voice. "Whatever made you switch on your torch when you strangled her? Oh, what a fool you are! With mug like yours, you shouldn't go about picking pockets, to say nothing of murder. She recognised your photograph. Now you've had it, Genka. It's the firing squad for you, as sure as daylight." Aniskin shook his head ruefully. "I've been militia inspector in this village for thirty-two years, but I've never seen a murderer yet. There have been fights and stealing, but no murders. You are my first murderer, Genka."

"Don't arrest me, Uncle Aniskin, don't give me up to the district station," Genka's head pleaded piteously and passionately. "Don't give me up."

There was a rural silence all around, with not a sound to be heard, except the cockroaches scuttling behind the stove.

"I've never given up any of the village folk to the district station for a small thing," Aniskin said. "You just try and think of somebody I have given up for a small thing."

"No, you haven't," Genka's swollen lips whispered. "Not one."

"I've got to arrest you, Genka," Aniskin went on quietly. "I have no choice but to arrest you, but I shall give you a chance to escape and prove your worth if only you get the better of your cowardice. But if your cowardice is stronger than you are, then you've had it. So decide for yourself whether you accept my condition or not."

"What condition?"

"I'll tell you."

Aniskin walked across the room to the window, and looked out leaning against the frame. He saw the Ob almost colourless in the sun, the blue cedars on the other bank and the empty space beyond them: the river was a mile across and there was an even wider expanse beyond it, the Vasyugansky marshes which stretched for hundreds of miles, a monotonous cheerless plain. Clouds of mosquitoes hovered over the marshes, the long-legged snipe squealed plaintively and the sun seemed to have got stuck in one position.

"Here is my condition, Genka," said Aniskin. "I am giving you till twelve o'clock tonight to leave the village. I haven't seen you and you haven't seen me. Now get out."

"Will you give me a canoe?" Genka whispered.

"No, I won't give you a canoe, or a boat either," Aniskin answered in a hard voice. "You know I put someone to keep an eye on them. You'll have to walk."

Paltsev sprawled on his stool, his face turned to the window, the Ob, the cedars and the expanse beyond.

"But it's the same as the firing squad," Genka whispered.

"And what did you think?" Aniskin responded after a pause. "What did you think when you strangled the mother of two children? Go away into the marshes and may God help you. If you get through alive, there's a chance that you will make good after all. If you don't make it, that's as it should be, too. You are your own master now, Genka. And there is nothing more to talk about."

Paltsev remained motionless, numb all over. His muscles lay flaccid on the bones, a trapped beast's torment flowed from the icon eyes down to his chest.

"You're a terrible man, Genka," Aniskin said sucking his tooth. "People usually turn pale with fear, but you've gone red all over as though you'd drunk a glass of vodka."

Some five minutes later Genka rose and stumbled over to the door.

"Have you got a knife?" Aniskin suddenly asked him in polite tones. "Eh, Genka?"

"The things you go thinking up, Uncle Aniskin," Genka chanted into the door. "Where would I get a knife from, how can you invent such a thing, really, it's quite insulting, it is."

On and on he chanted, but the inspector was not listening. He felt Genka all over with his eyes and nodded with satisfaction as he noticed a wave pass down Genka's back from the shoulders to the hips and to the left pocket of his breeches.

"Why you rotten bastard!" Aniskin said delightedly. "You have a revolver in your left pocket, can you beat it? You are a dangerous criminal alright!"

2

The old poplar on the bank whispered day-time story, the Ob was turning a deeper blue, the children no longer swam at the bottom of the high bank for it was already past five; lorries were giving impatient hoots in nearby meadows where the haymaking was in progress and women's voices were raised as they rounded up the work. It is always like this towards evening when the air becomes clear and light and carries every sound. If it is quiet in the village, one can hear the chugging of a boat's engine beyond the far bend, the cries of cormorants above the shallows four miles away and the cuckoo's lament in the birches of the graveyard.

It was quiet in the village, and Aniskin, standing in the middle of the road, his hands clasped on his paunch, and twiddling his thumbs, thought, "It's been such a hard day that I don't know which way to go." He stood in the dusty road for another minute, then nodded and went towards the house made of pine logs, the home of schoolteacher Filatov. Instead of entering the yard, he walked over to an open window, listened in frowning concentration, unable to place the sound coming from within, and then smiled broadly.

"Vladimir!" he called. "Would you mind coming out for a minute. I'd like to have a talk with you."

The whining of the electric razor stopped, there was an annoyed creaking of a chair, the hasty slapping of bare feet on the floor and the teacher poked his head out of the window. A small man, flecked with sun-spots like freckles, he averted his unshaven cheek from the inspector.

"Good afternoon," Aniskin greeted him. "Shaving, are you?"

"Good afternoon, Inspector," the teacher answered unenthusiastically and gestured with his hand. "Come inside, please." Instead of doing so, Aniskin took a step towards the window and peered into the teacher's face. Of course, the teacher's left cheek had been left unshaven, but that was nothing compared to the fact that his eyelids were as swollen as if they had been stung by a bee, his cheeks were puffy and purple and his hands shook so badly that the razor clutched in his fingers made a tattoo against the window-sill. Noticing this the teacher smiled wryly and put his hands behind his back.

"Vladimir, my dear man," said Aniskin. "Why don't you sit down on the sill, while I stand here outside."

"Thank you," answered the teacher hoarsely, "thank you, but I have no intention of sitting on the sill."

The teacher spoke defiantly, but he did not dare to look Aniskin in the eye, using the pretext of his unshaven cheek to turn further and further away from him until he presented to the inspector's gaze an ear pierced through by the sunrays and therefore of a bright scarlet colour.

"It was a good idea, Vladimir," Aniskin said gayly. "A very good idea to use an electric razor."

"Excuse me, Comrade Aniskin, but I don't get your meaning."

"There is nothing to get," Aniskin answered, growing serious. "Clear as day."

The inspector grew as subdued as a village of an evening. He turned away from the teacher, too, leaned his back against the log wall, hands drooping, head to one side. His breathing was laboured and wheezy, the skin on his face was grey and the collar of his shirt was open revealing a chest covered with grey hairs. It was a long time since the inspector had been seen in such a condition in the village, and the teacher threw him a glance out of the corner of his eye.

"I can't sleep, Vladimir, I have not been sleeping for the last three nights," he complained miserably. "I walk the street at night and examine my life from all angles. I turn myself inside out like a sheepskin coat, Vladimir, and it makes me restless. I regret something, fear something, want something. . . . The dogs bark, the moon shines, the Ob flows on its way. . . . I feel sick at heart, when I look behind me." He paused, sucked his tooth and added, "This is because a terrible thing has happened in our village."

Aniskin raised his head, gave a forced smile, smoothed his grey hair and stood silent and subdued for another minute, as though coming back from very far away, from an incomprehensible distance to this house made of fresh pine logs, this window, and the teacher at whom he stared unseeingly. It took him a long time, but he came back at last.

"You know what I meant about the razor," he went on. "I meant that it was much safer to use an electric razor when one has a bad hangover. You won't cut yourself."

"Comrade Aniskin!" the teacher said.

"I've been 'Comrade Aniskin' for sixty years now," the inspector said drily. "But I shall have to tell you the truth to your face, Comrade Filatov, since it's such a bad day anyway. I would probably have left you alone yesterday, but today. . . . Why do you drink and quarrel with your wife at night?" Aniskin demanded fiercely, goggling at the teacher lobster fashion. "What right have you to drink 600 grams of vodka an evening and raise a row at home?"

"I am not going to answer your questions," replied the teacher with a sarcastic smile. "Don't you think you are exceeding your rights and duties?"

The teacher no longer averted his face from Aniskin, he no longer hid his shaking hands behind his back, but stretched out his thin neck and hissed like an angry goose. He was a puny man and Aniskin, looking at him, thought with an inward smile, "Why is it always like this? A chicken of a man will strut before his wife!" But Aniskin did not smile outwardly, only shook his head and said:

"And don't you take it into your head that your wife has been complaining to me. She had nothing to do with it. I heard you shouting myself as I was roaming around in the moonlight. You made a terrific racket. It could be heard for miles around."

With these words Aniskin walked away from the window and sat down on a bit of wood that the builders had cut off a huge beam. The sunrays slanted onto him, forming a big square on his back that looked like a yellow patch. He was silent, and so was the teacher. The teacher's head was still raised haughtily and his eyes were narrowed, but colour was creeping into his blue cheeks and his lips trembled as though they kept back words with difficulty.

"I know how you started drinking, Vladimir," Aniskin said quietly. "That soak Cherkashin drags you into his house every Saturday, gives you some filthy muck to drink and complains that he was sacked from the chairman's post through intrigue." Aniskin snorted bitterly. "Cherkashin is a vicious and spiteful man, and you, Vladimir, are beginning to get like him."

"How? Can you be more specific?" the teacher asked with a crooked smile and an ironic shrug of his shoulders, though he realised that Aniskin was behaving strangely today. There were no golden sparks dancing in his grey eyes, he did not respond with his usual, reflective "Ho-ho!" and did not turn his face to the Ob to catch the cool breeze.

"You are like Cherkashin, Vladimir, in that you only see the bad in people. This is why you heap foul abuse on your wife, and why your class has seven unsatisfactory marks in arithmetic, and only four in Russian. Your opinion of people is by three marks lower than Yevgeni Samoilovich's who teaches the kids Russian."

Aniskin fell silent. The yellow patch lay on his back, his big gnarled hands hung between his legs, his dead tooth could be seen through his parted lips. He sat thus for some ten seconds, then said with a laugh:

"You are unjust to me too, Vladimir. Whatever did you call me Corporal Prishibeyev* for last Saturday in Cherkashin's company? Cherkashin has a bone to pick with me because I did a lot to get him sacked. Did you want to make him happy? You used to treat me fairly enough, Vladimir." Aniskin did not raise his head, but he was aware nonetheless that the teacher bit his lower lip, put the razor quietly on the window-sill and gripped the wooden frame warmed by the sun. Aniskin knew that the teacher's face had turned red, his dark eyes had become moist with shame and his hands had ceased to shake.

"Fyodor Ivanovich," the teacher whispered. "Fyodor Ivanovich. . . ."

"As for Fyodor Ivanovich, I've been called that for the last twenty years at least," Aniskin said with a smile. "Before that people called me Fyodor, and before that Fedka."

The inspector rose from the stump and put his hands behind his back slowly, but instead of starting down the street turned his face towards the Ob, for the first time since the conversation began. There was, as usual, a

---

* Corporal Prishibeyev is a character from Chekhov's story of the same title who keeps pulling people up and playing a volunteer policeman in the hope of introducing his beloved army order everywhere.—Tr.

moist breeze coming from the river and it blew at Aniskin's cheeks, strong neck and open chest. The same wind from the Ob ruffled his hair which was a solid grey but as thick as in his youth now long past.

"I don't hold it against you, Vladimir, that you called me Corporal Prishibeyev, for you are still young and silly. You don't even understand how things have changed since Corporal Prishibeyev's time. If you called a police officer that in those days . . ." Aniskin gave a listless wave of his hand. "Oh well, what's the use. . . . You wouldn't understand."

Without another glance at the teacher, Aniskin plodded down the village street, leaving round tracks in the dust with his sandals and shaking his head every three steps. He did not hurry, but his stride was long and he soon disappeared in the sun's rosy glow.

3

Aniskin awoke about eight o'clock in the evening, his usual time, opened his eyes, lay for a while silently, without stirring, listening to the noises inside the house, the tread of his wife Glafira on the floorboards, his youngest daughter Zinaida whispering with a girl-friend in the next room and the cow chewing its cud in the shed. It was hot and stuffy under the cotton bed-curtain, but Aniskin was not sweaty, for he had not been making any strenuous movements in his sleep.

The inspector thought about this and that: the Kolotovkins had been missing a calf these five days; the Murzins were expecting a son to come on leave from his military service and could well be planning to make some illicit homebrew; the first team had two harrows missing, old ones, to be true, but quite good, with a horse; Vanka, the tractor-driver, had again spent the night at Panka Voloshina's; the lad was nearing twenty and his parents hoped he would marry soon; Grandfather Anisim, the fisherman, was selling sterlet on the sly and it was the forbidden season for sterlet fishing. A lot of thoughts crowded into Aniskin's head, but one was uppermost, and only now he admitted to himself that ever since the morning he had been turning it over in his big head, as incessantly and heavily as the river current rolls over smooth stone, "Will he go or won't he?"

All the while Aniskin was making his way to the teacher's house, talking to him, thinking about things past or lying down for his afternoon nap, the same thought was boring into his mind, "Will he go or won't he?" But if he had avoided thinking about it all day and chased the thought away, now, as he lay under the curtain cool with inactivity, he began thinking about Genka Paltsev full blast. And as soon as he let his thoughts dwell on him, he understood that his visit to the teacher and his sleep under the curtain and his present meaningless lolling were all manoeuvres to escape Genka Paltsev.

The last thought stuck with Aniskin, and he kept turning it this way and that, letting it sink in and then discarding it to snatch it back again the next moment. Thousands of threads took him back into the past, hit at him and caressed him, lulled him and roused him. One moment Aniskin turned himself inside out, as it were, the next he shrank into a ball. The thought puzzled and baffled him and he was caught in a mass of inexplicables.

"Damn," he swore finally in a whisper and suddenly noticed that he was covered with sticky sweat. It appeared that, while thinking about Genka, he had been tossing about in bed and making unnecessary movements with his arms and legs.

"Glafira!" he called out.

Nobody answered, there were no steps heard, but a tawny gypsy face appeared in the parting of the curtain and the sullen eyes gleamed inquiringly:

"Well?"

"I'm getting up. Put on the samovar."

"The samovar is ready."

Glafira disappeared as noiselessly as she had come, and Aniskin shook his finger at her back.

"She always knows everything," he thought in resentful wonderment, lowering his legs and pushing them into his well-worn sandals.

Silence rolled about the rooms of the house, a usual but always unpleasant fact for Aniskin. Somehow it so happened that he was always busy and the life of his own family went on irrespective of him, not around him, but along some distant parallel. Nobody ever stopped to ask himself whether it was good or bad, for the divisional militia inspector lived a mysterious and unusual kind of life not only in the eyes of his family but of all the villagers. He was as enigmatic and removed from everyday human pursuits as a high-ranking general who spent all days behind the doors of his office.

As usual Aniskin had his tea by himself. His red face expressed bliss, delight and contentment. Everything was as usual, but he had his tea in the kitchen instead of in the yard. And Glafira, knowing that the only time he felt at home was during his meals, came into the kitchen and sat down in front of him. She sat quietly, resting, and her face was blissful too. Strangely enough, the thin bony Glafira and her stout husband were somehow alike, either in their manner of looking at people, or in the frown of the eyebrows, or in the vertical furrow over the bridge of the nose.

"Finished weeding the tomatoes?" Aniskin asked looking sideways at her.

"Yes."

Long comfortable minutes floated by. Aniskin drank one glass of tea after another, bit the sugar noisily, champed at a piece of bacon and puffed right and left. Glafira sat silent, gazing down, but one could see from the restful look of her ear, the strand of dark hair and the curved toe on her foot that she enjoyed these minutes alone with her husband.

"Bought boots for Fedka?" Aniskin asked her lazily.

"No."

"Why not?"

"What does he want pigskin boots for?"

Again there was a spell of silence, the special kind characteristic of this house. Aniskin listened to it, opened his mouth to say something, but changed his mind and only waved his arm.

"I'll buy him boots next week," Glafira explained. "Duska sent an order to the district when she heard Fedka needed some. Have you been after her again?"

"She has been cheating children out of their change. The day before yesterday she robbed Petka Surov of three kopecks."

"And Darya's Luska of five kopecks," Glafira volunteered after some consideration.

"Five kopecks?" Aniskin asked, placing his glass on the table and turning to his wife heavily. "Five kopecks!"

"Yes. She thinks that because I've quarrelled with Darya I won't find out about the five kopecks. But Darya is not a fool, she came and told me. 'All right,' she said, 'you and I had a quarrel, but it's real shameless to cheat a child out of five kopecks.' I'm sure Duska knows that she complained, so she's in a hurry to get Fedka real nice boots."

"I'll keep it in mind," Aniskin said smiling and shaking his head. "Duska, Duska, funny woman! What does she want all that money for?"

"She is making herself a new coat. Remember they delivered three fur collars to the shop and she bought one of them."

"I know about that."

"Then why do you ask what she wants the money for? D'you think she'd let that collar lie another winter?"

"Oh, you always know everything," Aniskin said with sudden severity and turned away from his wife, who did not react to his change of tone in any way, however, but sat there as happy and relaxed as before. She simply stared more intently down at the floor and bent her scrawny neck lower. Suddenly her sunken cheeks moved in a smile.

"You know, Fedka is already wearing size nine. Can you imagine it?"

"Take ten then," Aniskin responded after a pause. "I suppose you were going to anyway?"

"Yes."

And again the room was immersed in silence. Aniskin drank two more glasses of tea, then upturned his empty glass resolutely and rose with a springy motion. The table and the stool creaked, the floorboards groaned under his elephant weight, Glafira started and then relaxed again, reluctant to put an end to the blissful interlude of inactivity.

"It's a quarter to nine," said Aniskin. "I'll go to the farm board. There is some important business to discuss. Make me up a bed in the outhouse, will you."

He wiped his sweaty face with a towel, dropped the towel on the window-sill and waddled to the door. He walked in his usual unhurried manner. Glafira did not change her posture and still sat with her head bent low, her eyes staring at the floor. But she obviously was aware that her husband was at the door for she suddenly called out:

"Aniskin!"

"What is it?"

"You'd better take your gun along," she said very quietly.

Aniskin stopped in the doorway, turned to her slowly as though his hinges were too stiff, and said after a considering pause with a wave of his arm:

"No, I won't. I'm not thinking of killing him."

4

At a quarter to twelve the moon was suspended high over the village, and its shadows had grown so short that they were no longer dogging Aniskin's steps. The moon was yellow like a piece of cheap amber inserted into a dark fabric sprinkled with stars. The night was cool and bright.

Aniskin felt fine at night. His heart did not ache, his legs did not hurt, there was no gnawing feeling in the pit of his stomach; he felt healthy, cheerful and strong and so perceived everything with youthful freshness of feeling. He liked the moon, enjoyed the distant sounds of the accordion and looked with pleasure at the silver zigzag of the moonlit Ob.

The accordion sang the moving old song about young Komsomol lovers parted by the Civil War, about him pressing her hand and looking tenderly into the girl's eyes. Aniskin stopped for a while listening to the accordion singing about himself, his own youth. "I am a cunning fox," he thought of himself admiringly. "I certainly picked the right time for Genka's arrest—at midnight." The accordion made the inspector feel young and even handsome.

Genka's house was the last in the row. An empty bird box was nailed to an old willow tree. The young bull uttered short restless moos in the shed. The windows were gilded all over with moonlight. The yard was crowded with shadows thrown by the well pole, the numerous sheds, barns and outhouses. These shadows, dark-grey and shapeless, lived a life of their own, unconnected, as it were, with the moon. Aniskin walked up to the house and gazed at it for a while.

"Here we meet again, Dmitri," he thought.

Nobody in the village knew why starlings never made nests in the little boxes put up by Dmitri Paltsev or his son Genka. The excited birds, reaching home after their long flight from the south, fought among themselves for the possession of every little box available, but, for some reason, gave a wide berth to the Paltsevs' yard.

"Eh, Dmitri," Aniskin thought ruefully, "millions of people have been won over by Soviet power, but you remained what you have always been, a miserable, tight-fisted kulak."

Aniskin opened the gate soundlessly and entered the yard, dragging his dark-grey legless shadow along. The shadow went across the yard, winded its way among the outhouses and barns and stopped in front of the big shed. Moonlight made its way gladly and confidently into the opened door of the shed lighting its interior with pale mat reflection. In this paleness Aniskin could see two green dots and a strip of white.

Entering the shed, Aniskin made out what they were, the two green dots and the strip of white. Genka was sitting on an upturned tub, staring glassily, his teeth bared in a snarl. He was holding a gleaming revolver in his hand, his arm bent at an awkward angle so that it was hard to say where the revolver was pointing. When Aniskin crunched his way across the sandy floor and stopped, the barrel of the revolver turned on the inspector. Turned and remained in that position.

"I'll kill you!" said Genka.

"No, you won't," replied Aniskin with a grim smile. "If you aren't gone, that means you won't kill me. You are a coward, same as your father. That is why I gave you a chance, to see if there is anything of a man in you. There isn't. I never really believed you would go, that's why I gave you the chance. Now I see that you deserve the firing squad. Murderers never escape us."

Aniskin waddled his way unhurriedly towards Genka, scraping on the ground with his worn sandals. He went straight to meet the ominous hole of the revolver, a big, stout man who looked like an enigmatic Oriental deity.

NIKOLAI GOGOL

THE PORTRAIT

One of Russia's most important writers, Nikolai Vasilyevich Gogol-Yanovsky (1809–1852) may be credited for helping to lay the foundations of the development of the Russian realistic novel, though he was not himself a realist. Powerfully influenced by Alexander Pushkin, many of his early works were based on Russian folk tales, combining mythology and fantasy, and his later works were perceived as satires, though he saw them more as reflections of society. Profoundly, even fanatically, religious and nationalistic during much of his life, he dropped the Polish-sounding second part of his last name due to its Catholic, non-Russian, overtones.

His earliest work was so disastrously received that he fled St. Petersburg but, after a short stay in Germany, he returned to write *Evenings on the Farm Near Dikanka* (1831), a romantic picture of Ukrainian life that was widely praised. His most famous and lasting works followed, notably *Arabesques* (1835), which included such stories as "The Diary of a Madman" and "The Portrait"; *Mirgorod* (1836), containing "Taras Bulba," a historical romance about Ukrainian Cossacks which was filmed in 1962 with Yul Brynner and Tony Curtis; the 1836 satiric comedy *The Inspector General* (made into an unlikely musical comedy vehicle for Danny Kaye in 1949); and his masterpiece, *Dead Souls* (1842), often seen as a satire but in actuality a reflection of Gogol's dismal view of humanity. There were supposed to be additional tales about his hero, showing his gradual reformation, but none were published and, as the author descended into madness, he burned virtually all of his late writings.

THE PORTRAIT

"The Portrait" is about the possibility of evil and the mysterious effect a painting has on two artists, one of whom it corrupts while the other is lifted by it, though both suffer consequences. It was first published in a collection titled *Arabesques* in 1835; a somewhat different version was published in 1842. It was translated by Constance Garnett in 1922.

PART I

Nowhere did so many people pause as before the little picture-shop in the Shtchukinui Dvor. This little shop contained, indeed, the most varied collection of curiosities. The pictures were chiefly oil-paintings covered with dark varnish, in frames of dingy yellow. Winter scenes with white trees; very red sunsets, like raging conflagrations, a Flemish boor, more like a turkey-cock in cuffs than a human being, were the prevailing subjects. To these must be added a few engravings, such as a portrait of Khozreff-Mirza in a sheepskin cap, and some generals with three-cornered hats and hooked noses. Moreover, the doors of such shops are usually festooned with bundles of those publications, printed on large sheets of bark, and then coloured by hand, which bear witness to the native talent of the Russian.

On one was the Tzarevna Miliktrisa Kirbitievna; on another the city of Jerusalem. There are usually but few purchasers of these productions, but gazers are many. Some truant lackey probably yawns in front of them, holding in his hand the dishes containing dinner from the cook-shop for his master, who will not get his soup very hot. Before them, too, will most likely be standing a soldier wrapped in his cloak, a dealer from the old-clothes mart, with a couple of penknives for sale, and a huckstress, with a basketful of shoes. Each expresses admiration in his own way. The muzhiks generally touch them with their fingers; the dealers gaze seriously at them; serving boys and apprentices laugh, and tease each other with the coloured caricatures; old lackeys in frieze cloaks look at them merely for the sake of yawning away their time somewhere; and the hucksters, young Russian women, halt by instinct to hear what people are gossiping about, and to see what they are looking at.

At the time our story opens, the young painter, Tchartkoff, paused involuntarily as he passed the shop. His old cloak and plain attire showed him to be a man who was devoted to his art with self-denying zeal, and who had no time to trouble himself about his clothes. He halted in front of the little shop, and at first enjoyed an inward laugh over the monstrosities in the shape of pictures.

At length he sank unconsciously into a reverie, and began to ponder as to what sort of people wanted these productions? It did not seem remarkable to him that the Russian populace should gaze with rapture upon "Eruslanoff Lazarevitch," on "The Glutton" and "The Carouser," on "Thoma and Erema." The delineations of these subjects were easily intelligible to the masses. But where were there purchases for those streaky, dirty oil-paintings? Who needed those Flemish boors, those red and blue landscapes, which put forth some claims to a higher stage of art, but which really expressed the depths of its degradation? They did not appear the works of a self-taught child. In that case, in spite of the caricature of drawing, a sharp distinction would have manifested itself. But here were visible only simple dullness, steady-going incapacity, which stood, through self-will, in the ranks of art, while its true place was among the lowest trades. The same colours, the same manner, the same practised hand, belonging rather to a manufacturing automaton than to a man!

He stood before the dirty pictures for some time, his thoughts at length wandering to other matters. Meanwhile the proprietor of the shop, a little grey man, in a frieze cloak, with a beard which had not been shaved since Sunday, had been urging him to buy for some time, naming prices, without even knowing what pleased him or what he wanted. "Here, I'll take a silver piece for these peasants and this little landscape. What painting! it fairly dazzles one; only just received from the factory; the varnish isn't dry yet. Or here is a winter scene—take the winter scene; fifteen rubles; the frame alone is worth it. What a winter scene!" Here the merchant gave a slight fillip to the canvas, as if to demonstrate all the merits of the winter scene. "Pray have them put up and sent to your house. Where do you live? Here, boy, give me some string!"

"Hold, not so fast!" said the painter, coming to himself, and perceiving that the brisk dealer was beginning in earnest to pack some pictures up. He was rather ashamed not to take anything after standing so long in front of the shop; so saying, "Here, stop! I will see if there is anything I want here!" he stooped and began to pick up from the floor, where they were thrown in a heap, some worn, dusty old paintings. There were old family portraits, whose descendants, probably could not be found on earth; with torn canvas and frames minus their gilding; in short, trash. But the painter began his search, thinking to himself, "Perhaps I may come across something." He had heard stories about pictures of the great masters having been found among the rubbish in cheap print-sellers' shops.

The dealer, perceiving what he was about, ceased his importunities, and took up his post again at the door, hailing the passers-by with, "Hither, friends, here are pictures; step in, step in; just received from the makers!" He shouted his fill, and generally in vain, had a long talk with a rag-merchant, standing opposite, at the door of his shop; and finally, recollecting that he had a customer in his shop, turned his back on the public and went inside. "Well, friend, have you chosen anything?" said he. But the painter had already been standing motionless for some time before a portrait in a large and originally magnificent frame, upon which, however, hardly a trace of gilding now remained.

It represented an old man, with a thin, bronzed face and high cheek-bones; the features seemingly depicted in a moment of convulsive agitation. He wore a flowing Asiatic costume. Dusty and defaced as the portrait was, Tchartkoff saw, when he had succeeded in removing the dirt from the face, traces of the work of a great artist. The portrait appeared to be unfinished, but the power of the handling was striking. The eyes were the most remarkable picture of all: it seemed as though the full power of the artist's brush had been lavished upon them. They fairly gazed out of the portrait, destroying its harmony with their strange liveliness. When he carried the portrait to the door, the eyes gleamed even more penetratingly. They produced nearly the same impression on the public. A woman standing behind him exclaimed, "He is looking, he is looking!" and jumped back. Tchartkoff experienced an unpleasant feeling, inexplicable even to himself, and placed the portrait on the floor.

"Well, will you take the portrait?" said the dealer.

"How much is it?" said the painter.

"Why chaffer over it? give me seventy-five kopeks."

"No."

"Well, how much will you give?"

"Twenty kopeks," said the painter, preparing to go.

"What a price! Why, you couldn't buy the frame for that! Perhaps you will decide to purchase to-morrow. Sir, sir, turn back! Add ten kopeks. Take it, take it! give me twenty kopeks. To tell the truth, you are my only customer to-day, and that's the only reason."

Thus Tchartkoff quite unexpectedly became the purchaser of the old portrait, and at the same time reflected, "Why have I bought it? What is it to me?" But there was nothing to be done. He pulled a twenty-kopek piece from his pocket, gave it to the merchant, took the portrait under his arm, and carried it home. On the way thither, he remembered that the twenty-kopek piece he had given for it was his last. His thoughts at once became gloomy. Vexation and careless indifference took possession of him at one and the same moment. The red light of sunset still lingered in one half the sky; the houses facing that way still gleamed with its warm light; and meanwhile the cold blue light of the moon grew brighter. Light, half-transparent shadows fell in bands upon the ground. The painter began by degrees to glance up at the sky, flushed with a transparent light; and at the same moment from his mouth fell the words, "What a delicate tone! What a nuisance! Deuce take it!" Re-adjusting the portrait, which kept slipping from under his arm, he quickened his pace.

Weary and bathed in perspiration, he dragged himself to Vasilievsky Ostroff. With difficulty and much panting he made his way up the stairs flooded with soap-suds, and adorned with the tracks of dogs and cats. To his knock there was no answer: there was no one at home. He leaned against the window, and disposed himself to wait patiently, until at last there resounded behind him the footsteps of a boy in a blue blouse, his servant, model, and colour-grinder. This boy was called Nikita, and spent all his time in the streets when his master was not at home. Nikita tried for a long time to get the key into the lock, which was quite invisible, by reason of the darkness.

Finally the door was opened. Tchartkoff entered his ante-room, which was intolerably cold, as painters' rooms always are, which fact, however, they do not notice. Without giving Nikita his coat, he went on into his studio, a large room, but low, fitted up with all sorts of artistic rubbish—plaster hands, canvases, sketches begun and discarded, and draperies thrown over chairs. Feeling very tired, he took off his cloak, placed the portrait abstractedly between two small canvases, and threw himself on the narrow divan. Having stretched himself out, he finally called for a light.

"There are no candles," said Nikita.

"What, none?"

"And there were none last night," said Nikita. The artist recollected that, in fact, there had been no candles the previous evening, and became silent. He let Nikita take his coat off, and put on his old worn dressing-gown.

"There has been a gentleman here," said Nikita.

"Yes, he came for money, I know," said the painter, waving his hand.

"He was not alone," said Nikita.

"Who else was with him?"

"I don't know, some police officer or other."

"But why a police officer?"

"I don't know why, but he says because your rent is not paid."

"Well, what will come of it?"

"I don't know what will come of it: he said, 'If he won't pay, why, let him leave the rooms.' They are both coming again to-morrow."

"Let them come," said Tchartkoff, with indifference; and a gloomy mood took full possession of him.

Young Tchartkoff was an artist of talent, which promised great things: his work gave evidence of observation, thought, and a strong inclination to approach nearer to nature.

"Look here, my friend," his professor said to him more than once, "you have talent; it will be a shame if you waste it: but you are impatient; you have but to be attracted by anything, to fall in love with it, you become engrossed with it, and all else goes for nothing, and you won't even look at it. See to it that you do not become a fashionable artist. At present your colouring begins to assert itself too loudly; and your drawing is at times quite weak; you are already striving after the fashionable style, because it strikes the eye at once. Have a care! society already begins to have its attraction for you: I have seen you with a shiny hat, a foppish neckerchief. . . . It is seductive to paint fashionable little pictures and portraits for money; but talent is ruined, not developed, by that means. Be patient; think out every piece of work, discard your foppishness; let others amass money, your own will not fail you."

The professor was partly right. Our artist sometimes wanted to enjoy himself, to play the fop, in short, to give vent to his youthful impulses in some way or other; but he could control himself withal. At times he would forget everything, when he had once taken his brush in his hand, and could not tear himself from it except as from a delightful dream. His taste perceptibly developed. He did not as yet understand all the depths of Raphael, but he was attracted by Guido's broad and rapid handling, he paused before Titian's portraits, he delighted in the Flemish masters. The dark veil enshrouding the ancient pictures had not yet wholly passed away from before them; but he already saw something in them, though in private he did not agree with the professor that the secrets of the old masters are irremediably lost to us. It seemed to him that the nineteenth century had improved upon them considerably, that the delineation of nature was more clear, more vivid, more close. It sometimes vexed him when he saw how a strange artist, French or German, sometimes not even a painter by profession, but only a skilful dauber, produced, by the celerity of his brush and the vividness of his colouring, a universal commotion, and amassed in a twinkling a funded capital. This did not occur to him when fully occupied with his own work, for then he forgot food and drink and all the world. But when dire want arrived, when he had no money wherewith to buy brushes and colours, when his implacable landlord came ten times a day to demand the rent for his rooms, then did the luck of the wealthy artists recur to his hungry imagination; then did the thought which so often traverses Russian minds, to give up altogether, and go down hill, utterly to the bad, traverse his. And now he was almost in this frame of mind.

"Yes, it is all very well, to be patient, be patient!" he exclaimed, with vexation; "but there is an end to patience at last. Be patient! but what money have I to buy a dinner with to-morrow? No one will lend me any. If I did bring myself to sell all my pictures and sketches, they would not give me twenty kopeks for the whole of them. They are useful; I feel that not one of them has been undertaken in vain; I have learned something from each one. Yes, but of what use is it? Studies, sketches, all will be studies, trial-sketches to the end. And who will buy, not even knowing me by name? Who wants drawings from the antique, or the life class, or my unfinished love of a Psyche, or the interior of my room, or the portrait of Nikita, though it is better, to tell the truth, than the portraits by any of the fashionable artists? Why do I worry, and toil like a learner over the alphabet, when I might shine as brightly as the rest, and have money, too, like them?"

Thus speaking, the artist suddenly shuddered, and turned pale. A convulsively distorted face gazed at him, peeping forth from the surrounding canvas; two terrible eyes were fixed straight upon him; on the mouth was written a menacing command of silence. Alarmed, he tried to scream and summon Nikita, who already was snoring in the ante-room; but he suddenly paused and laughed. The sensation of fear died away in a moment; it was the portrait he had bought, and which he had quite forgotten. The light of the moon illuminating the chamber had fallen upon it, and lent it a strange likeness to life.

He began to examine it. He moistened a sponge with water, passed it over the picture several times, washed off nearly all the accumulated and incrusted dust and dirt, hung it on the wall before him, wondering yet more at the remarkable workmanship. The whole face had gained new life, and the eyes gazed at him so that he shuddered; and, springing back, he exclaimed in a voice of surprise: "It looks with human eyes!" Then suddenly there occurred to him a story he had heard long before from his professor, of a certain portrait by the renowned Leonardo da Vinci, upon which the great master laboured several years, and still regarded as incomplete, but which, according to Vasari, was nevertheless deemed by all the most complete and finished product of his art. The most finished thing about it was the eyes, which amazed his contemporaries; the very smallest, barely visible veins in them being reproduced on the canvas.

But in the portrait now before him there was something singular. It was no longer art; it even destroyed the harmony of the portrait; they were living, human eyes! It seemed as though they had been cut from a living man and inserted. Here was none of that high enjoyment which takes possession of the soul at the sight of an artist's production, no matter how terrible the subject he may have chosen.

Again he approached the portrait, in order to observe those wondrous eyes, and perceived, with terror, that they were gazing at him. This was no copy from Nature; it was life, the strange life which might have lighted up the face of a dead man, risen from the grave. Whether it was the effect of the moonlight, which brought with it fantastic thoughts, and transformed things into strange likenesses, opposed to those of matter-of-fact day, or from some other cause, but it suddenly became terrible to him, he knew not why, to sit alone in the room. He draw back from the portrait, turned aside, and tried not to look at it; but his eye involuntarily, of its own accord, kept glancing sideways towards it. Finally, he became afraid to walk about the room. It seemed as though some one were on the point of stepping up behind him; and every time he turned, he glanced timidly back. He had never been a coward; but his imagination and nerves were sensitive, and that evening he could not explain his involuntary fear. He seated himself in one corner, but even then it seemed to him that some one was peeping over his shoulder into his face. Even Nikita's snores, resounding from the ante-room, did not chase away his fear. At length he rose from the seat, without raising his eyes, went behind a screen, and lay down on his bed. Through the cracks of the screen he saw his room lit up by the moon, and the portrait hanging stiffly on the wall. The eyes were fixed upon him in a yet more terrible and significant manner, and it seemed as if they would not look at anything but himself. Overpowered with a feeling of oppression, he decided to rise from his bed, seized a sheet, and, approaching the portrait, covered it up completely.

Having done this, he lay down more at ease on his bed, and began to meditate upon the poverty and pitiful lot of the artist, and the thorny path lying before him in the world. But meanwhile his eye glanced involuntarily through the joint of the screen at the portrait muffled in the sheet. The light of the moon heightened the whiteness of the sheet, and it seemed to him as though those terrible eyes shone through the cloth. With terror he fixed his eyes more steadfastly on the spot, as if wishing to convince himself that it was all nonsense. But at length he saw—saw clearly; there was no longer a sheet—the portrait was quite uncovered, and was gazing beyond everything around it, straight at him; gazing as it seemed fairly into his heart. His heart grew cold. He watched anxiously; the old man moved, and suddenly, supporting himself on the frame with both arms, raised himself by his hands, and, putting forth both feet, leapt out of the frame. Through the crack of the screen, the empty frame alone was now visible. Footsteps resounded through the room, and approached nearer and nearer to the screen. The poor artist's heart began beating fast. He expected every moment, his breath failing for fear, that the old man would look round the screen at him. And lo! he did look from behind the screen, with the very same bronzed face, and with his big eyes roving about.

Tchartkoff tried to scream, and felt that his voice was gone; he tried to move; his limbs refused their office. With open mouth, and failing breath, he gazed at the tall phantom, draped in some kind of a flowing Asiatic robe, and waited for what it would do. The old man sat down almost on his very feet, and then pulled out something from among the folds of his wide garment. It was a purse. The old man untied it, took it by the end, and shook it. Heavy rolls of coin fell out with a dull thud upon the floor. Each was wrapped in blue paper, and on each was marked, "1000 ducats." The old man protruded his long, bony hand from his wide sleeves, and began to undo the rolls. The gold glittered. Great as was the artist's unreasoning fear, he concentrated all his attention upon the gold, gazing motionless, as it made its appearance in the bony hands, gleamed, rang lightly or dully, and was wrapped up again. Then he perceived one packet which had rolled farther than the rest, to the very leg of his bedstead, near his pillow. He grasped it almost convulsively, and glanced in fear at the old man to see whether he noticed it.

But the old man appeared very much occupied: he collected all his rolls, replaced them in the purse, and went outside the screen without looking at him. Tchartkoff's heart beat wildly as he heard the rustle of the retreating footsteps sounding through the room. He clasped the roll of coin more closely in his hand, quivering in every limb. Suddenly he heard the footsteps approaching the screen again. Apparently the old man had recollected that one roll was missing. Lo! again he looked round the screen at him. The artist in despair grasped the roll with all his strength, tried with all his power to make a movement, shrieked—and awoke.

He was bathed in a cold perspiration; his heart beat as hard as it was possible for it to beat; his chest was oppressed, as though his last breath was about to issue from it. "Was it a dream?" he said, seizing his head with both hands. But the terrible reality of the apparition did not resemble a dream. As he woke, he saw the old man step into the frame: the skirts of the flowing garment even fluttered, and his hand felt plainly that a moment before it had held something heavy. The moonlight lit up the room, bringing out from the dark corners here a canvas, there the model of a hand: a drapery thrown over a chair; trousers and dirty boots. Then he perceived that he was not lying in his bed, but standing upright in front of the portrait. How he had come there, he could not in the least comprehend. Still more surprised was he to find the portrait uncovered, and with actually no sheet over it. Motionless with terror, he gazed at it, and perceived that the living, human eyes were fastened upon him. A cold perspiration broke out upon his forehead. He wanted to move away, but felt that his feet had in some way become rooted to the earth. And he felt that this was not a dream. The old man's features moved, and his lips began to project towards him, as though he wanted to suck him in. With a yell of despair he jumped back—and awoke.

"Was it a dream?" With his heart throbbing to bursting, he felt about him with both hands. Yes, he was lying in bed, and in precisely the position in which he had fallen asleep. Before him stood the screen. The moonlight flooded the room. Through the crack of the screen, the portrait was visible, covered with the sheet, as it should be, just as he had covered it. And so that, too, was a dream? But his clenched fist still felt as though something had been held in it. The throbbing of his heart was violent, almost terrible; the weight upon his breast intolerable. He fixed his eyes upon the crack, and stared steadfastly at the sheet. And lo! he saw plainly the sheet begin to open, as though hands were pushing from underneath, and trying to throw it off. "Lord God, what is it!" he shrieked, crossing himself in despair—and awoke.

And was this, too, a dream? He sprang from his bed, half-mad, and could not comprehend what had happened to him. Was it the oppression of a nightmare, the raving of fever, or an actual apparition? Striving to calm, as far as possible, his mental tumult, and stay the wildly rushing blood, which beat with straining pulses in every vein, he went to the window and opened it. The cool breeze revived him. The moonlight lay on the roofs and the white walls of the houses, though small clouds passed frequently across the sky. All was still: from time to time there struck the ear the distant rumble of a carriage. He put his head out of the window, and gazed for some time. Already the signs of approaching dawn were spreading over the sky. At last he felt drowsy, shut the window, stepped back, lay down in bed, and quickly fell, like one exhausted, into a deep sleep.

He awoke late, and with the disagreeable feeling of a man who has been half-suffocated with coal-gas: his head ached painfully. The room was dim: an unpleasant moisture pervaded the air, and penetrated the cracks of his windows. Dissatisfied and depressed as a wet cock, he seated himself on his dilapidated divan, not knowing what to do, what to set about, and at length remembered the whole of his dream. As he recalled it, the dream presented itself to his mind as so oppressively real that he even began to wonder whether it were a dream, whether there were not something more here, whether it were not really an apparition. Removing the sheet, he looked at the terrible portrait by the light of day. The eyes were really striking in their liveliness, but he found nothing particularly terrible about them, though an indescribably unpleasant feeling lingered in his mind. Nevertheless, he could not quite convince himself that it was a dream. It struck him that there must have been some terrible fragment of reality in the vision. It seemed as though there were something in the old man's very glance and expression which said that he had been with him that night: his hand still felt the weight which had so recently lain in it as if some one had but just snatched it from him. It seemed to him that, if he had only grasped the roll more firmly, it would have remained in his hand, even after his awakening.

"My God, if I only had a portion of that money!" he said, breathing heavily; and in his fancy, all the rolls of coin, with their fascinating inscription, "1000 ducats," began to pour out of the purse. The rolls opened, the gold glittered, and was wrapped up again; and he sat motionless, with his eyes fixed on the empty air, as if he were incapable of tearing himself from such a sight, like a child who sits before a plate of sweets, and beholds, with watering mouth, other people devouring them.

At last there came a knock on the door, which recalled him unpleasantly to himself. The landlord entered with the constable of the district, whose presence is even more disagreeable to poor people than is the presence of a beggar to the rich. The landlord of the little house in which Tchartkoff lived resembled the other individuals who own houses anywhere in the Vasilievsky Ostroff, on the St. Petersburg side, or in the distant regions of Kolomna—individuals whose character is as difficult to define as the colour of a threadbare surtout. In his youth he had been a captain and a braggart, a master in the art of flogging, skilful, foppish, and stupid; but in his old age he combined all these various qualities into a kind of dim indefiniteness. He was a widower, already on the retired list, no longer boasted, nor was dandified, nor quarrelled, but only cared to drink tea and talk all sorts of nonsense over it. He walked about his room, and arranged the ends of the tallow candles; called punctually at the end of each month upon his lodgers for money; went out into the street, with the key in his hand, to look at the roof of his house, and sometimes chased the porter out of his den, where he had hidden himself to sleep. In short, he was a man on the retired list, who, after the turmoils and wildness of his life, had only his old-fashioned habits left.

"Please to see for yourself, Varukh Kusmitch," said the landlord, turning to the officer, and throwing out his hands, "this man does not pay his rent, he does not pay."

"How can I when I have no money? Wait, and I will pay."

"I can't wait, my good fellow," said the landlord angrily, making a gesture with the key which he held in his hand. "Lieutenant-Colonel Potogonkin has lived with me seven years, seven years already; Anna Petrovna Buchmisteroff rents the coach-house and stable, with the exception of two stalls, and has three household servants: that is the kind of lodgers I have. I say to you frankly, that this is not an establishment where people do not pay their rent. Pay your money at once, please, or else clear out."

"Yes, if you rented the rooms, please to pay," said the constable, with a slight shake of the head, as he laid his finger on one of the buttons of his uniform.

"Well, what am I to pay with? that's the question. I haven't a groschen just at present."

"In that case, satisfy the claims of Ivan Ivanovitch with the fruits of your profession," said the officer: "perhaps he will consent to take pictures."

"No, thank you, my good fellow, no pictures. Pictures of holy subjects, such as one could hang upon the walls, would be well enough; or some general with a star, or Prince Kutusoff's portrait. But this fellow has painted that muzhik, that muzhik in his blouse, his servant who grinds his colours! The idea of painting his portrait, the hog! I'll thrash him well: he took all the nails out of my bolts, the scoundrel! Just see what subjects! Here he has drawn his room. It would have been well enough had he taken a clean, well-furnished room; but he has gone and drawn this one, with all the dirt and rubbish he has collected. Just see how he has defaced my room! Look for yourself. Yes, and my lodgers have been with me seven years, the lieutenant-colonel, Anna Petrovna Buchmisteroff. No, I tell you, there is no worse lodger than a painter: he lives like a pig—God have mercy!"

The poor artist had to listen patiently to all this. Meanwhile the officer had occupied himself with examining the pictures and studies, and showed that his mind was more advanced than the landlord's, and that he was not insensible to artistic impressions.

"Heh!" said he, tapping one canvas, on which was depicted a naked woman, "this subject is—lively. But why so much black under her nose? did she take snuff?"

"Shadow," answered Tchartkoff gruffly, without looking at him.

"But it might have been put in some other place: it is too conspicuous under the nose," observed the officer. "And whose likeness is this?" he continued, approaching the old man's portrait. "It is too terrible. Was he really so dreadful? Ah! why, he actually looks at one! What a thundercloud! From whom did you paint it?"

"Ah! it is from a—" said Tchartkoff, but did not finish his sentence: he heard a crack. It seems that the officer had pressed too hard on the frame of the portrait, thanks to the weight of his constable's hands. The small boards at the side caved in, one fell on the floor, and with it fell, with a heavy crash, a roll of blue paper. The inscription caught Tchartkoff's eye— "1000 ducats." Like a madman, he sprang to pick it up, grasped the roll, and gripped it convulsively in his hand, which sank with the weight.

"Wasn't there a sound of money?" inquired the officer, hearing the noise of something falling on the floor, and not catching sight of it, owing to the rapidity with which Tchartkoff had hastened to pick it up.

"What business is it of yours what is in my room?"

"It's my business because you ought to pay your rent to the landlord at once; because you have money, and won't pay, that's why it's my business."

"Well, I will pay him to-day."

"Well, and why wouldn't you pay before, instead of giving trouble to your landlord, and bothering the police to boot?"

"Because I did not want to touch this money. I will pay him in full this evening, and leave the rooms to-morrow. I will not stay with such a landlord."

"Well, Ivan Ivanovitch, he will pay you," said the constable, turning to the landlord. "But in case you are not satisfied in every respect this evening, then you must excuse me, Mr. Painter." So saying, he put on his three-cornered hat, and went into the ante-room, followed by the landlord hanging his head, and apparently engaged in meditation.

"Thank God, Satan has carried them off!" said Tchartkoff, as he heard the outer door of the ante-room close. He looked out into the ante-room, sent Nikita off on some errand, in order to be quite alone, fastened the door behind him, and, returning to his room, began with wildly beating heart to undo the roll.

In it were ducats, all new, and bright as fire. Almost beside himself, he sat down beside the pile of gold, still asking himself, "Is not this all a dream?" There were just a thousand in the roll, the exterior of which was precisely like what he had seen in his dream. He turned them over, and looked at them for some minutes. His imagination recalled up all the tales he had heard of hidden hoards, cabinets with secret drawers, left by ancestors for their spendthrift descendants, with firm belief in the extravagance of their life. He pondered this: "Did not some grandfather, in the present instance, leave a gift for his grandchild, shut up in the frame of a family portrait?" Filled with romantic fancies, he began to think whether this had not some secret connection with his fate? whether the existence of the portrait was not bound up with his own, and whether his acquisition of it was not due to a kind of predestination?

He began to examine the frame with curiosity. On one side a cavity was hollowed out, but concealed so skilfully and neatly by a little board, that, if the massive hand of the constable had not effected a breach, the ducats might have remained hidden to the end of time. On examining the portrait, he marvelled again at the exquisite workmanship, the extraordinary treatment of the eyes. They no longer appeared terrible to him; but, nevertheless, each time he looked at them a disagreeable feeling involuntarily lingered in his mind.

"No," he said to himself, "no matter whose grandfather you were, I'll put a glass over you, and get you a gilt frame." Then he laid his hand on the golden pile before him, and his heart beat faster at the touch. "What shall I do with them?" he said, fixing his eyes on them. "Now I am independent for at least three years: I can shut myself up in my room and work. I have money for colours now; for food and lodging—no one will annoy and disturb me now. I will buy myself a first-class lay figure, I will order a plaster torso, and some model feet, I will have a Venus. I will buy engravings of the best pictures. And if I work three years to satisfy myself, without haste or with the idea of selling, I shall surpass all, and may become a distinguished artist."

Thus he spoke in solitude, with his good judgment prompting him; but louder and more distinct sounded another voice within him. As he glanced once more at the gold, it was not thus that his twenty-two years and fiery youth reasoned. Now everything was within his power on which he had hitherto gazed with envious eyes, had viewed from afar with longing. How his heart beat when he thought of it! To wear a fashionable coat, to feast after long abstinence, to hire handsome apartments, to go at once to the theatre, to the confectioner's, to . . . other places; and seizing his money, he was in the street in a moment.

First of all he went to the tailor, was clothed anew from head to foot, and began to look at himself like a child. He purchased perfumes and pomades; hired the first elegant suite of apartments with mirrors and plateglass windows which he came across in the Nevsky Prospect, without haggling about the price; bought, on the impulse of the moment, a costly eye-glass; bought, also on the impulse, a number of neckties of every description, many more than he needed; had his hair curled at the hairdresser's; rode through the city twice without any object whatever; ate an immense quantity of sweetmeats at the confectioner's; and went to the French Restaurant, of which he had heard rumours as indistinct as though they had concerned the Empire of China. There he dined, casting proud glances at the other visitors, and continually arranging his curls in the glass. There he drank a bottle of champagne, which had been known to him hitherto only by hearsay. The wine rather affected his head; and he emerged into the street, lively, pugnacious, and ready to raise the Devil, according to the Russian expression. He strutted along the pavement, levelling his eye-glass at everybody. On the bridge he caught sight of his former professor, and slipped past him neatly, as if he did not see him, so that the astounded professor stood stock-still on the bridge for a long time, with a face suggestive of a note of interrogation.

All his goods and chattels, everything he owned, easels, canvas, pictures, were transported that same evening to his elegant quarters. He arranged the best of them in conspicuous places, threw the worst into a corner, and promenaded up and down the handsome rooms, glancing constantly in the mirrors. An unconquerable desire to take the bull by the horns, and show himself to the world at once, had arisen in his mind. He already heard the shouts, "Tchartkoff! Tchartkoff! Tchartkoff paints! What talent Tchartkoff has!" He paced the room in a state of rapture.

The next day he took ten ducats, and went to the editor of a popular journal asking his charitable assistance. He was joyfully received by the journalist, who called him on the spot, "Most respected sir," squeezed both his hands, and made minute inquiries as to his name, birthplace, residence. The next day there appeared in the journal, below a notice of some newly invented tallow candles, an article with the following heading:

"TCHARTKOFF'S IMMENSE TALENT

"We hasten to delight the cultivated inhabitants of the capital with a discovery which we may call splendid in every respect. All are agreed that there are among us many very handsome faces, but hitherto there has been no means of committing them to canvas for transmission to posterity. This want has now been supplied: an artist has been found who unites in himself all desirable qualities. The beauty can now feel assured that she will be depicted with all the grace of her charms, airy, fascinating, butterfly-like, flitting among the flowers of spring. The stately father of a family can see himself surrounded by his family. Merchant, warrior, citizen, statesman—hasten one and all, wherever you may be. The artist's magnificent establishment [Nevsky Prospect, such and such a number] is hung with portraits from his brush, worthy of Van Dyck or Titian. We do not know which to admire most, their truth and likeness to the originals, or the wonderful brilliancy and freshness of the colouring. Hail to you, artist! you have drawn a lucky number in the lottery. Long live Andrei Petrovitch!" (The journalist evidently liked familiarity.) "Glorify yourself and us. We know how to prize you. Universal popularity, and with it wealth, will be your meed, though some of our brother journalists may rise against you."

The artist read this article with secret satisfaction; his face beamed. He was mentioned in print; it was a novelty to him: he read the lines over several times. The comparison with Van Dyck and Titian flattered him extremely. The praise, "Long live Andrei Petrovitch," also pleased him greatly: to be spoken of by his Christian name and patronymic in print was an honour hitherto totally unknown to him. He began to pace the chamber briskly, now he sat down in an armchair, now he sprang up, and seated himself on the sofa, planning each moment how he would receive visitors, male and female; he went to his canvas and made a rapid sweep of the brush, endeavouring to impart a graceful movement to his hand

The next day, the bell at his door rang. He hastened to open it. A lady entered, accompanied by a girl of eighteen, her daughter, and followed by a lackey in a furred livery-coat.

"You are the painter Tchartkoff?"

The artist bowed.

"A great deal is written about you: your portraits, it is said, are the height of perfection." So saying, the lady raised her glass to her eyes and glanced rapidly over the walls, upon which nothing was hanging. "But where are your portraits?"

"They have been taken away" replied the artist, somewhat confusedly: "I have but just moved into these apartments; so they are still on the road, they have not arrived."

"You have been in Italy?" asked the lady, levelling her glass at him, as she found nothing else to point it at.

"No, I have not been there; but I wish to go, and I have deferred it for a while. Here is an arm-chair, madame: you are fatigued?"

"Thank you: I have been sitting a long time in the carriage. Ah, at last I behold your work!" said the lady, running to the opposite wall, and bringing her glass to bear upon his studies, sketches, views and portraits which were standing there on the floor. "It is charming. Lise! Lise, come here. Rooms in the style of Teniers. Do you see? Disorder, disorder, a table with a bust upon it, a hand, a palette; dust, see how the dust is painted! It is charming. And here on this canvas is a woman washing her face. What a pretty face! Ah! a little muzhik! So you do not devote yourself exclusively to portraits?"

"Oh! that is mere rubbish. I was trying experiments, studies."

"Tell me your opinion of the portrait painters of the present day. Is it not true that there are none now like Titian? There is not that strength of colour, that—that— What a pity that I cannot express myself in Russian." The lady was fond of paintings, and had gone through all the galleries in Italy with her eye-glass. "But Monsieur Nohl—ah, how well he paints! what remarkable work! I think his faces have more expression than Titian's. You do not know Monsieur Nohl?"

"Who is Nohl?" inquired the artist.

"Monsieur Nohl. Ah, what talent! He painted her portrait when she was only twelve years old. You must certainly come to see us. Lise, you shall show him your album. You know, we came expressly that you might begin her portrait immediately."

"What? I am ready this very moment." And in a trice he pulled forward an easel with a canvas already prepared, grasped his palette, and fixed his eyes on the daughter's pretty little face. If he had been acquainted with human nature, he might have read in it the dawning of a childish passion for balls, the dawning of sorrow and misery at the length of time before dinner and after dinner, the heavy traces of uninterested application to various arts, insisted upon by her mother for the elevation of her mind. But the artist saw only the tender little face, a seductive subject for his brush, the body almost as transparent as porcelain, the delicate white neck, and the aristocratically slender form. And he prepared beforehand to triumph, to display the delicacy of his brush, which had hitherto had to deal only with the harsh features of coarse models, and severe antiques and copies of classic masters. He already saw in fancy how this delicate little face would turn out.

"Do you know," said the lady with a positively touching expression of countenance, "I should like her to be painted simply attired, and seated among green shadows, like meadows, with a flock or a grove in the distance, so that it could not be seen that she goes to balls or fashionable entertainments. Our balls, I must confess, murder the intellect, deaden all remnants of feeling. Simplicity! would there were more simplicity!" Alas, it was stamped on the faces of mother and daughter that they had so overdanced themselves at balls that they had become almost wax figures.

Tchartkoff set to work, posed his model, reflected a bit, fixed upon the idea, waved his brush in the air, settling the points mentally, and then began and finished the sketching within an hour. Satisfied with it, he began to paint. The task fascinated him; he forgot everything, forgot the very existence of the aristocratic ladies, began even to display some artistic tricks, uttering various odd sounds and humming to himself now and then as artists do when immersed heart and soul in their work. Without the slightest ceremony, he made the sitter lift her head, which finally began to express utter weariness.

"Enough for the first time," said the lady.

"A little more," said the artist, forgetting himself.

"No, it is time to stop. Lise, three o'clock!" said the lady, taking out a tiny watch which hung by a gold chain from her girdle. "How late it is!"

"Only a minute," said Tchartkoff innocently, with the pleading voice of a child.

But the lady appeared to be not at all inclined to yield to his artistic demands on this occasion; she promised, however, to sit longer the next time.

"It is vexatious, all the same," thought Tchartkoff to himself: "I had just got my hand in"; and he remembered no one had interrupted him or stopped him when he was at work in his studio on Vasilievsky Ostroff. Nikita sat motionless in one place. You might even paint him as long as you pleased; he even went to sleep in the attitude prescribed him. Feeling dissatisfied, he laid his brush and palette on a chair, and paused in irritation before the picture.

The woman of the world's compliments awoke him from his reverie. He flew to the door to show them out: on the stairs he received an invitation to dine with them the following week, and returned with a cheerful face to his apartments. The aristocratic lady had completely charmed him. Up to that time he had looked upon such beings as unapproachable, born solely to ride in magnificent carriages, with liveried footmen and stylish coachmen, and to cast indifferent glances on the poor man travelling on foot in a cheap cloak. And now, all of a sudden, one of these very beings had entered his room; he was painting her portrait, was invited to dinner at an aristocratic house. An unusual feeling of pleasure took possession of him: he was completely intoxicated, and rewarded himself with a splendid dinner, an evening at the theatre, and a drive through the city in a carriage, without any necessity whatever.

But meanwhile his ordinary work did not fall in with his mood at all. He did nothing but wait for the moment when the bell should ring. At last the aristocratic lady arrived with her pale daughter. He seated them, drew forward the canvas with skill, and some efforts of fashionable airs, and began to paint. The sunny day and bright light aided him not a little: he saw in his dainty sitter much which, caught and committed to canvas, would give great value to the portrait. He perceived that he might accomplish something good if he could reproduce, with accuracy, all that nature then offered to his eyes. His heart began to beat faster as he felt that he was expressing something which others had not even seen as yet. His work engrossed him completely: he was wholly taken up with it, and again forgot the aristocratic origin of the sitter. With heaving breast he saw the delicate features and the almost transparent body of the fair maiden grow beneath his hand. He had caught every shade, the slight sallowness, the almost imperceptible blue tinge under the eyes—and was already preparing to put in the tiny mole on the brow, when he suddenly heard the mother's voice behind him.

"Ah! why do you paint that? it is not necessary: and you have made it here, in several places, rather yellow; and here, quite so, like dark spots."

The artist undertook to explain that the spots and yellow tinge would turn out well, that they brought out the delicate and pleasing tones of the face. He was informed that they did not bring out tones, and would not turn out well at all. It was explained to him that just to-day Lise did not feel quite well; that she never was sallow, and that her face was distinguished for its fresh colouring.

Sadly he began to erase what his brush had put upon the canvas. Many a nearly imperceptible feature disappeared, and with it vanished too a portion of the resemblance. He began indifferently to impart to the picture that commonplace colouring which can be painted mechanically, and which lends to a face, even when taken from nature, the sort of cold ideality observable on school programmes. But the lady was satisfied when the objectionable tone was quite banished. She merely expressed surprise that the work lasted so long, and added that she had heard that he finished a portrait completely in two sittings. The artist could not think of any answer to this. The ladies rose, and prepared to depart. He laid aside his brush, escorted them to the door, and then stood disconsolate for a long while in one spot before the portrait.

He gazed stupidly at it; and meanwhile there floated before his mind's eye those delicate features, those shades, and airy tints which he had copied, and which his brush had annihilated. Engrossed with them, he put the portrait on one side and hunted up a head of Psyche which he had some time before thrown on canvas in a sketchy manner. It was a pretty little face, well painted, but entirely ideal, and having cold, regular features not lit up by life. For lack of occupation, he now began to tone it up, imparting to it all he had taken note of in his aristocratic sitter. Those features, shadows, tints, which he had noted, made their appearance here in the purified form in which they appear when the painter, after closely observing nature, subordinates himself to her, and produces a creation equal to her own.

Psyche began to live: and the scarcely dawning thought began, little by little, to clothe itself in a visible form. The type of face of the fashionable young lady was unconsciously transferred to Psyche, yet nevertheless she had an expression of her own which gave the picture claims to be considered in truth an original creation. Tchartkoff gave himself up entirely to his work. For several days he was engrossed by it alone, and the ladies surprised him at it on their arrival. He had not time to remove the picture from the easel. Both ladies uttered a cry of amazement, and clasped their hands.

"Lise, Lise! Ah, how like! Superb, superb! What a happy thought, too, to drape her in a Greek costume! Ah, what a surprise!"

The artist could not see his way to disabuse the ladies of their error. Shamefacedly, with drooping head, he murmured, "This is Psyche."

"In the character of Psyche? Charming!" said the mother, smiling, upon which the daughter smiled too. "Confess, Lise, it pleases you to be painted in the character of Psyche better than any other way? What a sweet idea! But what treatment! It is Correggio himself. I must say that, although I had read and heard about you, I did not know you had so much talent. You positively must paint me too." Evidently the lady wanted to be portrayed as some kind of Psyche too.

"What am I to do with them?" thought the artist. "If they will have it so, why, let Psyche pass for what they choose:" and added aloud, "Pray sit a little: I will touch it up here and there."

"Ah! I am afraid you will . . . it is such a capital likeness now!"

But the artist understood that the difficulty was with respect to the sallowness, and so he reassured them by saying that he only wished to give more brilliancy and expression to the eyes. In truth, he was ashamed, and wanted to impart a little more likeness to the original, lest any one should accuse him of actual barefaced flattery. And the features of the pale young girl at length appeared more closely in Psyche's countenance.

"Enough," said the mother, beginning to fear that the likeness might become too decided. The artist was remunerated in every way, with smiles, money, compliments, cordial pressures of the hand, invitations to dinner: in short, he received a thousand flattering rewards.

The portrait created a furore in the city. The lady exhibited it to her friends, and all admired the skill with which the artist had preserved the likeness, and at the same time conferred more beauty on the original. The last remark, of course, was prompted by a slight tinge of envy. The artist was suddenly overwhelmed with work. It seemed as if the whole city wanted to be painted by him. The door-bell rang incessantly. From one point of view, this might be considered advantageous, as presenting to him endless practice in variety and number of faces. But, unfortunately, they were all people who were hard to get along with, either busy, hurried people, or else belonging to the fashionable world, and consequently more occupied than any one else, and therefore impatient to the last degree. In all quarters, the demand was merely that the likeness should be good and quickly executed. The artist perceived that it was a simple impossibility to finish his work; that it was necessary to exchange power of treatment for lightness and rapidity, to catch only the general expression, and not waste labour on delicate details.

Moreover, nearly all of his sitters made stipulations on various points. The ladies required that mind and character should be represented in their portraits; that all angles should be rounded, all unevenness smoothed away, and even removed entirely if possible; in short, that their faces should be such as to cause every one to stare at them with admiration, if not fall in love with them outright. When they sat to him, they sometimes assumed expressions which greatly amazed the artist; one tried to express melancholy; another, meditation; a third wanted to make her mouth appear small on any terms, and puckered it up to such an extent that it finally looked like a spot about as big as a pinhead. And in spite of all this, they demanded of him good likenesses and unconstrained naturalness. The men were no better: one insisted on being painted with an energetic, muscular turn to his head; another, with upturned, inspired eyes; a lieutenant of the guard demanded that Mars should be visible in his eyes; an official in the civil service drew himself up to his full height in order to have his uprightness expressed in his face, and that his hand might rest on a book bearing the words in plain characters, "He always stood up for the right."

At first such demands threw the artist into a cold perspiration. Finally he acquired the knack of it, and never troubled himself at all about it. He understood at a word how each wanted himself portrayed. If a man wanted Mars in his face, he put in Mars: he gave a Byronic turn and attitude to those who aimed at Byron. If the ladies wanted to be Corinne, Undine, or Aspasia, he agreed with great readiness, and threw in a sufficient measure of good looks from his own imagination, which does no harm, and for the sake of which an artist is even forgiven a lack of resemblance. He soon began to wonder himself at the rapidity and dash of his brush. And of course those who sat to him were in ecstasies, and proclaimed him a genius.

Tchartkoff became a fashionable artist in every sense of the word. He began to dine out, to escort ladies to picture galleries, to dress foppishly, and to assert audibly that an artist should belong to society, that he must uphold his profession, that artists mostly dress like showmakers, do not know how to behave themselves, do not maintain the highest tone, and are lacking in all polish. At home, in his studio, he carried cleanliness and spotlessness to the last extreme, set up two superb footmen, took fashionable pupils, dressed several times a day, curled his hair, practised various manners of receiving his callers, and busied himself in adorning his person in every conceivable way, in order to produce a pleasing impression on the ladies. In short, it would soon have been impossible for any one to have recognised in him the modest artist who had formerly toiled unknown in his miserable quarters in the Vasilievsky Ostroff.

He now expressed himself decidedly concerning artists and art; declared that too much credit had been given to the old masters; that even Raphael did not always paint well, and that fame attached to many of his works simply by force of tradition: that Michael Angelo was a braggart because he could boast only a knowledge of anatomy; that there was no grace about him, and that real brilliancy and power of treatment and colouring were to be looked for in the present century. And there, naturally, the question touched him personally. "I do not understand," said he, "how others toil and work with difficulty: a man who labours for months over a picture is a dauber, and no artist in my opinion; I don't believe he has any talent: genius works boldly, rapidly. Here is this portrait which I painted in two days, this head in one day, this in a few hours, this in little more than an hour. No, I confess I do not recognise as art that which adds line to line; that is a handicraft, not art." In this manner did he lecture his visitors; and the visitors admired the strength and boldness of his works, uttered exclamations on hearing how fast they had been produced, and said to each other, "This is talent, real talent! see how he speaks, how his eyes gleam! There is something really extraordinary in his face!"

It flattered the artist to hear such reports about himself. When printed praise appeared in the papers, he rejoiced like a child, although this praise was purchased with his money. He carried the printed slips about with him everywhere, and showed them to friends and acquaintances as if by accident. His fame increased, his works and orders multiplied. Already the same portraits over and over again wearied him, by the same attitudes and turns, which he had learned by heart. He painted them now without any great interest in his work, brushing in some sort of a head, and giving them to his pupils to finish. At first he had sought to devise a new attitude each time. Now this had grown wearisome to him. His brain was tired with planning and thinking. It was out of his power; his fashionable life bore him far away from labour and thought. His work grew cold and colourless; and he betook himself with indifference to the reproduction of monotonous, well-worn forms. The eternally spic-and-span uniforms, and the so-to-speak buttoned-up faces of the government officials, soldiers, and statesmen, did not offer a wide field for his brush: it forgot how to render superb draperies and powerful emotion and passion. Of grouping, dramatic effect and its lofty connections, there was nothing. In face of him was only a uniform, a corsage, a dress-coat, and before which the artist feels cold and all imagination vanishes. Even his own peculiar merits were no longer visible in his works, yet they continued to enjoy renown; although genuine connoisseurs and artists merely shrugged their shoulders when they saw his latest productions. But some who had known Tchartkoff in his earlier days could not understand how the talent of which he had given such clear indications in the outset could so have vanished; and strove in vain to divine by what means genius could be extinguished in a man just when he had attained to the full development of his powers.

But the intoxicated artist did not hear these criticisms. He began to attain to the age of dignity, both in mind and years: to grow stout, and increase visibly in flesh. He often read in the papers such phrases as, "Our most respected Andrei Petrovitch; our worthy Andrei Petrovitch." He began to receive offers of distinguished posts in the service, invitations to examinations and committees. He began, as is usually the case in maturer years, to advocate Raphael and the old masters, not because he had become thoroughly convinced of their transcendent merits, but in order to snub the younger artists. His life was already approaching the period when everything which suggests impulse contracts within a man; when a powerful chord appeals more feebly to the spirit; when the touch of beauty no longer converts virgin strength into fire and flame, but when all the burnt-out sentiments become more vulnerable to the sound of gold, hearken more attentively to its seductive music, and little by little permit themselves to be completely lulled to sleep by it. Fame can give no pleasure to him who has stolen it, not won it; so all his feelings and impulses turned towards wealth. Gold was his passion, his ideal, his fear, his delight, his aim. The bundles of bank-notes increased in his coffers; and, like all to whose lot falls this fearful gift, he began to grow inaccessible to every sentiment except the love of gold. But something occurred which gave him a powerful shock, and disturbed the whole tenor of his life.

One day he found upon his table a note, in which the Academy of Painting begged him, as a worthy member of its body, to come and give his opinion upon a new work which had been sent from Italy by a Russian artist who was perfecting himself there. The painter was one of his former comrades, who had been possessed with a passion for art from his earliest years, had given himself up to it with his whole soul, estranged himself from his friends and relatives, and had hastened to that wonderful Rome, at whose very name the artist's heart beats wildly and hotly. There he buried himself in his work from which he permitted nothing to entice him. He visited the galleries unweariedly, he stood for hours at a time before the works of the great masters, seizing and studying their marvellous methods. He never finished anything without revising his impressions several times before these great teachers, and reading in their works silent but eloquent counsels. He gave each impartially his due, appropriating from all only that which was most beautiful, and finally became the pupil of the divine Raphael alone, as a great poet, after reading many works, at last made Homer's "Iliad" his only breviary, having discovered that it contains all one wants, and that there is nothing which is not expressed in it in perfection. And so he brought away from his school the grand conception of creation, the mighty beauty of thought, the high charm of that heavenly brush.

When Tchartkoff entered the room, he found a crowd of visitors already collected before the picture. The most profound silence, such as rarely settles upon a throng of critics, reigned over all. He hastened to assume the significant expression of a connoisseur, and approached the picture; but, O God! what did he behold!

Pure, faultless, beautiful as a bride, stood the picture before him. The critics regarded this new hitherto unknown work with a feeling of involuntary wonder. All seemed united in it: the art of Raphael, reflected in the lofty grace of the grouping; the art of Correggio, breathing from the finished perfection of the workmanship. But more striking than all else was the evident creative power in the artist's mind. The very minutest object in the picture revealed it; he had caught that melting roundness of outline which is visible in nature only to the artist creator, and which comes out as angles with a copyist. It was plainly visible how the artist, having imbibed it all from the external world, had first stored it in his mind, and then drawn it thence, as from a spiritual source, into one harmonious, triumphant song. And it was evident, even to the uninitiated, how vast a gulf there was fixed between creation and a mere copy from nature. Involuntary tears stood ready to fall in the eyes of those who surrounded the picture. It seemed as though all joined in a silent hymn to the divine work.

Motionless, with open mouth, Tchartkoff stood before the picture. At length, when by degrees the visitors and critics began to murmur and comment upon the merits of the work, and turning to him, begged him to express an opinion, he came to himself once more. He tried to assume an indifferent, everyday expression; strove to utter some such commonplace remark as; "Yes, to tell the truth, it is impossible to deny the artist's talent; there is something in it;" but the speech died upon his lips, tears and sobs burst forth uncontrollably, and he rushed from the room like one beside himself.

In a moment he stood in his magnificent studio. All his being, all his life, had been aroused in one instant, as if youth had returned to him, as if the dying sparks of his talent had blazed forth afresh. The bandage suddenly fell from his eyes. Heavens! to think of having mercilessly wasted the best years of his youth, of having extinguished, trodden out perhaps, that spark of fire which, cherished in his breast, might perhaps have been developed into magnificence and beauty, and have extorted too, its meed of tears and admiration! It seemed as though those impulses which he had known in other days re-awoke suddenly in his soul.

He seized a brush and approached his canvas. One thought possessed him wholly, one desire consumed him; he strove to depict a fallen angel. This idea was most in harmony with his frame of mind. The perspiration started out upon his face with his efforts; but, alas! his figures, attitudes, groups, thoughts, arranged themselves stiffly, disconnectedly. His hand and his imagination had been too long confined to one groove; and the fruitless effort to escape from the bonds and fetters which he had imposed upon himself, showed itself in irregularities and errors. He had despised the long, wearisome ladder to knowledge, and the first funda-mental law of the future great man, hard work. He gave vent to his vex-ation. He ordered all his later productions to be taken out of his studio, all the fashionable, lifeless pictures, all the portraits of hussars, ladies, and councillors of state.

He shut himself up alone in his room, would order no food, and devoted himself entirely to his work. He sat toiling like a scholar. But how pitifully wretched was all which proceeded from his hand! He was stopped at every step by his ignorance of the very first principles: simple ignorance of the mechanical part of his art chilled all inspiration and formed an impassable barrier to his imagination. His brush returned involuntarily to hackneyed forms: hands folded themselves in a set atti-tude; heads dared not make any unusual turn; the very garments turned out commonplace, and would not drape themselves to any unaccustomed posture of the body. And he felt and saw this all himself.

"But had I really any talent?" he said at length: "did not I deceive myself?" Uttering these words, he turned to the early works which he had painted so purely, so unselfishly, in former days, in his wretched cabin yonder in lonely Vasilievsky Ostroff. He began attentively to examine them all; and all the misery of his former life came back to him. "Yes," he cried despairingly, "I had talent: the signs and traces of it are everywhere visible—"

He paused suddenly, and shivered all over. His eyes encountered other eyes fixed immovably upon him. It was that remarkable portrait which he had bought in the Shtchukinui Dvor. All this time it had been covered up, concealed by other pictures, and had utterly gone out of his mind. Now, as if by design, when all the fashionable portraits and paintings had been removed from the studio, it looked forth, together with the productions of his early youth. As he recalled all the strange events connected with it; as he remembered that this singular portrait had been, in a manner, the cause of his errors; that the hoard of money which he had obtained in such peculiar fashion had given birth in his mind to all the wild caprices which had destroyed his talent—madness was on the point of taking possession of him. At once he ordered the hateful portrait to be removed.

But his mental excitement was not thereby diminished. His whole being was shaken to its foundation; and he suffered that fearful torture which is sometimes exhibited when a feeble talent strives to display itself on a scale too great for it and cannot do so. A horrible envy took possession of him—an envy which bordered on madness. The gall flew to his heart when he beheld a work which bore the stamp of talent. He gnashed his teeth, and devoured it with the glare of a basilisk. He conceived the most devilish plan which ever entered into the mind of man, and he hastened with the strength of madness to carry it into execution. He began to purchase the best that art produced of every kind. Having bought a picture at a great price, he transported it to his room, flung himself upon it with the ferocity of a tiger, cut it, tore it, chopped it into bits, and stamped upon it with a grin of delight.

The vast wealth he had amassed enabled him to gratify this devilish desire. He opened his bags of gold and unlocked his coffers. No monster of ignorance ever destroyed so many superb productions of art as did this raging avenger. At any auction where he made his appearance, every one despaired at once of obtaining any work of art. It seemed as if an angry heaven had sent this fearful scourge into the world expressly to destroy all harmony. Scorn of the world was expressed in his countenance. His tongue uttered nothing save biting and censorious words. He swooped down like a harpy into the street: and his acquaintances, catching sight of him in the distance, sought to turn aside and avoid a meeting with him, saying that it poisoned all the rest of the day.

Fortunately for the world and art, such a life could not last long: his passions were too overpowering for his feeble strength. Attacks of madness began to recur more frequently, and ended at last in the most frightful illness. A violent fever, combined with galloping consumption, seized upon him with such violence, that in three days there remained only a shadow of his former self. To this was added indications of hopeless insanity. Sometimes several men were unable to hold him. The long-forgotten, living eyes of the portrait began to torment him, and then his madness became dreadful. All the people who surrounded his bed seemed to him horrible portraits. The portrait doubled and quadrupled itself; all the walls seemed hung with portraits, which fastened their living eyes upon him; portraits glared at him from the ceiling, from the floor; the room widened and lengthened endlessly, in order to make room for more of the motionless eyes. The doctor who had undertaken to attend him, having learned something of his strange history, strove with all his might to fathom the secret connection between the visions of his fancy and the occurrences of his life, but without the slightest success. The sick man understood nothing, felt nothing, save his own tortures, and gave utterance only to frightful yells and unintelligible gibberish. At last his life ended in a final attack of unutterable suffering. Nothing could be found of all his great wealth; but when they beheld the mutilated fragments of grand works of art, the value of which exceeded a million, they understood the terrible use which had been made of it.

PART II

A throng of carriages and other vehicles stood at the entrance of a house in which an auction was going on of the effects of one of those wealthy art-lovers who have innocently passed for Maecenases, and in a simple-minded fashion expended, to that end, the millions amassed by their thrifty fathers, and frequently even by their own early labours. The long saloon was filled with the most motley throng of visitors, collected like birds of prey swooping down upon an unburied corpse. There was a whole squadron of Russian shop-keepers from the Gostinnui Dvor, and from the old-clothes mart, in blue coats of foreign make. Their faces and expressions were a little more natural here, and did not display that fictitious desire to be subservient which is so marked in the Russian shop-keeper when he stands before a customer in his shop. Here they stood upon no ceremony, although the saloons were full of those very aristocrats before whom, in any other place, they would have been ready to sweep, with reverence, the dust brought in by their feet. They were quite at their ease, handling pictures and books without ceremony, when desirous of ascertaining the value of the goods, and boldly upsetting bargains mentally secured in advance by noble connoisseurs. There were many of those infallible attendants of auctions who make it a point to go to one every day as regularly as to take their breakfast; aristocratic connoisseurs who look upon it as their duty not to miss any opportunity of adding to their collections, and who have no other occupation between twelve o'clock and one; and noble gentlemen, with garments very threadbare, who make their daily appearance without any selfish object in view, but merely to see how it all goes off.

A quantity of pictures were lying about in disorder: with them were mingled furniture, and books with the cipher of the former owner, who never was moved by any laudable desire to glance into them. Chinese vases, marble slabs for tables, old and new furniture with curving lines, with griffins, sphinxes, and lions' paws, gilded and ungilded, chandeliers, sconces, all were heaped together in a perfect chaos of art.

The auction appeared to be at its height.

The surging throng was competing for a portrait which could not but arrest the attention of all who possessed any knowledge of art. The skilled hand of an artist was plainly visible in it. The portrait, which had apparently been several times restored and renovated, represented the dark features of an Asiatic in flowing garments, and with a strange and remarkable expression of countenance; but what struck the buyers more than anything else was the peculiar liveliness of the eyes. The more they were looked at, the more did they seem to penetrate into the gazer's heart. This peculiarity, this strange illusion achieved by the artist, attracted the attention of nearly all. Many who had been bidding gradually withdrew, for the price offered had risen to an incredible sum. There remained only two well-known aristocrats, amateurs of painting, who were unwilling to forego such an acquisition. They grew warm, and would probably have run the bidding up to an impossible sum, had not one of the onlookers suddenly exclaimed, "Permit me to interrupt your competition for a while: I, perhaps, more than any other, have a right to this portrait."

These words at once drew the attention of all to him. He was a tall man of thirty-five, with long black curls. His pleasant face, full of a certain bright nonchalance, indicated a mind free from all wearisome, worldly excitement; his garments had no pretence to fashion: all about him indicated the artist. He was, in fact, B. the painter, a man personally well known to many of those present.

"However strange my words may seem to you," he continued, perceiving that the general attention was directed to him, "if you will listen to a short story, you may possibly see that I was right in uttering them. Everything assures me that this is the portrait which I am looking for."

A natural curiosity illuminated the faces of nearly all present; and even the auctioneer paused as he was opening his mouth, and with hammer uplifted in the air, prepared to listen. At the beginning of the story, many glanced involuntarily towards the portrait; but later on, all bent their attention solely on the narrator, as his tale grew gradually more absorbing.

"You know that portion of the city which is called Kolomna," he began. "There everything is unlike anything else in St. Petersburg.

Retired officials remove thither to live; widows; people not very well off, who have acquaintances in the senate, and therefore condemn themselves to this for nearly the whole of their lives; and, in short, that whole list of people who can be described by the words ash-coloured—people whose garments, faces, hair, eyes, have a sort of ashy surface, like a day when there is in the sky neither cloud nor sun. Among them may be retired actors, retired titular councillors, retired sons of Mars, with ruined eyes and swollen lips.

"Life in Kolomna is terribly dull: rarely does a carriage appear, except, perhaps, one containing an actor, which disturbs the universal stillness by its rumble, noise, and jingling. You can get lodgings for five rubles a month, coffee in the morning included. Widows with pensions are the most aristocratic families there; they conduct themselves well, sweep their rooms often, chatter with their friends about the dearness of beef and cabbage, and frequently have a young daughter, a taciturn, quiet, sometimes pretty creature; an ugly dog, and wall-clocks which strike in a melancholy fashion. Then come the actors whose salaries do not permit them to desert Kolomna, an independent folk, living, like all artists, for pleasure. They sit in their dressing-gowns, cleaning their pistols, gluing together all sorts of things out of cardboard, playing draughts and cards with any friend who chances to drop in, and so pass away the morning, doing pretty nearly the same in the evening, with the addition of punch now and then. After these great people and aristocracy of Kolomna, come the rank and file. It is as difficult to put a name to them as to remember the multitude of insects which breed in stale vinegar. There are old women who get drunk, who make a living by incomprehensible means, like ants, dragging old clothes and rags from the Kalinkin Bridge to the old clothes-mart, in order to sell them for fifteen kopeks—in short, the very dregs of mankind, whose conditions no beneficent, political econo- mist has devised any means of ameliorating.

"I have mentioned them in order to point out how often such people find themselves under the necessity of seeking immediate temporary assistance and having recourse to borrowing. Hence there settles among them a peculiar race of money-lenders who lend small sums on security at an enormous percentage. Among these usurers was a certain . . . but I must not omit to mention that the occurrence which I have undertaken to relate occurred the last century, in the reign of our late Empress Catherine the Second. So, among the usurers, at that epoch, was a certain person—an extraordinary being in every respect, who had settled in that quarter of the city long before. He went about in flowing Asiatic garb; his dark complexion indicated a Southern origin, but to what particular nation he belonged, India, Greece, or Persia, no one could say with certainty. Of tall, almost colossal stature, with dark, thin, ardent face, heavy overhanging brows, and an indescribably strange colour in his large eyes of unwonted fire, he differed sharply and strongly from all the ash-coloured denizens of the capital.

"His very dwelling was unlike the other little wooden houses. It was of stone, in the style of those formerly much affected by Genoese merchants, with irregular windows of various sizes, secured with iron shutters and bars. This usurer differed from other usurers also in that he could furnish any required sum, from that desired by the poor old beggar-woman to that demanded by the extravagant grandee of the court. The most gorgeous equipages often halted in front of his house, and from their windows sometimes peeped forth the head of an elegant high-born lady. Rumour, as usual, reported that his iron coffers were full of untold gold, treasures, diamonds, and all sorts of pledges, but that, nevertheless, he was not the slave of that avarice which is characteristic of other usurers. He lent money willingly, and on very favourable terms of payment apparently, but, by some curious method of reckoning, made them mount to an incredible percentage. So said rumour, at any rate. But what was strangest of all was the peculiar fate of those who received money from him: they all ended their lives in some unhappy way. Whether this was simply the popular superstition, or the result of reports circulated with an object, is not known. But several instances which happened within a brief space of time before the eyes of every one were vivid and striking.

"Among the aristocracy of that day, one who speedily drew attention to himself was a young man of one of the best families who had made a figure in his early years in court circles, a warm admirer of everything true and noble, zealous in his love for art, and giving promise of becoming a Maecenas. He was soon deservedly distinguished by the Empress, who conferred upon him an important post, fully proportioned to his deserts—a post in which he could accomplish much for science and the general welfare. The youthful dignitary surrounded himself with artists, poets, and learned men. He wished to give work to all, to encourage all. He undertook, at his own expense, a number of useful publications; gave numerous orders to artists; offered prizes for the encouragement of different arts; spent a great deal of money, and finally ruined himself. But, full of noble impulses, he did not wish to relinquish his work, sought to raise a loan, and finally betook himself to the well-known usurer. Having borrowed a considerable sum from him, the man in a short time changed completely. He became a persecutor and oppressor of budding talent and intellect. He saw the bad side in everything produced, and every word he uttered was false.

"Then, unfortunately, came the French Revolution. This furnished him with an excuse for every kind of suspicion. He began to discover a revolutionary tendency in everything; to concoct terrible and unjust accusations, which made scores of people unhappy. Of course, such conduct could not fail in time to reach the throne. The kind-hearted Empress was shocked; and, full of the noble spirit which adorns crowned heads, she uttered words still engraven on many hearts. The Empress remarked that not under a monarchical government were high and noble impulses persecuted; not there were the creations of intellect, poetry, and art contemned and oppressed. On the other hand, monarchs alone were their protectors. Shakespeare and Moliere flourished under their magnanimous protection, while Dante could not find a corner in his republican birthplace. She said that true geniuses arise at the epoch of brilliancy and power in emperors and empires, but not in the time of monstrous political apparitions and republican terrorism, which, up to that time, had never given to the world a single poet; that poet-artists should be marked out for favour, since peace and divine quiet alone compose their minds, not excitement and tumult; that learned men, poets, and all producers of art are the pearls and diamonds in the imperial crown: by them is the epoch of the great ruler adorned, and from them it receives yet greater brilliancy.

"As the Empress uttered these words she was divinely beautiful for the moment, and I remember old men who could not speak of the occurrence without tears. All were interested in the affair. It must be remarked, to the honour of our national pride, that in the Russian's heart there always beats a fine feeling that he must adopt the part of the persecuted. The dignitary who had betrayed his trust was punished in an exemplary manner and degraded from his post. But he read a more dreadful punishment in the faces of his fellow-countrymen: universal scorn. It is impossible to describe what he suffered, and he died in a terrible attack of raving madness.

"Another striking example also occurred. Among the beautiful women in which our northern capital assuredly is not poor, one decidedly surpassed the rest. Her loveliness was a combination of our Northern charms with those of the South, a gem such as rarely makes its appearance on earth. My father said that he had never beheld anything like it in the whole course of his life. Everything seemed to be united in her, wealth, intellect, and wit. She had throngs of admirers, the most distinguished of them being Prince R., the most noble-minded of all young men, the finest in face, and an ideal of romance in his magnanimous and knightly sentiments. Prince R. was passionately in love, and was requited by a like ardent passion.

"But the match seemed unequal to the parents. The prince's family estates had not been in his possession for a long time, his family was out of favour, and the sad state of his affairs was well known to all. Of a sudden the prince quitted the capital, as if for the purpose of arranging his affairs, and after a short interval reappeared, surrounded with luxury and splendour. Brilliant balls and parties made him known at court. The lady's father began to relent, and the wedding took place. Whence this change in circumstances, this unheard-of-wealth, came, no one could fully explain; but it was whispered that he had entered into a compact with the mysterious usurer, and had borrowed money of him. However that may have been, the wedding was a source of interest to the whole city, and the bride and bridegroom were objects of general envy. Every one knew of their warm and faithful love, the long persecution they had had to endure from every quarter, the great personal worth of both. Ardent women at once sketched out the heavenly bliss which the young couple would enjoy. But it turned out very differently.

"In the course of a year a frightful change came over the husband. His character, up to that time so noble, became poisoned with jealous suspicions, irritability, and inexhaustible caprices. He became a tyrant to his wife, a thing which no one could have foreseen, and indulged in the most inhuman deeds, and even in blows. In a year's time no one would have recognised the woman who, such a little while before, had dazzled and drawn about her throngs of submissive adorers. Finally, no longer able to endure her lot, she proposed a divorce. Her husband flew into a rage at the very suggestion. In the first outburst of passion, he chased her about the room with a knife, and would doubtless have murdered her then and there, if they had not seized him and prevented him. In a fit of madness and despair he turned the knife against himself, and ended his life amid the most horrible sufferings.

"Besides these two instances which occurred before the eyes of all the world, stories circulated of many more among the lower classes, nearly all of which had tragic endings. Here an honest sober man became a drunkard; there a shopkeeper's clerk robbed his master; again, a driver who had conducted himself properly for a number of years cut his passenger's throat for a groschen. It was impossible that such occurrences, related, not without embellishments, should not inspire a sort of involuntary horror amongst the sedate inhabitants of Kolomna. No one entertained any doubt as to the presence of an evil power in the usurer. They said that he imposed conditions which made the hair rise on one's head, and which the miserable wretch never afterward dared reveal to any other being; that his money possessed a strange power of attraction; that it grew hot of itself, and that it bore strange marks. And it is worthy of remark, that all the colony of Kolomna, all these poor old women, small officials, petty artists, and insignificant people whom we have just recapitulated, agreed that it was better to endure anything, and to suffer the extreme of misery, rather than to have recourse to the terrible usurer. Old women were even found dying of hunger, who preferred to kill their bodies rather than lose their soul. Those who met him in the street experienced an involuntary sense of fear. Pedestrians took care to turn aside from his path, and gazed long after his tall, receding figure. In his face alone there was sufficient that was uncommon to cause any one to ascribe to him a supernatural nature. The strong features, so deeply chiselled; the glowing bronze of his complexion; the incredible thickness of his brows; the intolerable, terrible eyes—everything seemed to indicate that the passions of other men were pale compared to those raging within him. My father stopped short every time he met him, and could not refrain each time from saying, 'A devil, a perfect devil!' But I must introduce you as speedily as possible to my father, the chief character of this story.

"My father was a remarkable man in many respects. He was an artist of rare ability, a self-taught artist, without teachers or schools, principles and rules, carried away only by the thirst for perfection, and treading a path indicated by his own instincts, for reasons unknown, perchance, even to himself. Through some lofty and secret instinct he perceived the presence of a soul in every object. And this secret instinct and personal conviction turned his brush to Christian subjects, grand and lofty to the last degree. His was a strong character: he was an honourable, upright, even rough man, covered with a sort of hard rind without, not entirely lacking in pride, and given to expressing himself both sharply and scornfully about people. He worked for very small results; that is to say, for just enough to support his family and obtain the materials he needed; he never, under any circumstances, refused to aid any one, or to lend a helping hand to a poor artist; and he believed with the simple, reverent faith of his ancestors. At length, by his unintermitting labour and perseverance in the path he had marked out for himself, he began to win the approbation of those who honoured his self-taught talent. They gave him constant orders for churches, and he never lacked employment.

"One of his paintings possessed a strong interest for him. I no longer recollect the exact subject: I only know that he needed to represent the Spirit of Darkness in it. He pondered long what form to give him: he wished to concentrate in his face all that weighs down and oppresses a man. In the midst of his meditations there suddenly occurred to his mind the image of the mysterious usurer; and he thought involuntarily, 'That's how I ought to paint the Devil!' Imagine his amazement when one day, as he was at work in his studio, he heard a knock at the door, and directly after there entered that same terrible usurer.

"'You are an artist?' he said to my father abruptly.

"'I am,' answered my father in surprise, waiting for what should come next.

"'Good! Paint my portrait. I may possibly die soon. I have no children; but I do not wish to die completely, I wish to live. Can you paint a portrait that shall appear as though it were alive?'

"My father reflected, 'What could be better! he offers himself for the Devil in my picture.' He promised. They agreed upon a time and price; and the next day my father took palette and brushes and went to the usurer's house. The lofty court-yard, dogs, iron doors and locks, arched windows, coffers, draped with strange covers, and, last of all, the remarkable owner himself, seated motionless before him, all produced a strange impression on him. The windows seemed intentionally so encumbered below that they admitted the light only from the top. 'Devil take him, how well his face is lighted!' he said to himself, and began to paint assiduously, as though afraid that the favourable light would disappear. 'What power!' he repeated to himself. 'If I only accomplish half a likeness of him, as he is now, it will surpass all my other works: he will simply start from the canvas if I am only partly true to nature. What remarkable features!' He redoubled his energy; and began himself to notice how some of his sitter's traits were making their appearance on the canvas.

"But the more closely he approached resemblance, the more conscious he became of an aggressive, uneasy feeling which he could not explain to himself. Notwithstanding this, he set himself to copy with literal accuracy every trait and expression. First of all, however, he busied himself with the eyes. There was so much force in those eyes, that it seemed impossible to reproduce them exactly as they were in nature. But he resolved, at any price, to seek in them the most minute characteristics and shades, to penetrate their secret. As soon, however, as he approached them in resemblance, and began to redouble his exertions, there sprang up in his mind such a terrible feeling of repulsion, of inexplicable expression, that he was forced to lay aside his brush for a while and begin anew. At last he could bear it no longer: he felt as if these eyes were piercing into his soul, and causing intolerable emotion. On the second and third days this grew still stronger. It became horrible to him. He threw down his brush, and declared abruptly that he could paint the stranger no longer. You should have seen how the terrible usurer changed countenance at these words. He threw himself at his feet, and besought him to finish the portrait, saying that his fate and his existence depended on it; that he had already caught his prominent features; that if he could reproduce them accurately, his life would be preserved in his portrait in a supernatural manner; that by that means he would not die completely; that it was necessary for him to continue to exist in the world.

"My father was frightened by these words: they seemed to him strange and terrible to such a degree, that he threw down his brushes and palette and rushed headlong from the room.

"The thought of it troubled him all day and all night; but the next morning he received the portrait from the usurer, by a woman who was the only creature in his service, and who announced that her master did not want the portrait, and would pay nothing for it, and had sent it back. On the evening of the same day he learned that the usurer was dead, and that preparations were in progress to bury him according to the rites of his religion. All this seemed to him inexplicably strange. But from that day a marked change showed itself in his character. He was possessed by a troubled, uneasy feeling, of which he was unable to explain the cause; and he soon committed a deed which no one could have expected of him. For some time the works of one of his pupils had been attracting the attention of a small circle of connoisseurs and amateurs. My father had perceived his talent, and manifested a particular liking for him in consequence. Suddenly the general interest in him and talk about him became unendurable to my father who grew envious of him. Finally, to complete his vexation, he learned that his pupil had been asked to paint a picture for a recently built and wealthy church. This enraged him. 'No, I will not permit that fledgling to triumph!' said he: 'it is early, friend, to think of consigning old men to the gutters. I still have powers, God be praised! We'll soon see which will put down the other.'

"And this straightforward, honourable man employed intrigues which he had hitherto abhorred. He finally contrived that there should be a competition for the picture which other artists were permitted to enter into. Then he shut himself up in his room, and grasped his brush with zeal. It seemed as if he were striving to summon all his strength up for this occasion. And, in fact, the result turned out to be one of his best works. No one doubted that he would bear off the palm. The pictures were placed on exhibition, and all the others seemed to his as night to day. But of a sudden, one of the members present, an ecclesiastical personage if I mistake not, made a remark which surprised every one. 'There is certainly much talent in this artist's picture,' said he, 'but no holiness in the faces: there is even, on the contrary, a demoniacal look in the eyes, as though some evil feeling had guided the artist's hand.' All looked, and could not but acknowledge the truth of these words. My father rushed forward to his picture, as though to verify for himself this offensive remark, and perceived with horror that he had bestowed the usurer's eyes upon nearly all the figures. They had such a diabolical gaze that he involuntarily shuddered. The picture was rejected; and he was forced to hear, to his indescribable vexation, that the palm was awarded to his pupil.

"It is impossible to describe the state of rage in which he returned home. He almost killed my mother, he drove the children away, broke his brushes and easels, tore down the usurer's portrait from the wall, demanded a knife, and ordered a fire to be built in the chimney, intending to cut it in pieces and burn it. A friend, an artist, caught him in the act as he entered the room—a jolly fellow, always satisfied with himself, inflated by unattainable wishes, doing daily anything that came to hand, and taking still more gaily to his dinner and little carouses.

"'What are you doing? What are you preparing to burn?' he asked, and stepped up to the portrait. 'Why, this is one of your very best works. It is the usurer who died a short time ago: yes, it is a most perfect likeness. You did not stop until you had got into his very eyes. Never did eyes look as these do now.'

"'Well, I'll see how they look in the fire!' said my father, making a movement to fling the portrait into the grate.

"'Stop, for Heaven's sake!' exclaimed his friend, restraining him: 'give it to me, rather, if it offends your eyes to such a degree.' My father resisted, but yielded at length; and the jolly fellow, well pleased with his acquisition, carried the portrait home with him.

"When he was gone, my father felt more calm. The burden seemed to have disappeared from his soul in company with the portrait. He was surprised himself at his evil feelings, his envy, and the evident change in his character. Reviewing his acts, he became sad at heart; and not without inward sorrow did he exclaim, 'No, it was God who punished me! my picture, in fact, was meant to ruin my brother-man. A devilish feeling of envy guided my brush, and that devilish feeling must have made itself visible in it.'

"He set out at once to seek his former pupil, embraced him warmly, begged his forgiveness, and endeavoured as far as possible to excuse his own fault. His labours continued as before; but his face was more frequently thoughtful. He prayed more, grew more taciturn, and expressed himself less sharply about people: even the rough exterior of his character was modified to some extent. But a certain occurrence soon disturbed him more than ever. He had seen nothing for a long time of the comrade who had begged the portrait of him. He had already decided to hunt him up, when the latter suddenly made his appearance in his room. After a few words and questions on both sides, he said, 'Well, brother, it was not without cause that you wished to burn that portrait. Devil take it, there's something horrible about it! I don't believe in sorcerers; but, begging your pardon, there's an unclean spirit in it.'

"'How so?' asked my father.

"'Well, from the very moment I hung it up in my room I felt such depression—just as if I wanted to murder some one. I never knew in my life what sleeplessness was; but I suffered not from sleeplessness alone, but from such dreams!—I cannot tell whether they were dreams, or what; it was as if a demon were strangling one: and the old man appeared to me in my sleep. In short, I can't describe my state of mind. I had a sensation of fear, as if expecting something unpleasant. I felt as if I could not speak a cheerful or sincere word to any one: it was just as if a spy were sitting over me. But from the very hour that I gave that portrait to my nephew, who asked for it, I felt as if a stone had been rolled from my shoulders, and became cheerful, as you see me now. Well, brother, you painted the very Devil!'

"During this recital my father listened with unswerving attention, and finally inquired, 'And your nephew now has the portrait?'

"'My nephew, indeed! he could not stand it!' said the jolly fellow:'do you know, the soul of that usurer has migrated into it; he jumps out of the frame, walks about the room; and what my nephew tells of him is simply incomprehensible. I should take him for a lunatic, if I had not undergone a part of it myself. He sold it to some collector of pictures; and he could not stand it either, and got rid of it to some one else.'

"This story produced a deep impression on my father. He grew seriously pensive, fell into hypochondria, and finally became fully convinced that his brush had served as a tool of the Devil; and that a portion of the usurer's vitality had actually passed into the portrait, and was now troubling people, inspiring diabolical excitement, beguiling painters from the true path, producing the fearful torments of envy, and so forth. Three catastrophes which occurred afterwards, three sudden deaths of wife, daughter, and infant son, he regarded as a divine punishment on him, and firmly resolved to withdraw from the world.

"As soon as I was nine years old, he placed me in an academy of painting, and, paying all his debts, retired to a lonely cloister, where he soon afterwards took the vows. There he amazed every one by the strictness of his life, and his untiring observance of all the monastic rules. The prior of the monastery, hearing of his skill in painting, ordered him to paint the principal picture in the church. But the humble brother said plainly that he was unworthy to touch a brush, that his was contaminated, that with toil and great sacrifice must he first purify his spirit in order to render himself fit to undertake such a task. He increased the rigours of monastic life for himself as much as possible. At last, even they became insufficient, and he retired, with the approval of the prior, into the desert, in order to be quite alone. There he constructed himself a cell from branches of trees, ate only uncooked roots, dragged about a stone from place to place, stood in one spot with his hands lifted to heaven, from the rising until the going down of the sun, reciting prayers without cessation. In this manner did he for several years exhaust his body, invigorating it, at the same time, with the strength of fervent prayer.

"At length, one day he returned to the cloister, and said firmly to the prior, 'Now I am ready. If God wills, I will finish my task.' The subject he selected was the Birth of Christ. A whole year he sat over it, without leaving his cell, barely sustaining himself with coarse food, and praying incessantly. At the end of the year the picture was ready. It was a really wonderful work. Neither prior nor brethren knew much about painting; but all were struck with the marvellous holiness of the figures. The expression of reverent humility and gentleness in the face of the Holy Mother, as she bent over the Child; the deep intelligence in the eyes of the Holy Child, as though he saw something afar; the triumphant silence of the Magi, amazed by the Divine Miracle, as they bowed at his feet: and finally, the indescribable peace which emanated from the whole picture—all this was presented with such strength and beauty, that the impression it made was magical. All the brethren threw themselves on their knees before it; and the prior, deeply affected, exclaimed, 'No, it is impossible for any artist, with the assistance only of earthly art, to produce such a picture: a holy, divine power has guided thy brush, and the blessing of Heaven rested upon thy labour!'

"By that time I had completed my education at the academy, received the gold medal, and with it the joyful hope of a journey to Italy—the fairest dream of a twenty-year-old artist. It only remained for me to take leave of my father, from whom I had been separated for twelve years. I confess that even his image had long faded from my memory. I had heard somewhat of his grim saintliness, and rather expected to meet a hermit of rough exterior, a stranger to everything in the world, except his cell and his prayers, worn out, tried up, by eternal fasting and penance. But how great was my surprise when a handsome old man stood before me! No traces of exhaustion were visible on his countenance: it beamed with the light of a heavenly joy. His beard, white as snow, and his thin, almost transparent hair of the same silvery hue, fell picturesquely upon his breast, and upon the folds of his black gown, even to the rope with which his poor monastic garb was girded. But most surprising to me of all was to hear from his mouth such words and thoughts about art as, I confess, I long shall bear in mind, and I sincerely wish that all my comrades would do the same.

"'I expected you, my son,' he said, when I approached for his blessing. 'The path awaits you in which your life is henceforth to flow. Your path is pure—desert it not. You have talent: talent is the most price-less of God's gifts—destroy it not. Search out, subject all things to your brush; but in all see that you find the hidden soul, and most of all, strive to attain to the grand secret of creation. Blessed is the elect one who mas-ters that! There is for him no mean object in nature. In lowly themes the artist creator is as great as in great ones: in the despicable there is nothing for him to despise, for it passes through the purifying fire of his mind. An intimation of God's heavenly paradise is contained for the artist in art, and by that alone is it higher than all else. But by as much as triumphant rest is grander than every earthly emotion, by so much is the lofty creation of art higher than everything else on earth. Sacrifice everything to it, and love it with passion—not with the passion breathing with earthly desire, but a peaceful, heavenly passion. It cannot plant discord in the spirit, but ascends, like a resounding prayer, eternally to God. But there are moments, dark moments—' He paused, and I observed that his bright face darkened, as though some cloud crossed it for a moment. 'There is one incident of my life,' he said. 'Up to this moment, I cannot understand what that terrible being was of whom I painted a likeness. It was certainly some diabolical apparition. I know that the world denies the existence of the Devil, and therefore I will not speak of him. I will only say that I painted him with repugnance: I felt no liking for my work, even at the time. I tried to force myself, and, stifling every emotion in a hard-hearted way, to be true to nature. I have been informed that this portrait is passing from hand to hand, and sowing unpleasant impressions, inspiring artists with feelings of envy, of dark hatred towards their brethren, with mali-cious thirst for persecution and oppression. May the Almighty preserve you from such passions! There is nothing more terrible.'

"He blessed and embraced me. Never in my life was I so grandly moved. Reverently, rather than with the feeling of a son, I leaned upon his breast, and kissed his scattered silver locks.

"Tears shone in his eyes. 'Fulfil my one request, my son,' said he, at the moment of parting. 'You may chance to see the portrait I have mentioned somewhere. You will know it at once by the strange eyes, and their peculiar expression. Destroy it at any cost.'

"Judge for yourselves whether I could refuse to promise, with an oath, to fulfil this request. In the space of fifteen years I had never succeeded in meeting with anything which in any way corresponded to the description given me by my father, until now, all of a sudden, at an auction—"

The artist did not finish his sentence, but turned his eyes to the wall in order to glance once more at the portrait. The entire throng of auditors made the same movement, seeking the wonderful portrait with their eyes. But, to their extreme amazement, it was no longer on the wall. An indistinct murmur and exclamation ran through the crowd, and then was heard distinctly the word, "stolen." Some one had succeeded in carrying it off, taking advantage of the fact that the attention of the spectators was distracted by the story. And those present long remained in a state of surprise, not knowing whether they had really seen those remarkable eyes, or whether it was simply a dream which had floated for an instant before their eyesight, strained with long gazing at old pictures.

ANTON CHEKHOV

THE SWEDISH MATCH

Generally regarded as one of the world's greatest short story writers and playwrights, Anton Pavlovitch Chekhov (1860–1904) was extremely prolific in his short life, finding success as a writer of popular humor, horror and crime stories, selling his first, "What Is Met in the Novels" just before his twentieth birthday while a medical student at Moscow University. His stories number in the hundreds, many of which have never been translated and some never even included in his collected works in Russia. His only novel, *The Shooting Party* (1884) was published in the same year that he took his medical degree, and a story collection, *Motley Stories* (1886) garnered critical acclaim. He was already suffering from tuberculosis and soon moved to a farm in the countryside. As his health deteriorated, he made frequent trips to warmer climates, befriending Leo Tolstoy on one trip to Yalta. He shared some of Tolstoy's views of simple Christianity and anarchy for a short while, then broke with the philosophy, famously declaring: "Reason and justice tell me that there is more humanity in electricity and steam than in chastity and vegetarianism." In the last decade of his life, he wrote his four greatest plays, *The Sea Gull* (1896), *Uncle Vanya* (1899), *The Three Sisters* (1901) and *The Cherry Orchard* (1904). His collected works were translated into English by Constance Garnett and published in thirteen volumes (1916–1922).

"The Swedish Match" was first published in 1884. It has also been published as "The Match" and "The Safety Match."

I

On the morning of October 6, 1885, a well-dressed young man presented himself at the office of the police superintendent of the 2nd division of the S. district, and announced that his employer, a retired cornet of the guards, called Mark Ivanovitch Klyauzov, had been murdered. The young man was pale and extremely agitated as he made this announcement. His hands trembled and there was a look of horror in his eyes.

"To whom have I the honour of speaking?" the superintendent asked him.

"Psyekov, Klyauzov's steward. Agricultural and engineering expert."

The police superintendent, on reaching the spot with Psyekov and the necessary witnesses, found the position as follows.

Masses of people were crowding about the lodge in which Klyauzov lived. The news of the event had flown round the neighbourhood with the rapidity of lightning, and, thanks to its being a holiday, the people were flocking to the lodge from all the neighbouring villages. There was a regular hubbub of talk. Pale and tearful faces were to be seen here and there. The door into Klyauzov's bedroom was found to be locked. The key was in the lock on the inside.

"Evidently the criminals made their way in by the window" Psyekov observed, as they examined the door.

They went into the garden into which the bedroom window looked. The window had a gloomy, ominous air. It was covered by a faded green curtain. One corner of the curtain was slightly turned back, which made it possible to peep into the bedroom.

"Has anyone of you looked in at the window?" inquired the superintendent.

"No, your honour," said Yefrem, the gardener, a little, grey-haired old man with the face of a veteran non-commissioned officer. "No one feels like looking when they are shaking in every limb!"

"Ech, Mark Ivanitch! Mark Ivanitch!" sighed the superintendent, as he looked at the window. "I told you that you would come to a bad end! I told you, poor dear—you wouldn't listen! Dissipation leads to no good!"

"It's thanks to Yefrem," said Psyekov. "We should never have guessed it but for him. It was he who first thought that something was wrong. He came to me this morning and said: 'Why is it our master hasn't waked up for so long? He hasn't been out of his bedroom for a whole week!' When he said that to me I was struck all of a heap. . . . The thought flashed through my mind at once. He hasn't made an appearance since Saturday of last week, and to-day's Sunday. Seven days is no joke!"

"Yes, poor man," the superintendent sighed again. "A clever fellow, well-educated, and so good-hearted. There was no one like him, one may say, in company. But a rake; the kingdom of heaven be his! I'm not surprised at anything with him! Stepan," he said, addressing one of the witnesses, "ride off this minute to my house and send Andryushka to the police captain's, let him report to him. Say Mark Ivanitch has been murdered! Yes, and run to the inspector—why should he sit in comfort doing nothing? Let him come here. And you go yourself as fast as you can to the examining magistrate, Nikolay Yermolaitch, and tell him to come here. Wait a bit, I will write him a note."

The police superintendent stationed watchmen round the lodge, and went off to the steward's to have tea. Ten minutes later he was sitting on a stool, carefully nibbling lumps of sugar, and sipping tea as hot as a red-hot coal.

"There it is! . . ." he said to Psyekov, "there it is! . . . a gentleman, and a well-to-do one, too . . . a favourite of the gods, one may say, to use Pushkin's expression, and what has he made of it? Nothing! He gave himself up to drinking and debauchery, and . . . here now . . . he has been murdered!"

Two hours later the examining magistrate drove up. Nikolay Yermolaitch Tchubikov (that was the magistrate's name), a tall, thick-set old man of sixty, had been hard at work for a quarter of a century. He was known to the whole district as an honest, intelligent, energetic man, devoted to his work. His invariable companion, assistant, and secretary, a tall young man of six and twenty, called Dyukovsky, arrived on the scene of action with him.

"Is it possible, gentlemen?" Tchubikov began, going into Psyekov's room and rapidly shaking hands with everyone. "Is it possible? Mark Ivanitch? Murdered? No, it's impossible! Imposs-i-ble!"

"There it is," sighed the superintendent

"Merciful heavens! Why I saw him only last Friday. At the fair at Tarabankovo! Saving your presence, I drank a glass of vodka with him!"

"There it is," the superintendent sighed once more.

They heaved sighs, expressed their horror, drank a glass of tea each, and went to the lodge.

"Make way!" the police inspector shouted to the crowd.

On going into the lodge the examining magistrate first of all set to work to inspect the door into the bedroom. The door turned out to be made of deal, painted yellow, and not to have been tampered with. No special traces that might have served as evidence could be found. They proceeded to break open the door.

"I beg you, gentlemen, who are not concerned, to retire," said the examining magistrate, when, after long banging and cracking, the door yielded to the axe and the chisel. "I ask this in the interests of the investigation. . . . Inspector, admit no one!"

Tchubikov, his assistant, and the police superintendent opened the door and hesitatingly, one after the other, walked into the room. The following spectacle met their eyes. In the solitary window stood a big wooden bedstead with an immense feather bed on it. On the rumpled feather bed lay a creased and crumpled quilt. A pillow, in a cotton pillow case—also much creased, was on the floor. On a little table beside the bed lay a silver watch, and silver coins to the value of twenty kopecks. Some sulphur matches lay there too. Except the bed, the table, and a solitary chair, there was no furniture in the room.

Looking under the bed, the superintendent saw two dozen empty bottles, an old straw hat, and a jar of vodka. Under the table lay one boot, covered with dust. Taking a look round the room, Tchubikov frowned and flushed crimson.

"The blackguards!" he muttered, clenching his fists.

"And where is Mark Ivanitch?" Dyukovsky asked quietly.

"I beg you not to put your spoke in," Tchubikov answered roughly. "Kindly examine the floor. This is the second case in my experience, Yevgraf Kuzmitch," he added to the police superintendent, dropping his voice. "In 1870 I had a similar case. But no doubt you remember it. . . . The murder of the merchant Portretov. It was just the same. The blackguards murdered him, and dragged the dead body out of the window."

Tchubikov went to the window, drew the curtain aside, and cautiously pushed the window. The window opened.

"It opens, so it was not fastened. . . . H'm there are traces on the window-sill. Do you see? Here is the trace of a knee. . . . Some one climbed out. . . . We shall have to inspect the window thoroughly."

"There is nothing special to be observed on the floor," said Dyukovsky. "No stains, nor scratches. The only thing I have found is a used Swedish match. Here it is. As far as I remember, Mark Ivanitch didn't smoke; in a general way he used sulphur ones, never Swedish matches. This match may serve as a clue. . . ."

"Oh, hold your tongue, please!" cried Tchubikov, with a wave of his hand. "He keeps on about his match! I can't stand these excitable people! Instead of looking for matches, you had better examine the bed!"

On inspecting the bed, Dyukovsky reported:

"There are no stains of blood or of anything else. . . . Nor are there any fresh rents. On the pillow there are traces of teeth. A liquid, having the smell of beer and also the taste of it, has been spilt on the quilt. . . . The general appearance of the bed gives grounds for supposing there has been a struggle."

"I know there was a struggle without your telling me! No one asked you whether there was a struggle. Instead of looking out for a struggle you had better be . . ."

"One boot is here, the other one is not on the scene."

"Well, what of that?"

"Why, they must have strangled him while he was taking off his boots. He hadn't time to take the second boot off when . . . ."

"He's off again! . . . And how do you know that he was strangled?"

"There are marks of teeth on the pillow. The pillow itself is very much crumpled, and has been flung to a distance of six feet from the bed."

"He argues, the chatterbox! We had better go into the garden. You had better look in the garden instead of rummaging about here. . . . I can do that without your help."

When they went out into the garden their first task was the inspection of the grass. The grass had been trampled down under the windows. The clump of burdock against the wall under the window turned out to have been trodden on too. Dyukovsky succeeded in finding on it some broken shoots, and a little bit of wadding. On the topmost burrs, some fine threads of dark blue wool were found.

"What was the colour of his last suit?" Dyukovsky asked Psyekov.

"It was yellow, made of canvas."

"Capital! Then it was they who were in dark blue. . . ."

Some of the burrs were cut off and carefully wrapped up in paper. At that moment Artsybashev-Svistakovsky, the police captain, and Tyutyuev, the doctor, arrived. The police captain greeted the others, and at once proceeded to satisfy his curiosity; the doctor, a tall and extremely lean man with sunken eyes, a long nose, and a sharp chin, greeting no one and asking no questions, sat down on a stump, heaved a sigh and said:

"The Serbians are in a turmoil again! I can't make out what they want! Ah, Austria, Austria! It's your doing!"

The inspection of the window from outside yielded absolutely no result; the inspection of the grass and surrounding bushes furnished many valuable clues. Dyukovsky succeeded, for instance, in detecting a long, dark streak in the grass, consisting of stains, and stretching from the window for a good many yards into the garden. The streak ended under one of the lilac bushes in a big, brownish stain. Under the same bush was found a boot, which turned out to be the fellow to the one found in the bedroom.

"This is an old stain of blood," said Dyukovsky, examining the stain.

At the word "blood," the doctor got up and lazily took a cursory glance at the stain.

"Yes, it's blood," he muttered.

"Then he wasn't strangled since there's blood," said Tchubikov, looking malignantly at Dyukovsky.

"He was strangled in the bedroom, and here, afraid he would come to, they stabbed him with something sharp. The stain under the bush shows that he lay there for a comparatively long time, while they were trying to find some way of carrying him, or something to carry him on out of the garden."

"Well, and the boot?"

"That boot bears out my contention that he was murdered while he was taking off his boots before going to bed. He had taken off one boot, the other, that is, this boot he had only managed to get half off. While he was being dragged and shaken the boot that was only half on came off of itself. . . ."

"What powers of deduction! Just look at him!" Tchubikov jeered. "He brings it all out so pat! And when will you learn not to put your theories forward? You had better take a little of the grass for analysis instead of arguing!"

After making the inspection and taking a plan of the locality they went off to the steward's to write a report and have lunch. At lunch they talked.

"Watch, money, and everything else . . . are untouched," Tchubikov began the conversation. "It is as clear as twice two makes four that the murder was committed not for mercenary motives."

"It was committed by a man of the educated class," Dyukovsky put in.

"From what do you draw that conclusion?"

"I base it on the Swedish match which the peasants about here have not learned to use yet. Such matches are only used by landowners and not by all of them. He was murdered, by the way, not by one but by three, at least: two held him while the third strangled him. Klyauzov was strong and the murderers must have known that."

"What use would his strength be to him, supposing he were asleep?"

"The murderers came upon him as he was taking off his boots. He was taking off his boots, so he was not asleep."

"It's no good making things up! You had better eat your lunch!"

"To my thinking, your honour," said Yefrem, the gardener, as he set the samovar on the table, "this vile deed was the work of no other than Nikolashka."

"Quite possible," said Psyekov.

"Who's this Nikolashka?"

"The master's valet, your honour," answered Yefrem. "Who else should it be if not he? He's a ruffian, your honour! A drunkard, and such a dissipated fellow! May the Queen of Heaven never bring the like again! He always used to fetch vodka for the master, he always used to put the master to bed. . . . Who should it be if not he? And what's more, I venture to bring to your notice, your honour, he boasted once in a tavern, the rascal, that he would murder his master. It's all on account of Akulka, on account of a woman. . . . He had a soldier's wife. . . . The master took a fancy to her and got intimate with her, and he . . . was angered by it, to be sure. He's lolling about in the kitchen now, drunk. He's crying . . . making out he is grieving over the master. . . ."

"And anyone might be angry over Akulka, certainly," said Psyekov.

"She is a soldier's wife, a peasant woman, but . . . Mark Ivanitch might well call her Nana. There is something in her that does suggest Nana . . . fascinating . . ."

"I have seen her . . . I know . . ." said the examining magistrate, blowing his nose in a red handkerchief.

Dyukovsky blushed and dropped his eyes. The police superintendent drummed on his saucer with his fingers. The police captain coughed and rummaged in his portfolio for something. On the doctor alone the mention of Akulka and Nana appeared to produce no impression. Tchubikov ordered Nikolashka to be fetched. Nikolashka, a lanky young man with a long pock-marked nose and a hollow chest, wearing a reefer jacket that had been his master's, came into Psyekov's room and bowed down to the ground before Tchubikov. His face looked sleepy and showed traces of tears. He was drunk and could hardly stand up.

"Where is your master?" Tchubikov asked him.

"He's murdered, your honour."

As he said this Nikolashka blinked and began to cry.

"We know that he is murdered. But where is he now? Where is his body?"

"They say it was dragged out of window and buried in the garden."

"H'm . . . the results of the investigation are already known in the kitchen then. . . . That's bad. My good fellow, where were you on the night when your master was killed? On Saturday, that is?"

Nikolashka raised his head, craned his neck, and pondered.

"I can't say, your honour," he said. "I was drunk and I don't remember."

"An alibi!" whispered Dyukovsky, grinning and rubbing his hands.

"Ah! And why is it there's blood under your master's window!"

Nikolashka flung up his head and pondered.

"Think a little quicker," said the police captain.

"In a minute. That blood's from a trifling matter, your honour. I killed a hen; I cut her throat very simply in the usual way, and she fluttered out of my hands and took and ran off. . . . That's what the blood's from."

Yefrem testified that Nikolashka really did kill a hen every evening and killed it in all sorts of places, and no one had seen the half-killed hen running about the garden, though of course it could not be positively denied that it had done so.

"An alibi," laughed Dyukovsky, "and what an idiotic alibi."

"Have you had relations with Akulka?"

"Yes, I have sinned."

"And your master carried her off from you?"

"No, not at all. It was this gentleman here, Mr. Psyekov, Ivan Mihalitch, who enticed her from me, and the master took her from Ivan Mihalitch. That's how it was."

Psyekov looked confused and began rubbing his left eye. Dyukovsky fastened his eyes upon him, detected his confusion, and started. He saw on the steward's legs dark blue trousers which he had not previously noticed. The trousers reminded him of the blue threads found on the burdock. Tchubikov in his turn glanced suspiciously at Psyekov.

"You can go!" he said to Nikolashka. "And now allow me to put one question to you, Mr. Psyekov. You were here, of course, on the Saturday of last week?"

"Yes, at ten o'clock I had supper with Mark Ivanitch."

"And afterwards?"

Psyekov was confused, and got up from the table.

"Afterwards . . . afterwards . . . I really don't remember," he muttered. "I had drunk a good deal on that occasion. . . . I can't remember where and when I went to bed. . . . Why do you all look at me like that? As though I had murdered him!"

"Where did you wake up?"

"I woke up in the servants' kitchen on the stove. . . . They can all confirm that. How I got on to the stove I can't say. . . ."

"Don't disturb yourself . . . Do you know Akulina?"

"Oh well, not particularly."

"Did she leave you for Klyauzov?"

"Yes. . . . Yefrem, bring some more mushrooms! Will you have some tea, Yevgraf Kuzmitch?"

There followed an oppressive, painful silence that lasted for some five minutes. Dyukovsky held his tongue, and kept his piercing eyes on Psyekov's face, which gradually turned pale. The silence was broken by Tchubikov.

"We must go to the big house," he said, "and speak to the deceased's sister, Marya Ivanovna. She may give us some evidence."

Tchubikov and his assistant thanked Psyekov for the lunch, then went off to the big house. They found Klyauzov's sister, a maiden lady of five and forty, on her knees before a high family shrine of ikons. When she saw portfolios and caps adorned with cockades in her visitors' hands, she turned pale.

"First of all, I must offer an apology for disturbing your devotions, so to say," the gallant Tchubikov began with a scrape. "We have come to you with a request. You have heard, of course, already. . . . There is a suspicion that your brother has somehow been murdered. God's will, you know. . . . Death no one can escape, neither Tsar nor ploughman. Can you not assist us with some fact, something that will throw light?"

"Oh, do not ask me!" said Marya Ivanovna, turning whiter still, and hiding her face in her hands. "I can tell you nothing! Nothing! I implore you! I can say nothing . . . What can I do? Oh, no, no . . . not a word . . . of my brother! I would rather die than speak!"

Marya Ivanovna burst into tears and went away into another room. The officials looked at each other, shrugged their shoulders, and beat a retreat.

"A devil of a woman!" said Dyukovsky, swearing as they went out of the big house. "Apparently she knows something and is concealing it. And there is something peculiar in the maid-servant's expression too. . . . You wait a bit, you devils! We will get to the bottom of it all!"

In the evening, Tchubikov and his assistant were driving home by the light of a pale-faced moon; they sat in their waggonette, summing up in their minds the incidents of the day. Both were exhausted and sat silent. Tchubikov never liked talking on the road. In spite of his talkativeness, Dyukovsky held his tongue in deference to the old man. Towards the end of the journey, however, the young man could endure the silence no longer, and began:

"That Nikolashka has had a hand in the business," he said, "*non dubitandum est*. One can see from his mug too what sort of a chap he is. . . . His alibi gives him away hand and foot. There is no doubt either that he was not the instigator of the crime. He was only the stupid hired tool. Do you agree? The discreet Psyekov plays a not unimportant part in the affair too. His blue trousers, his embarrassment, his lying on the stove from fright after the murder, his alibi, and Akulka."

"Keep it up, you're in your glory! According to you, if a man knows Akulka he is the murderer. Ah, you hot-head! You ought to be sucking your bottle instead of investigating cases! You used to be running after Akulka too, does that mean that you had a hand in this business?"

"Akulka was a cook in your house for a month, too, but . . . I don't say anything. On that Saturday night I was playing cards with you, I saw you, or I should be after you too. The woman is not the point, my good sir. The point is the nasty, disgusting, mean feeling. . . . The discreet young man did not like to be cut out, do you see. Vanity, do you see. . . . He longed to be revenged. Then . . . His thick lips are a strong indication of sensuality. Do you remember how he smacked his lips when he compared Akulka to Nana? That he is burning with passion, the scoundrel, is beyond doubt! And so you have wounded vanity and unsatisfied passion. That's enough to lead to murder. Two of them are in our hands, but who is the third? Nikolashka and Psyekov held him. Who was it smothered him? Psyekov is timid, easily embarrassed, altogether a coward. People like Nikolashka are not equal to smothering with a pillow, they set to work with an axe or a mallet. . . . Some third person must have smothered him, but who?"

Dyukovsky pulled his cap over his eyes, and pondered. He was silent till the waggonette had driven up to the examining magistrate's house.

"Eureka!" he said, as he went into the house, and took off his overcoat. "Eureka, Nikolay Yermolaitch! I can't understand how it is it didn't occur to me before. Do you know who the third is?"

"Do leave off, please! There's supper ready. Sit down to supper!"

Tchubikov and Dyukovsky sat down to supper. Dyukovsky poured himself out a wine-glassful of vodka, got up, stretched, and with sparkling eyes, said:

"Let me tell you then that the third person who collaborated with the scoundrel Psyekov and smothered him was a woman! Yes! I am speaking of the murdered man's sister, Marya Ivanovna!"

Tchubikov coughed over his vodka and fastened his eyes on Dyukovsky.

"Are you . . . not quite right? Is your head . . . not quite right? Does it ache?"

"I am quite well. Very good, suppose I have gone out of my mind, but how do you explain her confusion on our arrival? How do you explain her refusal to give information? Admitting that that is trivial—very good! All right!—but think of the terms they were on! She detested her brother! She is an Old Believer, he was a profligate, a godless fellow . . . that is what has bred hatred between them! They say he succeeded in persuading her that he was an angel of Satan! He used to practise spiritualism in her presence!"

"Well, what then?"

"Don't you understand? She's an Old Believer, she murdered him through fanaticism! She has not merely slain a wicked man, a profligate, she has freed the world from Antichrist—and that she fancies is her merit, her religious achievement! Ah, you don't know these old maids, these Old Believers! You should read Dostoevsky! And what does Lyeskov say . . . and Petchersky! It's she, it's she, I'll stake my life on it.

She smothered him! Oh, the fiendish woman! Wasn't she, perhaps, standing before the ikons when we went in to put us off the scent? 'I'll stand up and say my prayers,' she said to herself, 'they will think I am calm and don't expect them.' That's the method of all novices in crime. Dear Nikolay Yermolaitch! My dear man! Do hand this case over to me! Let me go through with it to the end! My dear fellow! I have begun it, and I will carry it through to the end."

Tchubikov shook his head and frowned.

"I am equal to sifting difficult cases myself," he said. "And it's your place not to put yourself forward. Write what is dictated to you, that is your business!"

Dyukovsky flushed crimson, walked out, and slammed the door.

"A clever fellow, the rogue," Tchubikov muttered, looking after him. "Ve-ery clever! Only inappropriately hasty. I shall have to buy him a cigar-case at the fair for a present."

Next morning a lad with a big head and a hare lip came from Klyauzovka. He gave his name as the shepherd Danilko, and furnished a very interesting piece of information.

"I had had a drop," said he. "I stayed on till midnight at my crony's. As I was going home, being drunk, I got into the river for a bathe. I was bathing and what do I see! Two men coming along the dam carrying something black. 'Tyoo!' I shouted at them. They were scared, and cut along as fast as they could go into the Makarev kitchen-gardens. Strike me dead, if it wasn't the master they were carrying!"

Towards evening of the same day Psyekov and Nikolashka were arrested and taken under guard to the district town. In the town they were put in the prison tower.

II

Twelve days passed.

It was morning. The examining magistrate, Nikolay Yermolaitch, was sitting at a green table at home, looking through the papers, relating to

the "Klyauzov case"; Dyukovsky was pacing up and down the room rest-
lessly, like a wolf in a cage.

"You are convinced of the guilt of Nikolashka and Psyekov," he said,
nervously pulling at his youthful beard. "Why is it you refuse to be convinced of the guilt of Marya Ivanovna? Haven't you evidence enough?"

"I don't say that I don't believe in it. I am convinced of it, but
somehow I can't believe it. . . . There is no real evidence. It's all theoretical, as it were. . . . Fanaticism and one thing and another. . . ."

"And you must have an axe and bloodstained sheets! . . .You lawyers!
Well, I will prove it to you then! Do give up your slip-shod attitude to
the psychological aspect of the case. Your Marya Ivanovna ought to be in
Siberia! I'll prove it. If theoretical proof is not enough for you, I have
something material. . . . It will show you how right my theory is! Only
let me go about a little!"

"What are you talking about?"

"The Swedish match! Have you forgotten? I haven't forgotten it! I'll
find out who struck it in the murdered man's room! It was not struck
by Nikolashka, nor by Psyekov, neither of whom turned out to have
matches when searched, but a third person, that is Marya Ivanovna. And
I will prove it! . . . Only let me drive about the district, make some
inquiries. . . ."

"Oh, very well, sit down. . . . Let us proceed to the examination."

Dyukovsky sat down to the table, and thrust his long nose into the
papers.

"Bring in Nikolay Tetchov!" cried the examining magistrate.

Nikolashka was brought in. He was pale and thin as a chip. He was
trembling.

"Tetchov!" began Tchubikov. "In 1879 you were convicted of theft
and condemned to a term of imprisonment. In 1882 you were condemned for theft a second time, and a second time sent to prison . . . We
know all about it. . . ."

A look of surprise came up into Nikolashka's face. The examining magistrate's omniscience amazed him, but soon wonder was replaced by an expression of extreme distress. He broke into sobs, and asked leave to go to wash, and calm himself. He was led out.

"Bring in Psyekov!" said the examining magistrate.

Psyekov was led in. The young man's face had greatly changed during those twelve days. He was thin, pale, and wasted. There was a look of apathy in his eyes.

"Sit down, Psyekov," said Tchubikov. "I hope that to-day you will be sensible and not persist in lying as on other occasions. All this time you have denied your participation in the murder of Klyauzov, in spite of the mass of evidence against you. It is senseless. Confession is some mitigation of guilt. To-day I am talking to you for the last time. If you don't confess to-day, to-morrow it will be too late. Come, tell us. . . ."

"I know nothing, and I don't know your evidence," whispered Psyekov.

"That's useless! Well then, allow me to tell you how it happened. On Saturday evening, you were sitting in Klyauzov's bedroom drinking vodka and beer with him." (Dyukovsky riveted his eyes on Psyekov's face, and did not remove them during the whole monologue.) "Nikolay was waiting upon you. Between twelve and one Mark Ivanitch told you he wanted to go to bed. He always did go to bed at that time. While he was taking off his boots and giving you some instructions regarding the estate, Nikolay and you at a given signal seized your intoxicated master and flung him back upon the bed. One of you sat on his feet, the other on his head. At that moment the lady, you know who, in a black dress, who had arranged with you beforehand the part she would take in the crime, came in from the passage. She picked up the pillow, and proceeded to smother him with it. During the struggle, the light went out. The woman took a box of Swedish matches out of her pocket and lighted the candle. Isn't that right? I see from your face that what I say is true. Well, to proceed. . . . Having smothered him, and being convinced that he had ceased to breathe, Nikolay and you dragged him out of window and put him down near the burdocks. Afraid that he might regain consciousness, you struck him with something sharp. Then you carried him, and laid him for some time under a lilac bush. After resting and considering a little, you carried him . . . lifted him over the hurdle. . . . Then went along the road. . . Then comes the dam; near the dam you were frightened by a peasant. But what is the matter with you?"

Psyekov, white as a sheet, got up, staggering.

"I am suffocating!" he said. "Very well. . . . So be it. . . . Only I must go. . . . Please."

Psyekov was led out.

"At last he has admitted it!" said Tchubikov, stretching at his ease. "He has given himself away! How neatly I caught him there."

"And he didn't deny the woman in black!" said Dyukovsky, laughing. "I am awfully worried over that Swedish match, though! I can't endure it any longer. Good-bye! I am going!"

Dyukovsky put on his cap and went off. Tchubikov began interrogating Akulka.

Akulka declared that she knew nothing about it. . . .

"I have lived with you and with nobody else!" she said.

At six o'clock in the evening Dyukovsky returned. He was more excited than ever. His hands trembled so much that he could not unbutton his overcoat. His cheeks were burning. It was evident that he had not come back without news.

"Veni, vidi, vici!" he cried, dashing into Tchubikov's room and sinking into an arm-chair. "I vow on my honour, I begin to believe in my own genius. Listen, damnation take us! Listen and wonder, old friend! It's comic and it's sad. You have three in your grasp already . . . haven't you? I have found a fourth murderer, or rather murderess, for it is a woman! And what a woman! I would have given ten years of my life merely to touch her shoulders. But . . . listen. I drove to Klyauzovka and proceeded to describe a spiral round it. On the way I visited all the shopkeepers and innkeepers, asking for Swedish matches. Everywhere I was told 'No.' I have been on my round up to now. Twenty times I lost hope, and as many times regained it. I have been on the go all day long, and only an hour ago came upon what I was looking for. A couple of miles from here they gave me a packet of a dozen boxes of matches. One box was missing . . . I asked at once: 'Who bought that box?' 'So-and-so. She took a fancy to them. . . They crackle.' My dear fellow! Nikolay Yermolaitch! What can sometimes be done by a man who has been expelled from a seminary and studied Gaboriau is beyond all conception! From to-day I shall began to respect myself! . . . Ough. . . . Well, let us go!"

"Go where?"

"To her, to the fourth. . . . We must make haste, or . . . I shall explode with impatience! Do you know who she is? You will never guess. The young wife of our old police superintendent, Yevgraf Kuzmitch, Olga Petrovna; that's who it is! She bought that box of matches!"

"You . . . you. . . . Are you out of your mind?"

"It's very natural! In the first place she smokes, and in the second she was head over ears in love with Klyauzov. He rejected her love for the sake of an Akulka. Revenge. I remember now, I once came upon them behind the screen in the kitchen. She was cursing him, while he was smoking her cigarette and puffing the smoke into her face. But do come along; make haste, for it is getting dark already. . . . Let us go!"

"I have not gone so completely crazy yet as to disturb a respectable, honourable woman at night for the sake of a wretched boy!"

"Honourable, respectable. . . . You are a rag then, not an examining magistrate! I have never ventured to abuse you, but now you force me to it! You rag! you old fogey! Come, dear Nikolay Yermolaitch, I entreat you!"

The examining magistrate waved his hand in refusal and spat in disgust.

"I beg you! I beg you, not for my own sake, but in the interests of justice! I beseech you, indeed! Do me a favour, if only for once in your life!"

Dyukovsky fell on his knees.

"Nikolay Yermolaitch, do be so good! Call me a scoundrel, a worthless wretch if I am in error about that woman! It is such a case, you know! It is a case! More like a novel than a case. The fame of it will be all over Russia. They will make you examining magistrate for particularly important cases! Do understand, you unreasonable old man!"

The examining magistrate frowned and irresolutely put out his hand towards his hat.

"Well, the devil take you!" he said, "let us go."

It was already dark when the examining magistrate's waggonette rolled up to the police superintendent's door.

"What brutes we are!" said Tchubikov, as he reached for the bell. "We are disturbing people."

"Never mind, never mind, don't be frightened. We will say that one of the springs has broken."

Tchubikov and Dyukovsky were met in the doorway by a tall, plump woman of three and twenty, with eyebrows as black as pitch and full red lips. It was Olga Petrovna herself.

"Ah, how very nice," she said, smiling all over her face. "You are just in time for supper. My Yevgraf Kuzmitch is not at home. . . . He is staying at the priest's. But we can get on without him. Sit down. Have you come from an inquiry?"

"Yes. . . . We have broken one of our springs, you know," began Tchubikov, going into the drawing-room and sitting down in an easy-chair.

"Take her by surprise at once and overwhelm her," Dyukovsky whispered to him.

"A spring . . . er . . . yes. . . . We just drove up. . . ."

"Overwhelm her, I tell you! She will guess if you go drawing it out."

"Oh, do as you like, but spare me," muttered Tchubikov, getting up and walking to the window. "I can't! You cooked the mess, you eat it!"

"Yes, the spring," Dyukovsky began, going up to the superinten- dent's wife and wrinkling his long nose. "We have not come in to . . . er-er-er . . . supper, nor to see Yevgraf Kuzmitch. We have come to ask you, madam, where is Mark Ivanovitch whom you have murdered?"

"What? What Mark Ivanovitch?" faltered the superintendent's wife, and her full face was suddenly in one instant suffused with crimson. "I . . . don't understand."

"I ask you in the name of the law! Where is Klyauzov? We know all about it!"

"Through whom?" the superintendent's wife asked slowly, unable to face Dyukovsky's eyes.

"Kindly inform us where he is!"

"But how did you find out? Who told you?"

"We know all about it. I insist in the name of the law."

The examining magistrate, encouraged by the lady's confusion, went up to her.

"Tell us and we will go away. Otherwise we . . ."

"What do you want with him?"

"What is the object of such questions, madam? We ask you for information. You are trembling, confused. . . . Yes, he has been mur- dered, and if you will have it, murdered by you! Your accomplices have betrayed you!"

The police superintendent's wife turned pale.

"Come along," she said quietly, wringing her hands. "He is hidden in the bath-house. Only for God's sake, don't tell my husband! I implore you! It would be too much for him."

The superintendent's wife took a big key from the wall, and led her visitors through the kitchen and the passage into the yard. It was dark in the yard. There was a drizzle of fine rain. The superintendent's wife went on ahead. Tchubikov and Dyukovsky strode after her through the long grass, breathing in the smell of wild hemp and slops, which made a squelching sound under their feet. It was a big yard. Soon there were no more pools of slops, and their feet felt ploughed land. In the darkness they saw the silhouette of trees, and among the trees a little house with a crooked chimney.

"This is the bath-house," said the superintendent's wife, "but, I implore you, do not tell anyone."

Going up to the bath-house, Tchubikov and Dyukovsky saw a large padlock on the door.

"Get ready your candle-end and matches," Tchubikov whispered to his assistant.

The superintendent's wife unlocked the padlock and let the visitors into the bath-house. Dyukovsky struck a match and lighted up the entry. In the middle of it stood a table. On the table, beside a podgy little samovar, was a soup tureen with some cold cabbage-soup in it, and a dish with traces of some sauce on it.

"Go on!"

They went into the next room, the bathroom. There, too, was a table. On the table there stood a big dish of ham, a bottle of vodka, plates, knives and forks.

"But where is he . . . where's the murdered man?"

"He is on the top shelf," whispered the superintendent's wife, turning paler than ever and trembling.

Dyukovsky took the candle-end in his hand and climbed up to the upper shelf. There he saw a long, human body, lying motionless on a big feather bed. The body emitted a faint snore. . . .

"They have made fools of us, damn it all!" Dyukovsky cried. "This is not he! It is some living blockhead lying here. Hi! who are you, damnation take you!"

The body drew in its breath with a whistling sound and moved. Dyukovsky prodded it with his elbow. It lifted up its arms, stretched, and raised its head.

"Who is that poking?" a hoarse, ponderous bass voice inquired. "What do you want?"

Dyukovsky held the candle-end to the face of the unknown and uttered a shriek. In the crimson nose, in the ruffled, uncombed hair, in the pitch-black moustaches of which one was jauntily twisted and pointed insolently towards the ceiling, he recognised Cornet Klyauzov.

"You. . . . Mark . . . Ivanitch! Impossible!"

The examining magistrate looked up and was dumbfounded.

"It is I, yes. . . . And it's you, Dyukovsky! What the devil do you want here? And whose ugly mug is that down there? Holy Saints, it's the examining magistrate! How in the world did you come here?"

Klyauzov hurriedly got down and embraced Tchubikov. Olga Petrovna whisked out of the door.

"However did you come? Let's have a drink!—dash it all! Tra-ta-ti-to-tom. . . . Let's have a drink! Who brought you here, though? How did you get to know I was here? It doesn't matter, though! Have a drink!"

Klyauzov lighted the lamp and poured out three glasses of vodka.

"The fact is, I don't understand you," said the examining magistrate, throwing out his hands. "Is it you, or not you?"

"Stop that. . . . Do you want to give me a sermon? Don't trouble yourself! Dyukovsky boy, drink up your vodka! Friends, let us pass the . . . What are you staring at . . . ? Drink!"

"All the same, I can't understand," said the examining magistrate, mechanically drinking his vodka. "Why are you here?"

"Why shouldn't I be here, if I am comfortable here?"

Klyauzov sipped his vodka and ate some ham.

"I am staying with the superintendent's wife, as you see. In the wilds among the ruins, like some house goblin. Drink! I felt sorry for her, you know, old man! I took pity on her, and, well, I am living here in the deserted bath-house, like a hermit. . . . I am well fed. Next week I am thinking of moving on. . . . I've had enough of it. . . ."

"Inconceivable!" said Dyukovsky.

"What is there inconceivable in it?"

"Inconceivable! For God's sake, how did your boot get into the garden?"

"What boot?"

"We found one of your boots in the bedroom and the other in the garden."

"And what do you want to know that for? It is not your business. But do drink, dash it all. Since you have waked me up, you may as well drink! There's an interesting tale about that boot, my boy. I didn't want to come to Olga's. I didn't feel inclined, you know, I'd had a drop too much. . . . She came under the window and began scolding me. . . .You know how women . . . as a rule. Being drunk, I up and flung my boot at her. Ha ha! . . . 'Don't scold,' I said. She clambered in at the window, lighted the lamp, and gave me a good drubbing, as I was drunk. I have plenty to eat here. . . . Love, vodka, and good things! But where are you off to? Tchubikov, where are you off to?"

The examining magistrate spat on the floor and walked out of the bath-house. Dyukovsky followed him with his head hanging. Both got into the waggonette in silence and drove off. Never had the road seemed so long and dreary. Both were silent. Tchubikov was shaking with anger all the way. Dyukovsky hid his face in his collar as though he were afraid the darkness and the drizzling rain might read his shame on his face.

On getting home the examining magistrate found the doctor, Tyutyuev, there. The doctor was sitting at the table and heaving deep sighs as he turned over the pages of the *Neva*.

"The things that are going on in the world," he said, greeting the examining magistrate with a melancholy smile. "Austria is at it again . . . and Gladstone, too, in a way. . . ."

Tchubikov flung his hat under the table and began to tremble.

"You devil of a skeleton! Don't bother me! I've told you a thousand times over, don't bother me with your politics! It's not the time for politics! And as for you," he turned upon Dyukovsky and shook his fist at him, "as for you. . . . I'll never forget it, as long as I live!"

"But the Swedish match, you know! How could I tell. . . ."

"Choke yourself with your match! Go away and don't irritate me, or goodness knows what I shall do to you. Don't let me set eyes on you."

Dyukovsky heaved a sigh, took his hat, and went out.

"I'll go and get drunk!" he decided, as he went out of the gate, and he sauntered dejectedly towards the tavern.

When the superintendent's wife got home from the bath-house she found her husband in the drawing-room.

"What did the examining magistrate come about?" asked her husband.

"He came to say that they had found Klyauzov. Only fancy, they found him staying with another man's wife."

"Ah, Mark Ivanitch, Mark Ivanitch!" sighed the police superintendent, turning up his eyes. "I told you that dissipation would lead to no good! I told you so—you wouldn't heed me!"

ANTON CHEKHOV

SLEEPY

Typical of many Russian stories, "Sleepy" is filled with despair and a sympathetic look at the crushing plight of a poor servant girl. It was first published in 1888. It has also been published as "Let Me Sleep," "Hush-a-bye, My Baby" and "Sleepyhead."

NIGHT

Varka, the little nurse, a girl of thirteen, is rocking the cradle in which the baby is lying, and humming hardly audibly:

"Hush-a-bye, my baby wee,
While I sing a song for thee."

A little green lamp is burning before the ikon; there is a string stretched from one end of the room to the other, on which baby-clothes and a pair of big black trousers are hanging. There is a big patch of green on the ceiling from the ikon lamp, and the baby-clothes and the trousers throw long shadows on the stove, on the cradle, and on

Varka. . . . When the lamp begins to flicker, the green patch and the shadows come to life, and are set in motion, as though by the wind. It is stuffy. There is a smell of cabbage soup, and of the inside of a boot-shop.

The baby's crying. For a long while he has been hoarse and exhausted with crying; but he still goes on screaming, and there is no knowing when he will stop. And Varka is sleepy. Her eyes are glued together, her head droops, her neck aches. She cannot move her eyelids or her lips, and she feels as though her face is dried and wooden, as though her head has become as small as the head of a pin.

"Hush-a-bye, my baby wee," she hums, "while I cook the groats for thee. . . ."

A cricket is churring in the stove. Through the door in the next room the master and the apprentice Afanasy are snoring. . . . The cradle creaks plaintively, Varka murmurs—and it all blends into that soothing music of the night to which it is so sweet to listen, when one is lying in bed. Now that music is merely irritating and oppressive, because it goads her to sleep, and she must not sleep; if Varka—God forbid!—should fall asleep, her master and mistress would beat her.

The lamp flickers. The patch of green and the shadows are set in motion, forcing themselves on Varka's fixed, half-open eyes, and in her half slumbering brain are fashioned into misty visions. She sees dark clouds chasing one another over the sky, and screaming like the baby. But then the wind blows, the clouds are gone, and Varka sees a broad high road covered with liquid mud; along the high road stretch files of wagons, while people with wallets on their backs are trudging along and shadows flit backwards and forwards; on both sides she can see forests through the cold harsh mist. All at once the people with their wallets and their shadows fall on the ground in the liquid mud. "What is that for?" Varka asks. "To sleep, to sleep!" they answer her. And they fall sound asleep, and sleep sweetly, while crows and magpies sit on the telegraph wires, scream like the baby, and try to wake them.

"Hush-a-bye, my baby wee, and I will sing a song to thee," murmurs Varka, and now she sees herself in a dark stuffy hut.

Her dead father, Yefim Stepanov, is tossing from side to side on the floor. She does not see him, but she hears him moaning and rolling on the floor from pain. "His guts have burst," as he says; the pain is so violent that he cannot utter a single word, and can only draw in his breath and clack his teeth like the rattling of a drum:

"Boo—boo—boo—boo. . . ."

Her mother, Pelageya, has run to the master's house to say that Yefim is dying. She has been gone a long time, and ought to be back. Varka lies awake on the stove, and hears her father's "boo—boo—boo." And then she hears someone has driven up to the hut. It is a young doctor from the town, who has been sent from the big house where he is staying on a visit. The doctor comes into the hut; he cannot be seen in the darkness, but he can be heard coughing and rattling the door.

"Light a candle," he says.

"Boo—boo—boo," answers Yefim.

Pelageya rushes to the stove and begins looking for the broken pot with the matches. A minute passes in silence. The doctor, feeling in his pocket, lights a match.

"In a minute, sir, in a minute," says Pelageya. She rushes out of the hut, and soon afterwards comes back with a bit of candle.

Yefim's cheeks are rosy and his eyes are shining, and there is a peculiar keenness in his glance, as though he were seeing right through the hut and the doctor.

"Come, what is it? What are you thinking about?" says the doctor, bending down to him. "Aha! have you had this long?"

"What? Dying, your honour, my hour has come. . . . I am not to stay among the living."

"Don't talk nonsense! We will cure you!"

"That's as you please, your honour, we humbly thank you, only we understand. . . . Since death has come, there it is."

The doctor spends a quarter of an hour over Yefim, then he gets up and says:

"I can do nothing. You must go into the hospital, there they will operate on you. Go at once . . . You must go! It's rather late, they will all be asleep in the hospital, but that doesn't matter, I will give you a note. Do you hear?"

"Kind sir, but what can he go in?" says Pelageya. "We have no horse."

"Never mind. I'll ask your master, he'll let you have a horse."

The doctor goes away, the candle goes out, and again there is the sound of "boo—boo—boo." Half an hour later someone drives up to the hut. A cart has been sent to take Yefim to the hospital. He gets ready and goes. . . .

But now it is a clear bright morning. Pelageya is not at home; she has gone to the hospital to find what is being done to Yefim. Somewhere there is a baby crying, and Varka hears someone singing with her own voice:

"Hush-a-bye, my baby wee, I will sing a song to thee."

Pelageya comes back; she crosses herself and whispers:

"They put him to rights in the night, but towards morning he gave up his soul to God. . . . The Kingdom of Heaven be his and peace everlasting. . . . They say he was taken too late. . . . He ought to have gone sooner. . . ."

Varka goes out into the road and cries there, but all at once someone hits her on the back of her head so hard that her forehead knocks against a birch tree. She raises her eyes, and sees facing her, her master, the shoemaker.

"What are you about, you scabby slut?" he says. "The child is crying, and you are asleep!"

He gives her a sharp slap behind the ear, and she shakes her head, rocks the cradle, and murmurs her song. The green patch and the shadows from the trousers and the baby-clothes move up and down, nod to her, and soon take possession of her brain again. Again she sees the high road covered with liquid mud. The people with wallets on their backs and the shadows have lain down and are fast asleep. Looking at them, Varka has a passionate longing for sleep; she would lie down with enjoyment, but her mother Pelageya is walking beside her, hurrying her on. They are hastening together to the town to find situations.

"Give alms, for Christ's sake!" her mother begs of the people they meet. "Show us the Divine Mercy, kind-hearted gentlefolk!"

"Give the baby here!" a familiar voice answers. "Give the baby here!" the same voice repeats, this time harshly and angrily. "Are you asleep, you wretched girl?"

Varka jumps up, and looking round grasps what is the matter: there is no high road, no Pelageya, no people meeting them, there is only her mistress, who has come to feed the baby, and is standing in the middle of the room. While the stout, broad-shouldered woman nurses the child and soothes it, Varka stands looking at her and waiting till she has done. And outside the windows the air is already turning blue, the shadows and the green patch on the ceiling are visibly growing pale, it will soon be morning.

"Take him," says her mistress, buttoning up her chemise over her bosom; "he is crying. He must be bewitched."

Varka takes the baby, puts him in the cradle and begins rocking it again. The green patch and the shadows gradually disappear, and now there is nothing to force itself on her eyes and cloud her brain. But she is as sleepy as before, fearfully sleepy! Varka lays her head on the edge of the cradle, and rocks her whole body to overcome her sleepiness, but yet her eyes are glued together, and her head is heavy.

"Varka, heat the stove!" she hears the master's voice through the door.

So it is time to get up and set to work. Varka leaves the cradle, and runs to the shed for firewood. She is glad. When one moves and runs about, one is not so sleepy as when one is sitting down. She brings the wood, heats the stove, and feels that her wooden face is getting supple again, and that her thoughts are growing clearer.

"Varka, set the samovar!" shouts her mistress.

Varka splits a piece of wood, but has scarcely time to light the splinters and put them in the samovar, when she hears a fresh order:

"Varka, clean the master's goloshes!"

She sits down on the floor, cleans the goloshes, and thinks how nice it would be to put her head into a big deep golosh, and have a little nap in it. . . . And all at once the golosh grows, swells, fills up the whole room. Varka drops the brush, but at once shakes her head, opens her eyes wide, and tries to look at things so that they may not grow big and move before her eyes.

"Varka, wash the steps outside; I am ashamed for the customers to see them!"

Varka washes the steps, sweeps and dusts the rooms, then heats another stove and runs to the shop. There is a great deal of work: she hasn't one minute free.

But nothing is so hard as standing in the same place at the kitchen table peeling potatoes. Her head droops over the table, the potatoes dance before her eyes, the knife tumbles out of her hand while her fat, angry mistress is moving about near her with her sleeves tucked up, talking so loud that it makes a ringing in Varka's ears. It is agonising, too, to wait at dinner, to wash, to sew, there are minutes when she longs to flop on to the floor regardless of everything, and to sleep.

The day passes. Seeing the windows getting dark, Varka presses her temples that feel as though they were made of wood, and smiles, though she does not know why. The dusk of evening caresses her eyes that will hardly keep open, and promises her sound sleep soon. In the evening visitors come.

"Varka, set the samovar!" shouts her mistress. The samovar is a little one, and before the visitors have drunk all the tea they want, she has to heat it five times. After tea Varka stands for a whole hour on the same spot, looking at the visitors, and waiting for orders.

"Varka, run and buy three bottles of beer!"

She starts off, and tries to run as quickly as she can, to drive away sleep.

"Varka, fetch some vodka! Varka, where's the corkscrew? Varka, clean a herring!"

But now, at last, the visitors have gone; the lights are put out, the master and mistress go to bed.

"Varka, rock the baby!" she hears the last order.

The cricket churrs in the stove; the green patch on the ceiling and the shadows from the trousers and the baby-clothes force themselves on Varka's half-opened eyes again, wink at her and cloud her mind.

"Hush-a-bye, my baby wee," she murmurs, "and I will sing a song to thee."

And the baby screams, and is worn out with screaming. Again Varka sees the muddy high road, the people with wallets, her mother Pelageya, her father Yefim. She understands everything, she recognizes everyone, but through her half sleep she cannot understand the force which binds her, hand and foot, weighs upon her, and prevents her from living. She looks round, searches for that force that she may escape from it, but she cannot find it. At last, tired to death, she does her very utmost, strains her eyes, looks up at the flickering green patch, and listening to the screaming, finds the foe who will not let her live.

That foe is the baby.

She laughs. It seems strange to her that she has failed to grasp such a simple thing before. The green patch, the shadows, and the cricket seem to laugh and wonder too.

The hallucination takes possession of Varka. She gets up from her stool, and with a broad smile on her face and wide unblinking eyes, she walks up and down the room. She feels pleased and tickled at the thought that she will be rid directly of the baby that binds her hand and foot. . . . Kill the baby and then sleep, sleep, sleep. . . .

Laughing and winking and shaking her fingers at the green patch, Varka steals up to the cradle and bends over the baby. When she has strangled him, she quickly lies down on the floor, laughs with delight that she can sleep, and in a minute is sleeping as sound as the dead.

THE HEAD-GARDENER'S STORY

A tiny masterpiece of absurdist literature, "The Head-Gardener's Story" was first published in 1894.

A sale of flowers was taking place in Count N.'s greenhouses. The purchasers were few in number—a landowner who was a neighbor of mine, a young timber-merchant, and myself. While the workmen were carrying out our magnificent purchases and packing them into the carts, we sat at the entry of the greenhouse and chatted about one thing and another. It is extremely pleasant to sit in a garden on a still April morning, listening to the birds, and watching the flowers brought out into the open air and basking in the sunshine.

The head-gardener, Mihail Karlovitch, a venerable old man with a full shaven face, wearing a fur waistcoat and no coat, superintended the packing of the plants himself, but at the same time he listened to our conversation in the hope of hearing something new. He was an intelli-gent, very good-hearted man, respected by everyone. He was for some reason looked upon by everyone as a German, though he was in reality on his father's side Swedish, on his mother's side Russian, and attended the Orthodox church. He knew Russian, Swedish, and German. He had read a good deal in those languages, and nothing one could do gave him greater pleasure than lending him some new book or talking to him, for instance, about Ibsen.

He had his weaknesses, but they were innocent ones: he called himself the head-gardener, though there were no under-gardeners; the expression of his face was unusually dignified and haughty; he could not endure to be contradicted, and liked to be listened to with respect and attention.

"That young fellow there I can recommend to you as an awful rascal," said my neighbor, pointing to a laborer with a swarthy, gipsy face, who drove by with the water-barrel. "Last week he was tried in the town for burglary and was acquitted; they pronounced him mentally deranged, and yet look at him, he is the picture of health. Scoundrels are very often acquitted nowadays in Russia on grounds of abnormality and aberration, yet these acquittals, these unmistakable proofs of an indulgent attitude to crime, lead to no good. They demoralize the masses, the sense of justice is blunted in all as they become accustomed to seeing vice unpunished, and you know in our age one may boldly say in the words of Shakespeare that in our evil and corrupt age virtue must ask forgiveness of vice."

"That's very true," the merchant assented. "Owing to these frequent acquittals, murder and arson have become much more common. Ask the peasants."

Mihail Karlovitch turned towards us and said:

"As far as I am concerned, gentlemen, I am always delighted to meet with these verdicts of not guilty. I am not afraid for morality and justice when they say 'Not guilty,' but on the contrary I feel pleased. Even when my conscience tells me the jury have made a mistake in acquitting the criminal, even then I am triumphant. Judge for yourselves, gentlemen; if the judges and the jury have more faith in *man* than in evidence, material proofs, and speeches for the prosecution, is not that faith *in man* in itself higher than any ordinary considerations? Such faith is only attainable by those few who understand and feel Christ."

"A fine thought," I said.

"But it's not a new one. I remember a very long time ago I heard a legend on that subject. A very charming legend," said the gardener, and he smiled. "I was told it by my grandmother, my father's mother, an excellent old lady. She told me it in Swedish, and it does not sound so fine, so classical, in Russian."

But we begged him to tell it and not to be put off by the coarseness of the Russian language. Much gratified, he deliberately lighted his pipe, looked angrily at the laborers, and began:

"There settled in a certain little town a solitary, plain, elderly gentleman called Thomson or Wilson—but that does not matter; the surname is not the point. He followed an honorable profession: he was a doctor. He was always morose and unsociable, and only spoke when required by his profession. He never visited anyone, never extended his acquaintance beyond a silent bow, and lived as humbly as a hermit. The fact was, he was a learned man, and in those days learned men were not like other people. They spent their days and nights in contemplation, in reading and in healing disease, looked upon everything else as trivial, and had no time to waste a word. The inhabitants of the town understood this, and tried not to worry him with their visits and empty chatter. They were very glad that God had sent them at last a man who could heal diseases, and were proud that such a remarkable man was living in their town. 'He knows everything,' they said about him.

"But that was not enough. They ought to have also said, 'He loves everyone.' In the breast of that learned man there beat a wonderful angelic heart. Though the people of that town were strangers and not his own people, yet he loved them like children, and did not spare himself for them. He was himself ill with consumption, he had a cough, but when he was summoned to the sick he forgot his own illness; he did not spare himself and, gasping for breath, climbed up the hills however high they might be. He disregarded the sultry heat and the cold, despised thirst and hunger. He would accept no money and strange to say, when one of his patients died, he would follow the coffin with the relations, weeping.

"And soon he became so necessary to the town that the inhabitants wondered how they could have got on before without the man. Their gratitude knew no bounds. Grown-up people and children, good and bad alike, honest men and cheats—all in fact, respected him and knew his value. In the little town and all the surrounding neighborhood there was no man who would allow himself to do anything disagreeable to him; indeed, they would never have dreamed of it. When he came out of his lodging, he never fastened the doors or windows, in complete confidence that there was no thief who could bring himself to do him wrong. He often had in the course of his medical duties to walk along the highroads, through the forests and mountains haunted by numbers of hungry vagrants; but he felt that he was in perfect security.

"One night he was returning from a patient when robbers fell upon him in the forest, but when they recognized him, they took off their hats respectfully and offered him something to eat. When he answered that he was not hungry, they gave him a warm wrap and accompanied him as far as the town, happy that fate had given them the chance in some small way to show their gratitude to the benevolent man. Well, to be sure, my grandmother told me that even the horses and the cows and the dogs knew him and expressed their joy when they met him.

"And this man who seemed by his sanctity to have guarded himself from every evil, to whom even brigands and frenzied men wished nothing but good, was one fine morning found murdered. Covered with blood, with his skull broken, he was lying in a ravine, and his pale face wore an expression of amazement. Yes, not horror but amazement was the emotion that had been fixed upon his face when he saw the murderer before him. You can imagine the grief that overwhelmed the inhabitants of the town and the surrounding districts. All were in despair, unable to believe their eyes, wondering who could have killed the man. The judges who conducted the inquiry and examined the doctor's body said: 'Here we have all the signs of a murder, but as there is not a man in the world capable of murdering our doctor, obviously it was not a case of murder, and the combination of evidence is due to simple chance. We must suppose that in the darkness he fell into the ravine of himself and was mortally injured.'

"The whole town agreed with this opinion. The doctor was buried, and nothing more was said about a violent death. The existence of a man who could have the baseness and wickedness to kill the doctor seemed incredible. There is a limit even to wickedness, isn't there?

"All at once, would you believe it, chance led them to discovering the murderer. A vagrant who had been many times convicted, notorious for his vicious life, was seen selling for drink a snuff-box and watch that had belonged to the doctor. When he was questioned he was confused, and answered with an obvious lie. A search was made, and in his bed was found a shirt with stains of blood on the sleeves, and a doctor's lancet set in gold. What more evidence was wanted? They put the criminal in prison. The inhabitants were indignant, and at the same time said:

"'It's incredible! It can't be so! Take care that a mistake is not made; it does happen, you know, that evidence tells a false tale.'

"At his trial the murderer obstinately denied his guilt. Everything was against him, and to be convinced of his guilt was as easy as to believe that this earth is black; but the judges seem to have gone mad: they weighed every proof ten times, looked distrustfully at the witnesses, flushed crimson and sipped water. . . . The trial began early in the morning and was only finished in the evening.

"'Accused!' the chief judge said, addressing the murderer, 'the court has found you guilty of murdering Dr. So-and-so, and has sentenced you to. . . .'

"The chief judge meant to say 'to the death penalty,' but he dropped from his hands the paper on which the sentence was written, wiped the cold sweat from his face, and cried out:

"'No! May God punish me if I judge wrongly, but I swear he is not guilty. I cannot admit the thought that there exists a man who would dare to murder our friend the doctor! A man could not sink so low!'

"'There cannot be such a man!' the other judges assented.

"'No,' the crowd cried. 'Let him go!'

"The murderer was set free to go where he chose, and not one soul blamed the court for an unjust verdict. And my grandmother used to say that for such faith in humanity God forgave the sins of all the inhabitants of that town. He rejoices when people believe that man is His image and semblance, and grieves if, forgetful of human dignity, they judge worse of men than of dogs. The sentence of acquittal may bring harm to the inhabitants of the town, but on the other hand, think of the beneficial influence upon them of that faith in man—a faith which does not remain dead, you know; it raises up generous feelings in us, and always impels us to love and respect every man. Every man! And that is important."

Mihail Karlovitch had finished. My neighbor would have urged some objection, but the head-gardener made a gesture that signified that he did not like objections; then he walked away to the carts, and, with an expression of dignity, went on looking after the packing.

ANTON CHEKHOV

THE BET

While nothing illegal occurs in this powerful tale, one of Chekhov's most
admired, it is as terrible a crime story as one is likely to read. "The Bet" was
first published in 1889.

I t was a dark autumn night. The old banker was walking up and down
his study and remembering how, fifteen years before, he had given a
party one autumn evening. There had been many clever men there,
and there had been interesting conversations. Among other things they
had talked of capital punishment. The majority of the guests, among
whom were many journalists and intellectual men, disapproved of the
death penalty. They considered that form of punishment out of date,
immoral, and unsuitable for Christian States. In the opinion of some of
them the death penalty ought to be replaced everywhere by imprisonment for life.

"I don't agree with you," said their host the banker. "I have not
tried either the death penalty or imprisonment for life, but if one may
judge *a priori*, the death penalty is more moral and more humane than

imprisonment for life. Capital punishment kills a man at once, but life-long imprisonment kills him slowly. Which executioner is the more humane, he who kills you in a few minutes or he who drags the life out of you in the course of many years?"

"Both are equally immoral," observed one of the guests, "for they both have the same object—to take away life. The State is not God. It has not the right to take away what it cannot restore when it wants to."

Among the guests was a young lawyer, a young man of five-and-twenty. When he was asked his opinion, he said:

"The death sentence and the life sentence are equally immoral, but if I had to choose between the death penalty and imprisonment for life, I would certainly choose the second. To live anyhow is better than not at all."

A lively discussion arose. The banker, who was younger and more nervous in those days, was suddenly carried away by excitement; he struck the table with his fist and shouted at the young man:

"It's not true! I'll bet you two millions you wouldn't stay in solitary confinement for five years."

"If you mean that in earnest," said the young man, "I'll take the bet, but I would stay not five but fifteen years."

"Fifteen? Done!" cried the banker. "Gentlemen, I stake two millions!"

"Agreed! You stake your millions and I stake my freedom!" said the young man.

And this wild, senseless bet was carried out! The banker, spoilt and frivolous, with millions beyond his reckoning, was delighted at the bet. At supper he made fun of the young man, and said:

"Think better of it, young man, while there is still time. To me two millions are a trifle, but you are losing three or four of the best years of your life. I say three or four, because you won't stay longer. Don't forget either, you unhappy man, that voluntary confinement is a great deal harder to bear than compulsory. The thought that you have the right to step out in liberty at any moment will poison your whole existence in prison. I am sorry for you."

And now the banker, walking to and fro, remembered all this, and asked himself: "What was the object of that bet? What is the good of that man's losing fifteen years of his life and my throwing away two millions? Can it prove that the death penalty is better or worse than imprisonment for life? No, no. It was all nonsensical and meaningless. On my part it was the caprice of a pampered man, and on his part simple greed for money. . . ."

Then he remembered what followed that evening. It was decided that the young man should spend the years of his captivity under the strictest supervision in one of the lodges in the banker's garden. It was agreed that for fifteen years he should not be free to cross the threshold of the lodge, to see human beings, to hear the human voice, or to receive letters and newspapers. He was allowed to have a musical instrument and books, and was allowed to write letters, to drink wine, and to smoke. By the terms of the agreement, the only relations he could have with the outer world were by a little window made purposely for that object. He might have anything he wanted—books, music, wine, and so on—in any quantity he desired by writing an order, but could only receive them through the window. The agreement provided for every detail and every trifle that would make his imprisonment strictly solitary, and bound the young man to stay there *exactly* fifteen years, beginning from twelve o'clock of November 14, 1870, and ending at twelve o'clock of November 14, 1885. The slightest attempt on his part to break the conditions, if only two minutes before the end, released the banker from the obligation to pay him two millions.

For the first year of his confinement, as far as one could judge from his brief notes, the prisoner suffered severely from loneliness and depression. The sounds of the piano could be heard continually day and night from his lodge. He refused wine and tobacco. Wine, he wrote, excites the desires, and desires are the worst foes of the prisoner; and besides, nothing could be more dreary than drinking good wine and seeing no one. And tobacco spoilt the air of his room. In the first year the books he sent for were principally of a light character; novels with a complicated love plot, sensational and fantastic stories, and so on.

In the second year the piano was silent in the lodge, and the prisoner asked only for the classics. In the fifth year music was audible again, and the prisoner asked for wine. Those who watched him through the window said that all that year he spent doing nothing but eating and drinking and lying on his bed, frequently yawning and angrily talking to himself. He did not read books. Sometimes at night he would sit down to write; he would spend hours writing, and in the morning tear up all that he had written. More than once he could be heard crying.

In the second half of the sixth year the prisoner began zealously studying languages, philosophy, and history. He threw himself eagerly into these studies—so much so that the banker had enough to do to get him the books he ordered. In the course of four years some six hundred volumes were procured at his request. It was during this period that the banker received the following letter from his prisoner:

"My dear Jailer, I write you these lines in six languages. Show them to people who know the languages. Let them read them. If they find not one mistake I implore you to fire a shot in the garden. That shot will show me that my efforts have not been thrown away. The geniuses of all ages and of all lands speak different languages, but the same flame burns in them all. Oh, if you only knew what unearthly happiness my soul feels now from being able to understand them!" The prisoner's desire was fulfilled. The banker ordered two shots to be fired in the garden.

Then after the tenth year, the prisoner sat immovably at the table and read nothing but the Gospel. It seemed strange to the banker that a man who in four years had mastered six hundred learned volumes should waste nearly a year over one thin book easy of comprehension. Theology and histories of religion followed the Gospels.

In the last two years of his confinement the prisoner read an immense quantity of books quite indiscriminately. At one time he was busy with the natural sciences, then he would ask for Byron or Shakespeare. There were notes in which he demanded at the same time books on chemistry, and a manual of medicine, and a novel, and some treatise on philosophy or theology. His reading suggested a man swimming in the sea among the wreckage of his ship, and trying to save his life by greedily clutching first at one spar and then at another.

II

The old banker remembered all this, and thought:

"To-morrow at twelve o'clock he will regain his freedom. By our agreement I ought to pay him two millions. If I do pay him, it is all over with me: I shall be utterly ruined."

Fifteen years before, his millions had been beyond his reckoning; now he was afraid to ask himself which were greater, his debts or his assets. Desperate gambling on the Stock Exchange, wild speculation and the excitability which he could not get over even in advancing years, had by degrees led to the decline of his fortune and the proud, fearless, self-confident millionaire had become a banker of middling rank, trembling at every rise and fall in his investments. "Cursed bet!" muttered the old man, clutching his head in despair. "Why didn't the man die? He is only forty now. He will take my last penny from me, he will marry, will enjoy life, will gamble on the Exchange; while I shall look at him with envy like a beggar, and hear from him every day the same sentence: 'I am indebted to you for the happiness of my life, let me help you!' No, it is too much! The one means of being saved from bankruptcy and disgrace is the death of that man!"

It struck three o'clock, the banker listened; everyone was asleep in the house and nothing could be heard outside but the rustling of the chilled trees. Trying to make no noise, he took from a fireproof safe the key of the door which had not been opened for fifteen years, put on his overcoat, and went out of the house.

It was dark and cold in the garden. Rain was falling. A damp cutting wind was racing about the garden, howling and giving the trees no rest. The banker strained his eyes, but could see neither the earth nor the white statues, nor the lodge, nor the trees. Going to the spot where the lodge stood, he twice called the watchman. No answer followed. Evidently the watchman had sought shelter from the weather, and was now asleep somewhere either in the kitchen or in the greenhouse.

"If I had the pluck to carry out my intention," thought the old man, "suspicion would fall first upon the watchman."

He felt in the darkness for the steps and the door, and went into the entry of the lodge. Then he groped his way into a little passage and lighted a match. There was not a soul there. There was a bedstead with no bedding on it, and in the corner there was a dark cast-iron stove. The seals on the door leading to the prisoner's rooms were intact.

When the match went out the old man, trembling with emotion, peeped through the little window. A candle was burning dimly in the prisoner's room. He was sitting at the table. Nothing could be seen but his back, the hair on his head, and his hands. Open books were lying on the table, on the two easy-chairs, and on the carpet near the table.

Five minutes passed and the prisoner did not once stir. Fifteen years' imprisonment had taught him to sit still. The banker tapped at the window with his finger, and the prisoner made no movement whatever in response. Then the banker cautiously broke the seals off the door and put the key in the keyhole. The rusty lock gave a grating sound and the door creaked. The banker expected to hear at once footsteps and a cry of astonishment, but three minutes passed and it was as quiet as ever in the room. He made up his mind to go in.

At the table a man unlike ordinary people was sitting motionless. He was a skeleton with the skin drawn tight over his bones, with long curls like a woman's and a shaggy beard. His face was yellow with an earthy tint in it, his cheeks were hollow, his back long and narrow, and the hand on which his shaggy head was propped was so thin and delicate that it was dreadful to look at it. His hair was already streaked with silver, and seeing his emaciated, aged-looking face, no one would have believed that he was only forty. He was asleep. . . . In front of his bowed head there lay on the table a sheet of paper on which there was something written in fine handwriting.

"Poor creature!" thought the banker, "he is asleep and most likely dreaming of the millions. And I have only to take this half-dead man, throw him on the bed, stifle him a little with the pillow, and the most conscientious expert would find no sign of a violent death. But let us first read what he has written here. . . ."

The banker took the page from the table and read as follows:

"To-morrow at twelve o'clock I regain my freedom and the right to associate with other men, but before I leave this room and see the sunshine, I think it necessary to say a few words to you. With a clear conscience I tell you, as before God, who beholds me, that I despise freedom and life and health, and all that in your books is called the good things of the world.

"For fifteen years I have been intently studying earthly life. It is true I have not seen the earth nor men, but in your books I have drunk fragrant wine, I have sung songs, I have hunted stags and wild boars in the forests, have loved women. . . . Beauties as ethereal as clouds, created by the magic of your poets and geniuses, have visited me at night, and have whispered in my ears wonderful tales that have set my brain in a whirl. In your books I have climbed to the peaks of Elburz and Mont Blanc, and from there I have seen the sun rise and have watched it at evening flood the sky, the ocean, and the mountain-tops with gold and crimson. I have watched from there the lightning flashing over my head and cleaving the storm-clouds. I have seen green forests, fields, rivers, lakes, towns. I have heard the singing of the sirens, and the strains of the shepherds' pipes; I have touched the wings of comely devils who flew down to converse with me of God. . . . In your books I have flung myself into the bottomless pit, performed miracles, slain, burned towns, preached new religions, conquered whole kingdoms. . . .

"Your books have given me wisdom. All that the unresting thought of man has created in the ages is compressed into a small compass in my brain. I know that I am wiser than all of you.

"And I despise your books, I despise wisdom and the blessings of this world. It is all worthless, fleeting, illusory, and deceptive, like a mirage. You may be proud, wise, and fine, but death will wipe you off the face of the earth as though you were no more than mice burrowing under the floor, and your posterity, your history, your immortal geniuses will burn or freeze together with the earthly globe.

"You have lost your reason and taken the wrong path. You have taken lies for truth, and hideousness for beauty. You would marvel if, owing to strange events of some sorts, frogs and lizards suddenly grew on apple and orange trees instead of fruit, or if roses began to smell like a sweating horse; so I marvel at you who exchange heaven for earth. I don't want to understand you.

"To prove to you in action how I despise all that you live by, I renounce the two millions of which I once dreamed as of paradise and which now I despise. To deprive myself of the right to the money I shall go out from here five hours before the time fixed, and so break the compact. . . ."

When the banker had read this he laid the page on the table, kissed the strange man on the head, and went out of the lodge, weeping. At no other time, even when he had lost heavily on the Stock Exchange, had he felt so great a contempt for himself. When he got home he lay on his bed, but his tears and emotion kept him for hours from sleeping.

Next morning the watchmen ran in with pale faces, and told him they had seen the man who lived in the lodge climb out of the window into the garden, go to the gate, and disappear. The banker went at once with the servants to the lodge and made sure of the flight of his prisoner. To avoid arousing unnecessary talk, he took from the table the writing in which the millions were renounced, and when he got home locked it up in the fireproof safe.

ALEXANDER PUSHKIN

THE QUEEN OF SPADES

Admired by Russians as the greatest poet the country ever produced, Aleksandr Sergevich Pushkin (1799–1837) led a less than successful life. Although born to a noble family on his father's side, most of the money had been lost over the centuries so the family was merely minor nobility. On his mother's side, his great grandfather was the son of an Abyssinian prince, and Pushkin was interested enough in his heritage to begin work on a long novel about his ancestor titled *The Negro of Peter the Great.* He led a relatively liberal and dissolute early life, followed by minor government positions and exile. He was killed when he challenged a young French nobleman who engaged in a flirtation with his pretty young wife to a duel.

In spite of his wild youth, there was no denying Pushkin's genius, as his first poem was published in the most influential Russian literary magazine when he was barely fifteen. Among his greatest poetic successes were *Rusland and Ludmila* (1820), a romance in the form of a fairy tale; *The Prisoner of the Caucasus* (1821), which was heavily influenced by Byron; and *The Gypsies* (1824), about a young Russian seeking freedom and, when he finds it, his unwillingness to allow it to others. His masterpiece, *Eugene Onegin*, was begun in 1823 and was completed in eight cantos in 1830. While writing his epic poem, he wrote his most famous work, the play *Boris Godunov* (1825), about the difficult Russian history after the death of Ivan the Terrible. Later in life, he began to produce prose works in a clear and simple style, many of which have as their theme the notion of unpredictable fate.

ALEXANDER PUSHKIN

Pushkin's most famous and often reprinted story is "The Queen of Spades," a powerful tale of self-destructive greed. It was first published in Russia in 1833; its first English translation was published in *Chambers' Papers* in 1850. It was made into an opera by Pyotr Ilyich Tchaikovsky which premiered in St. Petersburg in 1890.

A t the house of Naroumov, a cavalry officer, the long winter night had been passed in gambling. At five in the morning breakfast was served to the weary players. The winners ate with relish; the losers, on the contrary, pushed back their plates and sat brooding gloomily. Under the influence of the good wine, however, the conversation then became general.

"Well, Sourine?" said the host inquiringly.

"Oh, I lost as usual. My luck is abominable. No matter how cool I keep, I never win."

"How is it, Herman, that you never touch a card?" remarked one of the men, addressing a young officer of the Engineering Corps. "Here you are with the rest of us at five o'clock in the morning, and you have neither played nor bet all night."

"Play interests me greatly," replied the person addressed, "but I hardly care to sacrifice the necessaries of life for uncertain superfluities."

"Herman is a German, therefore economical; that explains it," said Tomsky. "But the person I can't quite understand is my grandmother, the Countess Anna Fedorovna."

"Why?" inquired a chorus of voices.

"I can't understand why my grandmother never gambles."

"I don't see anything very striking in the fact that a woman of eighty refuses to gamble," objected Naroumov.

"Have you never heard her story?"

"No—"

"Well, then, listen to it. To begin with, sixty years ago my grandmother went to Paris, where she was all the fashion. People crowded each other in the streets to get a chance to see the 'Muscovite Venus,' as she was called. All the great ladies played faro, then. On one occasion, while playing with the Duke of Orleans, she lost an enormous sum. She told her husband of the debt, but he refused outright to pay it. Nothing could induce him to change his mind on the subject, and grandmother was at her wits' ends. Finally, she remembered a friend of hers, Count Saint-Germain. You must have heard of him, as many wonderful stories have been told about him. He is said to have discovered the elixir of life, the philosopher's stone, and many other equally marvelous things. He had money at his disposal, and my grandmother knew it. She sent him a note asking him to come to see her. He obeyed her summons and found her in great distress. She painted the cruelty of her husband in the darkest colors, and ended by telling the Count that she depended upon his friendship and generosity.

" 'I could lend you the money,' replied the Count, after a moment of thoughtfulness, 'but I know that you would not enjoy a moment's rest until you had returned it; it would only add to your embarrassment. There is another way of freeing yourself.'

"'But I have no money at all,' insisted my grandmother.

"'There is no need of money. Listen to me.'

"The Count then told her a secret which any of us would give a good deal to know."

The young gamesters were all attention. Tomsky lit his pipe, took a few whiffs, then continued:

"The next evening, grandmother appeared at Versailles at the Queen's gaming-table. The Duke of Orleans was the dealer. Grandmother made some excuse for not having brought any money, and began to punt. She chose three cards in succession, again and again, winning every time, and was soon out of debt."

"A fable," remarked Herman; "perhaps the cards were marked."

"I hardly think so," replied Tomsky, with an air of importance.

"So you have a grandmother who knows three winning cards, and you haven't found out the magic secret."

"I must say I have not. She had four sons, one of them being my father, all of whom are devoted to play; she never told the secret to one of them. But my uncle told me this much, on his word of honor. Tchaplitzky, who died in poverty after having squandered millions, lost at one time, at play, nearly three hundred thousand rubles. He was desperate and grandmother took pity on him. She told him the three cards, making him swear never to use them again. He returned to the game, staked fifty thousand rubles on each card, and came out ahead, after paying his debts."

As day was dawning the party now broke up, each one draining his glass and taking his leave.

The Countess Anna Fedorovna was seated before her mirror in her dressing-room. Three women were assisting at her toilet. The old Countess no longer made the slightest pretensions to beauty, but she still clung to all the habits of her youth, and spent as much time at her toilet as she had done sixty years before. At the window a young girl, her ward, sat at her needlework.

"Good afternoon, grandmother," cried a young officer, who had just entered the room. "I have come to ask a favor of you."

"What, Pavel?"

"I want to be allowed to present one of my friends to you, and to take you to the ball on Tuesday night."

"Take me to the ball and present him to me there."

After a few more remarks the officer walked up to the window where Lisaveta Ivanovna sat.

"Whom do you wish to present?" asked the girl.

"Naroumov; do you know him?"

"No; is he a soldier?"

"Yes."

"An engineer?"

"No; why do you ask?"

The girl smiled and made no reply.

Pavel Tomsky took his leave, and, left to herself, Lisaveta glanced out of the window. Soon, a young officer appeared at the corner of the street; the girl blushed and bent her head low over her canvas.

This appearance of the officer had become a daily occurrence. The man was totally unknown to her, and as she was not accustomed to coquetting with the soldiers she saw on the street, she hardly knew how to explain his presence. His persistence finally roused an interest entirely strange to her. One day, she even ventured to smile upon her admirer, for such he seemed to be.

The reader need hardly be told that the officer was no other than Herman, the would-be gambler, whose imagination had been strongly excited by the story told by Tomsky of the three magic cards.

"Ah," he thought, "if the old Countess would only reveal the secret to me. Why not try to win her good-will and appeal to her sympathy?"

With this idea in mind, he took up his daily station before the house, watching the pretty face at the window, and trusting to fate to bring about the desired acquaintance.

One day, as Lisaveta was standing on the pavement about to enter the carriage after the Countess, she felt herself jostled and a note was thrust into her hand. Turning, she saw the young officer at her elbow. As quick as thought, she put the note in her glove and entered the carriage. On her return from the drive, she hastened to her chamber to read the missive, in a state of excitement mingled with fear. It was a tender and respectful declaration of affection, copied word for word from a German novel. Of this fact, Lisa was, of course, ignorant.

The young girl was much impressed by the missive, but she felt that the writer must not be encouraged. She therefore wrote a few lines of explanation and, at the first opportunity, dropped it, with the letter, out of the window. The officer hastily crossed the street, picked up the papers and entered a shop to read them.

In no wise daunted by this rebuff, he found the opportunity to send her another note in a few days. He received no reply, but, evidently understanding the female heart, he persevered, begging for an interview. He was rewarded at last by the following:

"To-night we go to the ambassador's ball. We shall remain until two o'clock. I can arrange for a meeting in this way. After our departure, the servants will probably all go out, or go to sleep. At half-past eleven enter the vestibule boldly, and if you see any one, inquire for the Countess; if not, ascend the stairs, turn to the left and go on until you come to a door, which opens into her bedchamber. Enter this room and behind a screen you will find another door leading to a corridor; from this a spiral staircase leads to my sitting-room. I shall expect to find you there on my return."

Herman trembled like a leaf as the appointed hour drew near. He obeyed instructions fully, and, as he met no one, he reached the old lady's bedchamber without difficulty. Instead of going out of the small door behind the screen, however, he concealed himself in a closet to await the return of the old Countess.

The hours dragged slowly by; at last he heard the sound of wheels. Immediately lamps were lighted and servants began moving about. Finally the old woman tottered into the room, completely exhausted. Her women removed her wraps and proceeded to get her in readiness for the night. Herman watched the proceedings with a curiosity not unmingled with superstitious fear. When at last she was attired in cap and gown, the old woman looked less uncanny than when she wore her ball-dress of blue brocade.

She sat down in an easy chair beside a table, as she was in the habit of doing before retiring, and her women withdrew. As the old lady sat swaying to and fro, seemingly oblivious to her surroundings, Herman crept out of his hiding-place.

At the slight noise the old woman opened her eyes, and gazed at the intruder with a half-dazed expression.

"Have no fear, I beg of you," said Herman, in a calm voice. "I have not come to harm you, but to ask a favor of you instead."

The Countess looked at him in silence, seemingly without comprehending him. Herman thought she might be deaf, so he put his lips close to her ear and repeated his remark. The listener remained perfectly mute.

"You could make my fortune without its costing you anything," pleaded the young man; "only tell me the three cards which are sure to win, and—"

Herman paused as the old woman opened her lips as if about to speak.

"It was only a jest; I swear to you, it was only a jest," came from the withered lips.

"There was no jesting about it. Remember Tchaplitzky, who, thanks to you, was able to pay his debts."

An expression of interior agitation passed over the face of the old woman; then she relapsed into her former apathy.

"Will you tell me the names of the magic cards, or not?" asked Herman after a pause.

There was no reply.

The young man then drew a pistol from his pocket, exclaiming: "You old witch, I'll force you to tell me!"

At the sight of the weapon the Countess gave a second sign of life. She threw back her head and put out her hands as if to protect herself; then they dropped and she sat motionless.

Herman grasped her arm roughly, and was about to renew his threats, when he saw that she was dead!

—·—

Seated in her room, still in her ball-dress, Lisaveta gave herself up to her reflections. She had expected to find the young officer there, but she felt relieved to see that he was not.

Strangely enough, that very night at the ball, Tomsky had rallied her about her preference for the young officer, assuring her that he knew more than she supposed he did.

"Of whom are you speaking?" she had asked in alarm, fearing her adventure had been discovered.

"Of the remarkable man," was the reply. "His name is Herman."

Lisa made no reply.

"This Herman," continued Tomsky, "is a romantic character; he has the profile of a Napoleon and the heart of a Mephistopheles. It is said he has at least three crimes on his conscience. But how pale you are."

"It is only a slight headache. But why do you talk to me of this Herman?"

"Because I believe he has serious intentions concerning you."

"Where has he seen me?"

"At church, perhaps, or on the street."

The conversation was interrupted at this point, to the great regret of the young girl. The words of Tomsky made a deep impression upon her, and she realized how imprudently she had acted. She was thinking of all this and a great deal more when the door of her apartment suddenly opened, and Herman stood before her. She drew back at sight of him, trembling violently.

"Where have you been?" she asked in a frightened whisper.

"In the bedchamber of the Countess. She is dead," was the calm reply.

"My God! What are you saying?" cried the girl.

"Furthermore, I believe that I was the cause of her death."

The words of Tomsky flashed through Lisa's mind.

Herman sat down and told her all. She listened with a feeling of terror and disgust. So those passionate letters, that audacious pursuit were not the result of tenderness and love. It was money that he desired. The poor girl felt that she had in a sense been an accomplice in the death of her benefactress. She began to weep bitterly. Herman regarded her in silence.

"You are a monster!" exclaimed Lisa, drying her eyes.

"I didn't intend to kill her; the pistol was not even loaded."

"How are you going to get out of the house?" inquired Lisa. "It is nearly daylight. I intended to show you the way to a secret staircase, while the Countess was asleep, as we would have to cross her chamber. Now I am afraid to do so."

"Direct me, and I will find the way alone," replied Herman.

She gave him minute instructions and a key with which to open the street door. The young man pressed the cold, inert hand, then went out.

The death of the Countess had surprised no one, as it had long been expected. Her funeral was attended by every one of note in the vicinity. Herman mingled with the throng without attracting any especial attention. After all the friends had taken their last look at the dead face, the young man approached the bier. He prostrated himself on the cold floor, and remained motionless for a long time. He rose at last with a face almost as pale as that of the corpse itself, and went up the steps to look into the casket. As he looked down it seemed to him that the rigid face returned his glance mockingly, closing one eye. He turned abruptly away, made a false step, and fell to the floor. He was picked up, and, at the same moment, Lisaveta was carried out in a faint.

Herman did not recover his usual composure during the entire day. He dined alone at an out-of-the-way restaurant, and drank a great deal, in the hope of stifling his emotion. The wine only served to stimulate his imagination. He returned home and threw himself down on his bed without undressing.

During the night he awoke with a start; the moon shone into his chamber, making everything plainly visible. Some one looked in at the window, then quickly disappeared. He paid no attention to this, but soon he heard the vestibule door open. He thought it was his orderly, returning late, drunk as usual. The step was an unfamiliar one, and he heard the shuffling sound of loose slippers.

The door of his room opened, and a woman in white entered. She came close to the bed, and the terrified man recognized the Countess.

"I have come to you against my will," she said abruptly; "but I was commanded to grant your request. The trey, seven, and ace in succession are the magic cards. Twenty-four hours must elapse between the use of each card, and after the three have been used you must never play again."

The fantom then turned and walked away. Herman heard the outside door close, and again saw the form pass the window.

He rose and went out into the hall, where his orderly lay asleep on the floor. The door was closed. Finding no trace of a visitor, he returned to his room, lit his candle, and wrote down what he had just heard.

Two fixed ideas cannot exist in the brain at the same time any more than two bodies can occupy the same point in space. The trey, seven, and ace soon chased away the thoughts of the dead woman, and all other thoughts from the brain of the young officer. All his ideas merged into a single one: how to turn to advantage the secret paid for so dearly. He even thought of resigning his commission and going to Paris to force a fortune from conquered fate. Chance rescued him from his embarrassment.

Tchekalinsky, a man who had passed his whole life at cards, opened a club at St. Petersburg. His long experience secured for him the confidence of his companions, and his hospitality and genial humor conciliated society.

The gilded youth flocked around him, neglecting society, preferring the charms of faro to those of their sweethearts. Naroumov invited Herman to accompany him to the club, and the young man accepted the invitation only too willingly.

The two officers found the apartments full. Generals and statesmen played whist; young men lounged on sofas, eating ices or smoking. In the principal salon stood a long table, at which about twenty men sat playing faro, the host of the establishment being the banker.

He was a man of about sixty, gray-haired and respectable. His ruddy face shone with genial humor; his eyes sparkled and a constant smile hovered around his lips.

Naroumov presented Herman. The host gave him a cordial handshake, begged him not to stand upon ceremony, and returned, to his dealing. More than thirty cards were already on the table. Tchekalinsky paused after each coup, to allow the punters time to recognize their gains or losses, politely answering all questions and constantly smiling.

After the deal was over, the cards were shuffled and the game began again.

"Permit me to choose a card," said Herman, stretching out his hand over the head of a portly gentleman, to reach a livret. The banker bowed without replying.

Herman chose a card, and wrote the amount of his stake upon it with a piece of chalk.

"How much is that?" asked the banker; "excuse me, sir, but I do not see well."

"Forty thousand rubles," said Herman coolly.

All eyes were instantly turned upon the speaker.

"He has lost his wits," thought Naroumov.

"Allow me to observe," said Tchekalinsky, with his eternal smile, "that your stake is excessive."

"What of it?" replied Herman, nettled. "Do you accept it or not?"

The banker nodded in assent. "I have only to remind you that the cash will be necessary; of course your word is good, but in order to keep the confidence of my patrons, I prefer the ready money."

Herman took a bank-check from his pocket and handed it to his host. The latter examined it attentively, then laid it on the card chosen.

He began dealing: to the right, a nine; to the left, a trey.

"The trey wins," said Herman, showing the card he held—a trey.

A murmur ran through the crowd. Tchekalinsky frowned for a second only, then his smile returned. He took a roll of bank-bills from his pocket and counted out the required sum. Herman received it and at once left the table.

The next evening saw him at the place again. Every one eyed him curiously, and Tchekalinsky greeted him cordially.

He selected his card and placed upon it his fresh stake. The banker began dealing: to the right, a nine; to the left, a seven.

Herman then showed his card—a seven spot. The onlookers exclaimed, and the host was visibly disturbed. He counted out ninety-four-thousand rubles and passed them to Herman, who accepted them without showing the least surprise, and at once withdrew.

The following evening he went again. His appearance was the signal for the cessation of all occupation, every one being eager to watch the developments of events. He selected his card—an ace.

The dealing began: to the right, a queen; to the left, an ace.

"The ace wins," remarked Herman, turning up his card without glancing at it.

"Your queen is killed," remarked Tchekalinsky quietly.

Herman trembled; looking down, he saw, not the ace he had selected, but the queen of spades. He could scarcely believe his eyes. It seemed impossible that he could have made such a mistake. As he stared at the card it seemed to him that the queen winked one eye at him mockingly.

"The old woman!" he exclaimed involuntarily.

The croupier raked in the money while he looked on in stupid terror. When he left the table, all made way for him to pass; the cards were shuffled, and the gambling went on.

Herman became a lunatic. He was confined at the hospital at Oboukov, where he spoke to no one, but kept constantly murmuring in a monotonous tone: "The trey, seven, ace! The trey, seven, queen!"

LEV SHEININ

THE HUNTING KNIFE

Writing was only a secondary career for Lev Romanovich Sheinin
(1906–1967) who, at the age of seventeen, was appointed by the Communist Party to be a Regional Court Investigator. Later, he was trained in
Criminal, Legal, Civil and Labor Codes, becoming a leading criminologist in
the Soviet Union. In the 1930s, he was a prosecutor and aide to the notorious State Prosecutor Andrei Y. Vyshinsky, who conducted most of the
purge trials for Josef Stalin in the 1930s. These infamous trials convicted
hundreds of thousands of people on transparently trumped-up charges,
facilitating the spread of the Great Terror.

Born in Belarus, Sheinin had been studying to be a writer when, with
no legal education of any kind, he began his criminal career, which culmi-
nated, late in life, with a position as senior criminologist for the NKVD, the
state public (and secret) police force which was the predecessor of the
KGB. His experiences were later published as fictional accounts in *Pravda*,
Izvestia and various Soviet magazines, then collected in *Diary of a Criminologist*, published in Moscow in 1956. He also wrote *The People's Court in the
U.S.S.R.*, published in Moscow in 1957, a sympathetic view of the court
system in the Soviet Union.

"The Hunting Knife" was first published in a Russian periodical, then
collected in *Diary of a Criminologist*; it was first translated into English and
published in the July 1965 issue of *Ellery Queen's Mystery Magazine*.

T he papers were finally signed and there it stood, black on white, that A. Burov, Professor of Zoology, and his assistant Voronov were being sent to Kolguyev Island in the Barents Sea to conduct scientific research for one year.

Their colleagues at the University read the notice and laughed. The teachers and students knew only too well that the Professor and his assistant could not bear the sight of each other. The news that these two were to be sent to a deserted island for a year, where they would be thrown together twenty-four hours a day, prompted shrugs and smiles. Some said it had been done on purpose—a scheme to cool their tempers with the harsh climate.

"They'll come back friends," they said. "Just you wait and see— they'll be the best of pals."

But the two most surprised by the news were the men involved. It became known at the University that the Professor had spent a sleepless night when he discovered the name of his companion for the winter. And Voronov was no less upset.

Still, orders were orders, and several weeks later the two men set out for an island in the far-off Barents Sea, where they were to spend a long Arctic year together.

Their first letters arrived a month later. They wrote of their first impressions, the details of their journey, and their plans for the future.

"Everything would be fine," read the Professor's letter, "if not for the constant presence of this character, who definitely qualifies as a subject for scientific study by any zoologist. This young man continues to get on my nerves. Being here and unfortunately having to see him constantly, I am once again convinced that my original dislike of him was well founded."

Voronov, in turn, complained of "the absolute intolerance of the old grouch and the torture of being with him, day in and day out."

At the University they read the letters, chuckled, and wondered at the stubbornness of these two men in their indefatigable dislike of each other.

The other Professors argued about how long the groundless feud would last. The optimists said both would finally make up and even come to like each other; the pessimists contended it would be just the opposite. Several bets were made, and two quarrels broke out.

A month later, however, a brief telegram from Kolguyev Island informed the University that Professor Burov had been murdered by Assistant Professor Voronov.

The special investigator assigned to the case began by looking for a means of reaching the island. Meteorological conditions, unfortunately, made the journey impossible at that time of the year.

The investigator then radioed instructions to the Captain of an icebreaker cruising near the island. The Captain was to deliver the frozen corpse to Moscow, to interrogate the witnesses—if there were any—and to search the scene of the crime thoroughly. Voronov was to be brought to Moscow with all due precautions.

Three weeks later, the Captain delivered to the special investigator's office a man in his thirties with a lost and frightened expression—the chief, and only suspect, Assistant Professor Voronov.

"Please be seated," the detective said, looking Voronov over with cold curiosity.

"Thank you," Voronov answered quietly.

The detective had carefully studied the records of Voronov's past. In his thirty-two years, Voronov had lived honestly until the day he killed Burov. Voronov was undoubtedly a talented scientist. He had written several scientific papers and was firmly on the road to professional acclaim.

The questioning began.

"What in God's name made you murder the Professor?" the detective, usually a calm and self-controlled man, exclaimed.

Voronov shrugged helplessly.

"You see," he said in an apologetic, hesitant voice, "you see—well, the thing is, I didn't murder him."

"But he *was* killed?"

"Yes."

"Was there anyone at the scene of the crime except the two of you?"

"No, only the two of us. No one else was there—no one else could possibly have been there."

"In that case I can't see why you don't confess. You'll have to agree that if only two people are together and one of them is murdered, the murderer—"

"—must be the other," Voronov finished the sentence. "It's undoubtedly so. But I did not kill him. The terrible thing is that I realize the utter hopelessness of my situation. I have no chance in the world to defend myself. Of course, I've been—what is it you call it?— caught red-handed. If I were in your shoes, I'd never have a moment's doubt. I understand. I'm prepared for the worst—for the very worst. But I did *not* kill him."

And Voronov began to weep. He sobbed as strangely as he had spoken. This tall calm, cultured man wept like a child, helplessly, without anger, and touchingly. He did not at all intend his tears to move his interrogator. On the other hand, he made no attempt to hide them. He wept as simply as he had spoken, and just as unaffectedly.

"Pull yourself together," the detective said gruffly. "If you murdered him—and everything points to that—it's best to confess. If you did *not,* then defend yourself. Refute my arguments, explain your actions, present your side of the story."

Voronov's guilt seemed too obvious, too incontrovertible. All the evidence pointed to the fact that Burov had been murdered by Voronov and no one else. But to the investigator's amazement, Voronov, far from trying to defend himself, provided additional and extremely incriminating information without the slightest prompting. While continuing to deny his guilt, he went on hurriedly to disclose new circumstances, new facts, all piling up further evidence against him.

"When we came to the island," he said, "our animosity grew sharper.

We tried to keep our emotions in check, but our hatred of each other entered every word, look, and gesture. It was very difficult to keep oneself always in control, and that, unfortunately, did nothing to help the situation. Professor Burov couldn't stand the sight of me, and I felt the same way about him. To tell you the truth, there were moments when I had half a mind to strike him, even to kill him. These thoughts began to torment me. They even found their way into my diary. I've brought it along. Here, read it."

With these words Voronov handed the detective a large notebook. True enough, among other entries were those which showed that more and more often Voronov had kept playing with the thought of killing Professor Burov.

"I really don't know," he continued, "but perhaps in the end I might actually have killed the Professor. Perhaps! But I did *not* kill him. This is what happened.

"That morning we decided to go duck hunting on a small lake in the center of the island. We went there by dogsled. Our driver was a Nenets named Vasya. Halfway there the sled broke down. We had about two miles to go, so we decided to continue on foot, while Vasya stayed behind to fix the sled.

"We arrived at the lake and began shooting. Then the ducks swam off to the far shore. I suggested that the Professor remain where he was while I went round to the other side to shoot from there. He agreed, and I set off for the opposite shore.

"I had a clear view of the Professor as he stood all alone on the other side of the lake, not far away. There was no one near him, and no one could have been. Of this I was sure. Then a shot rang out from the area where he was standing. I saw him jerk strangely and fall, and I ran back to him, wondering what had happened.

"When I reached him, the Professor was still alive, but unconscious. A hunting knife was plunged into his left eye to the very hilt. His rifle lay beside him.

"I lost my head, not knowing what to do for the unfortunate man. I tried to pull the knife from his eye, but could not—it had been driven in with great force. Then I ran back to where we had left the sled. Vasya was just finishing his repairs. I told him there had been a terrible accident. By the time we reached the lake, the Professor was dead. We took his body to camp, where we finally managed to get the knife out of the eye with great difficulty. That's all."

Voronov lit a cigarette, inhaling hungrily. After a brief pause he spoke again.

"So you see, it's hard for me to defend myself. I'm intelligent enough to see that everything in this case points to my guilt. In fact, I may even stand a better chance in court—for clemency—by confessing, by making a clean breast of it and sincerely repenting my crime. Yet I cannot do that. I did *not* kill him. I did not commit murder, although I can't prove my innocence. I have only one request before you arrest me. These letters are from my fiancee, and this is a letter I've written to her. Will you please send them to her?"

"No, I won't," the detective replied bluntly. "You can give the letters to her yourself. I'm not going to arrest you, Voronov."

There are cases in which the unusual solution, the sudden conclusion, does not spring from a chain of formal clues and evidence, from a logical sequence of data already established, from a final summary of the events. Often there are such dark and tangled labyrinths of facts and details of human relations, such a terrible piling up of all sorts of circumstantial evidence and chance occurrences, that the most experienced investigator finds himself ready to throw up his hands. In such cases his guiding lights are his intuition and experience, his perseverence and conscience, and above all, his humaneness. These will surely lead him to the truth in the end . . .

The detective had put himself in a very awkward position by releasing Voronov. On the one hand, Voronov's guilt seemed indisputable; on the other hand, the freeing of Voronov had been prompted solely by the investigator's intuition—by the fact that he believed the man's story despite all proofs to the contrary. He based his belief on those dim, vague, and unclear grounds which are formed within the soul, which do not always seem logical, which are so difficult to express in words, which appear as a result of the investigator's psychological and professional insight, and the keenness of his intuition. They are the fruitful outcome of many years of thoughtful and tireless work, of training in observation, of experience in criminology, and of the constant habit of analyzing events and characters.

The detective was convinced that Voronov had not murdered Professor Burov. But he had to prove it, and what is more, he had to solve the mystery of the Professor's death. Certainly Voronov could not be cleared of the murder charge simply because the detective was emotionally convinced of his innocence.

The autopsy was performed by Dr. Semyonov with his usual skill and care. His findings boiled down to two points. First, Professor Burov died as a result of injuries caused by the blow of a hunting knife, plunged into the victim's left eye; and second, the blow had been inflicted with a force greater than that of a human being's.

"What do you mean by 'greater than that of a human being's'?" the detective asked.

"I mean," Dr. Semyonov answered, "that the strength with which the blow was struck was greater than could be expected from an average person. But just how great that force was I cannot tell."

The detective examined the Professor's rifle. It was a Winchester and supplied nothing of interest to the case. The knife which inflicted the fatal blow was also quite ordinary—a cheap hunting knife with a wooden handle. But on examining it more closely, the detective discovered a small fault in the end of the handle, obviously the result of poor workmanship. The tiny tip of the metal rod by which the handle was attached to the blade protruded as a sharp point from the end of the wood, though it was barely perceptible.

The investigator ran his finger over the tiny point of metal, then suddenly sprang to his feet.

An hour later a group of hastily summoned experts—gunsmiths and hunters—crowded the detective's office.

"Tell me," he asked them, "what would a hunter do if he had a hunting knife with a wooden handle in his belt and found that a cartridge in his rifle had stuck in the magazine? For instance, if the cartridge became slightly enlarged from dampness or had a flaw—what would a hunter do then?"

The experts began to whisper among themselves.

"In such a case," one said, when they had finally come to a unanimous decision, "he would probably take his hunting knife and carefully tap its smooth wooden handle on the cartridge to ease it into the magazine."

"That's what I thought, too," the investigator said. "Well, now, have a look at this knife. Notice the tiny metal point sticking out of the wood. Now, imagine that a hunter were to try to push the cartridge in with this knife. What do you think would happen?"

The experts examined the knife, noted the tiny metal protuberance, and reached agreement.

"This bit of metal," they said, "sharp and strong as it is, could easily play the part of a firing pin. If this knife were used to tap the cartridge, it might cause an explosion that would fire the rifle."

The detective turned to the gunsmiths.

"Tell me," he said, "if the cartridge had not fully entered the magazine and if, as a result of the hunter's carelessness, the rifle were fired, where would the main force of the explosion be directed? And how great would that force be?"

"The force of the explosion would be directed backwards, throwing the hand holding the knife back to the face. The force of the shot would be very great."

The detective heaved a sigh of relief. His theory had been confirmed.

Just then Dr. Semyonov entered the office. The investigator showed him the knife and told him what the experts had concluded.

"That's all very clever," Dr. Semyonov said slowly, "and even quite believable, if not for one small detail. Considering the length of the Professor's arm, his height, and the correlation of various parts of his body, his right hand would have wounded him in the right eye. And as you know, Professor Burov was killed by the knife entering his left eye."

The detective's solution, which had seemed so clear and correct, had fallen to pieces. But he was a stubborn man, so he continued his investigation. Back he went to the family of the dead Professor.

"Was there anything peculiar about Professor Burov physically?"

"No—nothing peculiar."

"Did you ever see the Professor use a scalpel?"

"Yes, certainly—he often worked at home."

"In which hand did he hold the scalpel?"

"In his left hand—the Professor was left-handed."

The detective almost danced with joy. There, at last, was the final clue!

Now everything seemed in order. The truth had been uncovered. Professor Burov's death was explained, and Voronov was cleared completely. The case could now be closed "For lack of evidence attesting to a crime."

But the Professor's brother came to see the investigator.

"I'm ready to agree that you are right and that my brother died as a result of his own carelessness," he said. "But where did the knife come from? My brother did not own such a knife. Whose knife was it? Until you answer that question, Inspector, I cannot consider the case closed."

Professor Burov's brother was certainly entitled to an answer.

The detective checked the supply list. In the huge pile of bills, lists, and receipts, among hundreds of items including ammunition, rifles, tents, canned goods, binoculars, pans, thermos bottles, axes, pliers, hammers, metal cans, kerosene stoves, thermometers, dishes, and a multitude of other things, the detective searched in vain for an item marked: *Hunting knife—4 rubles.*

Recalling that the expedition had sailed from Archangel after stopping there for several days, the investigator decided to go to that city and see what he could learn there.

He arrived in Archangel the next morning and immediately started on a tour of all stores that sold hunting knives. He was shown hundreds of hunting knives, expensive and cheap, Finnish knives, knives from Vologda, Kostroma, Vyatka, and Pavlovo-Posad—but not one of the kind he was looking for. Salesmen eyed their fussy customer in dismay; store managers shrugged, cashiers giggled—but nowhere could he find the knife he was seeking.

Finally, toward evening, he wandered into a small sporting goods shop on the Dvina Embankment. Almost the first thing he noticed was a hunting knife with a wooden handle—exactly like the one that had killed the Professor.

"How much does this knife cost?" the investigator asked.

"Three seventy-five," the salesman answered.

The detective called the manager and learned that only one cooperative made such knives, sending its entire output to this store. And yes, the knives had been on sale when the University expedition was in Archangel.

"We have sold many of them," the manager said, "but we can't remember all our customers."

The detective returned to Moscow. There, in Professor Burov's notebook, among hundreds of entries, he found the following: *Archangel. Hunting kniife—3 rub. 75 kop. . . .*

"Sit down, Comrade Voronov," the detective said, smiling. "This is the last time I'll be summoning you. Kindly read the order to close the case. Sign here, to show you've received your copy."

Voronov took up the pen. Suddenly everything seemed to swim before him—the pen, the inkwell, the face of the investigator sitting across the table. But the investigator's words finally sank in. The young scientist realized that his horrible experience was now a thing of the past, that his innocence had been proved, that the uncommunicative man sitting across the desk from him had saved his life and his honor.

IVAN BUNIN

THE GENTLEMAN FROM SAN FRANCISCO

When Ivan Alexeyevich Bunin (1870–1953) was told in 1933 that he had won the Nobel Prize for Literature, he asked what the amount was. Living in France at the time, he was told it was 600,000 francs (about $38,000). He said he was lucky, but then pointed out that a barber from Tarascon had won 5,000,000. His move to Paris, followed by one to the French Riviera, had been necessitated when he sided with the reactionary forces at the outbreak of the Russian Revolution and fled the country in May 1918.

The precocious author and poet began writing poetry at the age of eight, heavily influenced by his mother's reading Pushkin aloud to him. His tutor taught him to read and write with the aid of such books as *Don Quixote*, *Robinson Crusoe* and the stories of Gogol, convincing him that he wanted to be a writer. His poetry and translations of Longfellow's *Hiawatha* and Byron's *Cain* earned him the Pushkin Prize in 1903, the highest literary award given by the Russian Academy; he was elected to its literary division in 1909. The following year, he wrote *The Village*, the novel that brought him international renown. It was his first major work to use as its theme one he used frequently in other books: the trials and complex, often tragic, lives of the Russian people under the Czar.

"The Gentleman from San Francisco" is regarded as one of the greatest short stories of all time. Whether a crime occurs may be left to the reader to decide. It was first published in Russia in 1915; the first English language translation appeared in the January 1922 issue of *The Dial*.

"Alas, alas, that great city Babylon, that mighty city!"
—Revelation of St. John.

T he Gentleman from San Francisco—neither at Naples nor on Capri
could any one recall his name—with his wife and daughter, was on
his way to Europe, where he intended to stay for two whole years,
solely for the pleasure of it.

He was firmly convinced that he had a full right to a rest, enjoyment, a long comfortable trip, and what not. This conviction had a two-
fold reason: first he was rich, and second, despite his fifty-eight years, he
was just about to enter the stream of life's pleasures. Until now he had
not really lived, but simply existed, to be sure—fairly well, yet putting
off his fondest hopes for the future. He toiled unweariedly—the Chinese, whom he imported by thousands for his works, knew full well
what it meant,—and finally he saw that he had made much, and that
he had nearly come up to the level of those whom he had once taken
as a model, and he decided to catch his breath. The class of people to
which he belonged was in the habit of beginning its enjoyment of life
with a trip to Europe, India, Egypt. He made up his mind to do the
same. Of course, it was first of all himself that he desired to reward for
the years of toil, but he was also glad for his wife and daughter's sake.
His wife was never distinguished by any extraordinary impressionability,
but then, all elderly American women are ardent travelers. As for his
daughter, a girl of marriageable age, and somewhat sickly,—travel was
the very thing she needed. Not to speak of the benefit to her health,
do not happy meetings occur during travels? Abroad, one may chance
to sit at the same table with a prince, or examine frescoes side by side
with a multi-millionaire.

The itinerary the Gentleman from San Francisco planned out was
an extensive one. In December and January he expected to relish the sun
of southern Italy, monuments of antiquity, the tarantella, serenades of
wandering minstrels, and that which at his age is felt most keenly—the

love, not entirely disinterested though, of young Neapolitan girls. The Carnival days he planned to spend at Nice and Monte-Carlo, which at that time of the year is the meeting-place of the choicest society, the society upon which depend all the blessings of civilization: the cut of dress suits, the stability of thrones, the declaration of wars, the prosperity of hotels. Some of these people passionately give themselves over to automobile and boat races, others to roulette, others, again, busy themselves with what is called flirtation, and others shoot pigeons, which soar so beautifully from the dove-cote, hover a while over the emerald lawn, on the background of the forget-me-not colored sea, and then suddenly hit the ground, like little white lumps. Early March he wanted to devote to Florence, and at Easter, to hear the Miserere in Paris. His plans also included Venice, Paris, bull-baiting at Seville, bathing on the British Islands, also Athens, Constantinople, Palestine, Egypt, and even Japan, of course, on the way back... And at first things went very well indeed.

It was the end of November, and all the way to Gibraltar the ship sailed across seas which were either clad by icy darkness or swept by storms carrying wet snow. But there were no accidents, and the vessel did not even roll. The passengers,—all people of consequence—were numerous, and the steamer the famous "Atlantis," resembled the most expensive European hotel with all improvements: a night refreshment-bar, Oriental baths, even a newspaper of its own. The manner of living was a most aristocratic one; passengers rose early, awakened by the shrill voice of a bugle, filling the corridors at the gloomy hour when the day broke slowly and sulkily over the grayish-green watery desert, which rolled heavily in the fog. After putting on their flannel pajamas, they took coffee, chocolate, cocoa; they seated themselves in marble baths, went through their exercises, whetting their appetites and increasing their sense of well-being, dressed for the day, and had their breakfast. Till eleven o'clock they were supposed to stroll on the deck, breathing in the chill freshness of the ocean, or they played table-tennis, or other games which arouse the appetite. At eleven o'clock a collation was served consisting of sandwiches and bouillon, after which people read their newspapers, quietly waiting for luncheon, which was more nourishing and varied than the breakfast. The next two hours were given to rest; all the decks were crowded then with steamer chairs, on which the passengers, wrapped in plaids, lay stretched, dozing lazily, or watching the cloudy sky and the foamy-fringed water hillocks flashing beyond the sides of the vessel. At five o'clock, refreshed and gay, they drank strong, fragrant tea; at seven the sound of the bugle announced a dinner of nine courses... Then the Gentleman from San Francisco, rubbing his hands in an onrush of vital energy, hastened to his luxurious state-room to dress.

In the evening, all the decks of the "Atlantis" yawned in the darkness, shone with their innumerable fiery eyes, and a multitude of servants worked with increased feverishness in the kitchens, dish-washing compartments, and wine-cellars. The ocean, which heaved about the sides of the ship, was dreadful, but no one thought of it. All had faith in the controlling power, of the captain, a red-headed giant, heavy and very sleepy, who, clad in a uniform with broad golden stripes, looked like a huge idol, and but rarely emerged, for the benefit of the public, from his mysterious retreat. On the fore-castle, the siren gloomily roared or screeched in a fit of mad rage, but few of the diners heard the siren: its hellish voice was covered by the sounds of an excellent string orchestra, which played ceaselessly and exquisitely in a vast hall, decorated with marble and spread with velvety carpets. The hall was flooded with torrents of light, radiated by crystal lustres and gilt chandeliers; it was filled with a throng of bejeweled ladies in low-necked dresses, of men in dinner-coats, graceful waiters, and deferential maîtres-d'hôtel. One of these,—who accepted wine orders exclusively—wore a chain on his neck like some lord-mayor. The evening dress, and the ideal linen made the Gentleman from San Francisco look very young. Dry-skinned, of average height, strongly, though irregularly built, glossy with thorough washing and cleaning, and moderately animated, he sat in the golden splendor of this palace. Near him stood a bottle of amber-colored Johannisberg, and goblets of most delicate glass and of varied sizes, surmounted by a frizzled bunch of fresh hyacinths. There was something Mongolian in his yellowish face with its trimmed silvery moustache; his large teeth glimmered with gold fillings, and his strong, bald head had a dull glow, like old ivory. His wife, a big, broad and placid woman, was dressed richly, but in keeping with her age. Complicated, but light, transparent, and innocently immodest was the dress of his daughter, tall and slender, with magnificent hair gracefully combed; her breath was sweet with violet-scented tablets, and she had a number of tiny and most delicate pink dimples near her lips and between her slightly-powdered shoulder blades. . .

The dinner lasted two whole hours, and was followed by dances in the dancing hall, while the men—the Gentleman from San Francisco among them—made their way to the refreshment bar, where negros in red jackets and with eye-balls like shelled hard-boiled eggs, waited on them. There, with their feet on tables, smoking Havana cigars, and drinking themselves purple in the face, they settled the destinies of nations on the basis of the latest political and stock-exchange news. Outside, the ocean tossed up black mountains with a thud; and the snowstorm hissed furiously in the rigging grown heavy with slush; the ship trembled in every limb, struggling with the storm and ploughing with difficulty the shifting and seething mountainous masses that threw far and high their foaming tails; the siren groaned in agony, choked by storm and fog; the watchmen in their towers froze and almost went out of their minds under the superhuman stress of attention. Like the gloomy and sultry mass of the inferno, like its last, ninth circle, was the submersed womb of the steamer, where monstrous furnaces yawned with red-hot open jaws, and emitted deep, hooting sounds, and where the stokers, stripped to the waist, and purple with the reflected flames, bathed in their own dirty, acid sweat. And here, in the refreshment-bar, carefree men, with their feet, encased in dancing shoes, on the table, sipped cognac and liqueurs, swam in waves of spiced smoke, and exchanged subtle remarks, while in the dancing-hall everything sparkled and radiated light, warmth and joy. The couples now turned around in a waltz, now swayed in the tango; and the music, sweetly shameless and sad, persisted in its ceaseless entreaties . . . There were many persons of note in this magnificent crowd; an ambassador, a dry, modest old man; a great millionaire, shaved, tall, of an indefinite age, who, in his old-fashioned dress-coat, looked like a prelate; also a famous Spanish writer, and an international belle, already slightly faded and of dubious morals. There was also among them a loving pair, exquisite and refined, whom everybody watched with curiosity and who did not conceal their bliss; he danced only with her, sang—with great skill— only to her accompaniment, and they were so charming, so graceful. The captain alone knew that they had been hired by the company at a good salary to play at love, and that they had been sailing now on one, now on another steamer, for quite a long time.

In Gibraltar everybody was gladdened by the sun, and by the weather which was like early Spring. A new passenger appeared aboard the "Atlantis" and aroused everybody's interest. It was the crown-prince of an Asiatic state, who traveled incognito, a small man, very nimble, though looking as if made of wood, broad-faced, narrow-eyed, in gold-rimmed glasses, somewhat disagreeable because of his long black moustache, which was sparse like that of a corpse, but otherwise—charming, plain, modest. In the Mediterranean the breath of winter was again felt. The seas were heavy and motley like a peacock's tail and the waves stirred up by the gay gusts of the tramontane, tossed their white crests under a sparkling and perfectly clear sky. Next morning, the sky grew paler and the skyline misty. Land was near. Then Ischia and Capri came in sight, and one could descry, through an opera-glass, Naples, looking like pieces of sugar strewn at the foot of an indistinct dove-colored mass, and above them, a snow-covered chain of distant mountains. The decks were crowded, many ladies and gentlemen put on light fur-coats;

Chinese servants, bandy-legged youths—with pitch black braids down to the heels and with girlish, thick eyelashes,—always quiet and speaking in a whisper, were carrying to the foot of the staircases, plaid wraps, canes, and crocodile-leather valises and hand-bags. The daughter of the Gentleman from San Francisco stood near the prince, who, by a happy chance, had been introduced to her the evening before, and feigned to be looking steadily at something far-off, which he was pointing out to her, while he was, at the same time, explaining something, saying something rapidly and quietly. He was so small that he looked like a boy among other men, and he was not handsome at all. And then there was something strange about him; his glasses, derby and coat were most commonplace, but there was something horse-like in the hair of his sparse moustache, and the thin, tanned skin of his flat face looked as though it were somewhat stretched and varnished. But the girl listened to him, and so great was her excitement that she could hardly grasp the meaning of his words, her heart palpitated with incomprehensible rapture and with pride that he was standing and speaking with her and nobody else. Everything about him was different: his dry hands, his clean skin, under which flowed ancient kingly blood, even his light shoes and his European dress, plain, but singularly tidy—everything hid an inexplicable fascination and engendered thoughts of love. And the Gentleman from San Francisco, himself, in a silk-hat, gray leggings, patent leather shoes, kept eyeing the famous beauty who was standing near him, a tall, stately blonde, with eyes painted according to the latest Parisian fashion, and a tiny, bent peeled-off pet-dog, to whom she addressed herself. And the daughter, in a kind of vague perplexity, tried not to notice him.

Like all wealthy Americans he was very liberal when traveling, and believed in the complete sincerity and good-will of those who so painstakingly fed him, served him day and night, anticipating his slightest desire, protected him from dirt and disturbance, hauled things for him, hailed carriers, and delivered his luggage to hotels; so it was everywhere, and it had to be so at Naples. Meanwhile, Naples grew and came nearer. The musicians, with their shining brass instruments had already formed a group on the deck, and all of a sudden deafened everybody with the triumphant sounds of a ragtime march. The giant captain, in his full uniform appeared on the bridge and like a gracious Pagan idol, waved his hands to the passengers,—and it seemed to the Gentleman from San Francisco,—as it did to all the rest,—that for him alone thundered the march, so greatly loved by proud America, and that him alone did the captain congratulate on the safe arrival. And when the "Atlantis" had finally entered the port and all its many-decked mass leaned against the quay, and the gang-plank began to rattle heavily,—what a crowd of porters, with their assistants, in caps with golden galloons, what a crowd of various boys and husky ragamuffins with pads of colored postal cards attacked the Gentleman from San Francisco, offering their services! With kindly contempt he grinned at these beggars, and, walking towards the automobile of the hotel where the prince might stop, muttered between his teeth, now in English, now in Italian—"Go away! Via . . ."

Immediately, life at Naples began to follow a set routine. Early in the morning breakfast was served in the gloomy dining-room, swept by a wet draught from the open windows looking upon a stony garden, while outside the sky was cloudy and cheerless, and a crowd of guides swarmed at the door of the vestibule. Then came the first smiles of the warm roseate sun, and from the high suspended balcony, a broad vista unfolded itself: Vesuvius, wrapped to its base in radiant morning vapors; the pearly ripple, touched to silver, of the bay, the delicate outline of Capri on the skyline; tiny asses dragging twowheeled buggies along the soft, sticky embankment, and detachments of little soldiers marching somewhere to the tune of cheerful and defiant music.

Next on the day's program was a slow automobile ride along crowded, narrow, and damp corridors of streets, between high, many-windowed buildings. It was followed by visits to museums, lifelessly clean and lighted evenly and pleasantly, but as though with the dull light cast by snow;—then to churches, cold, smelling of wax, always alike: a majestic entrance, closed by a ponderous, leather curtain, and inside—a vast void, silence, quiet flames of seven-branched candlesticks, sending forth a red glow from where they stood at the farther end, on the bedecked altar,—a lonely, old woman lost among the dark wooden benches, slippery gravestones under the feet, and somebody's "Descent from the Cross," infallibly famous. At one o'clock—luncheon, on the mountain of San-Martius, where at noon the choicest people gathered, and where the daughter of the Gentleman from San Francisco once almost fainted with joy, because it seemed to her that she saw the Prince in the hall, although she had learned from the newspapers that he had temporarily left for Rome. At five o'clock it was customary to take tea at the hotel, in a smart *salon*, where it was far too warm because of the carpets and the blazing fireplaces; and then came dinner-time—and again did the mighty, commanding voice of the gong resound throughout the building, again did silk rustle and the mirrors reflect files of ladies in low-necked dresses ascending the staircases, and again the splendid palatial dining hall opened with broad hospitality, and again the musicians' jackets formed red patches on the estrade, and the black figures of the waiters swarmed around the maître-d'hôtel, who, with extraordinary skill, poured a thick pink soup into plates . . . As everywhere, the dinner was the crown of the day. People dressed for it as for a wedding, and so abundant was it in food, wines, mineral waters, sweets and fruits, that about eleven o'clock in the evening chamber-maids would carry to all the rooms hot-water bags.

That year, however, December did not happen to be a very propitious one. The doormen were abashed when people spoke to them about the weather, and shrugged their shoulders guiltily, mumbling that they could not recollect such a year, although, to tell the truth, it was not the first year they mumbled those words, usually adding that "things are terrible everywhere": that unprecedented showers and storms had broken out on the Riviera, that it was snowing in Athens, that Aetna, too, was all blocked up with snow, and glowed brightly at night, and that tourists were fleeing from Palermo to save themselves from the cold spell . . .

That winter, the morning sun daily deceived Naples: toward noon the sky would invariably grow gray, and a light rain would begin to fall, growing thicker and duller. Then the palms at the hotel-porch glistened disagreeably like wet tin, the town appeared exceptionally dirty and congested, the museums too monotonous, the cigars of the drivers in their rubber raincoats, which flattened in the wind like wings, intolerably stinking, and the energetic flapping of their whips over their thin-necked nags—obviously false. The shoes of the signors, who cleaned the streetcar tracks, were in a frightful state, the women who splashed in the mud, with black hair unprotected from the rain, were ugly and short-legged, and the humidity mingled with the foul smell of rotting fish, that came from the foaming sea, was simply disheartening. And so, early-morning quarrels began to break out between the Gentleman from San Francisco and his wife; and their daughter now grew pale and suffered from headaches, and now became animated, enthusiastic over everything, and at such times was lovely and beautiful. Beautiful were the tender, complex feelings which her meeting with the ungainly man aroused in her,— the man in whose veins flowed unusual blood, for, after all, it does not matter what in particular stirs up a maiden's soul: money, or fame, or nobility of birth . . . Everybody assured the tourists that it was quite different at Sorrento and on Capri, that lemon-trees were blossoming there, that it was warmer and sunnier there, the morals purer, and the wine less adulterated. And the family from San Francisco decided to set out with all their luggage for Capri. They planned to settle down at Sorrento, but first to visit the island, tread the stones where stood Tiberius's palaces, examine the fabulous wonders of the Blue Grotto, and listen to the bagpipes of Abruzzi, who roam about the island during the whole month preceding Christmas and sing the praises of the Madonna.

On the day of departure—a very memorable day for the family from

San Francisco—the sun did not appear even in the morning. A heavy winter fog covered Vesuvius down to its very base and hung like a gray curtain low over the leaden surge of the sea, hiding it completely at a distance of half a mile. Capri was completely out of sight, as though it had never existed on this earth. And the little steamboat which was making for the island tossed and pitched so fiercely that the family lay prostrated on the sofas in the miserable cabin of the little steamer, with their feet wrapped in plaids and their eyes shut because of their nausea. The older lady suffered, as she thought, most; several times she was overcome with sea-sickness, and it seemed to her then she was dying, but the chambermaid, who repeatedly brought her the basin, and who for many years, in heat and in cold, had been tossing on these waves, ever on the alert, ever kindly to all,—the chambermaid only laughed. The lady's daughter was frightfully pale and kept a slice of lemon between her teeth. Not even the hope of an unexpected meeting with the prince at Sorrento, where he planned to arrive on Christmas, served to cheer her. The Gentleman from San Francisco, who was lying on his back, dressed in a large overcoat and a big cap, did not loosen his jaws throughout the voyage. His face grew dark, his moustache white, and his head ached heavily; for the last few days, because of the bad weather, he had drunk far too much in the evenings.

And the rain kept on beating against the rattling window panes, and water dripped down from them on the sofas; the howling wind attacked the masts, and sometimes, aided by a heavy sea, it laid the little steamer on its side, and then something below rolled about with a rattle.

While the steamer was anchored at Castellamare and Sorrento, the situation was more cheerful; but even here the ship rolled terribly, and the coast with all its precipices, gardens and pines, with its pink and white hotels and hazy mountains clad in curling verdure, flew up and down as if it were on swings. The rowboats hit against the sides of the steamer, the sailors and the deck passengers shouted at the top of their voices, and somewhere a baby screamed as if it were being crushed to pieces. A wet wind blew through the door, and from a wavering barge flying the flag of the Hotel Royal, an urchin kept on unwearyingly shouting "Kgoyal-al! Hotel Kgoyal-al! . . ." inviting tourists. And the Gentleman from San Francisco felt like the old man that he was,—and it was with weariness and animosity that he thought of all these "Royals," "Splendids," "Excelsiors," and of all those greedy bugs, reeking with garlic, who are called Italians. Once, during a stop, having opened his eyes and half-risen from the sofa, he noticed in the shadow of the rock beach a heap of stone huts, miserable, mildewed through and through, huddled close by the water, near boats, rags, tin-boxes, and brown fishing nets,—and as he remembered that this was the very Italy he had come to enjoy, he felt a great despair . . . Finally, in twilight, the black mass of the island began to grow nearer, as though burrowed through at the base by red fires, the wind grew softer, warmer, more fragrant; from the dock-lanterns huge golden serpents flowed down the tame waves which undulated like black oil . . . Then, suddenly, the anchor rumbled and fell with a splash into the water, the fierce yells of the boatman filled the air,—and at once everyone's heart grew easy. The electric lights in the cabin grew more brilliant, and there came a desire to eat, drink, smoke, move . . . Ten minutes later the family from San Francisco found themselves in a large ferry-boat; fifteen minutes later they trod the stones of the quay, and then seated themselves in a small lighted car, which, with a buzz, started to ascend the slope, while vineyard stakes, half-ruined stone fences, and wet, crooked lemon-trees, in spots shielded by straw sheds, with their glimmering orange-colored fruit and thick glossy foliage, were sliding down past the open car windows. . . After rain, the earth smells sweetly in Italy, and each of her islands has a fragrance of its own.

The Island of Capri was dark and damp on that evening. But for a while it grew animated and let up, in spots, as always in the hour of the steamer's arrival. On the top of the hill, at the station of the *funiculaire*, there stood already the crowd of those whose duty it was to receive properly the Gentleman from San Francisco. The rest of the tourists hardly deserved any attention. There were a few Russians, who had settled on Capri, untidy, absent-minded people, absorbed in their bookish thoughts, spectacled, bearded, with the collars of their cloth overcoats raised. There was also a company of long-legged, long-necked, round-headed German youths in Tyrolean costume, and with linen bags on their backs, who need no one's services, are everywhere at home, and are by no means liberal in their expenses. The Gentleman from San Francisco, who quietly kept aloof from both the Russians and the Germans, was noticed at once. He and his ladies were hurriedly helped from the car, a man ran before them to show them the way, and they were again surrounded by boys and those thickset Caprean peasant women, who carry on their heads the trunks and valises of wealthy travelers. Their tiny, wooden, foot-stools rapped against the pavement of the small square, which looked almost like an opera square, and over which an electric lantern swung in the damp wind; the gang of urchins whistled like birds and turned somersaults, and as the Gentleman from San Francisco passed among them, it all looked like a stage scene; he went first under some kind of mediaeval archway, beneath houses huddled close together, and then along a steep echoing lane which led to the hotel entrance, flooded with light. At the left, a palm tree raised its tuft above the flat roofs, and higher up, blue stars burned in the black sky. And again things looked as though it was in honor of the guests from San Francisco that the stony damp little town had awakened on its rocky island in the Mediterranean, that it was they who had made the owner of the hotel so happy and beaming, and that the Chinese gong, which had sounded the call to dinner through all the floors as soon as they entered the lobby, had been waiting only for them.

The owner, an elegant young man, who met the guests with a polite and exquisite bow, for a moment startled the Gentleman from San Francisco. Having caught sight of him, the Gentleman from San Francisco suddenly recollected that on the previous night, among other confused images which disturbed his sleep, he had seen this very man. His vision resembled the hotel keeper to a dot, had the same head, the same hair, shining and scrupulously combed, and wore the same frock-coat with rounded skirts. Amazed, he almost stopped for a while. But as there was not a mustard-seed of what is called mysticism in his heart, his surprise subsided at once; in passing the corridor of the hotel he jestingly told his wife and daughter about this strange coincidence of dream and reality. His daughter alone glanced at him with alarm, longing suddenly compressed her heart, and such a strong feeling of solitude on this strange, dark island seized her that she almost began to cry. But, as usual, she said nothing about her feelings to her father.

A person of high dignity, Rex XVII, who had spent three entire weeks on Capri, had just left the island, and the guests from San Francisco were given the apartments he had occupied. At their disposal was put the most handsome and skillful chambermaid, a Belgian, with a figure rendered slim and firm by her corset, and with a starched cap, shaped like a small, indented crown; and they had the privilege of being served by the most well-appearing and portly footman, a black, fiery-eyed Sicilian, and by the quickest waiter, the small, stout Luigi, who was a fiend at cracking jokes and had changed many places in his life. Then the maitre-d'hôtel, a Frenchman, gently rapped at the door of the American gentleman's room. He came to ask whether the gentleman and the ladies would dine, and in case they would, which he did not doubt, to report that there was to be had that day lobsters, roast beef, asparagus, pheasants, etc., etc.

The floor was still rocking under the Gentleman from San Francisco —so sea-sick had the wretched Italian steamer made him—yet, he slowly, though awkwardly, shut the window which had banged when the maître-d'hôtel entered, and which let in the smell of the distant kitchen and wet flowers in the garden, and answered with slow distinctness, that they would dine, that their table must be placed farther away from the door, in the depth of the hall, that they would have local wine and champagne, moderately dry and but slightly cooled. The maître-d'hôtel approved the words of the guest in various intonations, which all meant, however, only one thing; there is and can be no doubt that the desires of the Gentleman from San Francisco are right, and that everything would be carried out, in exact conformity with his words. At last he inclined his head and asked delicately:

"Is that all, sir?"

And having received in reply a slow "Yes," he added that to-day they were going to have the tarantella danced in the vestibule by Carmella and Giuseppe, known to all Italy and to "the entire world of tourists."

"I saw her on post-card pictures," said the Gentleman from San Francisco in a tone of voice which expressed nothing. "And this Giuseppe, is he her husband?"

"Her cousin, sir," answered the maître-d'hôtel.

The Gentleman from San Francisco tarried a little, evidently musing on something, but said nothing, then dismissed him with a nod of his head.

Then he started making preparations, as though for a wedding: he turned on all the electric lamps, and filled the mirrors with reflections of light and the sheen of furniture, and opened trunks; he began to shave and to wash himself, and the sound of his bell was heard every minute in the corridor, crossing with other impatient calls which came from the rooms of his wife and daughter. Luigi, in his red apron, with the ease characteristic of stout people, made funny faces at the chambermaids, who were dashing by with tile buckets in their hands, making them laugh until the tears came. He rolled head over heels to the door, and, tapping with his knuckles, asked with feigned timidity and with an obsequious-ness which he knew how to render idiotic:

"Ha sonata, Signore?" (Did you ring, sir?)

And from behind the door a slow, grating, insultingly polite voice, answered:

"Yes, come in."

What did the Gentleman from San Francisco think and feel on that evening forever memorable to him? It must be said frankly: absolutely nothing exceptional. The trouble is that everything on this earth appears too simple. Even had he felt anything deep in his heart, a premonition that something was going to happen, he would have imagined that it was not going to happen so soon, at least not at once. Besides, as is usually the case just after sea-sickness is over, he was very hungry, and he anticipated with real delight the first spoonful of soup, and the first gulp of wine; therefore, he was performing the habitual process of dressing, in a state of excitement which left no time for reflection.

Having shaved and washed himself, and dexterously put in place a few false teeth, he then, standing before the mirror, moistened and vigorously plastered what was left of his thick pearly-colored hair, close to his tawny-yellow skull. Then he put on, with some effort, a tight-fitting undershirt of cream-colored silk, fitted tight to his strong, aged body with its waist swelling out because of an abundant diet; and he pulled black silk socks and patent-leather dancing shoes on his dry feet with their fallen arches. Squatting down, he set right his black trousers, drawn high by means of silk suspenders, adjusted his snow-white shirt with its bulging front, put the buttons into the shining cuffs, and began the painful process of hunting up the front button under the hard collar. The floor was still swaying under him, the tips of his fingers hurt terribly, the button at times painfully pinched the flabby skin in the depression under his Adam's apple, but he persevered, and finally, with his eyes shining from the effort, his face blue because of the narrow collar which squeezed his neck, he triumphed over the difficulties—and all exhausted, he sat down before the glass-pier, his reflected image repeating itself in all the mirrors.

"It's terrible!" he muttered, lowering his strong, bald head and making no effort to understand what was terrible; then, with a careful and habitual gesture, he examined his short fingers with gouty callosities in the joints, and their large, convex, almond-colored nails, and repeated with conviction, "It's terrible!"

But here the stentorian voice of the second gong sounded throughout the house, as in a heathen temple. And having risen hurriedly, the Gentleman from San Francisco drew his tie more taut and firm around his collar, and pulled together his abdomen by means of a tight waistcoat, put on a dinner-coat, set to rights the cuffs, and for the last time he examined himself in the mirror . . . This Carnella, tawny as a mulatto, with fiery eyes, in a dazzling dress in which orange-color predominated, must be an extraordinary dancer,—it occurred to him. And cheerfully leaving his room, he walked on the carpet, to his wife's chamber, and asked in a loud tone of voice if they would be long.

"In five minutes, papa!" answered cheerfully and gaily a girlish voice. "I am combing my hair."

"Very well," said the Gentleman from San Francisco.

And thinking of her wonderful hair, streaming on her shoulders, he slowly walked down along corridors and staircases, spread with red velvet carpets,—looking for the library. The servants he met hugged the walls, and he walked by as if not noticing them. An old lady, late for dinner, already bowed with years, with milk-white hair, yet bare-necked, in a light-gray silk dress, hurried at top speed, but she walked in a mincing, funny, hen-like manner, and he easily overtook her. At the glass door of the dining hall where the guests had already gathered and started eating, he stopped before the table crowded with boxes of matches and Egyptian cigarettes, took a great Manilla cigar, and threw three liras on the table. On the winter veranda he glanced into the open window; a stream of soft air came to him from the darkness, the top of the old palm loomed up before him afar-off, with its boughs spread among the stars and looking gigantic, and the distant even noise of the sea reached his ear. In the library-room, snug, quiet, a German in round silver-bowed glasses and with crazy, wondering eyes—stood turning the rustling pages of a newspaper. Having coldly eyed him, the Gentleman from San Francisco seated himself in a deep leather arm-chair near a lamp under a green hood, put on his pince-nez and twitching his head because of the collar which choked him, hid himself from view behind a newspaper. He glanced at a few headlines, read a few lines about the interminable Balkan war, and turned over the page with an habitual gesture. Suddenly, the lines blazed up with a glassy sheen, the veins of his neck swelled, his eyes bulged out, the pince-nez fell from his nose . . . He dashed forward, wanted to swallow air—and made a wild, rattling noise; his lower jaw dropped, dropped on his shoulder and began to shake, the shirt-front bulged out,—and the whole body, writhing, the heels catching in the carpet, slowly fell to the floor in a desperate struggle with an invisible foe . . .

Had not the German been in the library, this frightful accident would have been quickly and adroitly hushed up. The body of the Gentleman from San Francisco would have been rushed away to some far corner—and none of the guests would have known of the occurrence. But the German dashed out of the library with outcries and spread the alarm all over the house. And many rose from their meal, upsetting chairs, others growing pale, ran along the corridors to the library, and the question, asked in many languages, was heard: "What is it? What has happened?" And no one was able to answer it clearly, no one understood anything, for until this very day men still wonder most at death and most absolutely refuse to believe in it. The owner rushed from one guest to another, trying to keep back those who were running and soothe them with hasty assurances, that this was nothing, a mere trifle, a little fainting-spell by which a Gentleman from San Francisco had been overcome. But no one listened to him, many saw how the footmen and waiters tore from the gentleman his tie, collar, waistcoat, the rumpled evening coat, and even—for no visible reason—the dancing shoes from his black silk-covered feet. And he kept on writhing. He obstinately struggled with death, he did not want to yield to the foe that attacked him so unexpectedly and grossly. He shook his head, emitted rattling sounds like one throttled, and turned up his eyeballs like one drunk with wine. When he was hastily brought into

Number Forty-three,—the smallest, worst, dampest, and coldest room at the end of the lower corridor,—and stretched on the bed,—his daughter came running, her hair falling over her shoulders, the skirts of her dressing-gown thrown open, with bare breasts raised by the corset. Then came his wife, big, heavy, almost completely dressed for dinner, her mouth round with terror.

In a quarter of an hour all was again in good trim at the hotel. But the evening was irreparably spoiled. Some tourists returned to the dining-hall and finished their dinner, but they kept silent, and it was obvious that they took the accident as a personal insult, while the owner went from one guest to another, shrugging his shoulders in impotent and appropriate irritation, feeling like one innocently victimized, assuring everyone that he understood perfectly well "how disagreeable this is," and giving his word that he would take all "the measures that are within his power" to do away with the trouble. Yet it was found necessary to cancel the tarantella. The unnecessary electric lamps were put out, most of the guests left for the beer-hall, and it grew so quiet in the hotel that one could distinctly hear the tick-tock of the clock in the lobby, where a lonely parrot babbled something in its expressionless manner, stirring in its cage, and trying to fall asleep with its paw clutching the upper perch in a most absurd manner. The Gentleman from San Francisco lay stretched in a cheap iron bed, under coarse woolen blankets, dimly lighted by a single gasburner fastened in the ceiling. An ice-bag slid down on his wet, cold forehead. His blue, already lifeless face grew gradually cold; the hoarse, rattling noise which came from his mouth, lighted by the glimmer of the golden fillings, gradually weakened. It was not the Gentleman from San Francisco that was emitting those weird sounds; he was no more,—someone else did it. His wife and daughter, the doctor, the servants were standing and watching him apathetically. Suddenly, that which they expected and feared happened. The rattling sound ceased. And slowly, slowly, in everybody's sight a pallor stole over the face of the dead man, and his features began to grow thinner and more luminous, beautiful with the beauty that he had long shunned and that became him well . . .

The proprietor entered. "Gia e morto," whispered the doctor to him. The proprietor shrugged his shoulders indifferently. The older lady, with tears slowly running down her cheeks, approached him and said timidly that now the deceased must be taken to his room.

"O no, madam," answered the proprietor politely, but without any amiability and not in English, but in French. He was no longer interested in the trifle which the guests from San Francisco could now leave at his cash-office. "This is absolutely impossible," he said, and added in the form of an explanation that he valued this apartment highly, and if he satisfied her desire, this would become known over Capri and the tourists would begin to avoid it.

The girl, who had looked at him strangely, sat down, and with her handkerchief to her mouth, began to cry. Her mother's tears dried up at once, and her face flared up. She raised her tone, began to demand, using her own language and still unable to realize that the respect for her was absolutely gone. The proprietor, with polite dignity, cut her short: "If madam does not like the ways of this hotel, he dare not detain her." And he firmly announced that the corpse must leave the hotel that very day, at dawn, that the police had been informed, that an agent would call immediately and attend to all the necessary formalities. . . "Is it possible to get on Capri at least a plain coffin?" madam asks. . . Unfortunately not; by no means, and as for making one, there will be no time. It will be necessary to arrange things some other way. . . For instance, he gets English soda-water in big, oblong boxes. . . The partitions could be taken out from such a box. . .

By night, the whole hotel was asleep. A waiter opened the window in Number 43—it faced a corner of the garden where a consumptive banana-tree grew in the shadow of a high stone wall set with broken glass on the top—turned out the electric light, locked the door, and went away. The deceased remained alone in the darkness. Blue stars looked down at him from the black sky, the cricket in the wall started his melancholy, care-free song. In the dimly lighted corridor two chambermaids were sitting on the window-sill, mending something. Then Luigi came in, in slippered feet, with a heap of clothes on his arm.

"Pronto?"—he asked in a stage whisper, as if greatly concerned, directing his eyes toward the terrible door, at the end of the corridor. And waving his free hand in that direction, *"Partenza!"* he cried out in a whisper, as if seeing off a train,—and the chambermaids, choking with noiseless laughter, put their heads on each other's shoulders.

Then, stepping softly, he ran to the door, slightly rapped at it, and inclining his ear, asked most obsequiously in a subdued tone of voice:

"Ha sonata, signore?"

And, squeezing his throat and thrusting his lower jaw forward, he answered himself in a drawling, grating, sad voice, as if from behind the door:

"Yes, come in . . ."

At dawn, when the window panes in Number Forty-three grew white, and a damp wind rustled in the leaves of the banana-tree, when the pale-blue morning sky rose and stretched over Capri, and the sun, rising from behind the distant mountains of Italy, touched into gold the pure, clearly outlined summit of Monte Solaro, when the masons, who mended the paths for the tourists on the island, went out to their work,—an oblong box was brought to room number forty-three. Soon it grew very heavy and painfully pressed against the knees of the assistant doorman who was conveying it in a one-horse carriage along the white highroad which winded on the slopes, among stone fences and vineyards, all the way down to the sea-coast. The driver, a sickly man, with red eyes, in an old short-sleeved coat and in worn-out shoes, had a drunken headache; all night long he had played dice at the eatinghouse—and he kept on flogging his vigorous little horse. According to Sicilian custom, the animal was heavily burdened with decorations: all sorts of bells tinkled on the bridle, which was ornamented with colored woolen fringes; there were bells also on the edges of the high saddle; and a bird's feather, two feet long, stuck in the trimmed crest of the horse, nodded up and down. The driver kept silence: he was depressed by his wrongheadedness and vices, by the fact that last night he had lost in gambling all the copper coins with which his pockets had been full,—neither more nor less than four liras and forty centesimi. But on such a morning, when the air is so fresh, and the sea stretches nearby, and the sky is serene with a morning serenity,—a headache passes rapidly and one becomes carefree again. Besides, the driver was also somewhat cheered by the unexpected earnings which the Gentleman from San Francisco, who bumped his dead head against the walls of the box behind his back, had brought him. The little steamer, shaped like a great bug, which lay far down, on the tender and brilliant blue filling to the brim the Neapolitan bay, was blowing the signal of departure,—and the sounds swiftly resounded all over Capri. Every bend of the island, every ridge and stone was seen as distinctly as if there were no air between heaven and earth. Near the quay the driver was overtaken by the head doorman who conducted in an auto the wife and daughter of the Gentleman from San Francisco. Their faces were pale and their eyes sunken with tears and a sleepless night. And in ten minutes the little steamer was again stirring up the water and picking its way toward Sorrento and Castellamare, carrying the American family away from Capri forever. . . . Meanwhile, peace and rest were restored on the island.

Two thousand years ago there had lived on that island a man who became utterly entangled in his own brutal and filthy actions. For some unknown reason he usurped the rule over millions of men and found himself bewildered by the absurdity of this power, while the fear that someone might kill him unawares, made him commit deeds inhuman beyond all measure. And mankind has forever retained his memory, and those who, taken together, now rule the world, as incomprehensibly and, essentially, as cruelly as he did,—come from all the corners of the earth to look at the remnants of the stone house he inhabited, which stands on one of the steepest cliffs of the island. On that wonderful morning the tourists, who had come to Capri for precisely that purpose, were still asleep in the various hotels, but tiny long-eared asses under red saddles were already being led to the hotel entrances. Americans and Germans, men and women, old and young, after having arisen and breakfasted heartily, were to scramble on them, and the old beggar-women of Capri, with sticks in their sinewy hands, were again to run after them along stony, mountainous paths, all the way up to the summit of Monte Tiberia. The dead old man from San Francisco, who had planned to keep the tourists company but who had, instead, only scared them by reminding them of death, was already shipped to Naples, and soothed by this, the travelers slept soundly, and silence reigned over the island. The stores in the little town were still closed, with the exception of the fish and greens market on the tiny square. Among the plain people who filled it, going about their business, stood idly by, as usual, Lorenzo, a tall old boatman, a carefree reveller and once a handsome man, famous all over Italy, who had many times served as a model for painters. He had brought and already sold—for a song—two big sea-crawfish, which he had caught at night and which were rustling in the apron of Don Cataldo, the cook of the hotel where the family from San Francisco had been lodged,—and now Lorenzo could stand calmly until nightfall, wearing princely airs, showing off his rags, his clay pipe with its long reed mouth-piece, and his red woolen cap, tilted on one ear. Meanwhile, among the precipices of Monte Solare, down the ancient Phoenician road, cut in the rocks in the form of a gigantic staircase, two Abruzzi mountaineers were coming from Anacapri. One carried under his leather mantle a bagpipe, a large goat's skin with two pipes; the other, something in the nature of a wooden flute. They walked, and the entire country, joyous, beautiful, sunny, stretched below them; the rocky shoulders of the island, which lay at their feet, the fabulous blue in which it swam, the shining morning vapors over the sea westward, beneath the dazzling sun, and the wavering masses of Italy's mountains, both near and distant, whose beauty human word is powerless to render. . . Midway they slowed up. Overshadowing the road stood, in a grotto of the rock wall of Monte Solare, the Holy Virgin, all radiant, bathed in the warmth and the splendor of the sun. The rust of her snow-white plaster-of-Paris vestures and queenly crown was touched into gold, and there were meekness and mercy in her eyes raised toward the heavens, toward the eternal and beatific abode of her thrice-blessed Son. They bared their heads, applied the pipes to their lips,—and praises flowed on, candid and humbly-joyous, praises to the sun and the morning, to Her, the Immaculate Intercessor for all who suffer in this evil and beautiful world, and to Him who had been born of her womb in the cavern of Bethlehem, in a hut of lowly shepherds in distant Judea.

As for the body of the dead Gentleman from San Francisco, it was on its way home, to the shores of the New World, where a grave awaited it. Having undergone many humiliations and suffered much human neglect, having wandered about a week from one port warehouse to another, it finally got on that same famous ship which had brought the family, such a short while ago and with such a pomp, to the Old World. But now he was concealed from the living: in a tar-coated coffin he was lowered deep into the black hold of the steamer. And again did the ship set out on its far sea journey. At night it sailed by the island of Capri, and, for those who watched it from the island, its lights slowly disappearing in the dark sea, it seemed infinitely sad. But there, on the vast steamer, in its lighted halls shining with brilliance and marble, a noisy dancing party was going on, as usual.

On the second and the third night there was again a ball—this time in mid-ocean, during a furious storm sweeping over the ocean, which roared like a funeral mass and rolled up mountainous seas fringed with mourning silvery foam. The Devil, who from the rocks of Gibraltar, the stony gateway of two worlds, watched the ship vanish into night and storm, could hardly distinguish from behind the snow the innumerable fiery eyes of the ship. The Devil was as huge as a cliff, but the ship was even bigger, a many-storied, many-stacked giant, created by the arrogance of the New Man with the old heart. The blizzard battered the ship's rigging and its broad-necked stacks, whitened with snow, but it remained firm, majestic—and terrible. On its uppermost deck, amidst a snowy whirlwind there loomed up in loneliness the cozy, dimly lighted cabin, where, only half awake, the vessel's ponderous pilot reigned over its entire mass, bearing the semblance of a pagan idol. He heard the wailing moans and the furious screeching of the siren, choked by the storm, but the nearness of that which was behind the wall and which in the last account was incomprehensible to him, removed his fears. He was reassured by the thought of the large, armored cabin, which now and then was filled with mysterious rumbling sounds and with the dry creaking of blue fires, flaring up and exploding around a man with a metallic headpiece, who was eagerly catching the indistinct voices of the vessels that hailed him, hundreds of miles away. At the very bottom, in the underwater womb of the "Atlantis," the huge masses of tanks and various other machines, their steel parts shining dully, wheezed with steam and oozed hot water and oil; here was the gigantic kitchen, heated by hellish furnaces, where the motion of the vessel was being generated; here seethed those forces terrible in their concentration which were transmitted to the keel of the vessel, and into that endless round tunnel, which was lighted by electricity, and looked like a gigantic cannon barrel, where slowly, with a punctuality and certainty that crushes the human soul, a colossal shaft was revolving in its oily nest, like a living monster stretching in its lair. As for the middle part of the "Atlantis," its warm, luxurious cabins, dining-rooms, and halls, they radiated light and joy, were astir with a chattering smartly-dressed crowd, were filled with the fragrance of fresh flowers, and resounded with a string orchestra. And again did the slender supple pair of hired lovers painfully turn and twist and at times clash convulsively amid the splendor of lights, silks, diamonds, and bare feminine shoulders: she—a sinfully modest pretty girl, with lowered eyelashes and an innocent hair-dressing, he—a tall, young man, with black hair, looking as if they were pasted, pale with powder, in most exquisite patent-leather shoes, in a narrow, long-skirted dresscoat,—a beautiful man resembling a leech. And no one knew that this couple has long since been weary of torturing themselves with a feigned beatific torture under the sounds of shamefully-melancholy music; nor did any one who know what lay deep, deep, beneath them, on the very bottom of the hold, in the neighborhood of the gloomy and sultry maw of the ship, that heavily struggled with the ocean, the darkness, and the storm. . .

P. NIKITIN

THE STRANGLER

Considering the fact that P. Nikitin was both a popular and, for a short time, prolific writer, it is perhaps surprising that nothing is known of him (or, possibly, her, as there is no information to suggest what the "P" stands for).

What is known is that in the short time after the turn of the century and the outbreak of World War I and the Russian Revolution, mass market pulp detective fiction became enormously popular, and a favorite character of Russian readers was Sherlock Holmes. On July 19, 1908, Nikitin published *The Latest Adventures of Sherlock Holmes in Russia: From the Notebooks of the Great Detective*, and he quickly published three more books in less than a year, concluding (as far as is known) his authorship of Holmes pastiches with the publication on May 30, 1909, of *On the Track of Criminals: The Adventures of the Resurrected Sherlock Holmes in Russia*; in all, Nikitin produced 21 Holmes stories.

Even in Russia, copies of these fragile paperbacks, designed to be read and thrown away, are almost non-existent. The Russian National Library in St. Petersburg, the greatest repository of Russian literature in the country, has only a single set of his stories.

This fragmentary information is due to the research efforts of George Piliev, a Russian scholar, editor, author, bibliographer and historian of detective fiction.

"The Strangler" was first published in English in *Sherlock Holmes in Russia* (London, Robert Hale, 2008) in a translation by Alex Auswaks.

THE STRANGLER

I

Sherlock Holmes was reading the papers when I came into his hotel room. Seeing me, he put aside the newspaper he was reading and said, "In the sort of life we lead, either we are asked to do something or, for some reason or another, we do it of our own accord."

"You are speaking of—" I prompted.

"I am speaking of our profession. More often than not, we are approached for assistance by others, but there are times when something crops up and investigating it is a positive joy, despite the fact that nobody has asked us to look into the matter."

"Do I take it that you've found something interesting in the papers today?" I asked.

"You are absolutely right, Watson," Holmes answered. "Today's papers are full of a particularly mysterious crime committed yesterday not far from Moscow and, if you are interested, let me read you one of the accounts of it."

"But, of course," I answered. "You know perfectly well that I am always interested in anything that interests you and you would be doing me a great favour if you were to read to me whatever it is that could intrigue you so much."

Instead of answering, Holmes picked up one of the newspapers and, finding the required item, began to read out aloud.

"Last night, 25 May, at 11 o'clock in the evening, the police began to investigate a highly mysterious crime which took place near Moscow on the estate of a member of the gentry, Sergey Sergeyevitch Kartzeff.

"At three o'clock in the afternoon, Sergey Sergeyevitch Kartzeff locked himself in his bedroom to rest, as he always did after having dined at home. Normally, his valet would wake him by knocking on the door after a couple of hours. This time, despite several attempts by the valet, there was no answer. Surprised at his master's failure to respond, the valet knocked harder, but there was still no response. The valet now became anxious, ran to fetch the cook and maid, and all three of them began to beat on the door, but there was still no response. Fearing that something untoward might have occurred, they broke it down and found Sergey Sergeyevitch Kartzeff dead. He was lying in his bed, his eyes bursting out of their sockets and his face blue. The district police and an investigator were immediately sent for and on arrival at the scene of the crime pronounced that Sergey Sergeyevitch had been strangled to death. A close inspection of the scene yielded only contradictory and incomprehensible results. First, it was established that at the time the crime was committed, the room was locked from the inside, though the lock was damaged because the staff had had to use force to break in. The window had been sealed for the winter and only a hinged pane in it could be opened, so small that a seven-year-old child could hardly squeeze through it. The room was on the second floor, and it had no other openings or apertures, even through the stove. Nevertheless, the old man's throat showed clear traces of a strangler's unusually long fingers. The face of the dead man was severely scratched in several places. An examination of the window, the windowsill and the ground beneath the window showed absolutely no clues of any sort. This might have been caused by a light drizzle which had been falling that day and most probably washed away all traces. The whole house stands in its own grounds. All that the investigators found were several strange traces on the wall outside of the room in which the corpse was found. These traces, most probably, belonged to some freak of nature whose fingers were inordinately long and left such strange prints. The staff were asked whether anyone in the house had deformed feet, but they all declared there never had been anyone like that. The investigators cross-examined the entire staff. Old man Kartzeff was a bit of a recluse, they said, enjoyed managing the estate, seldom received guests, visited neighbouring landowners and got along with everyone. He treated peasants and workers kindly, which ruled out revenge as a motive. Moreover, there is one other circumstance pointing to robbery as a motive. A drawer of the dead man's desk was open and there were many papers and objects strewn all over the floor as if in haste. Asked by the investigators who had recently visited the deceased, the servants testified that since the end of winter there had only been two visitors. One was his nephew, Boris Nikolayevitch Kartzeff, who lived on his own small estate, Igralino, not too far away, and another nephew, Nikolai Nikolayevitch Kartzeff, brother of Boris, had dropped in a couple of times. The latter was by no means a rich man and occupied himself with some sort of private business in Moscow. Further inquiries established that both nephews had each spent the night in his own home. Thus the investigation has produced no results and it seems that catching the perpetrator will be no easy matter.

"So, my dear chap, what have you to say to that?" asked Holmes putting down the newspaper.

"I can say that the perpetrator carefully considered every possible way in and out," I answered.

Holmes nodded, "I agree with you completely and, frankly, I wouldn't have stopped upon this crime were it not for those strange references to abnormal traces left by the strangler firstly on the neck of the victim and then by the wall in the garden below."

"My dear Holmes, from what you have said before and your reading of this account, I conclude that you wish to take up this case," I said with a smile. Knowing full well the character of my friend and his inordinate interest in every sort of mysterious crime, I knew Holmes could not pass up such a case.

"Do have in mind," I added, "that this case has intrigued not just you, but me as well. Hence, I volunteer in advance to be your assistant."

"Oh, I didn't have the least doubt on that score," exclaimed Holmes, gleefully rubbing his hands, "and anticipated that you would make the offer first and since you know me so well, you knew I would get on with it without more ado."

Instead of replying, I rose and began to put on my coat.

Seeing this, Holmes smiled and picked up his hat. "You are an indispensable assistant, my dear chap," pronounced Holmes with one of those good-natured glances that so gladdened me, "and when I am with you, the work advances thrice as quickly as with any other person."

"Just one thing," I asked, "are we going out of town now?"

"Yes," said Holmes, "I have to look at the scene of the crime and see everything for myself. That's why we are off to the Nikolayevsk station to undertake a short trip to not-so-distant parts."

Chatting thus, we went out and hired a hackney to take us to the station. We didn't have to wait long for a local train. We were told to get off after two stops and that the estate of Sergey Sergeyevitch Kartzeff was just over three miles from the station.

II

The journey passed swiftly. Getting off the train, we hired a coach to take us to Silver Slopes, the name of the estate belonging to Sergey Sergeyevitch Kartzeff. We arrived to find everyone rushing hither and thither in a scene of total chaos. Last night's crime was still too fresh in everyone's mind and, moreover, the corpse was still there amidst the chaos and the bustle.

The investigator was there, as were the local chief of police and Boris Nikolayevitch Kartzeff, who had come from home when informed of his uncle's sudden death.

Boris Nikolayevitch turned out to be a handsome man, some thirty-five years of age, with the outward appearance of a rake and gadabout. He was tall, with dark hair, an energetic look and a muscular body. His uncle's death had evidently upset him and he now issued orders nervously and absent-mindedly.

A moment before we came in, Holmes whispered in my ear, "Remember, Watson, we mustn't own up to our real names. Let's pretend, say, that we are real estate agents here for the purchase of the estate. Dear uncle is dead, nephews are stepping into their inheritance, and this seems the appropriate moment to ask whether they are prepared to sell as soon as it is in their ownership."

I nodded in agreement.

Our arrival was noted. Boris Nikolayevitch approached us first, asking who we are and what is our business.

On being told we are real estate agents working on commission, he involuntarily shrugged his shoulders. "Aren't you a little premature? You come to the funeral like carrion crows!"

Somewhat rude, but under the circumstances, still understandable. In any case, something even a well-mannered man might say. But in the confusion round the corpse, we were soon ignored. This was enough for Holmes to start investigating. He left me to myself, bidding me to keep out of sight, and left to return all of an hour later. He took me by the elbow and said, "Let's go, my dear chap. I've done everything I needed, but for the sake of appearances, let's intrude on Boris Nikolayevitch with our original inquiry."

Boris Nikolayevitch was pacing hither and thither, so intercepting him did not take long. But when we posed the same question to him again, he looked at us irritably and replied sharply, "It wouldn't come amiss if you were to make yourself scarce. But just in case, leave your address." Having said this, he looked intently at Holmes. He stared for some seconds, then his lips widened slightly in a little smile, "Perhaps I am wrong," he said, "but I suspect you are not whom you make yourselves out to be. There is something about you which reminds me of someone else I came across accidentally during my travels abroad."

For a few seconds Holmes was silent and now it was he who gazed intently at Boris Nikolayevitch Kartzeff. "I'd be interested to know where," he finally said.

"England," answered Kartzeff.

"In that case, no point in concealing our identities any further," said Holmes. "You guessed correctly and it is a great tribute to your memory. I am Sherlock Holmes and this is"—indicating me—"my friend Dr. Watson."

A look of unutterable joy came over the face of Boris Nikolayevitch

Kartzeff. "So I was right. The reason that I recognized you was that I saw you in London when you were a witness in an important case. But I felt too embarrassed to say so right away, and then I was completely taken aback by your superb Russian."

He came close and shook our hands warmly.

"But since this has happened and since you are here at your own initiative, it seems fate has brought you to our help and I cannot tell you how relieved I am, knowing full well that the villain who perpetrated this foul deed will not escape you. As of this moment, you are the most welcome, the most longed-for guests in this house, and I now beg your permission to present you to our investigator and the police authorities who are here."

Holmes bowed his consent. With an exchange of pleasantries we went into the dining-room which was full of people.

"Ladies and gentlemen, allow me to present Mr. Sherlock Holmes and Dr. Watson," Boris Nikolayevitch said loudly.

Our names created a sensation. Investigators and police jumped to their feet as if we were their superior officers. Compliments rained on Sherlock Holmes's head.

"This gives us fresh hope!" was heard on all sides.

We joined the company and the conversation soon turned to the murder. As was to be expected, there were many presuppositions, but they were to such an extent without foundation that neither Homes nor I paid much attention to them.

From their conversation, we learned that several people had been arrested, amongst them the valet, cook and maid.

"Are you sure that the valet and the cook together smashed a door definitely locked from within?" Homes asked the investigator.

"Oh, yes," the man answered with total conviction. "There is absolutely no doubt, as you will see for yourself from so much as a glance. Only a locked door could have been mangled in such a way."

"Then why did you arrest them?" Holmes asked in astonishment.

"More as a matter of form," was the answer. "I'm sure we'll have to let them go in a few days."

Having questioned the investigator and police chief concerning certain details, Holmes asked whether he could examine the dead man's room without wasting any further time. Needless to say, the request was granted, though I couldn't help but notice the smirk that appeared momentarily on both their faces.

We all went to the dead man's bedroom. It was just as we had been told. The door was smashed in and the key still stuck from the lock on the bedroom side.

Having examined this closely, Holmes said softly, "Yes, there is no doubt the bedroom was locked from inside and the door smashed in, in its locked form. This is apparent from the fact that the lock is twisted and the key is so jammed as a result that it would only be possible to take it out if the lock were to be taken apart."

Having done with the door, Holmes next approached the bed in which Sergey Sergeyevitch had been strangled and, taking his magnifying glass out of his pocket, he proceeded to examine the bedclothes closely. Knowing my friend as well as I did, I couldn't help noticing that he looked puzzled as he examined them.

Some minutes later he bent down to the floor and again began to examine something the others had missed. From the barely perceptible nod he gave, he had evidently found something.

We all watched with intense curiosity. From the bed he moved to the window. Here he pottered about for quite a while. It would appear he examined every little bit, even a little spot left by a fly. Gradually his face became more puzzled and more serious. And when Holmes finally moved away from the window, I could see that he was intensely absorbed.

Questions came at him from all sides.

"Not just yet, not just yet," Holmes said absent-mindedly as he turned to his questioners.

"Surely you don't intend to keep us in such a state of uncertainty?" asked Boris Nikolayevitch. "We're all closely connected to each other and to the case."

"There are certain matters it is sometimes premature to discuss," Holmes answered.

"But at least can you not point to anything suspicious, which may be a clue?" the investigator asked impatiently.

"Yes, there are one or two things," said Holmes enigmatically. "But, gentlemen, I repeat that, owing to certain considerations, I must refrain from further explanations."

Everyone shrugged at this reply and a brief look of distrust appeared once again on the faces of the investigator and the police chief.

And so silently and evidently very unhappy with Holmes, everyone returned to the dining-room. The rest of the evening passed in conversation to which neither Holmes nor I paid any attention. After eleven o'clock Holmes asked for us to be assigned a room and we retired.

III

When I awoke the following morning, Holmes wasn't in the room, although it was still early. As I had expected, he had been up at five, gone off somewhere and only returned at nine. This I found out only later from his own words. When he returned, I was awake.

"My dear chap, I didn't want to wake you," he said. "You were sleeping so soundly and so peacefully, I had no wish to disturb your slumber, but now that you are awake, I must ask you to dress quickly."

Much as I would have wanted to go on sleeping, I could hardly do so in the face of his demand. I jumped out of bed, washed and we sat down to breakfast which had been sent up to our room.

"Are we leaving?" I asked.

"Not entirely," answered Holmes. "It is very likely that we'll have to return, but in the meantime, I'd like to accept the kind invitation extended by Boris Nikolayevitch for us to visit his estate."

Chatting away, we drank several glasses of tea and when, at last, Boris Nikolayevitch knocked on our door, we were ready to leave.

Boris Nikolayevitch still appeared depressed, but was courteous and attentive. "I hope you slept well," he said, entering the room.

"Oh, yes, for which we wish to thank you," Sherlock Holmes answered on behalf of both of us.

"Is there anything else you would like," he asked. "Perhaps you are used to a hearty breakfast in the morning."

"I must confess that ham and eggs wouldn't go amiss," Holmes answered with a smile.

Boris Nikolayevitch Kartzeff was all attentiveness and a few minutes later returned with a servant carrying our breakfast and a bottle of sherry.

Thus fortified, we thanked our cordial host and rose from the table.

"Do you wish to come with me today," asked Kartzeff, "or do you wish to rest a while?"

"With your permission, we'd like to accept your invitation this very day," answered Sherlock Holmes. "We are very pressed for time and it is very likely that we have to return to England in a few days."

"In that case, I shall give instructions for the horses to be made ready as soon as the funeral is over," said our cordial host.

As he was about to leave, Holmes stopped him, "Another little request. With your permission, I'd like to see your late uncle again before we leave."

"But, of course," answered Boris Nikolayevitch. "Shall we do so this very minute?"

Holmes nodded. We left our room and made our way into the hall where the funeral service was in preparation.

Approaching the coffin, Sherlock Holmes carefully lifted the muslin cloth over the face of the dead man and proceeded to examine the corpse. Several minutes passed before he tore himself away. But when he moved away, one couldn't gather anything from the expression on his face.

Then the priests arrived and the usual service for that sort of event began. The reader began his doleful chant. The priest recited the service monotonously. And all was as if it was being done on a factory floor, unhurriedly, in a fixed manner but yet to some mysterious beat. Not particularly involved in the sacred service, we each stood sunk in his own thoughts.

The service over, we went out for some fresh air into the garden round the house. The garden was over ten hectares, i.e. nigh on ten acres in area. It was fully planted with fruit trees and truly magnificent. Here and there flowerbeds were scattered from which brightly coloured blossoms struck the eye. Yellow sand neatly covered the pathways and sculptures added to the sense of proportion of this lordly manor garden. We strolled silently through the alleyways and, from the look of intense concentration on the face of Sherlock Holmes, I could sense that a secret thought had lodged like a thorn in his brain.

A half hour later Boris Nikolayevitch followed us out. After the funeral service his mood seemed to have lifted. "I hope you won't refuse to attend the burial today," he said pleasantly. "We don't intend to let it drag on for long, especially as there will be no women present. I'm not particularly sentimental and am always against the dead being detained for long in the house of the living."

"How right you are," said Holmes. "The presence of the dead in a home is depressing, and as far as we in England are concerned, we always try to remove the body as quickly as possible to its place of burial."

"I'm sure you will excuse me for leaving you now," Kartzeff apologized. "I'm sure you will understand that all funeral arrangements are exclusively my responsibility."

"Oh, but of course," Sherlock Holmes nodded. "We'll stay here while you see to your duties and I beg you not to concern yourself with us."

Boris Nikolayevitch Kartzeff bowed himself away politely, while we continued our aimless meandering.

Several hours passed. At about two in the afternoon Boris

Nikolayevitch again reappeared and said that the body would be carried out in a quarter of an hour. We followed him inside.

We saw the corpse lifted up on a long piece of cloth and, accompanied by the clergy and choir, the sad procession moved to the village cemetery.

I won't describe the details of the burial as they are too well known to all. To the sad strains of the service and the wailing of the choir, the body was lowered into the ground. Heavy clods of damp earth thudded on the coffin lid and soon it vanished from sight. More and more damp earth was unevenly heaped over the grave and then, under the skilled hands of the gravediggers, evened out into the usual tidy mound.

The last note of the burial psalm and then all those present quietly trudged away, for some reason speaking of the departed in soft undertones. Sherlock Holmes and I also returned.

The dining-room table was already set and Boris Nikolayevitch, still preserving a look of sadness on his face, invited us to partake of refreshments.

In any wake, the faces of the guests begin by looking long and sad, but become merrier as the wine begins to flow until such time as the proceedings acquire the character of a proper binge.

It must have been all of seven o'clock, because the sun was beginning to set, when the guests and clergy rose from the table. At this point Boris Nikolayevitch approached Holmes saying, "I'm at your disposal now. And if you so wish, we can go to my place together."

"I am ready," answered Holmes. "Mind you, I see no reason for staying on. What I was able to find in the dead man's bedroom has little bearing on this scene and so, having rested at your place, we still have to return to Moscow, where I hope to find more reliable clues concerning this matter."

We didn't have much to pack. Boris Nikolayevitch gave final instructions and we got into an elegant landau harnessed to a troika, three horses harnessed abreast. The sun set completely.

The well cared for horses, energized by the cool evening air, rose to the occasion and our carriage sped merrily along the country road.

It was less than five miles to the estate of Boris Nikolayevitch. At first, the road passed through open fields in which ears of grain were like dark waves. Then it entered the forest. This was thick with fir trees that hadn't seen an axe for a long time, evidently protected for a long time by the late Sergey Sergeyevitch Kartzeff.

Now right, now left, the road wound through the dark forest lit by a patch of sky in which a myriad stars blazed. I don't know how others might be affected, but this mystery-laden road only served to depress me with its gloom.

We drove a mile and a half without encountering a living soul. There was something strange about this vast, unpopulated, silent country road which lay between the estate of the uncle and his nephew. I was unable to refrain from expressing my thoughts to Kartzeff who was sitting beside us.

"What's there to be surprised about?" he said, shrugging his shoulders. "This is a direct road joining our two estates and since time immemorial the peasants aren't permitted to drive along it."

Emerging from the forest, we again drove along open fields and, at last, the tall contours of the Igralino estate rose before us. We were met by the friendly barking of dogs, but as soon as they heard their master's voice, they fell silent. Our troika rolled up to the porch. An old retainer opened the door. He bowed low to his master, cast a suspicious look at the guests, let us through inside and helped us off with our outer garments.

The house did not overwhelm us with its opulence but, notwithstanding that, a glance into any of its rooms and you would conclude that a scion of the old gentry lived here. Not only were their portraits preserved, but their way of life. The house itself was too ordinary to be described as palatial. But the furnishings in any of the rooms had been selected with remarkable good taste and were far from cheap.

"First of all, gentlemen, abiding by a purely Russian tradition, I must show you to your quarters and then share with you whatever my humble abode is rich with," said the master of the house, cordially welcoming us.

With these words, he led us through several rooms and in one of them said, "I hope you will be comfortable here for the night."

The room was fairly large. Apart from two beds, there was a wash basin, cupboard, a chest of drawers, a comfortable divan and several cushioned and ordinary chairs. Needless to say, we were very satisfied with the arrangements.

We thanked Boris Nikolayevitch and followed him to the dining-room. It was decorated in the Russian style and dinner was already laid out. The cooking was out of the ordinary. Over dinner our host made every effort to appear bright and cheerful, but I couldn't help noticing that the events of the day were still with him. This was not unusual and so neither Holmes nor I paid much attention to that.

IV

"You're probably tired after such a day," said our host to Holmes, "which is why I don't feel I ought to tire you for long. Frankly, the day has worn me out, too, and so, if you don't wish to retire early, I'll have to apologize for leaving you to your own devices so soon."

"I do understand," said Holmes sympathetically. "I, too, would like to rest. Silly of me not to have said so earlier."

"In that case, I wish you a very good night," said Kartzeff.

He went off, leaving us to ourselves.

Holmes shut the door and carefully examined the room and window. This was the only window in the room and as in Russian houses it had the usual hinged ventilation pane set inside it.

"Perhaps the owner doesn't seem to be much bothered by draughts," Holmes said as if by the by, turning the catch now this way, now that. "It doesn't lock and the slightest breeze will blow it open."

From a small leather case in his pocket he took several nails and nailed them securely into the frame of the window pane. After that he locked the door, leaving the key in the lock and began to undress. I did the same and a few minutes later I was fast asleep. I don't recollect whether anything happened that night. All I know is that from the look on Holmes's face sitting at the table when I woke, I could see he had spent a sleepless night.

Seeing me open my eyes, he heaved a sigh of relief and then said in a tired voice, "Well, now, my dear chap, thank God that you're awake. This will give me a chance for a little rest. Stay awake, there's a good chap, and I suggest you pay special attention to this little window pane."

With these words he threw himself on the bed and a minute later he was already sleeping the sleep of the dead. Thoroughly puzzled, I sat there for a couple of hours, my gaze fixed on the window, but try as I might, I detected nothing suspicious.

The sun was already high in the heavens when Holmes awoke. He jumped out of bed, washed quickly and said cheerfully, "Well, my dear chap, I can now stay up for a couple of nights. That tired feeling is gone. Such tiredness is unforgivable and just this once, accidental."

"What's the matter?" I asked. "I suppose something unusual took place last night and you'll tell me what it was all about," I said.

"You'll allow me, my dear chap, to refrain from a direct answer," said Holmes solemnly. "It is very likely that in a few hours you will know more than you expected, and then your curiosity is bound to be satisfied."

We chatted about various trifles and the time passed unnoticed. At nine there was a knock on the door. The door opened and Boris Niko-layevitch came in. His eyes were baggy and his face somewhat drawn. He greeted us, asked how we had spent the night and, receiving a positive answer, appeared contented enough.

"Tea is served," he invited.

We nodded our acceptance. Over tea, Holmes, who was at first withdrawn, livened up and jokes, anecdotes and witticisms poured from him. When we had drunk our tea, he announced that it was imperative for him to go to Moscow.

"Surely you can stay longer," exclaimed Boris Nikolayevitch in a hurt tone.

Holmes gave a sad shrug. "Alas, I cannot. I did warn you yesterday that it is essential for me to be in Moscow today for pressing business and I hope you remember my words. This is why I must ask you to have horses made available immediately to get us to the station."

"Most certainly," exclaimed Kartzeff. "I will give the necessary orders at once." He went off but wasn't back for some considerable time.

Holmes sat there without stirring, his head in the palms of his hands. The rest of the time before lunch and the lunch itself passed slowly. After lunch we were told that the horses were ready and, having bidden farewell to our host, we departed for the station.

V

Arriving in town, we made straight for Nikolai Nikolayevitch Kartzeff, brother of Boris Nikolayevitch and whose address we had taken.

"It seems a little strange," said Holmes pensively along the way, "that the second nephew didn't even wish to attend his uncle's funeral."

"Yes, that is very strange," I agreed. "Could it be that we will find here some clues leading to the crime?"

Nikolai Nikolayevitch lived right on the edge of town, just before Sokolniki, so that it took a while to get to him.

Our ring was answered by a kindly sympathetic old woman, who asked the nature of our business. On being told that we had come to see Nikolai Nikolayevitch, she made a gesture expressing regret. "Oh, what a shame, what a really great shame that you missed him," she sighed good-naturedly. "We live so far away, and anyone who comes gets so upset when the master isn't home."

"And you are his *matushka?*" asked Holmes, using the Russian diminutive endearing form for mother.

"Nanny, sir, his nanny," she answered with a warm smile. "Brought him up as a little boy, spent my life by his side. He's such a good man, he is, and now he keeps me in my old age, where another would long since have thrown me out in the street."

"So where's he gone?" Holmes asked.

"Why, he left just before your arrival. He just got the news that his uncle had been strangled or was it knifed, in truth I don't know which it was. His own brother didn't tell him. I don't suppose he had time, with all the stir it must have caused."

"So how did he find out?"

"The newspaper, my dear sir. That's where he read it. It was all in the newspaper. Gentlemen, you will come in and rest a while. We may be poor, but there's always a cup of tea. Happy to share what God has given. That's how we do things. Should any friend of his not find him home, he'll always come in for a cuppa."

"Thank you, *nianushka,*" said Holmes, addressing her by the Russian diminutive endearment for nanny.

We entered the apartment. It wasn't very big, all of two small rooms, a kitchen and a tiny box room for the old woman. The furniture was not particularly ostentatious. There were only a few things, more the sort you would find in a country hut, anyway. It was all fairly typical of the domicile of a young artist.

In one room there was a bed, a wash basin in poor condition, several chairs, a writing desk, canvas concealed the walls. Paints, brushes and other painter's objects lay scattered everywhere.

The other room was filled with easels, picture frames with canvas stretched on them. Completed paintings and rough sketches hung on the walls, showing that Nikolai Nikolayevitch might be at the start of his career, but already showed great promise.

A great connoisseur, Sherlock Holmes examined the work of this beginner with considerable relish. The old woman was evidently very proud of her charge. She stood beside Holmes and with a smile watched him examine the work of her favourite.

"Why don't you sit down, sirs," she said warmly. "I'll get the samovar going. It will boil in no time at all."

"Thank you," said Holmes.

And shaking his head sadly, he said, "And so the uncle dies! How come his own brother didn't bother to tell him?"

The old woman shook her head sadly, too, "He's just a bad lot, is Boris Nikolayevitch, a bad lot. If he were a man like other men, of course he'd've told the master. I think he's got nothing inside his head except for the wind whistling."

"A bad lot, you say!"

The old woman gestured with her hand to show nothing could be done. "What is there to say," she sighed. "He's a born gambler. First he inherited an estate and a sizable capital sum. The capital sum he gambled away. He may have been a good-for-nothing, but he certainly knew how to ingratiate himself. My Nikolai Nikolayevitch was done out of his fair share because he wasn't one to bow and scrape. But the other fellow knew where and when to turn up and flatter relatives, who would give him a warm welcome. That's what happened with their grandmother. She included him in her will and left out Nikolai Nikolayevitch!"

"And did Nikolai Nikolayevitch often visit this departed uncle?" asked Sherlock Holmes.

"On the contrary! You have no idea how often he was invited. Mind you, he did go twice, but didn't stay long. No doubt he won't get anything there, either. You'll see, Boris Nikolayevitch will get the lot."

"To waste it on more carousing," said Holmes sympathetically.

"For sure! For sure!" said the old woman. "Nothing good will come out of the money that will come to him. He'll waste it on mam'selles, as he always has in the past and that's that! He did have a job, but got sacked for all those misdeeds."

"What was the job?" asked Holmes.

"He was a naval officer. Sailed as first officer on his own ship for some time. No less than ten years. And then he was kicked out. Thank God he wasn't tried. Mind you, even then, everyone said he couldn't evade being tried but luckily for him he wriggled out of that. They must've felt sorry for him."

She suddenly remembered the samovar and with a cry quickly ran out of the room. In no time tea appeared. We drank it with great pleasure and continued our interrupted conversation. Most of all, we spoke of Boris Nikolayevitch. The old woman spoke of him without evident rancour but in the sort of tone people use when speaking of someone of whom they disapprove.

From what she said, we pieced together the information that Boris Nikolayevitch, the older brother of Nikolai Nikolayevitch, graduated from a naval academy and had sailed far and wide on a ship which had been part of a squadron of the Russian navy. Then, for improper conduct and some sort of financial peculation, he was dismissed. After that he spent some years sailing the Indian Ocean on British ships plying between Bombay and Calcutta. Two years ago, Boris Nikolayevitch Kartzeff returned to Russia and the gossip amongst his friends was that he had been dismissed even from the ships of the private line by which he had been employed. During those two years he had managed to squander the remains of his small capital. As for the estate that had been left him, he'd brought it to the point where it was threatened with going under the hammer.

"But he's always been lucky, *batiushki,*" she said. "Born under a lucky star, he was," she said. "No sooner do things get bad, then uncle dies."

"Yes, it isn't the deserving who flourish on this earth," sighed Holmes.

"How right you are!" gestured the old woman. "Take our Nikolai Nikolayevitch. He doesn't get any assistance from anywhere. Pays for his own studies. Supports himself and me. Wonderful, wonderful young man!

While if ever a spare kopeck comes his way, it goes to a needy friend. He keeps nothing back for himself."

We sat there for a little while longer, thanked her for the welcome she had extended us, bade her farewell and left.

"So, what do you think of the young man?" Holmes asked me when we were outside.

"That this is not where we will find the criminal," I answered. "I think this is all a false lead."

Holmes said nothing. He paced along quickly, deep in thought.

Sokolniki was not a district with which we were familiar. We soon stopped a cabbie and Holmes directed him to take us to our hotel.

"Any post?" he asked the porter.

The porter rummaged round in a drawer and handed him a letter. Holmes opened it, read the contents quickly and then, having carefully examined the envelope, handed me a sheet of paper.

"Just look at this, if you please, my dear Watson," he said with a smile.

I read the following, "Dear Mr. Holmes, England has more than enough criminals of its own and your presence there would be immeasurably more beneficial for your fellow citizens than chasing fame in Russia. From the bottom of my heart, let me give you some good advice. Clear off home while you are still alive."

I glanced at the envelope and saw it had been posted locally.

"Well, what do you say?" asked Holmes with a disdainful smile.

"It looks as if our presence here is upsetting someone, and it seems that the letter has some connection with the mysterious crime at the Silver Slopes estate."

"Very probably," said Holmes indifferently, as he climbed up the stairs. "We've got enough time to change and get back on the train."

"Dare I ask where we are going?" I asked.

"Oh, we have to get back to Silver Slopes and Igralino once again. Nikolai Nikolayevich going there is just the perfect excuse for us."

Without further ado we changed and made our way to the station.

VI

Boris Nikolayevitch Kartzeff couldn't conceal his astonishment at seeing us back.

"What hand of fate brings you here?" he exclaimed, coming out on the porch. "I must confess I thought you have long since been in town."

"We've been there, too," answered Holmes, jumping from the carriage and greeting the owner. "But we were told that your brother, Nikolai Nikolayevitch, was on his way here and since we were interested in asking him a few questions, we hastened back."

"Not even stopping off wherever you were staying?"

"What's to be done! In our profession it isn't always possible to do as we please and it becomes necessary to accept the situation with all its inconveniences. I hope Nikolai Nikolayevitch is with you."

"Unfortunately not. He went to his uncle's graveside. But if you think it necessary, I'll send a carriage after him at once."

"Oh, no, please don't concern yourself. It'll keep. If you were to allow it, we would like to spend the night here and go tomorrow."

"But, of course. You know perfectly well that I am really glad of your company," exclaimed Boris Nikolayevitch.

Chatting away, we went in and sat down at the table which our host had ordered to be laid. At about four in the afternoon, Nikolai Nikolayevitch returned.

Told who we are, he didn't mince words, "Yes, it would be a good thing to catch the villain. I'd be the first to cut his throat with my own hands."

The death of his uncle had clearly affected him greatly.

"Say what you will, but this murder is beyond me," he began. "If anyone could wish his death, it would only be the two of us, as we are both his heirs and in the will found amongst uncle's things, his entire estate is to be equally divided between us. To tell you the truth, it doesn't give me any pleasure to receive this damned inheritance, coming as it does in such a manner. As far as I am concerned, I have always been used to living within my own means since I was quite young and even as things stand, I can support myself."

He lowered his head sadly without paying us any more attention.

Using his tiredness as an excuse, Holmes asked Boris Nikolayevitch's permission for us to retire. Our host personally escorted us to the door of our room and cordially asked whether there was anything more we required either that evening or for the night.

"No, thank you," said Holmes and we entered the room allocated us.

It was the same room we had occupied the previous night. Nonetheless, this did not prevent Holmes from conducting the most meticulous examination which included every little thing. Glancing at the small hinged pane in the window, Holmes gave a barely concealed smile, "Have a look, my dear Watson, at this example of gracious forethought. Of course, you do remember that when we first slept here, the pane was not secured. But now, just look at the improvements made by the host."

I looked and all I saw was the addition of a latch.

"Well, what about it?" asked Holmes. And clapping me on the back, he said with a smile, "I am just trying to test your powers of observation."

I gave a surprised shrug of my shoulders, "The latch has been repaired, that is all."

"And that is all?"

"I think so."

"But don't you detect anything special about the new arrangement?" asked Holmes with a smile.

"Absolutely none!"

"In that case, pay due attention to the following: for some unfathomable reason, the contraption actually goes right through the pane. Hence, it can be opened and shut from inside as well as outside the room."

"Do explain yourself."

"Why, only that I see such a contraption in a window pane for the first time in my life." Saying this, Holmes drew the heavy curtains over the window and lit the lamps.

It was already dark.

All was still outside, except for the soft lowing of cattle from afar. Very likely the herd was being driven to pasture.

"My dear Watson, I recommend the utmost care and vigilance tonight," said Holmes to me. "It is likely that the events of the night will tell us much, which is why it would be a good thing for you to abstain from sleep. Now, I suggest that you watch the inner courtyard, if you can. Actually, no. We'll go out for a little stroll in the field and then take up our watch."

With those words he opened the door and went out. I followed. Boris Nikolayevitch and his brother were sitting at the dining-room table.

"Have you already rested?" asked Boris Nikolayevitch.

"No, we thought we'd get a little fresh air," answered Holmes.

"Perhaps you'd like me to accompany you," our host offered graciously.

"Oh, no, we'll find our own way. We don't intend to go very far."

We went out and for half an hour strolled round the house. I saw that Holmes missed nothing, not the slightest detail. Soon we had gone round all the outhouses and seen where everything stood and what was kept where. An old man passed by. Holmes hailed him and proffered him half a rouble to show us the grounds in detail. The old fellow was delighted at his good fortune and couldn't thank us enough. He was a herdsman and told us he had lived there as long ago as the days of the late owner, the grandmother of Boris Nikolayevitch.

We wandered round the yard, examining whatever we saw, and eventually arrived in front of a small doorway. It was covered with metal and bolted with a large hanging lock. "Is this also a storehouse?" asked Holmes.

The old man's face took on an enigmatic appearance, "No, sir, not a barn. Mind you, when the late mistress was alive, oil paint was kept here for the roof, linseed oil as a base for varnish and other things. But since the new master took over, something strange seems to have appeared inside."

"Something strange, say you?" asked Holmes. "What could it possibly be?"

"How can I put it sir, since I don't know and neither does anyone else." The old man lowered his voice to a whisper. "Since the very day the new master arrived, none of us has been inside. I saw him drag in a huge chest, but nobody knows what was inside. He himself goes in twice daily, but none of us is allowed there."

"Well, I never!" said Holmes in a tone of evident disapproval.

"Oh, yes, sir! You can hear it moaning," whispered the old man enigmatically.

"What is it that is moaning?" asked a surprised Holmes.

"Whatever is locked in that chest. Some folk say that a man who has lost his mind is hidden inside. Someone possessed. Might be related to the master!"

"Where do you get all that from?"

"I'll tell you where from. Sometimes at night you can hear someone grunting or snarling. It is neither a human sound nor an animal's either."

"Maybe someone got frightened and just said it," suggested Holmes.

"Out of fright!" said the old man, this time truly aggrieved, "I heard it myself."

Holmes approached the door and looked at the lock. "Yes," he said thoughtfully, "this is no ordinary lock. You wouldn't easily find a key to fit it. In any case, if I were to decide to open it for myself, it would take a considerable while." He turned suddenly and looked at the big house.

I don't know what made me, but I automatically followed his example and that very moment I noticed the figure of Boris Nikolayevitch jumping back from the window as soon as we turned around. Actually, I don't know whether this was so or merely appeared so to me, but the expression on the nephew of the dead man was on this occasion particularly strange. It seemed to me that his eyes looked at us with an unnatural anger. But all this was only momentary.

Holmes turned away calmly from the mysterious shed and we continued on our way still interrogating the old man about any old trivia. Our stroll didn't last more than an hour. When we had had enough of the yard, we went in again and this time, meeting nobody, went to our room.

VII

We had just about retired, when there was a knock at the door. It was Boris Nikolayevitch, come to ask whether we'd like to have supper before retiring for the night. He looked perfectly content to accept our refusal, wished us a good night and departed.

We began to undress, but before we went to bed, Sherlock Holmes locked the door, leaving the key in the door and, approaching the window, began to look out carefully at the grounds. He stood like that for nigh on a quarter of an hour. Then he reached into his pocket for his leather case, took out a few nails and once again very carefully nailed them into the frame of the pane.

Next he put out the light, came up to my bed and leaning down to my ear whispered very softly, "My dear Watson, have your revolver at the ready and under no circumstances let go of it. In the meantime, I suggest that you part the curtains carefully and give your attention to anything that occurs anywhere near our window."

We tiptoed towards the curtains, parted them ever so slightly and put our eyes to the gap. A pale moon had risen and cast its mysterious light over the park. We tried to stand so quietly that the slightest move would not betray our vigil. A considerable time must have passed. I couldn't check the time in the dark, but it must have been all of two hours.

I became bored by the long silence and finally just had to ask Holmes, albeit softly, "What do you suppose is going on?"

"Quiet," he said. "This is no time for conjecture. We'll know everything in the morning."

And once again, hour after hour stretched past. My legs became numb from prolonged standing and I lost all sense of where I stood.

Suddenly, some object appeared at the window. A pole with an attachment! Holmes indicated I was to increase my vigilance, but my nerves were already stretched taut as it was. The pole was being slowly guided from below by some unseen hand and the attachment stopped at the level of the pane.

Whoever was below came nearer and the outer latch of the pane was now in the groove of whatever was on the end of the pole. It turned. Clearly, someone was trying to unlock it from down below. But now, just as it must have happened last time, the nails that Holmes had fixed with his usual foresight, proved too much of an impediment.

Someone below was trying hard to open the pane, but it would not give way. The effort lasted for nearly half an hour. The man seemed desperate to carry out his intention but eventually the pole was lowered beneath the level of the windowsill. We heard a slight noise from outside and below and then all was still. We waited in vain while another hour passed and then moved away from the window.

"There you are," said Sherlock Holmes, "you and I, my dear Watson, proved to be wiser, and as it seems to me, this time escaped certain death."

"What do you mean by that?" I asked.

"Someone was intent on opening the pane to let in a strange creature capable of squeezing through such a narrow aperture. Undoubtedly, it could not be a human being. The pane would have been too narrow."

He was silent for a moment and then added, "In any case, the morning brings wiser counsel, so it would be better for us to sleep. I'll tell you everything in the morning."

I was dying of curiosity, but I knew perfectly well that Holmes would never say anything till such time as he was good and ready, and so I did not insist.

VIII

Next morning, for a change, I was up before my friend. But I had hardly swung out of bed when Holmes opened his eyes. He was a remarkably light sleeper. No matter how tired out he had been, the slightest movement served to waken him.

"Aha, my friend," he exclaimed cheerfully. "I'm not quite myself this morning. Surely you couldn't have wakened before me." I gave an involuntary smile.

We began to dress. Our movements and voices must have come to the attention of the household. Hardly twenty minutes had gone by when there was a knock on the door. A servant had come to ask whether we'd like tea served up in our room.

"No thanks, my dear chap," Holmes answered. "We'll have it in the dining-room."

He waited till the servant had gone before giving me a look fraught with meaning, saying "It'll be safer this way, especially being able to see the host drink first."

Having completed our toilet, we entered the dining-room, where Boris Nikolayevitch and Nikolai Nikolayevitch were already sitting at breakfast.

There most probably had been a slight tiff between the brothers, at least judging from the end of the sentence uttered by Boris Nikolayevitch, "—you cannot possibly lay claim to any part of the inheritance. After all, you never paid so much as a visit to our uncle and he was entirely in my care."

"A will represents the will of the departed," Nikolai Nikolayevitch answered coldly. "Whether I visited him or not is beside the point. Since he left me a part of his estate, this is how it must be."

Boris Nikolayevitch was about to say something, but noticing our arrival, broke off the conversation abruptly, greeted me very cordially and offered tea. "I hope you slept well," he addressed us both.

"Oh, yes," I said. "I slept like a log till morning."

"And I, too," said Holmes. "Country air does predispose one to sleep, especially after an energetic stroll. And we must've strolled round your place at least a full hour before retiring."

"You have such a lovely nanny," he added, turning to Nikolai Niko-layevich.

"Oh, indeed!" answered the young man smiling happily. Evidently, he liked having the old lady praised. His face lit up with a kind and sympathetic smile. "I do love the old lady," he said tenderly, "for I have neither father nor mother. She is all I have left as the only loving reminder of my happy childhood."

The brothers reminisced about their childhood, their capers and pranks. Our presence didn't seem to divert them from their memories. However, when breakfast was over, before leaving the table, Boris Niko-layevitch turned to my friend, "You will allow me to ask a question, Mr. Holmes?"

"By all means," came the answer.

"Forgive me for what might be considered an insolent question, but I am curious to know how far advanced is your investigation into clearing up the mysterious murder. In fact, has it advanced at all?"

Holmes gave an enigmatic smile. "Yes, one could say that it is advancing and successfully so," he said. "But owing to certain circum-stances I have to be circumspect and consider the time is not yet ripe for me to reveal the results. Of course, while I know I can rely on your dis-cretion, nonetheless, an incautious word, involuntarily dropped, may serve to harm the course of events."

Boris Nikolayevitch shrugged, "Of course, you know best and it would be silly of me to insist. Sooner or later, however, you'll reveal all yourself, but since I do not belong amongst the ranks of the curious, I shall be silent, at least until such time as you yourself choose to share your secrets with me."

We exchanged various trivia and then Holmes announced he had to say something to me in private. We thanked our host for breakfast and left the dining-room. We went back to our room, put on our hats and went out, following the country road further out. Holmes glanced around him, saw that nobody followed and we lessened our pace. Well over a mile later, we threw ourselves on the soft grass beside the road.

"Well, then, my dear Holmes, last night you promised you'd reveal something interesting to me concerning your preliminary findings. We are all alone here, and since we cannot be overheard, there is nothing to prevent us from speaking loudly and clearly."

"True, true," said Holmes and stretched himself out with evident pleasure on the green sward. "When we set off, it was with the intention of sharing with you everything I have done up to this point. If you are ready, I'll begin."

"Of course," I said in joyful anticipation of a good story.

IX

Holmes stretched himself lazily, turned his head to face me and began his story.

"You probably remember, my dear Watson," he began, "our first arrival on the scene. As soon as we arrived at the scene of the crime, I was really amazed at the inadequate attention the investigative authorities had given the matter. It was as if the crime was of no particular interest. They didn't even bother to examine the room in which Kartzeff died. By the way, even from my initial glance at the bed on which he died, I was able to spot clues with the use of my magnifying glass and that put me on the right track. It was from that moment that I was convinced that the crime was committed not by a man, but by a beast.

"I spotted a few soft grey hairs on the blanket and the pillows. I examined them with a magnifying glass and established that they undoubtedly belonged to an animal. Then a close examination of the waxed parquet floor showed several traces of movement from the window to the bed and back again. These were long, with a narrow heel and long toes. They had definitely been made by an ape. I found the same sort of traces by the wall from which the window of the dead man looked out.

"It was clear that the ape had crept into Kartzeff's room through the window pane, strangled him, clambered up to the roof and then descended using the rain pipe attached to the wall.

"An examination of the corpse only confirmed my assumption, as there were traces of an ape's paws round the throat of the corpse.

"You know, of course, that I have often journeyed through India. I have covered nearly all the shores of the Indian Ocean, often travelling deep inland and, on several occasions, I saw the baboons which local Indians utilized for hunting. It was enough to show these dreaded animals the intended victim for them to leap on it with lightning-like agility, using their muscular paws to choke the life out of it. For some reason, these Indian baboons somehow came to mind when I looked at the scene of the crime.

"I have to admit that, at first, my suspicions fell strongly on Nikolai Nikolayevitch, of whom it was said that he visited his uncle extremely rarely and when departing never ever displayed any warmth. That's why I hastened away with you to test my suspicions. But the old nanny's account caused me to change my mind completely and all suspicions directed at Nikolai Nikolayevitch flew out of my mind.

"In fact, since then I had no doubt that his brother, Boris Nikolayevitch had committed the crime, although the latter hadn't betrayed guilt in the slightest manner. His service and dismissal from the navy and merchant marine, his poor reputation and finally his travels up and down the Indian Ocean gave rise to the first suspicions. Even then, the thought struck me that it could have been there that this sort of ape was acquired by him.

"The threatening letter which came to us in the hotel only strengthened my suspicion. That letter was a terrible blunder on the part of Boris Nikolayevitch and became the prime mover in establishing his guilt. Of course, it is possible to disguise handwriting, but I am certain that a handwriting expert will prove that it is that of Boris Kartzeff.

"And so, this was the course of my thinking: he'd lost everything in riotous living and now he couldn't wait for the death of his uncle. He knew about the will. And so, seeing that his own estate was about to go under the hammer, he decided to advance his way out of the situation.

"The fact is that from the moment of his arrival he had kept the ape under lock and key, let nobody see it, all this was a clear indication that he was up to no good. Evidently, that damned beast had been prepared for its task long before and all he had to do was point it at the victim for it to carry out its task. This is how Kartzeff distanced himself from the crime, substituting a creature that had no sense of what it was doing, thus guaranteeing his own safety from punishment.

"I fully comprehended his train of thought and action, but I have to admit that as an intelligent man he too read my mind and intuitively realized he could not escape from me. Of that he must actually have been convinced on the very first day we met, and when we arrived the very first time he immediately decided to put an end to us. You, of course, hadn't noticed that we had been assigned a room in which the window had a pane with a broken latch, nor that the room in which old Kartzeff had been strangled had a pane with a similarly broken latch.

"But on that occasion, his plan did not work. With foresight, I had nailed down the pane and for it to be opened there would have to be enough noise for us to be alerted. And that wasn't part of the villain's plan. I think you saw him in the window during our stroll last night—"

"Oh, I shall never forget that look, a mixture of fear and loathing," I said.

"If until then I had any reservations about his guilt, all doubt vanished from that moment. And so, during the night, I waited for confirmation of my presuppositions," said Holmes. "In any case, there's not much more to tell you about the most recent events. You saw for yourself how an invisible hand tried to open the pane for that cursed animal to get into our room. Now, Watson, all that's left is to lure him to a last desperate step. As soon as we return, I will announce that we have decided to depart for the city and, depending on how he reacts, we'll decide what to do next. In the meantime, let us take our time getting back."

X

We strolled back.

Boris Nikolayevitch was busy in the yard, handing out some sort of orders concerning household matters, when Sherlock Holmes approached and firmly stated that we had to return to Moscow this very day.

A hardly discernible gleam appeared in Kartzeff's glance. But it was only momentary and, taking himself in hand, he said indifferently, "I am so sorry you cannot stay longer, but it can't be helped. Work must come first. If you don't intend to stop off at Silver Slopes, I'll send you to the station by the direct road. I am only sorry that I cannot do so immediately. My horses are all out on the road and you'll have to wait a few hours."

"Oh, that's no problem," answered Sherlock Holmes.

"I'll give instructions for you to be driven to the ferry. It belongs to me, by the way. From there, the same horses will take you to the station."

"Excellent!" said Sherlock Holmes.

We thanked him again and went inside, where we chatted with Nikolai Nikolayevitch and Boris Nikolayevitch who occasionally dropped in on us. Nevertheless, hour after hour went by and no horses appeared.

At a convenient moment, when both brothers were out of the room at the same time, Holmes whispered to me softly, "I forgot to tell you another little detail. This morning a sock went missing. I deliberately placed my boots outside the door and stuffed my socks inside them. Tell me, why do you think a sock went missing?"

"I haven't a clue. Now why should he need an old sock of yours," I said with a smile.

"All the same, it is a serious matter," said Holmes. "I am nearly certain that he needed the sock for that ape to scent."

Dinner was served at five and went off normally. It was another two hours before the host informed us the horses were ready and awaited us by the porch. But even here there was a delay. Kartzeff examined the carriage and claimed it hadn't been properly oiled. He gave instructions for it to be oiled all over again. It was clearly a deliberate attempt to delay us further.

Night was beginning to fall when, at last, we thanked the brothers for their hospitality, bade them farewell and departed. After a mile along the road, the carriage entered a forest. Now the sun set and it became completely dark.

"Be even more on your guard and hold on to your revolver," Holmes whispered.

As we drove into the forest, the driver slowed down.

Holding his revolver in his hand, Holmes looked back and ordered me to do the same. The precaution was not wasted. A couple of miles into the forest, Holmes pressed my hand forcefully. Leaning over the seat with his outstretched hand holding a revolver, it was as if he was expecting some invisible foe. And suddenly, despite the darkness, I saw the fairly large, dark silhouette of some strange creature. It sped along the road after us in silent leaps. I had hardly become aware of what was going on, hardly had the thought flashed through my mind that this might be the ape-strangler, when the terrifying creature caught up with us and made a colossal flying leap.

Simultaneously, our shots rang out. The damned creature crashed to the ground.

At exactly the same moment the driver tumbled head over heels off the coach-box and vanished amongst the trees. The horses surged forward, only to be stopped by Holmes's powerful grip. He quickly passed the reins to me and, revolver in hand, jumped off the carriage. He ran a few quick steps towards the animal lying on the ground and a third shot rang out. He returned dragging the dead ape along with him. He threw it in, jumped on the coach-box, seized the reins and we galloped away. We raced through the forest with the speed of lightning. The foaming horses pulled up by the ferry.

We yelled and yelled, but nobody appeared. We had no idea how the ferry operated and ended up wasting the best part of an hour in fruitless activity, jumping on and off it and then alongside.

"The devil!" said Holmes fiercely. "He'll catch up with us."

We made another desperate attempt and this time success crowned our efforts. Just as we managed to find the end of the mooring rope, we heard the sound of horses galloping, but we had hardly managed to cast off when a troika came straight for us and into the water.

Two men leaped out and before we had time to gather ourselves together, they scrambled on board.

"Aha, so that's what you are up to," we heard a hoarse voice rage. In that moment I saw Boris Nikolayevitch leap like a cat at Holmes standing by the mooring rope. I threw myself to help him but powerful hands pinioned me.

The ferry forged ahead at full speed and there was nobody to see the life and death struggle being waged on board. We fought with every ounce of strength we possessed, we fought tooth and nail as we rolled over and over. In the heat of the struggle I couldn't see what was happening with Holmes. I gathered up my last reserves of strength, seized my opponent by the throat and with every ounce of strength bashed his head in the darkness against the wooden planking. He, too, made a desperate effort, slipped out of my hands to roll over and vanish beneath the waves.

I leapt to my feet to help Holmes. But it was too late. I was nearly at his side, but he was in a deathly embrace with Kartseff and they went overboard together. Holmes vanished out of sight.

I kept on yelling and screaming for him, but the river was as unresponsive as the grave. Somehow I managed to steer the craft to the opposite shore and at the first village I raised the alarm. I invoked the help of the villagers, and entreated them to find my friend.

All night and day we searched and searched. We even requested the help of the village downriver, but all was in vain. Holmes had irrevocably vanished. We searched a further five days but to no avail. I set off for Moscow, where I laid everything before the police. Soon I departed for England, grieving the premature end of my best friend.

VLADIMIR NABOKOV

REVENGE

Although Vladimir Vladimirovich Nabokov (1899–1977) became a naturalized American citizen in 1945, it is appropriate for him to be regarded as a Russian, too, having been born in St. Petersburg to an old family of nobility. In his childhood, he and his family spoke Russian, English and French fluently, and the boy was more comfortable in English during his pre-teen years. After his home was taken by the Bolsheviks, he left Russia, living in Germany and France from 1922 to 1940, when he moved to America. He earned his living by writing poetry and prose; his first nine novels were written in Russian, and subsequent work in English. Regarded as a major emigre Russian writer in the 1930s, his books were banned in the Soviet Union.

With the publication of *Lolita* in 1955 and its immediate (and enormous) success, he was able to retire from teaching (Russian and European literature at Cornell) and returned to Europe in 1961 to devote full time to writing. He settled into a luxury hotel in Switzerland and lived there for the rest of his life. *Lolita* is the famous novel of Humbert Humbert, a man who becomes obsessed with a 12-year-old girl, whose name has become part of the English language as a description of a sexually precocious girl. It was selected by the Modern Library as #4 on the list of the 100 greatest English language novels of the 20th century. His other major works include *Pnin* (1957), *Pale Fire* (1962) and *Ada, or Ardor: A Family Chronicle* (1969).

"Revenge" was written in Russian and first published in 1924; it is collected in *The Stories of Vladimir Nabokov* (New York, Knopf, 1995).

VLADIMIR NABOKOV

1

stend, the stone wharf, the gray strand, the distant row of hotels, were all slowly rotating as they receded into the turquoise haze of an autumn day.

The professor wrapped his legs in a tartan lap robe, and the chaise longue creaked as he reclined into its canvas comfort. The clean, ochre-red deck was crowded but quiet. The boilers heaved discreetly.

An English girl in worsted stockings, indicating the professor with a motion of her eyebrow, addressed her brother who was standing nearby: "Looks like Sheldon, doesn't he?"

Sheldon was a comic actor, a bald giant with a round, flabby face. "He's really enjoying the sea," the girl added sotto voce. Whereupon, I regret to say, she drops out of my story.

Her brother, an ungainly, red-haired student on his way back to his university after the summer holidays, took the pipe out of his mouth and said, "He's our biology professor. Capital old chap. Must say hello to him." He approached the professor, who, lifting his heavy eyelids, recognized one of the worst and most diligent of his pupils.

"Ought to be a splendid crossing," said the student, giving a light squeeze to the large, cold hand that was proffered him.

"I hope so," replied the professor, stroking his gray check with his fingers. "Yes, I hope so," he repeated, weightily, "I hope so."

The student gave the two suitcases standing next to the deck chair a cursory glance. One of them was a dignified veteran, covered with the white traces of old travel labels, like bird droppings on a monument. The other one—brand-new, orange-colored, with gleaming locks—for some reason caught his attention.

"Let me move that suitcase before it falls over," he offered, to keep up the conversation.

The professor chuckled. He did look like that silver-browed comic, or else like an aging boxer. . . .

"The suitcase, you say? Know what I have in it?" he inquired, with a hint of irritation in his voice. "Can't guess? A marvelous object! A special kind of coat hanger . . ."

"A German invention, sir?" the student prompted, remembering that the biologist had just been to Berlin for a scientific congress.

The professor gave a hearty, creaking laugh, and a golden tooth flashed like a flame. "A divine invention, my friend—divine. Something everybody needs. Why, you travel with the same kind of thing yourself. Eh? Or perhaps you're a polyp?" The student grinned. He knew that the professor was given to obscure jokes. The old man was the object of much gossip at the university. They said he tortured his spouse, a very young woman. The student had seen her once. A skinny thing, with incredible eyes. "And how is your wife, sir?" asked the red-haired student.

The professor replied, "I shall be frank with you, dear friend. I've been struggling with myself for quite some some time, but now I feel compelled to tell you. . . . My dear friend, I like to travel in silence. I trust you'll forgive me."

But here the student, whistling in embarrassment and sharing his sister's lot, departs forever from these pages.

The biology professor, meanwhile, pulled his black felt hat down over his bristly brows to shield his eyes against the sea's dazzling shimmer, and sank into a semblance of sleep. The sunlight falling on his gray, clean-shaven face, with its large nose and heavy chin, made it seem freshly modeled out of moist clay. Whenever a flimsy autumn cloud happened to screen the sun, the face would suddenly darken, dry out, and petrify. It was all, of course, alternating light and shade rather than a reflection of his thoughts. If his thoughts had indeed been reflected on his face, the professor would have hardly been a pretty sight. The trouble was that he had received a report the other day from the private detective he had hired in London that his wife was unfaithful to him. An intercepted letter, written in her minuscule familiar hand, began, *"My dear darling Jack, I am still all full of your last kiss."* The professor's name was certainly not Jack—that was the whole point. The perception made him feel neither surprise nor pain, not even masculine vexation, but only hatred, sharp and cold as a lancet. He realized with utter clarity that he would murder his wife. There could be no qualms. One had only to devise the most excruciating, the most ingenious method. As he reclined in the deck chair, he reviewed for the hundredth time all the methods of torture described by travelers and medieval scholars. Not one of them, so far, seemed adequately painful. In the distance, at the verge of the green shimmer, the sugary-white cliffs of Dover were materializing, and he had still not made a decision. The steamer fell silent and, gently rocking, docked. The professor followed his porter down the gangplank. The customs officer, after rattling off the items ineligible for import, asked him to open a suitcase—the new, orange one. The professor turned the lightweight key in its lock and swung open the leather flap. Some Russian lady behind him loudly exclaimed, "Good Lord!" and gave a nervous laugh. Two Belgians standing on either side of the professor cocked their heads and gave a kind of upward glance. He shrugged his shoulders and the other gave a soft whistle, while the English turned away with indifference. The official, dumbfounded, goggled his eyes at the suitcase's contents. Everybody felt very creepy and uncomfortable. The biologist phlegmatically gave his name, mentioning the university museum. Expressions cleared up. Only a few ladies were chagrined to learn that no crime had been committed.

"But why do you transport it in a suitcase?" inquired the official with respectful reproach, gingerly lowering the flap and chalking a scrawl on the bright leather. "I was in a hurry," said the professor with a fatigued squint. "No time to hammer together a crate. In any case it's a valuable object and not something I'd send in the baggage hold." And, with a stooped but springy gait, the professor crossed to the railway platform past a policeman who resembled a gargantuan toy. But suddenly he paused as if remembering something and mumbled with a radiant, kindly smile, "There—I have it. A most clever method." Whereupon he heaved a sigh of relief and purchased two bananas, a pack of cigarettes, newspapers reminiscent of crackling bedsheets, and, a few minutes later, was speeding in a comfortable compartment of the Continental Express along the scintillating sea, the white cliffs, the emerald pastures of Kent.

2

They were wonderful eyes indeed, with pupils like glossy inkdrops on dove-gray satin. Her hair was cut short and golden-pale in hue, a luxuriant topping of fluff. She was small, upright, flat-chested. She had been expecting her husband since yesterday, and knew for certain he would arrive today. Wearing a gray, open-necked dress and velvet slippers, she was sitting on a peacock ottoman in the parlor, thinking what a pity it was her husband did not believe in ghosts and openly despised the young medium, a Scot with pale, delicate eyelashes, who occasionally visited her. After all, odd things did happen to her. Recently, in her sleep, she had had a vision of a dead youth with whom, before she was married, she had strolled in the twilight, when the blackberry blooms seem so ghostly white. Next morning, still aquiver, she had penciled a letter to him—a letter to her dream. In this letter she had lied to poor Jack. She had, in fact, nearly forgotten about him; she loved her excruciating husband with a fearful but faithful love; yet she wanted to send a little warmth to this dear spectral visitor, to reassure him with some words from earth. The letter vanished mysteriously from her writing pad, and the same night she dreamt of a long table, from under which Jack suddenly emerged, nodding to her gratefully. Now, for some reason, she felt uneasy when recalling that dream, almost as if she had cheated on her husband with a ghost.

The drawing room was warm and festive. On the wide, low windowsill lay a silk cushion, bright yellow with violet stripes.

The professor arrived just when she had decided his ship must have gone to the bottom. Glancing out the window, she saw the black top of a taxi, the driver's proffered palm, and the massive shoulders of her husband who had bent down his head as he paid. She flew through the rooms and trotted downstairs swinging her thin, bared arms.

He was climbing toward her, stopped, in an ample coat. Behind him a servant carried his suitcases.

She pressed against his woolen scarf, playfully bending back the heel of one slender, gray-stockinged leg. He kissed her warm temple. With a good-natured smile he lifted away her arms. "I'm covered with dust. . . . Wait. . . . ," he mumbled, holding her by the wrists. Frowning, she tossed her head and the pale conflagration of her hair. The professor stooped and kissed her on the lips with another little grin.

At supper, thrusting out the white breastplate of his starched shirt and energetically moving his glossy cheekbones, he recounted his brief journey. He was reservedly jolly. The curved silk lapels of his dinner jacket, his bulldog jaw, his massive bald head with ironlike veins on its temples—all this aroused in his wife an exquisite pity: the pity she always felt because, as he studied the minutiae of life, he refused to enter her world, where the poetry of de la Mare flowed and infinitely tender astral spirits hurtled.

"Well, did your ghosts come knocking while I was away?" he asked, reading her thoughts. She wanted to tell him about the dream, the letter, but felt somehow guilty.

"You know something," he went on, sprinkling sugar on some pink rhubarb, "you and your friends are playing with fire. There can be really terrifying occurrences. One Viennese doctor told me about some incredible metamorphoses the other day. Some woman—some kind of fortune-telling hysteric—died, of a heart attack I think, and, when the doctor undressed her (it all happened in a Hungarian hut, by candle-light), he was stunned at the sight of her body; it was entirely covered with a reddish sheen, was soft and slimy to the touch, and, upon closer examination, he realized that this plump, taut cadaver consisted entirely of narrow, circular bands of skin, as if it were all bound evenly and tightly by invisible strings, something like that advertisement for French tires, the man whose body is all tires. Except that in her case these tires were very thin and pale red. And, as the doctor watched, the corpse gradually began to unwind like a huge ball of yarn. . . . Her body was a thin, endless worm, which was disentangling itself and crawling, slithering out through the crack under the door while, on the bed, there remained a naked, white, still humid skeleton. Yet this woman had a husband, who had once kissed her—kissed that worm."

The professor poured himself a glass of port the color of mahogany and began gulping the rich liquid, without taking his narrowed eyes off his wife's face. Her thin, pale shoulders gave a shiver. "You yourself don't realize what a terrifying thing you've told me," she said in agitation. "So the woman's ghost disappeared into a worm. It's all terrifying. . . ."

"I sometimes think," said the professor, ponderously shooting a cuff and examining his blunt fingers, "that, in the final analysis, my science is an idle illusion, that it is we who have invented the laws of physics, that anything—absolutely anything—can happen. Those who abandon themselves to such thoughts go mad. . . ."

He stifled a yawn, tapping his clenched fist against his lips.

"What's come over you, my dear?" his wife exclaimed softly. "You never spoke this way before. . . . I thought you knew everything, had everything mapped out. . . ."

For an instant the professor's nostrils flared spasmodically, and a gold fang flashed. But his face quickly regained its flabby state. He stretched and got up from the table. "I'm babbling nonsense," he said calmly and tenderly. "I'm tired. I'll go to bed. Don't turn on the light when you come in. Get right into bed with me—with me," he repeated meaningfully and tenderly, as he had not spoken for a long time.

These words resounded gently within her when she remained alone in the drawing room.

She had been married to him for five years and, despite her husband's capricious disposition, his frequent outbursts of unjustified jealousy, his silences, sullenness, and incomprehension, she felt happy, for she loved and pitied him. She, all slender and white, and he, massive, bald, with tufts of gray wool in the middle of his chest, made an impossible, monstrous couple—and yet she enjoyed his infrequent, forceful caresses.

A chrysanthemum, in its vase on the mantel, dropped several curled petals with a dry rustle. She gave a start and her heart jolted disagreeably as she remembered that the air was always filled with phantoms, that even her scientist husband had noted their fearsome apparitions.

She recalled how Jackie had popped out from under the table and started nodding his head with an eerie tenderness. It seemed to her that all the objects in the room were watching her expectantly. She was chilled by a wind of fear. She quickly left the drawing room, restraining an absurd cry. She caught her breath and thought, What a silly thing I am, really. . . . In the bathroom she spent a long time examining the sparkling pupils of her eyes. Her small face, capped by fluffy gold, seemed unfamiliar to her.

Feeling light as a young girl, with nothing on but a lace nightgown, trying not to brush against the furniture, she went to the darkened bedroom. She extended her arms to locate the headboard of the bed, and lay down on its edge. She knew she was not alone, that her husband was lying beside her. For a few instants she motionlessly gazed upward, feeling the fierce, muffled pounding of her heart.

When her eyes had become accustomed to the dark, intersected by the stripes of moonlight pouring through the muslin blind, she turned her head toward her husband. He was lying with his back to her, wrapped in the blanket. All she could see was the bald crown of his head, which seemed extraordinarily sleek and white in the puddle of moonlight.

He's not asleep, she thought affectionately; if he were, he would be snoring a little.

She smiled and, with her whole body, slid over toward her husband, spreading her arms under the covers for the familiar embrace.

Her fingers felt some smooth ribs. Her knee struck a smooth bone. A skull, its black eye sockets rotating, rolled from its pillow onto her shoulder.

Electric lights flooded the room. The professor, in his crude dinner jacket, his starched bosom, eyes, and enormous forehead glistening, emerged from behind a screen and approached the bed.

The blanket and sheets, jumbled together, slithered to the rug. His wife lay dead, embracing the white, hastily cobbled skeleton of a hunchback that the professor had acquired abroad for the university museum.

NIKOLAI LYESKOV

THE SENTRY

The controversial novelist and short story writer Nikolai Semyonovich Lyeskov (sometimes catalogued as Leskov) (1831–1895) refused to identify himself with any particular group in the literary world of mid-century Russia, though he took a strong view of the radical intelligentsia, to which he referred as nihilists, describing them as criminals and bloodthirsty monsters, causing him to be ostracized by progressive Russians. Along with his acquaintance, Fyodor Dostoevsky, Lyeskov maintained that the radicals had no knowledge of the ordinary Russian citizen. First as a business agent, then as a journalist, he traveled extensively in every part of Russia, where he became intimately familiar with the country's masses, about which he cared deeply. His observations about common people are seen most powerfully in his best work, the short stories set in various provinces, vividly portraying the people and the challenges of their difficult lives. Extremely religious, he depicted the provincial clergy in a positive light in his works, most notably in *Cathedral Folk* (1872) and *Odds and Ends from an Archbishop's Life* (1878). Among his other major works are *No Way Out* (also published as *Nowhere*, 1864), in which he describes radicals as cynics, profligates, parasites and traitors; *Enchanted Wanderer*, a series of Quixotic episodes describing life under the tsars; and *Lady Macbeth of the Mtsensk District* (1865), which was the basis for the 1934 Dimitri Shostakovich opera of the same title.

"The Sentry" was first published in English in *The Sentry and Other Stories* (London, The Bodley Head, 1922); it was translated by E.A. Chamot.

THE SENTRY

The events of the story which is now presented to the reader are so touching and terrible in their importance for the chief and heroic actor who took part in them and the issue of the affair was so unique, that anything similar could scarcely have occurred in another country than Russia.

It forms in part a court anecdote, in part a historic event that characterises fairly well the manners and the very strange tendency of the uneventful period comprised in the third decade of the nineteenth century.

There is no invention in the following story.

During the winter of 1839, just before the Festival of Epiphany, there was a great thaw in Petersburg. The weather was so warm, that it was almost like spring; the snow melted during the day, water dripped from the roofs, the ice on the rivers became blue, and just in front of the Winter Palace there was a large open space. A warm but very high wind blew from the west, the water was driven in from the gulf, and the signal guns were fired.

The guard at the Palace at that time was a company of the Ismailovsky regiment, commanded by a very brilliant well-educated officer named Nicolai Ivanovich Miller, a young man of the very best society (who subsequently rose to the rank of general and became the director of the Lyeium). He was a man of the so-called "humane tendencies," which had long since been noticed in him, and somewhat impaired his chances in the service, in the eyes of his superiors.

Miller was really an exact and trustworthy officer; the duty of the guard at the Palace was without any danger; the time was most uneventful and tranquil; the Palace sentries were only required to stand accurately at their posts. Nevertheless, just when Captain Miller was in command, a most extraordinary and very alarming event took place, which is probably scarcely remembered even by the few of his contemporaries who are now ending their days upon earth.

At first everything went well with the guard. The sentries were placed, the men were all at their posts and all was in the most perfect order. The Emperor Nikolai Pavlovich was well, he had been for a drive in the evening, returned home, and had gone to bed. The Palace slept, too. The night was most quiet. There was tranquility in the guard-room. Captain Miller had pinned his white pocket handkerchief to the back of the officer's chair, with its traditionally greasy morocco high back and had settled down to while away the time by reading.

Captain Miller had always been a passionate reader, and therefore was never dull; he read and did not notice how the night passed away. When suddenly at about three o'clock he was alarmed by a terrible anxiety. The sergeant on duty, pale and trembling with fear, stood before him, and stammered hurriedly:

"A calamity, your honor, a calamity!"

"What has happened?"

"A terrible misfortune has occurred."

Captain Miller jumped up in indescribable agitation and with difficulty was able to ascertain what really was the nature of the "calamity" and the "terrible misfortune."

The case was as follows: The sentry, a private of the Ismailovsky regiment named Postnikov, who was standing on guard at the outer door of the Palace, now called the "Jordan" entrance, heard that a man was drowning in the open spaces which had appeared in the ice just opposite the Palace, and was calling for help in his despair.

Private Postnikov, a domestic serf of some great family, was a very nervous and sensitive man. For a long time he listened to the distant cries and groans of the drowning man, and they seemed to benumb him with horror. He looked on all sides, but on the whole visible expanse of the quays and the Neva, as if on purpose, not a living soul could he see.

There was nobody who could give help to the drowning man, and he was sure to sink . . .

All this time the man struggled long and terribly.

It seemed as if there was but one thing left for him—to sink to the bottom without further struggle, but no! His cries of exhaustion were now broken and ceased, then were heard again, always nearer and nearer to the Palace quay. It was evident that the man had not lost his direction, but was making straight for the lights of the street lamps, but doubtless would perish because just in his path, he would fall into the "Jordan" (a hole made in the ice of the river for the consecration of the water on the 6th of January). There he would be drawn under the ice and it would be the end. Again he was quiet, but a minute later he began to splash through the water, and moan: "Save me, save me!" He was now so near that the splashing of the water could actually be heard as he waded along.

Private Postnikov began to realise that it would be quite easy to save this man. It was only necessary to run on to the ice, as the drowning man was sure to be there, throw him a rope, or stretch a pole or a gun towards him, and he could be saved. He was so near that he could take hold of it with his hand and save himself. But Postnikov remembered his service and his oath; he knew he was the sentry, and that the sentry dare not leave his sentry-box on any pretext, or for any reason whatever.

On the other hand, Postnikov's heart was not at all submissive; it gnawed, it throbbed, it sank. He would have been glad to tear it out and throw it at his feet—he had become so uneasy at the sound of these groans and sobs. It was terrible to hear another man perishing and not to stretch out a hand and save him, when really it was quite possible to do so, because the sentry-box would not run away, and no other harm could happen. "Shall I run down? Will anybody see it? Oh, Lord, if it could only end! He's groaning again!"

For a whole half hour, while this was going on, Private Postnikov's heart tormented him so much that he began to feel doubts of his own reason. He was a clever and conscientious soldier with a clear judgment, and he knew perfectly well that for a sentry to leave his post was a crime that would have to be tried by a court-martial, and he would afterwards have to run the gauntlet between two lines of cat-o'-nine-tails and then have penal servitude, or perhaps even be shot—but from the direction of the swollen river again there rose, always nearer and nearer, groans, mumblings and desperate struggles.

"I am drowning! Save me, I am drowning!"

Soon he would come to the Jordan cutting and then—the end.

Postnikov looked round once or twice on all sides. Not a soul was to be seen, only the lamps rattled, shook, and flickered in the wind, and on the wind were borne broken cries, perhaps the last cries . . .

There was another splash, a single sob and a gurgling in the water.

The sentry could bear it no longer, and left his post.

Postnikov rushed to the steps, with his heart beating violently, ran on to the ice, then into the water that had risen above it. He soon saw where the drowning man was struggling for life and held out the stock of his gun to him. The drowning man caught hold of the butt-end and Postnikov holding on to the bayonet, drew him to the bank.

Both the man who had been saved, and his rescuer were completely wet; the man who had been saved was in a state of great exhaustion, shivered and fell; his rescuer, Private Postnikov, could not make up his mind to abandon him on the ice, but led him to the quay, and began looking about for somebody to whom he could confide him. While all this was happening, a sledge in which an officer was sitting had appeared on the quay. He was an officer of the Palace Invalid Corps, a company which existed then, but has since been abolished.

This gentlemen who arrived at such an inopportune moment for Postnikov, was evidently a man of very heedless character, and besides a very muddle-headed and impudent person. He jumped out of his sledge and inquired:

"What man is this? Who are these people?"

"He was nearly drowned—he was sinking," began Postnikov.

"How was he drowning? Who was drowning? Was it you? Why is he here?"

But he only spluttered and panted, and Postnikov was no longer there; he had shouldered his gun and gone back to his sentry-box.

Possibly the officer understood what had happened, for he made no further inquiries, but at once took the man who had been rescued into his sledge and drove with him to the Admiralty Police Station in the Morskaia Street.

Here the officer made a statement to the inspector, that the dripping man he had brought had nearly drowned in one of the holes in the ice in front of the Palace, and that he, the officer, had saved him at the risk of his own life.

The man who had been saved was still quite wet, shivering and exhausted. From fright and owing to his terrific efforts he fell into a sort of unconsciousness, and it was quite indifferent to him who had saved him.

The sleepy police orderly hustled around him, while in the office a statement was drawn up from the officer's verbal deposition and, with the suspicion natural to members of the police, they were perplexed to understand how he had managed to come out of the water quite dry. The officer who was anxious to receive his life saving medal, tried to explain this happy concurrence of circumstance, but his explanation was incoherent and improbable. They went to wake the police inspector, and sent to make inquiries.

Meantime in the Palace this occurrence was the cause of another rapid series of events.

In the Palace guard-room all that had occurred since the officer took the half-drowned man into his sledge was unknown. There the Ismailovsky officer and the soldiers only knew that Postnikov, a private of their regiment, had left his sentry-box, and had hurried to save a man and, this being a great breach of military duty, Private Postnikov would certainly be tried by court-martial and have to undergo a thrashing, and all his superior officers, beginning from the commander of the company, would have to face terrible unpleasantness, to avert which they would have nothing to say, nor would they be able to defend themselves.

The wet and shivering soldier, Postnikov, was of course at once relieved from his post, and when he was brought to the guard-room frankly related to Captain Miller all that we already know, with all details to the moment when the officer of the Invalid Corps put the half-drowned man into his sledge, and ordered the coachman to drive to the Admiralty Police Station.

The danger grew greater and more unavoidable. It was certain the officer of the Invalid Corps would relate everything to the police inspector and the inspector would at once state all the facts to the chief of police, Kokoshkin, who in the morning would make his report to the Emperor, and then the trouble would begin.

There was no time for reflection; the advice of the superior officer must be obtained. Nicolai Ivanovich Miller forthwith sent an alarming note to his immediate superior, the commander of his battalion, Lieu-tenant Colonel Svinin, in which he begged him to come to the guard-room as soon as he could to take every possible measure to help him out of the terrible misfortune that had occurred.

It was already about three o'clock, and Kokoshkin had to present his report to the Emperor fairly early in the morning, so that but little time remained for reflection and action.

Lieutenant Colonel Svinin did not possess that compassion and tenderness of heart for which Nicolai Ivanovich Miller had always been distinguished. Svinin was known for his severity and he even liked to boast of his exacting discipline. He had no taste for evil, and never tried to cause anybody useless suffering, but when a man had violated any of the duties of the service, Svinin was inexorable. In the present case he considered it out of place to enter into the considera-tion of the causes that had guided the actions of the culprit, and held to the rule that every deviation from discipline was guilt. Therefore, in the company on guard, all knew that Private Postnikov would have to suffer what he deserved, for having left his post, and that Svinin would remain absolutely indifferent.

Such was the character by which the staff officer was known to his superiors, and also to his comrades, amongst whom there were men who did not sympathise with Svinin, because at that time "humaneness", and other similar delusions, had not entirely died out. Svinin was indifferent to whether he would be blamed or praised by the "humanitarians." To beg or entreat Svinin, or even try to move him to pity was quite useless. To all this he was hardened with the well-tempered armour of the people of those times, who wanted to make their way in the world, but even he, like Achilles, had a weak spot.

Svinin's career in the service had commenced well, and he of course greatly valued it and was very careful that on it, as on a full dress uniform, not a grain of dust should settle, and now this unfortunate action of one of the men of the battalion entrusted to him would certainly throw a shadow on the discipline of the whole company. Those on whom Svinin's well-started and carefully maintained military career depended, would not stop to inquire if the commander of the battalion was guilty or not guilty of what one of his men had done, while moved by the most honourable feelings of sympathy, and many would gladly have put a spoke in the wheel, so as to make way for their relations or to push forward some fine young fellow with high patronage. If the Emperor, who would certainly be angry, said to the commander of the regiment that he had feeble officers, that their men were undisciplined; who was the cause of it? Svinin. So it would be repeated that Svinin was feeble, and the reproach of feebleness would remain a stain on his reputation that could not be washed out. Then he would never be in any way remarkable among his comtemporaries, and he would not leave his portrait in the gallery of historical personages of the Russian Empire.

Although at that time but few cultivated the study of history, nevertheless they believed in it, and aspired, with special pleasure, to take part in its making.

At about three o'clock in the morning, as soon as Svinin received Captain Miller's disquieting letter, he at once jumped out of bed, put on his uniform and, swayed by fear and anger, arrived at the guard-room of the Winter Palace. Here he forthwith examined Private Postnikov, and assured himself that the extraordinary event had really taken place. Private Postnikov again frankly confirmed to the commander of his battalion all that had occurred while he was on guard duty, and what he (Postnikov) had already related to the commander of his company, Captain Miller. The soldier said that he was guilty before God and the Emperor, and could not expect mercy; that he, standing on guard, hearing the groans of a man who was drowning in the open places of ice, had suffered long, had struggled long between his sense of military duty and his feelings of compassion and at last he had yielded to temptation and not being able to stand the struggle, had left his sentry-box, jumped on the ice and had drawn the drowning man to the bank, and there to his misfortune, he had met an officer of the Palace Invalid Corps.

Lieutenant-Colonel Svinin was in despair; he gave himself the only possible satisfaction by wreaking his anger on Postnikov, whom he at once sent under arrest to the regimental prison, and then said some biting words to Miller, reproaching him with "humanitarianism," which was of no use at all in military service; but all this was of no avail, nor would it improve the matter. It was impossible to find any excuse, still less justification, for a sentry who had left his post, and there remained only one way of getting out of the difficulty—to conceal the whole affair from the Emperor. . .

But was it possible to conceal such an occurrence?

It was evident that this appeared to be impossible, as the rescue of the drowning man was known, not only to the whole rest of the guard, but also to that hateful officer of the Invalid Corps, who by now had certainly had time to report the whole matter to General Kokoshkin.

Which way was he to turn? To whom could he address himself? From whom could he obtain help and protection?

Svinin wanted to gallop off to the Grand Duke Michael Pavlovich and relate to him, quite frankly, all that had happened. Manoeuvres of this nature were then customary. The Grand Duke, who had a hot temper, would be angry and storm, but his humour and habits were such, that the greater the harshness he showed at first, even when he grievously insulted the offender, the sooner he would forgive him and take up his defence. Similar cases were not infrequent and they were even sometimes sought after. Words do not hurt; and Svinin was very anxious to bring the matter to a favourable conclusion; but was it possible at night to obtain entrance to the palace and disturb the Grand Duke? To wait for morning and appear before Michael Pavlovich, after Kokoshkin had made his report to the Emperor, would be too late.

While Svinin was agitated by these difficulties he became more subtle, and his mind began to see another issue, which till then had been hidden as if in a mist.

Among the well-know military tactics there is the following: at the moment when the greatest danger is threatened from the walls of a belea-guered fortress, not to retire, but to advance straight under its walls. Svinin decided not to do any of the things that had at first occurred to him, but to go straight to Kokoshkin.

Many terrible things were related at that time in Petersburg about the chief of police Kokoshkin, and many absurd things too, but among others it was affirmed that he possessed such wonderful resource and tact, that with the assistance of this tact he was not only able to make a mountain out of a molehill, but that he was able as easily to make a molehill out of a mountain.

Kokoshkin was really very stern and very terrible, and inspired great fear in all who came in contact with him, but he sometimes showed mercy to the gay young scamps among the officers and such young scamps were not few in those days, and they often found in him a mer-ciful and zealous protector. In a word, he was able to do much and knew how to do it, if only he chose. Both Svinin and Captain Miller knew this side of his character. Miller therefore encouraged his superior officer to risk going to Kokoshkin and trust to the General's magnanimity and resource and tact, which would probably suggest to him the means of getting out of this unpleasant situation without incurring the wrath of the Emperor, which Kokoshkin, to his honour be it said, always made great efforts to avoid.

Svinin put on his overcoat, looked up to heaven, murmured several times, "Good Lord! Good Lord!" and drove off to Kokoshkin.

It was already past four o'clock in the morning.

The chief of police, Kokoshkin, was aroused and the arrival of Svinin, who had come on important business, that could not be postponed, was reported to him.

The general got up at once and with an overcoat wrapped round him, wiping his forehead, yawning and stretching himself, came out to receive Svinin. Kokoshkin listened with great attention, but quite calmly, to all Svinin had to relate. During all these explanations and requests for indulgence he only said:

"The soldier left his sentry-box and saved a man?"

"Yes, sir," answered Svinin.

"And the sentry-box?"

"Remained empty during that time."

"Hm! I knew that it remained empty. I'm very pleased that nobody stole it."

Hearing this, Svinin felt certain that the General knew all about the case, and that he had already decided in what manner he would place the facts before the Emperor in his morning's report, and also that he would not alter this decision. Otherwise such an event as a soldier of the Palace Guard having left his post would, without doubt, have caused greater alarm to the energetic chief of police.

But Kokoshkin did not know anything about it. The police inspector to whom the officer of the Invalid Corps had conveyed the man saved from drowning, did not consider it a matter of great importance. In his sight it was not at all a subject that required him to awaken the weary chief of police in the middle of the night, and besides the whole event appeared to the inspector somewhat suspicious, because the officer of the Invalids was quite dry, which certainly could not have been the case if he had saved a man from drowning at the risk of his own life. The inspector looked upon the officer as an ambitious liar, who wanted to obtain another medal for his breast, and therefore detained him while the clerk on duty was taking down his statement, and tried to arrive at the truth by asking about all sorts of minute details.

It was disagreeable for the inspector that such an event should have occurred in his district, and that the man had been saved, not by a policeman but by an officer of the Palace Guard.

Kokoshkin's calmness could be explained very simply: first, by his terrible fatigue, after a day of anxiety and hard work, and by his having assisted in the night at the extinguishing of two fires, and secondly because the act of the sentry, Postnikov, did not concern him, as Chief of Police, at all.

Nevertheless, Kokoshkin at once gave the necessary instructions.

He sent to the Inspector of the Admiralty Quarter and ordered him to come at once and bring the officer of the Invalid Corps and the man who had been saved with him, and asked Svinin to remain in the small waiting-room adjoining his office. Then Kokoshkin went into his study, without closing the door, sat down at the table, and began to sign various papers, but he soon rested his head on his hand and fell asleep in his armchair at the table.

In those days there were neither municipal telegraphs nor telephones, and in order to transmit the commands of the chiefs the "forty thousand couriers," of whom Gogol has left a last memory in his comedy, had to ride post haste in all directions.

This, of course, was not so quickly done as by telegraph or telephone, but lent considerable animation to the town and proved that the authorities were indefatigably vigilant.

Before the breathless inspector, the life-saving officer, and the man rescued him from drowning had time to come from the Admiralty police station, the nervous and energetic Kokoshkin had time to have a snooze and refresh himself. This was seen in the expression of his face and by the revival of his mental faculties.

Kokoshkin ordered all who had arrived to come to his study and with them Svinin, too.

"The official report?" the General demanded of the inspector.

The latter silently handed a folded paper to the General and then whispered in a low voice:

"I must beg to permission to communicate a few words to your Excellency in private."

"Very well."

Kokoshkin went towards the bay-window, followed by the inspector.

"What is it?"

The inspector's indistinct whispers could be heard and the General's loud interjections.

"H'm, yes! Well, what then? . . . It is possible . . . They take care to come out dry . . . Anything more?"

"Nothing, sir."

The General came out of the bay-window, sat down at his desk, and began to read. He read the report in silence without showing any signs of uneasiness or suspicion, and then turning to the man who had been saved, asked in a loud voice:

"How comes it, my friend, that you got into the open places before the Palace?"

"Forgive me!"

"So! You were drunk?"

"Excuse me, I was not drunk, only tipsy."

"Why did you get into the water?"

"I wanted to cut across the ice, lost my way, and got into the water."

"That means it was dark before your eyes."

"It was dark; it was dark all around, your Excellency."

"And you were not able to notice who pulled you out?"

"Pardon me, I could not notice anything. I think it was he"—he pointed to the officer and added: "I could not distinguish anything. I was so scared."

"That's what it comes to. You were loafing about when you ought to have been asleep. Now look at him well and remember who was your benefactor. An honourable man risked his life to save you."

"I shall never forget it."

"Your name, sir?"

The officer mentioned his name.

"Do you hear?"

"I hear, your Excellency."

"You are Orthodox?"

"I am Orthodox, your Excellency."

"In your prayers for health, remember this man's name."

"I will write it down, your Excellency."

"Pray to God for him, and go away. You are no longer wanted."

He bowed to the ground and cleared off, immeasurably pleased that he was released.

Svinin stood there and could not understand how, by God's grace, things were taking such a turn.

Kokoshkin turned to the officer of the Invalid Corps.

"You saved this man, at the risk of your own life?"

"Yes, your Excellency."

"There were no witnesses to this occurrence, and owing to the late hour there could not have been any?"

"Yes, your Excellency, it was dark and on the quay there was nobody, except for the sentry."

"There is no need to mention the sentry; the sentry has to stand at his post and has no right to occupy himself with anything else. I believe what is written in this report. Was it not taken down from your own words?"

These words Kokoshkin pronounced with special emphasis, as if he were threatening or shouting.

The officer did not falter, but with staring eyes and expanded chest, standing at attention, answered:

"From my own words and quite correctly, your Excellency."

"Your action deserves a reward."

The officer bowed gracefully.

"There is nothing to thank for," continued Kokoshkin, "I shall report your self-sacrificing act to His Majesty the Emperor and your breast may be decorated with a medal even to-day. Now you may go home, have a warm drink, and don't leave the house, as perhaps you may be wanted."

The officer of the Invalid Corps beamed all over, bowed and retired.

Kokoshkin, looking after him, said:

"It is possible that the Emperor may wish to see him."

"I understand," answered the inspector, with apprehension.

"I do not require you any more."

The inspector left the room, closed the door, and in accordance with his religious habit, crossed himself.

The officer of the Invalids was waiting for the inspector below and they went away together, much better friends than when they had come.

Only Svinin remained in the study of the Chief of Police. Kokoshkin looked at him long and attentively and then asked:

"You have not been to the Grand Duke?"

At that time when the Grand Duke was mentioned everybody knew that it referred to the Grand Duke Michael.

"I came straight to you," answered Svinin.

"Who was the officer on guard?"

"Captain Miller."

Kokoshkin looked again at Svinin and said:

"I think you told me something different before."

Svinin did not understand to what this could refer and remained silent, and Kokoshkin added:

"Well, it's all the same; good night."

The audience was over.

About one o'clock the officer of the Invalids, was really sent for by Kokoshkin, who informed him most amiably the Emperor was most pleased that among the officers of the Invalids corps of his palace there were to be found such vigilant and self-sacrificing men, and had honoured him with the medal for saving life. Then Kokoshkin decorated the hero with his own hands and the officer went away to swagger about town with the medal on his breast.

The affair could therefore be considered as quite finished, but Lieutenant-Colonel Svinin felt that it was not concluded, and regarded himself as called upon to put the dots on the "i's."

He had been so much alarmed that he was ill for three days, and on the fourth, drove to the Peter House, had a service of Thanksgiving said for him before the icon of the Saviour, and returning home, sent to ask Captain Miller to come to him.

"Well, thank God, Nicolai Ivanovich," he said to Miller, "the storm that was hanging over us has been quite settled. I think we can now breathe freely. All this we owe without doubt, first to the mercy of God, and secondly to General Kokoshkin. Let people say he is not kind and heartless, but I am full of gratitude for his magnanimity and respect for his resourcefulness and tact. In what a masterly way he took advantage of that vainglorious Invalid swindler who, in truth, for his impudence ought to have received not a medal, but a good thrashing in the stable. There was nothing else for him to do; he had to take advantage of this to save many, and Kokoshkin manoeuvred the whole affair so cleverly that nobody had the slightest unpleasantness; on the contrary, all are very happy and contented. Between ourselves, I can tell you, I have been informed by a reliable person that Kokoshkin is very satisfied with me. He was pleased I had not gone anywhere else, but came straight to him, and that I did not argue with this swindler, who received a medal. In a word, nobody has suffered, and all has been done with so much tact that there can be no fear for the future; but there is one thing wanting on our side. We must follow Kokoshkin's example and finish the affair with tact on our side, so as to guarantee ourselves from any future occurrences. There is still one person whose position is not regulated. I speak of Private Postnikov. He is still lying in prison under arrest, no doubt troubled with thoughts of what will be done to him. We must put an end to his torments."

"Yes, it is time," said Miller, delighted.

"Well, certainly, and you are the best man to do it. Please go at once to the barracks, call your company together, lead Private Postnikov out of prison, and let him be punished with two hundred lashes before the whole company."

Miller was astonished, and made an attempt to persuade Svinin to complete the general happiness by showing mercy to Private Postnikov, and to pardon him as he had already suffered so much while lying in prison waiting his fate, but Svinin only got angry and did not allow Miller to continue.

"No," he broke in, "none of that! I have only just talked to you about tact and you at once are tactless! None of that!"

Svinin changed his tone to a dryer, more official one, and added sternly:

"An as in this affair you too are not quite in the right, but really much to blame because your softness of heart is quite unsuitable for a military man, and this deficiency of your character is reflected in your subordinates, therefore you are to be present personally at the execution of my orders and to see that the flogging is done seriously—as severely as possible. For this purpose have the goodness to give orders that the young soldiers who have just arrived from the army, shall do the whipping, because our old soldiers are all infected with the liberalism of the guards. They won't whip a comrade properly, but would only frighten the fleas away from his back. I myself will look in to see that they have done the guilty man properly."

To evade in any way instructions given by a superior officer was of course impossible, and kind-hearted Captain Miller was obliged to execute with exactitude the orders received from the commander of his battalion.

The company was drawn up in the courtyard of the Ismailovsky barracks; the rods were fetched in sufficient quantities from the stores, and Private Postnikov was brought out of his prison and "done properly" at the hands of the zealous comrades, who had just arrived from the army. These men, who had not yet been as tainted by the liberalism of the guards, put all the dots on the i's to the full, as ordered by the commander of the battalion. Then Postnikov, having received his punishment, was lifted up on the overcoat on which he had been whipped and carried to the hospital of the regiment.

The commander of the battalion, Svinin, as soon as he heard that the punishment had been inflicted, went away at once to visit Postnikov in the hospital in a most fatherly way, and to satisfy himself by a personal examination that his orders had been properly executed. Heartsore and nervous, Postnikov had been "done properly." Svinin was satisfied and ordered that Postnikov should receive, on his behalf, a pound of sugar and a quarter of a pound of tea with which to regale himself while he was recovering. Postnikov, from his bed, heard this order about tea and said:

"I am very contented, your honour. Thank you for your fatherly kindness."

And really he was contented, because while lying three days in prison he had expected something much worse. Two hundred lashes, according to the strict ideas of those days, was of very little consequence in comparison with the punishments that people suffered by order of the military courts; and that is the sort of punishment he would have awarded him if, by good luck, all the bold and tactful evolutions, which are related above, had not taken place.

But the number of persons who were pleased at the events just described was not limited to these.

The story of the exploit of Private Postnikov was secretly whispered in various circles of society in the capital, which in those days, when the public Press had no voice, lived in a world of endless gossip. In these verbal transmissions the name of the real hero, Private Postnikov, was lost, but instead of that the episode became embellished and received a very interesting and romantic character.

It was related that an extraordinary swimmer had swum from the side of the Peter and Paul Fortress, and had been fired at and wounded by one of the sentries stationed before the Winter Palace and an officer of the Invalid Guard, who was passing at the time, threw himself into the water and saved him from drowning, for which the one who had received the merited reward, and the other the punishment he deserved. These absurd reports even reached the Conventual House, inhabited at that time by His Eminence, a high ecclesiastic, who was cautious but not indifferent to worldly matters, and who was benevolently disposed towards, and a well-wisher of, the pious Moscow family, Svinin.

The story of the shot seemed improbable to the astute ecclesiastic. What nocturnal swimmer could it be? If he was an escaped prisoner, why was the sentry punished, for he had only done his duty in shooting at him, when he saw him swimming across the Neva from the Fortress. If he was not a prisoner, but another mysterious man, who had to be saved from the waves of the Neva, how could the sentry know anything about him? And then again, it could not have happened as it was whispered in frivolous society. In society much is accepted in a light-hearted and frivolous manner, but those who live in monasteries and conventual houses look upon all this much more seriously and are quite conversant with the real things of this world.

Once when Svinin happened to be at His Eminence's to receive his blessing, the distinguished dignitary began: "By the by, what about that shot?" Svinin related the whole truth, in which there was nothing whatever "about that shot."

The high ecclesiastic listened to the real story in silence, gently touching his white rosary and never taking his eyes off the narrator. When Svinin had finished, His Eminence quietly murmured in rippling speech:

"From all this one is obliged to conclude that in this matter the statements made were neither wholly nor on every occasion strictly true."

Svinin stammered and then answered with the excuse that it was not he but General Kokoshkin who had made the report.

His Eminence passed the rosary through his waxen fingers in silence, and then murmured:

"One must make a distinction between a lie and what is not wholly true."

Again the rosary, then silence, and at last a soft ripple of speech:

"A half truth is not a lie, but the less said about it the better."

Svinin was encouraged and said:

"That is certainly true. What troubles me most is that I had to inflict a punishment upon a soldier, who, although he had neglected his duty . . ."

The rosary and a soft rippling interruption:

"The duties of service must never be neglected."

"Yes, but it was done by him through magnanimity, through sympathy after such a struggle, and with danger. He understood that in saving the life of another man he was destroying himself. This is a high, holy feeling. . . ."

"Holiness is known to God; corporal punishment is not destruction for a common man, nor is it contrary to the customs of the nations, nor to the spirit of the Scriptures. The rod is easier borne by the coarse body than delicate suffering by the soul. In this case your justice has not suffered in the slightest degree."

"But he was deprived of the reward for saving one who was perishing."

"To save those who are perishing is not a merit, but rather a duty.

He who could save but did not save is liable to the punishment of the laws; but he who saves does his duty."

A pause, the rosary, and soft rippling speech:

"For a warrior to suffer degradation and wounds for his action is perhaps more profitable than marks of distinction. But what is most important is to be careful in this case, and never to mention anywhere or on any occasion what anybody said about it."

It was evident His Eminence was also satisfied.

If I had the temerity of the happy chosen of Heaven, who through their great faith are enabled to penetrate into the secrets of the Will of God, then I would perhaps dare to permit myself the supposition that probably God Himself was satisfied with the conduct of Postnikov's humble soul, which He had created. But my faith is small; it does not permit my mind to penetrate so high. I am of the earth, earthy. I think of those mortals who love goodness, simply because it is goodness and do not expect any reward for it, wherever it may be. I think these true and faithful people will also be entirely satisfied with this holy impulse of love, and not less holy endurance of the humble hero of my true and artless story.

MAXIM GORKY

A STRANGE MURDERER

Aleksey Maksimovich Peshkov (1868–1936) took the pseudonym Maxim Gorky because it means "the bitter one," a condemnation of the way he was treated after running away from an abusive home when he was twelve. He worked as a baker, dishwasher, dockworker, night watchman and other low level jobs, often starving and being beaten. When he was 21, he tried to commit suicide, shooting himself in the chest where the bullet punctured his lung. He recovered but suffered numerous bouts of tuberculosis in ensuing years. He then traveled extensively, mainly associating with the lowest members of society: thieves, derelicts and prostitutes. His experiences provided background material when he turned to journalism and short story writing at the age of 24, becoming the first Russian author to write sympathetically of this stratum of society. Although he was in frequent trouble and jailed by the police for his outspoken, revolutionary political views, he became a folk hero to the Russian people who sympathized with his advocacy of workers and ordinary citizens against the overwhelming power of the Czarist government. He was opposed to the Bolshevik takeover in 1917 and soon moved to Italy, but great public pressure forced his return to Russia in 1930. He died a few years later, almost certainly at the hands of a police chief who confessed to having ordered his murder, which was suspected (though not proven) to have been ordered by Josef Stalin himself.

"A Strange Murderer" was first published in America in the October 1924 issue of The Dial Magazine.

"I can kill you very gently, very softly—
allow you to say a prayer first, then kill you."

About two months before his death Judge L. N. Sviatoukhine said to me one day:

"Of all the murderers that have come before me during the last thirteen years, one only, the packhorse-driver Merkouloff, ever awoke a feeling of terror before man and for man. The ordinary murderer is a hopelessly dull and obtuse creature, half man, half beast, incapable of realising the significance of his crime; or else a sly little dirty fellow, a squealing fox caught in a trap; or else again an unsuccessful, hysterical mono-maniac, desperate and bitter. But when Merkouloff stood in front of me in the dock I instantly scented something weird and unusual about him."

Sviatoukhine half closed his eyes, recalling the picture to his memory.

"A large, broad-shouldered peasant of about forty-five, a thin, good-looking face, such a face as one usually sees on holy images. A long, grey beard, curly hair also grey, bald on the temples, and in the middle of the forehead, like a horn, a provocative, cossack forelock. From the deep orbits, quite out of keeping with that forelock, a pair of clever grey eyes glanced shrewdly at me, soft and full of pity."

Breathing a heavy, putrid breath—the judge was dying of cancer of the stomach—Sviatoukhine nervously wrinkled up his earthen-coloured, exhausted face.

"What startled me particularly was this expression of pity in his eyes—where could it have come from? And I confess that my official indifference disappeared, giving way to an anxious curiosity, a new and unpleasant experience for me.

"He answered my questions in the dull voice of a man who is not used to or does not like talking much—his answers were short and precise—it was clear that he intended to make a frank confession. I said something to him which I would never have said to any other man in the same circumstances:

"'You've got a fine face, Merkouloff; you do not look like a murderer.'

"At this he pulled up the chair in the dock, as though he were a guest there rather than a prisoner, sat down firmly on it, pressed his palms to his knees, and began to talk in a curiously melodious voice, as though he were playing on a reed-pipe. Perhaps that is not a very good simile, for a reed-pipe has also a dull note in it.

"'You think, sir, that if I have committed this murder it means that I am a beast? No—I am not one—and since you appear to be interested in me, I will tell you my story.'

"And he told it me, calmly, consecutively, as murderers usually do not do, without attempting to justify himself or to awaken compassion."

The judge spoke very slowly and indistinctly, his parched lips, covered with a kind of grey scale, moved with difficulty and he moistened them with his dark tongue, closing his eyes.

"I will try to recall his own words. There was a particular significance in them. They were words that amazed and shattered one. That compassionate glance of his, directed at me, crushed me, too. You understand? It was not plaintive but compassionate. He felt sorry for me, although I was in quite good health at that time.

"He committed his first murder in the following circumstances: He was carting some sacks of sugar from the harbour one autumn night when he noticed that a man was walking behind the cart and had made a rent in the sack and was filling his pockets with the sugar. Merkouloff got down, rushed at him, gave him a blow on the temple, and the man fell down.

"'Well,' said Merkouloff, 'I gave him another kick and began fixing the torn sack while all the time he lay under my feet, his face turned upwards, his eyes and mouth wide open. I felt frightened, so I knelt down and took his head in my hands, but it rolled from one side to the other, as heavy as lead, while his eyes seemed to wink at me and his nose bled all over my hands. I jumped up, crying: "My God, I've killed him." '

"Merkouloff then went off to the police-station, whence he was sent to prison.

"'Sitting in prison,' he said, 'and watching the criminals around me, I seemed to be looking at everything through a fog—I just couldn't take things in. I felt terrified, could not sleep or eat, but kept thinking: "How is it, how can it be? A man was walking along the road, I struck him— and—no more man. What does it mean? The soul—where is it? It isn't as though he were a sheep or a calf—he could do this and that and believed in God, no doubt; also, although his nature might have been different, he was just the same kind of being as I am. And I—don't you see?—crossed his life, killed him as though he were a beast, no more. If it's like that, why, then it might happen to me too any day: I might get a blow—and it's all up with me!" So terrified was I by such thoughts, sir, that I seemed to hear the very hairs on my head growing.'

"While telling his story, Merkouloff looked me straight in the face, but although his light eyes were motionless, I seemed to see the twinkle of dark fear in his grey pupils. He had folded his hands together, placed them between his knees, and was pressing them hard. For this unpremeditated crime he got a very mild punishment: his preliminary confinement was discounted and he was sent off to a monastery for penitence.

"'Over there,' Merkouloff continued, 'they appointed a little old monk to look after me. He was to teach me how to live. He was such gentle little man, who spoke of God in the finest way possible. A very fine character, he was; and like a father to me, always addressing me as: "My son, my son." Listening to him, I could not help asking myself sometimes: "Why, O God, is man so defenceless?" Then I would say to the monk, "Take yourself, Father Paul; you love God and He, most probably, loves you, too—yet I have merely to strike a blow at you and you'll die like a fly. Where then shall the gentle soul go? And the matter doesn't lie in your soul—it lies in my evil thought: I can kill you at any moment. And as a matter of fact my thought is not even an evil one. I can kill you very gently, very softly—allow you to say a prayer first, then kill you.

How do you explain that?"—But he couldn't, he only kept saying: "It's the Devil who rouses the beast in you. He's always goading you." I told him that it made no difference to me who was goading me; all I wanted him to teach me was how to avoid being goaded. "I'm not a beast," I told him, "there's nothing of the beast in me; it is only my soul that is frightened for itself."

""Pray," he said to me; "pray until you are exhausted." I did so, I got thin doing so, my temples went grey, although I was only twenty-eight at the time. But prayer could not still my fear; even during prayer I went on thinking: "Dear God, why is it? Here I can cause the death of any man at any moment, and any man can kill me at any moment he wants to! I can go to sleep and someone can draw a knife across my throat, or bring down a brick or a log on my head. Or any heavy weight. There are so many ways of doing it!" . . . These thoughts prevented me from sleeping, terrified me. At first I used to sleep with the novices, and as soon as one of them stirred, I'd jump up and shout out: "Who's fiddling about? Keep quiet, you hounds!" Everybody was afraid of me and I was afraid of everybody. They complained about me and I was sent off to the stables. There I grew quieter, with the horses—they're only soulless beasts. But all the same I only closed one eye when I slept. I was frightened.'

"After his penitence was over Merkouloff got another job as a driver, and lived in the market gardens outside the town, in a sober, detached way.

"'I lived like a man in a dream,' he told me. 'Just kept silent and avoided people. The other drivers used to ask me: "Why are you living so gloomily, Vassili? Are you preparing to take the cowl?" What should I want to take the cowl for? There are men in cloisters as well as outside them—and wherever there are men there is fear. I looked at people and thought: "God help you! Uncertain are your lives and you have no protection against me, just as I have none against you!" Just think, sir, how hard it was for me to live with such a weight on my heart.'"

Sviatoukhine sighed and adjusted the small black silk cap on his bald skull that shone like an old, bleached bone.

"At that moment, at those very words, Merkouloff smiled; and that unexpected, uncalled-for smile twisted and distorted his well-cut face so acutely that I was instantly convinced that the man was a fiend. Most probably he killed all his victims with precisely that smile. I experienced a most uncanny feeling. He continued with something like vexation in his voice:

"'So I went on walking about like a hen with an egg, the egg being rotten and I knowing it. The moment is bound to come when the egg inside me will burst, and what will happen to me then? I don't know— I daren't guess what it will be—but I can guess that it will be something terrible.'

"I asked him whether he had ever thought of committing suicide. He was silent for a moment, his eyebrows moved, and he answered: 'I can't remember—no—I don't think I ever have.' . . . Then he turned to me, wonderingly, with a look of inquiry in his eyes, and said, I think quite sincerely: 'How is it I never thought of that? That's a curious thing. . . .'

"He struck his knee with the palm of his hand, glanced vaguely at a corner of the court, and muttered pettishly:

"'Yes, yes, but don't you see, I didn't want to give my soul a free hand. I was so tormented in my heart with curiosity regarding other people and in the shameful cowardice of that soul of mine. I forgot about myself. As to my soul, it was just musing: what if I kill this fellow—what will happen then?'

"Two years later Merkouloff killed the half-witted girl Matreshka, the daughter of a gardener. He told me about her murder in a somewhat hazy manner, as though he himself hardly understood the motives of the crime. One could gather from his words that Matreshka was slightly crazy.

"'She used to have a kind of fits which blotted out her reason: she'd throw down her work of digging flower-beds or weeding and walk along smiling, with her mouth open, as though somebody unseen were beckoning to her to come. She'd knock against trees, hedges and walls, attempting to pass through them. One day she stepped on an upturned rake and hurt her foot; blood was flowing from the wound in a stream, but she still walked along, feeling no pain—didn't even wince. She was an ugly girl, very fat, and inclined to debauchery, owing to her silliness. She used to accost the peasants, and they, of course, took advantage of her silliness. She pestered me, too, with her attentions, but I had other things to think about. What fascinated me in her was the fact that nothing affected her: whether she fell into a ditch or down from a roof, she came up safe and sound. Anyone else would have sprained their foot or broken a bone, but nothing happened to her. She was all bruised and scratched, of course, but was as tough as could be. She seemed to live in absolute security.

"'I killed her in public, on a Sunday. I was sitting on a bench at the gate and she began to be amiable to me in a nasty manner—so I just struck her with a faggot. She rolled down and never moved. I glanced at her—she was dead. I sat down on the ground beside her and burst out crying: "God, oh God, what is the matter with me? Why this weakness, this helplessness?"'

"He spoke jerkily, as though in a delirium, for some time harping on the helplessness of men, and all the time a sullen fear shone in his eyes. His dry, ascetic face darkened as he said, hissing through his teeth:

"'Just you think, sir; here, at this very minute, I can strike you down dead! Just think of that! Who can forbid me to do it? What's to stop me? Nothing at all—nothing. . . .'

"He was punished for the murder of that girl by three years of prison—the mildness of the punishment being due, he explained, to the skill of his advocate—whom he did not hesitate to vilify: 'A young one, with dishevelled hair, a bawler. He kept on saying to the jury: "Who could possibly say a bad word against this man? Not one of the witnesses has been able to. Moreover it is admitted that the dead woman was half-witted and debauched." Oh, those lawyers! It's all tomfoolery, waste of time. I'll be defended from myself *before* the crime if you like, but once I've committed it I don't want anyone to help me. You can hold me while I stand still, but once I have started running you can't catch me! If I run I will go on running until I fall down with exhaustion. But prison!—tomfoolery, an idle man's job, too.

"'I came out from prison dazed—unable to understand anything. People walked past, drove past, worked, built houses, and all the time I kept thinking: "I can kill any man I choose and any man can kill me. Very terrible, this is." And it seemed as though my arms were growing, growing; becoming a stranger's arms. I started drinking, but I couldn't keep it up, it made me sick. As soon as I had had a drop too much I began to cry—hid in a dark corner and cried: "I am not a man but a maniac, there's no life for me." I drank—and didn't get drunk, and was worse than a drunkard when sober. I began to growl, growled at everyone, frightened people away, and was terrified of them. I kept thinking all the time: "Either he'll go for me, or I'll go for him."

"'And so I went on walking about, like a fly on a window-pane: the glass might break at any moment and I'd fall through, falling God knows where.

"'My boss, Ivan Kirilich, I killed for the same reason—curiosity. He was a cheerful, kind-hearted man, and wonderfully brave. When his neighbour's house was on fire he acted like an immortal hero—crawled right inside the flames to fetch out the old nurse, then back again for the nurse's trunk, just because she was crying for it. A happy man was Ivan Kirilich, God rest his soul. It is true that I tortured him a bit. The others I killed at once, but I tortured Ivan—I waited to see whether he would be frightened or not. Well, he had a weak constitution and was strangled very rapidly. People came running up at his cries, and wanted to beat and tie me up. But I said to them: "You'd better tie up my soul, not my hands, you fools!"'

"Merkouloff finished his story, wiped the perspiration from his face, and said, rather breathlessly:

"'You must punish me severely, your Honour, punish me with death, or else—what is the good of it all? I can't live with people, even in jail. I've got a crime against my soul. I'm fed up with it and afraid that I'll want to begin testing it again—and then more people will have to suffer for it. . . . You must put me away, sir, you must. . . .'"

Blinking with his dying eyes, the judge continued:

"He put himself away of his own accord—strangled himself in his cell, in a rather peculiar way—with the chains he was manacled with—the devil knows how! I didn't see it myself, but I was told about it by the governor of the prison. The latter said it needed great willpower to kill oneself in such a painful and unhandy manner. That's what he said: 'unhandy.'"

Then, closing his eyes, Sviatoukhine murmured:

"It was probably I who inspired Merkouloff with the idea of suicide. . . . Ye-es. . . . There, my dear friend, there's a simple Russian peasant for you, but all the same . . . Ye-es. . . . What do you think of it?"

BORIS SOKOLOFF

THE CRIME OF DR. GARINE

Born in St. Petersburg, Russia, Boris Sokoloff (1893–1979) devoted most of his life to biology and medicine, following his early years as a prominent socialist philosopher and writer. A prodigy, he published his first scientific study, *The Physiology of Protozoa*, at seventeen, and graduated from the University of St. Petersburg with a Doctor of Science degree at twenty. He was a professor of biology when the revolution broke out in 1917. Initially a member of forces that brought down the czar and a deputy of the convention which drafted the All-Russian Constitution, he did not agree with the Bolsheviks and fought against them. He was captured and sentenced to death but, as a doctor, was useful and transferred from one prison to another until he escaped from Russia, landing in Europe, where he worked in London, Brussels, Prague and Paris before moving permanently to America at the invitation of the Rocke-feller Institute. He also worked at Sloan-Kettering, the University of Wash-ington Cancer Research Center and was the head of the Cancer Research Laboratory at Florida Southern University. He was the editor of the scientific journal *Growth* and was the author of 27 books, mostly on cancer and other scientific subjects.

"The Crime of Dr. Garine" was first published in Russia in 1927 and in the U.S. in a collection titled *The Crime of Dr. Garine* (New York, Covici-Friede, 1928). Although not known as a fiction writer, the publisher evidently regarded it as a significant book because it bears an introduction by Theodore Dreiser, one of the most important authors in America at that time.

He refused to have an attorney.

"Idle chatterers! I will defend myself," he replied to the magistrate who questioned him. To his brother, who came to see him in prison, he said:

"Why did you come here? No good can come of your visit. You have already condemned me. Nothing worse could happen." Turning his back upon him he said to the guard: "Take me back to my cell. The interview is ended."

The crime of Dr. Garine had aroused general indignation, not only in his own city, but all over the country.

Public opinion loudly demanded the death penalty; "He is a brute, a beast, a madman who must be put out of the way."

Dimitrieff, the eminent psychologist, who had a short interview with the accused man, refused to take part in the proceedings: "He was rude, insulting, and even ridiculed my profession: 'Psychiatry, a science? Rather a collection of stupid anecdotes without which we could get along very nicely.' This was too much for me. He may be ill, I admit; but in spite of this, I do not see how he could have gone so far as to lose all sense of values. I prefer to make no definite statements."

The session of the Criminal Court of Riga opened at A—— one warm day in June.

A large crowd of people, who had come by boat from points all along the coast, completely filled the court room. Newspaper reporters and doctors were especially in evidence.

The accusation which was read, as usual, in a monotone, gave the details of a frightful murder.

The assembly expressed unanimous condemnation of the atrocious crime: "The prisoner is not a man, not even a beast, for no beast would have been so cruel." Even the criminal himself admitted this cynically.

"But why did he kill her?"

"If he could recall her to life, he would repeat the crime."

"What a monster!"

"Death for him! The most terrible tortures would be too good for him!"

The women in the audience were especially bitter in their denunciations, and unreservedly expressed their sentiments and their impressions after having heard the details of the autopsy findings.

"Prisoner at the bar."

The prisoner arose. "George Garine, age thirty years, doctor of medicine."

Orthodox, according to his passport.

"Married, no children."

Married! What irony!

"Was married," corrected the attorney severely.

The accused man shrugged his shoulders. "If you prefer; but what difference does it make?" and he sat down.

Then, as if suddenly remembering something, he arose again, and in a calm but aggressive voice said to the presiding judge:

"But why this comedy? You take it upon yourselves to judge me, who am already a condemned man in my own eyes. What right have you? What has attracted this crowd of embittered interlopers? What do you know about that which you commonly call a crime of passion? Suppose that I denied having killed her, my dear cherished wife whom I daily loved more and more. Suppose that I denied this, what would you know about it? I, a criminal! Empty words, stupid phrases! I, a criminal! Knowing you and your kind, I know full well what your verdict will be. Although I may not agree with you, I am here before you, ready to accept anything as another part of my Calvary." He sat down.

"Prisoner" . . .

Doctor Garine continued his story very slowly and deliberately, almost as though speaking to himself.

"Your Honor, do not interrupt me. Your nasal voice makes me nervous . . . well . . . she whom I killed . . . moaned something which remains ever with me ... sometimes it sounds like the droning of a bee, sometimes like a tolling bell at twilight! 'Forever—forever.' Do you know what she meant?" He was silent for a time. Then—"It is difficult for me to speak to-day. Perhaps another time."

The Chief of Police, Kotomkine, when called to the stand, declared that on the night of June 23rd he was awakened by the ringing of his telephone. Being very tired, having been on duty all evening at the celebration of a feast which had been organized by the inhabitants of the island, he took up the receiver most unwillingly. He heard the calm voice of a man.

"Good evening, Chief. Dr. Garine speaking. Will you please come to my house. I have just killed my wife."

Ten minutes later, Kotomkine, followed by his assistants, rang at the door of Dr. Garine's home. This was at two o'clock in the morning. No one replied. They entered the house and found the body of Mrs. Garine, the victim, lying on the bedroom floor.

She was clothed in a Japanese dressing-gown, which had been torn to shreds, and the terrified expression of the face presented a startling picture. Her face, her shoulders, and her arms bore traces of tooth marks, and were covered with blood. One eye had been put out and her right arm lay broken and deformed. Her throat gave evidence of strangulation, and the terribly bruised larynx showed the unusual strength of the murderer.

It required but an instant to discover that the victim had been ravished while dying or perhaps when already dead. The bruises, the echymoses, were more terrible than anything the witness had ever seen.

"Proceeding into the dressing-room," continued the policeman, "I found Dr. Garine seated before the mirror. He had just finished shaving. The expression on his face was extraordinary; he looked like a mask carved in stone. He calmly and politely asked me to wait until he had finished dressing, saying, 'Just a moment, I beg of you, sir. I am ill when I am unshaven. My bag is packed and I am ready to go to prison.'"

The murderer's testimony was brief.

"Yes, I killed her. I refuse to explain the motive. I remember nothing of the details."

He allowed himself to be led to prison without assistance. His correct manner was weirdly inhuman.

At the request of the prosecuting attorney, the policeman was asked to give any information he might have concerning the prisoner, whom he had known for about three years. At the completion of his testimony the man expressed his doubts as to the sanity of the prisoner, saying:

"During the journey from his home to the prison, Your Honor, he stopped suddenly and whispered to me confidentially, 'Do you hear the rolling wheels? It is the rhythm of life. I wanted to get away from it, but, vanquished, I return. The rolling of wheels——'"

Then came the testimony of Dr. Levitsky, Dr. Garine's young assistant. He was a handsome boy, slightly effeminate, with light hair, and a bit of down on his upper lip.

He was greatly embarrassed, and flushed deeply as he replied to the questions of the judge and of the prosecuting attorney.

"I live at the laboratory, about two kilometers from the Garines' home. On the evening of the twenty-third we had dined together to celebrate the feast of St. John. Mrs. Garine was very gay and happy. We danced together at the café. And the doctor joined in our merriment. He spoke of his life in South America. I returned home at about eleven o'clock after having accompanied Dr. and Mrs. Garine to their house. I undressed slowly and had great difficulty in getting to sleep.

"At one o'clock—I remember perfectly—I was awakened by an unusual noise in the laboratory. Fearing burglars, I grabbed a revolver and opened the laboratory door. Dr. Garine was standing near the thermostat with his back turned to me and was transplanting cultures. At the sound of my footsteps he turned around and gave his orders even more abruptly than usual. 'Culture A has been verified. I have finished the staining of culture B, which is very satisfactory. Here is a new case of tuberculous leprosy in which I have been able to make an exact diagnosis. Everything is in order. Be sure to give the exact dosage of injections.'

"His every word is firmly fixed in my mind. Then, looking straight into my eyes with a peculiar expression, he said to me: 'I entrust to you this little piece of work which is indispensable to humanity.' He placed his hand on my shoulder, and in an exceedingly clear and firm voice, added, 'I have just killed Nina. Forgive me, my friend, forgive me.' He kissed my forehead and abruptly left the laboratory. My strength failed me and I could not follow him. Later, I found myself in an armchair in my room."

In concluding his testimony, the witness dwelt at length and in great detail upon the doctor's scientific research work.

He had known him for almost three years and had found him to be an extraordinarily energetic man, with a calm, thoughtful disposition. The scientific world of Europe was unanimous in proclaiming his worth. His recent discoveries were exceedingly important. He had found a new method of diagnosis for the especially virulent type of tuberculous leprosy, and had discovered its contagiousness. He was a man of rare merit and of touching benevolence.

"Pardon me, Doctor," interrupted the judge, "what do you know of the family life of the prisoner and of his relations with the victim?"

Levitsky flushed suddenly and stuttered timidly in great confusion:

"Excellent relations, of course."

"Forgive me again, Doctor, but I have been told that you were on very intimate terms with Mrs. Garine."

"Not at all, not at all, your Honor," replied the witness, greatly embarrassed. "There was nothing of this kind. I admit that I was filled with respectful affection for Mrs. Garine. That was all, I swear it!"

"Is it true," asked the prosecuting attorney, "that you visited Mrs. Garine daily, sometimes even twice daily when her husband was away? Is it also true . . ."

"Levitsky," interrupted the prisoner, "don't answer the inane questions of these gentlemen. Tell them to go to the devil!"

"Prisoner," shouted the judge, "another interruption and you will be conducted to your cell."

"You would only be harming yourself," mumbled the prisoner between closed teeth.

Levitsky refused to answer all further questions.

The court room waited with great curiosity for the testimony of the only servant in Dr. Garine's household. She was an Esthonian of uncertain age.

She spoke most kindly of her unusual master. The doctor had been good to her, had been most generous with her, had given her money at frequent intervals, and had sent her to her people for vacations. Mrs. Garine, too, had been the kindest of mistresses.

"I have been with them for two years and they have never even spoken an impatient word to me. And they were so attentive to each other. It was really touching to see them. If Mrs. Garine was ill, the Doctor never left her bedside; he was constantly reading to her and heaping attentions upon her. As for the young doctor, he was always with us, it is true. But I think all of his loving gazes were lost upon Mrs. Garine."

In spite of the sly cleverness of the prosecuting attorney, it was impossible to obtain any details as to the exact character of the relations which had existed between Dr. Levitsky and the victim.

On the day of the tragedy both Mrs. Garine and the doctor had seemed to be very gay and happy. In the evening, the witness had left for Riga. This ended her testimony.

The deliveryman from the grocery declared that he had often met Mrs. Garine and the young doctor walking arm in arm along shady lanes.

The same statement was made by the priest's wife, who had twice met them in the city. She had been so interested that she had stood looking at them for a long time.

The prisoner's brother, a well-known architect in Moscow, gave an excited and incoherent history of the accused man's past life.

"We were the only children. Although I was the oldest, I was always dominated by him during my childhood and youth. He was most authoritative, audacious, and dominating; much like our father, who had been a big merchant at Perm, and who had risen from poverty to millions. My brother was his favorite and was literally adored by my father. They always went to the forest and mountains together to hunt, while I remained at home with my mother. My brother was very studious and always excelled in his studies. Being vain and proud, he was very reserved and avoided all quarrels. He was very much unlike our father in this respect, and had inherited this trait from our mother, whose maiden name was Karpoffs. Her family were chemists of Perm.

"Even in his early childhood my brother sought for the manifestations of the Creator, but he did this calmly and sanely. He attended social functions regularly in the afternoon, but preferred to remain in his room in the evening. Then, gradually, without a struggle, he lost his faith."

"No, Peter, you are mistaken when you say I lost my faith without a struggle."

"Yes, yes, I remember, George, I remember. What a time for you!— It is true, he did not eat, and I often heard him moan: 'I no longer believe in Thee, O God, but I know Thee.' No exterior change was noticeable in him, however. He passed his medical examinations brilliantly. He seemed especially fitted for scientific work. Politics did not interest him. His natural reserve did not allow him to make intimate friends, but he was highly esteemed by his classmates as well as by his professors. Naturally very obliging, he willingly performed little services for every one.

"He suffered cruelly through the death of our father, who died while he was still a student. He remained in his room for a week without taking any food, and refused to see or to speak to any one. This astonished us a great deal.

"When the will was opened and read, my father had left half of a fortune of several millions to my brother. But he obstinately refused to take his share of the inheritance. 'You and mother keep it, or build schools with it.' He accepted only a very small part of the fortune, and left for Petersburg.

"He passed his medical examinations not only brilliantly, but with exceptional distinction. People began to speak of him as a future scientist. He specialized in infectious diseases. He spent several years with Metchnikoff in Paris, then returned to Petersburg, where he was besieged by the ill and suffering.

"We scarcely ever heard from him; about three times a year. They were short, strange notes, in which he often spoke of our dead father, such as: 'Yesterday, while I was alone in my room, I thought of our father. Do you remember his well-known dear smile?'

"One day we heard that he had forsaken his work and his patients to fight an epidemic of eruptive typhus. Then he enlisted in the Russo-Japanese war, where he fought another epidemic.

"It was here that he distinguished himself, was wounded, and fell a victim to typhus. He recovered from this and came home for a period of rest.

"He had become more taciturn than ever, but also more thoughtful towards my wife and our old mother.

"He enjoyed talking to our priest, a learned man who led a very Christian life.

"At this time there began to be rumors of a revolution in Russia, but my brother refused to have anything to do with it: not because he was hostile to the cause, or a reactionary, but because he was indifferent to politics.

"Sometimes he liked to speak of human vanity, and tried to convince our priest that the lives of the saints were not free from it.

"People clamored for him at Petersburg, where he had been offered an important position. But my brother announced his intention of going to South America, much to our surprise and sorrow. 'What funny people you are,' said he to my mother with a smile which I still remember well. 'Must we not, each one of us, live our own lives, and find out where its harmony lies for us? Well, then, I must get away from the humdrum of daily existence. I must get away from hereditary influences.'

"These were literally his words. 'I must get away from hereditary influences.'

"From America we received one letter; but such a curious one. 'For hundreds of miles around me, it would be impossible to find one soul caught in the snares of daily routine. Here is another world, a people whose language is simple and primitive, who live only in the present hour. I have found peace of mind. This peace of mind and of soul I owe to my friends here. I am living life. I have attained the height of my desires. I have forgotten the meanness of trivialities.'

"We understood nothing in this letter.

"Suddenly, after spending six years in the forests of Brazil he returned to us unexpectedly. This was six years ago.

"He entertained us with tales of his life in South America, speaking enthusiastically in a language all his own. He told us of the morals and the customs of these primitive people among whom he had lived. But he never breathed a word about himself.

"Several weeks after his return, he accepted the position of chief physician to the leper colony.

"My mother and I were horrified. From this time on we heard no more from him.

"Through his associates, we heard of his marriage, of his devotion to his wife, and of a series of important discoveries which had made him famous in the scientific world.

"Then, suddenly, I learned of this tragedy through the newspapers. I hastened here immediately.

"My brother refused to see me.

"This is all I have to say."

The testimony of Peter Garine, which presented the murderer as a good, noble man, threw the court room into confusion, almost into anger.

Peter Garine's unquestionable sincerity left no room for doubt.

The prisoner himself listened indifferently to his brother's testimony, with half-closed eyes, but with clenched hands.

—"Pardon me, sir," said the foreman of the jury, "can you recall in the prisoner's past life any sudden burst of anger, any loss of self-control, or any acts of unusual cruelty?"

"Two occasions, gentlemen, remain firmly fixed in my mind. I have twice seen my brother, whose behavior was usually so faultlessly correct, beside himself with anger.

"The first time we were passing a tavern. I remember it was on a Saturday, when our attention was attracted by the yelping of a very young, half-blind dog, which had lost its mother. Two intoxicated young men came out of the tavern. They were in a very hilarious mood. One of them, seeing the poor beast, crushed its head with a savage kick, and uttering a frightful oath said:

"'That for you, you dirty little beast! Get out of my way!'

"My brother became livid when he saw this. His face assumed a terrible expression which I had never seen before; he threw himself upon the brute, sent him to earth with a terrific blow, and began to wring his neck in frenzied rage. He was fourteen years old at this time.

"The second time we were at Moscow.

"A policeman from the vice squad was beating a woman of the streets, who was greatly intoxicated. Covered with blood, unable to walk, she was trying to escape. Another terrible blow in the back sent the poor, muttering creature to the pavement.

"My brother, then a physician, seemed petrified. Suddenly he hurled himself upon the policeman, and after having knocked him down, began to stamp on him and kick him, uttering savage cries as he did so. We hushed up the affair with difficulty, and when I reproached him for his summary procedure in administering justice, he replied with an matic smile: 'It is the rebellion of the soul.'"

Then followed passages from the murdered woman's diary. These only confirmed the great, deep harmony which had existed between husband and wife. There was no word, no hint of any misunderstanding between them, not even in the last lines, which had been written on the day of her death.

Mrs. Garine, who had been married once before, had met Dr. Garine about two years previous to our story, under circumstances which had made a deep impression upon the young woman. She had been the spoiled, pleasure-loving wife of a captain of the Guards, and had been very prominent socially.

June 6th, 1910.

Last night I had an experience from which I have not yet recovered. Coming home rather late from a visit at the V—— home, I was walking along a narrow street when I heard steps behind me. I hastened my steps; my pursuers did the same. I could hear them whisper. I had almost reached the boulevards when two men attacked me from behind. I must have cried out in terror. The next thing I remember, my two aggressors were lying on the ground with battered faces, and my unexpected protector was putting on his silk hat and his overcoat.

I cannot forget how very calm he seemed. He bowed very formally to me and was about to go on his way. I begged him: "For Heaven's sake, take me to my door; it isn't very far."

He took my hand which I had held out to him, pressed it slightly as though it bored him to do so, and said: "I am Dr. Garine." Then something happened, the thought of which I had always ridiculed up to this time. Although I could not distinguish his features clearly, I felt that we were not strangers. He walked along beside me without speaking and was going to leave me without a word. "Thanks, thanks very much," I stammered. He raised his hat and said to me coldly and indifferently: "I am afraid you are losing your head. Don't do it. Good night, Madame."

June 17th.

I have told my husband everything.

I also asked him about Dr. Garine. It seems that he is a rather well-known scientist who lives alone and who seldom attends social functions. I asked my husband to go and thank him for having come to my aid.

June 23rd.

Tania and I went to see the fireworks in honor of the feast of St. John. We were bored, although there was a large crowd in the public gardens, and were just about to leave the place when we ran into Dr. Garine.

"Oh, Doctor!"

He hesitated, then bowed silently as though he had no desire to enter upon a conversation. I insisted, however, on his going to a café with us, where we spent the whole evening with him. He proved to be a brilliant conversationalist, and joked about the battle the other evening, in which I was the martyr and he the hero. He has an expressive face, an energetic mouth, and rather a heavy chin. I am glad he is smooth shaven. He scarcely looked at me, but he was very attentive to Tania. My cousin is very pretty.

July 10th.

We meet Dr. Garine occasionally. His attitude towards me is always discreetly correct. It is hard to believe that he really made that peculiar statement to me the first time we met. He is a man of great culture and is wonderfully intelligent. At times he is charmingly good-natured; at others, he is indifferent and taciturn and it is almost impossible to drag a word out of him. He pays absolutely no attention to me. I do not exist for him. I will admit that he troubles me and interests me very much, and that things seem wrong if I do not see him regularly.

July 25th.

My husband does not like Dr. Garine and tries to be most disagreeable to him. Dr. Garine is perfectly indifferent to this. I have never, in all my life, met a man so completely master of himself.

August 1ˢᵗ.

I passed last evening tête-à-tête with Dr. Garine. Contrary to his customary attitude, he surprised me by his unusual gentleness and thoughtfulness. He told me of his life in Paraguay. I am entering one of his statements in my diary. "Europeans pride themselves on their intelligence. A great deal of good it does them! True, they may be more developed than the primitive races, but the latter are unquestionably more vividly alive. They have made me understand the meaning of love, which is life!"

I did not ask him to explain what he meant.

August 20th.

An unbelievable thing happened to-day, which has completely upset me.

I have locked myself in my room, a prey to an awful presentiment.

We had Dr. Garine to dinner with us. The conversation turned to medicine, and my husband, as usual, tried to pick a quarrel with the doctor, saying: "Medicine is a fraud, and doctors are impostors." The doctor listened calmly to my husband's impertinences and continued peeling his apple. Finally, still intent upon his apple, he asked: "Dimitri Nikolaevitch, are you a brave man?" My husband was disconcerted for a moment, then replied angrily: "Certainly. I wear the Cross of St. George."

"That doesn't mean anything. I can't understand you; why this subterfuge? Do you fear the truth?"

"I don't know what you are talking about."

"Just a moment. You will know what I am talking about. You try to anger me in many different ways. Why? Naturally you are jealous. But you anticipate. No word of love has ever passed between your wife and myself. But, if you insist"—he smiled and put a piece of apple in his mouth—"there is only one thing left for you to do: that is to yield. I love Nina Petrovna."

"And she?" demanded my husband in a thick voice.

"And she," he replied calmly, "loves me. It cannot be otherwise."

"Nina, is this true?" My husband grasped my wrists. I was almost unconscious, could not say a word. My husband grabbed his revolver and rushed upon Garine. "Get out, you dog, or I'll kill you," he screamed savagely. Garine, as though trying to exasperate my husband, took another apple and started to cut it into pieces.

"Evidently, Dimitri Nikolaevitch, we are going to have a duel. It is rather a primitive way of settling an argument, but I am an advocate of primitive life. Only, I warn you, I will kill you. I see death written upon your face."

My husband, beside himself with rage, seized the doctor's shoulder, and I covered my face, expecting to hear a shot. But the doctor had seized Dimitri's arm and held it with such force as to cause him to drop the revolver. Then, slowly, authoritatively, he forced him into a chair, and left the house without a word.

September 10th.

I have not touched my diary for three weeks. Life is so strangely changed for me during this time that I sometimes believe that I am in a dream.

My husband and Garine have fought the duel. The doctor's assistant told me about it.

Garine exacted the most difficult conditions. Thirteen paces, and the mortal injury of one of the adversaries. Garine fired the first shot. An excellent shot, he wounded my husband's right arm, which forced Dimitri to fire with his left hand. This was a great disadvantage.

I know Dimitri did not want to kill Garine, as he said to me the evening before, as he left me, "If only I don't kill him!" Firing with his left hand, the shot was almost fatal. The ball had grazed the heart.

Garine fell.

"Dress the wound and give me a hypodermic. The duel will continue."

The assistant gave him an injection of morphine and ergotine.

"Even if my heart has been touched, I will live."

He was livid. His hand trembled with weakness.

"My whole being rebels at this butchery, but it must be done," said Dimitri.

"Fire more quickly!" said one of my husband's seconds.

"It is ended. I can't see," exclaimed Garine.

The assistant gave him an intravenous injection. He arose and fired, almost without aiming, then sank into unconsciousness.

For three weeks he hovered between life and death. I did not leave him for an instant, not even to go to my husband's funeral. Nothing matters now. I could not do otherwise. I am his.

The bullet is lodged dangerously near the heart. The doctors say he is very near death's door. But he lives. He must live. He is mine, my joy, my love, my all.

He talked to me in his delirium. He said peculiar things which made me love him all the more. I now partially understand this strange, distant being. Sometimes his words seem to be the only thing that matters.

"Do you hear the rolling of the wheels? Do you see the cable, the glowing water? I am heart-sick; I know what the wheels are saying. She laughs at them and at life.

"I am far, far away . . . and I laugh.

"I hear the sound of falling water . . . and I laugh.

"Love is all that remains. I see the narrow passage and hear the rolling wheels!"

Yesterday his temperature dropped and he regained consciousness.

"Where is the bullet?"

I was troubled and did not reply.

"I am not afraid of the truth. Can it be that you do not yet understand me?"

When I told him that it was impossible to remove it, he became silent and thoughtful.

"Very well. All is well; even that I still want to live."

October 15th.

He is a strange, enigmatic person. Usually taciturn, he never laughs, but often smiles a perfectly adorable smile. Occasionally he likes to talk; then he is all enthusiasm. More often he is calm, with the calmness of self-confidence and strength.

He works incessantly; too much, I think. He arises very early and goes to his laboratory. He often writes until late at night.

I cannot become accustomed to my present life after my past existence, which was filled with social obligations and so-called gayety and pleasure. We read a great deal, and sometimes it wearies me to do this, and to follow the trend of his thoughts.

I don't know whether he loves me, because he has never spoken to me of it: I say never; yes, once. It was during his convalescence. The doctor had permitted him to sit up in a chair.

It was evening and the whole house seemed to sleep the sleep of the dead. We seemed entirely alone in the world. He began to talk:

"Fire attracts me as it did the pagans. While still a boy, ten years or twelve years old, I used to run away to the country in search of bonfires.

"I used to go to the shepherds, taking no notice of their dogs, and sit long and silently, gazing dreamily into their fires.

"Little by little I seemed to become incorporated with the names. Child that I was, home seemed to me something distant, foreign, 'fiction'."

The coals in the fire-place were a golden glow. Garine bent over, took a burning coal into his hand, held it for a moment, and then threw it back into the fireplace.

"What are you doing? Did you burn yourself?" I cried.

I took his hand. He did not withdraw it and smiled. Then, tenderly, as though talking to a little girl, he said:

"It was only a little joke, a little, innocent ruse. I wanted you to hold my hand." Then he continued:

"As I have grown older I have lost the faculty of conforming objects and things to my will.

"I have ceased to be a primitive man. My mind has developed. It has reached the limits of intellectual development accorded to Europeans. But, on the other hand, my sensibilities have become dulled; I have lost one of the most essential characteristics of the human personality, intuition. Partly, at least, if not entirely." He smiled, then continued: "In spite of this atrophy, I am infinitely more sensitive than most people. This may be attributed, I think, to my childhood. I used to spend whole days and nights alone in the forests talking to the birds and trees. They seemed to understand my language. There I had friends and enemies. The ugly old oak was my most bitter enemy. The gentle lime-tree rejoiced my wild, incomprehensible, childish soul by its charming, tender murmurs. I was a part of the forest. When I returned to the city I discovered that the humdrum of daily existence deprived me of this faculty.

"The commotion of the city; society; in short, contact with human beings distressed me.

"Later, when as a student I returned to the forest, I could hear only the grumbling noises of city life in the whisperings of the trees and the songs of the birds, which had formerly been so dear to me.

"The rhythm of daily life, the cadence of time obsessed me, because I had lost all primitive impulses, having given myself over, body and soul, to human motives. Do you understand me?"

I waited attentively for him to explain his meaning to me. He gave as an example, the life of a citizen of our day, especially in America.

"The struggle for daily existence destroys all the rhythm of life, especially for the humble."

He spoke of the sick, who would be called by death to-morrow, perhaps even to-day. "They no longer belong to life, and yet they give themselves over to the joys of existence. Pitiful, wretched creatures swaying feebly to the sounds of the barbaric organ—life."

The most insignificant of his stories struck me, I don't know why, and made a powerful impression on me.

"I was consulted by one of my cousins, an engineer. 'I am tired, exhausted,' he told me. I examined him and was greatly distressed by my findings. He was completely gone. A radioscopic examination proved his case still more serious.

"His condition called for absolute rest. He should have ceased work immediately. I did not attempt to deceive him. We could have hoped to save him by patience and care.

"He was overwhelmed, not only because of his condition, but because of the necessity for immediate rest. He continually repeated: 'I have an important business deal for to-morrow, which will bring me a large fortune.' I became angry. To the devil with money! I again tried to convince him of the absolute necessity of entering a sanitarium. He promised me that he would go.

"At the end of three days he came back to me. He was a new man.

"'My deal has succeeded. I have two or three more like this. In a week I will begin to take care of myself.'

"He stopped speaking suddenly, swayed, and fell. For two hours I remained in silence beside his dead body.

"The next day I left for the Brazilian forests of South America. The bonds of civilization pursued me even there. For three years I wandered among the most primitive, the most savage of the natives. For three years I searched for freedom. But, city life held me in its tentacles.

"I experienced a sense of intuition for the first time when I met you.

Boresome trivialities were vanquished, and my sense of premonition had recovered its vitality."

He was silent for a long time. Then he caressed my hand and murmured:

"This is what is ordinarily called love, a word which, man has profaned long ago. My sentiment is not love. No, it is not love in the sense that the word is vulgarly used."

November 20th.

He overwhelms me with his tenderness. I am troubled and afraid in spite of the fact that he is always faultlessly correct. Our attitude towards each other, and our love-making are of a peculiar nature. I cannot become accustomed to it. After the joys and sensuality of my first marriage, the austerity of our life and the gravity of our love, of this super-love, sometimes depress me. And yet, I am entirely his, his slave, and I adore him.

I am angry with myself for my statement: "His slave!"

December 5th.

I am happy to-day, perhaps for the first time in my life. All of my past love is nothing as compared to that which I experienced yesterday. It was not passion, but a storm, a tempest, a something between life and death. I wept, I sobbed, I laughed.

How I pity those who have never experienced such ecstasy!

We had friends in to dinner, and he had drunk more than usual; he is ordinarily so temperate. The wine completely changed him—his correctness, his self-control, his cold, stern attitude, all this had disappeared, and he smiled and joked with excessive gayety.

After the departure of our guests he was maddened by an insatiable desire . . . as though he were trying to drain the cup of voluptuousness. He wept and he moaned as though his soul were wounded by the excess of his feelings, then yielded anew to his passions.

December 6th.

Yesterday he was cold, and more reserved than ever. He retired to his room very early in the evening. We did not even do any reading.

December 15th.

Life has become strangely monotonous. Sometimes I think he is one of those unfathomable beings whom it is impossible to understand. I often think of our one great experience. Will I ever know it again?

January 20th, 1911.

It is cold and windy. Sometimes Dr. Levitsky, my husband's assistant, comes and helps me, to a certain extent, to overcome my ennui. He is very gay and I think perhaps he is interested in me. We go riding occasionally. On Saturdays he dines with us and spends the evening. He is fond of music and sings rather well. He is very young and flushes delightfully if I happen to touch him.

February 5th.

Yesterday, a return of his "madness" brought us very close unto death.

To death, do I say? No, to resurrection. Joy and passion brought complete satiety. It was like a descent, into fathomless depths. Time and space were as nothing, and one thing only remained—eternity.

Is it possible that only the chosen few experience this supreme joy? Is this love? Then why is he depressed, displeased, and angry with himself afterwards?

February 22nd.

I notice that I am beginning to use my husband's language. This irritates and gladdens me. "Rejoice, O Slave!"

February 26th.

Levitsky has made a declaration of love. I was amused but also touched by it. He esteems and fears my husband greatly. "I implore you not to tell your husband of this," said he after his avowal. "This must be our secret." I stroked his silken hair—how soft it is!—and promised to say nothing.

That same evening, however, I could not keep from telling him all about it.

He did not seem surprised or angry.

"Very well," said he, "Levitsky is a nice young man. Be kind to him."

This is too much. He doesn't love me at all.

February 27th.

I have reread yesterday's notes and I am ashamed of myself. My heart is filled to overflowing with love for my husband. Yet, I am bored at times. Or, rather, I have dark presentiments. It is then that Levitsky is such a help to me. With him, I can laugh; I can joke and gossip; I can scold him and tease him.

Sometimes, I wonder whether I am happy.

March 10th.

Never, even in my innermost soul, not even in the moments of our most intimate tenderness, do I call him "George." However, I speak of Levitsky as Leon all of the time, whether he is present or not. My husband finds this entirely natural.

March 22nd.

Yesterday, Garine became very talkative while we were alone. "I cannot conceive of a future," he told me in a calm, indifferent voice. Sometimes I have the impression that he is dissatisfied with himself, at others, that he is not of this world. Just like every one else who knows him, I am surprised at the formidable amount of work he does.

When he comes home joyful and happy, I know that one of his experiments has succeeded, or that he is satisfied with a diagnosis he has made.

Yesterday, he was very enthusiastic. I heard him say several times: "Is it possible that I have succeeded!" He is experimenting with a serum, but I don't know what it is all about.

March 24th.

I have just returned from a long ride on horseback with our young friend. What a glorious spring day it has been! The stupid boy made love to me again. I became angry and threatened to tell my husband. He became very pale but said nothing. When he left me he implored fearfully: "Do not, I beg of you, speak of this to the Doctor."

April 6th.

Leon and I go riding almost daily. He is really a delightful boy, and so devoted to George. He never tires of talking about him. He considers him a great scientist. His patients, too, adore my husband.

Yesterday we were out riding and stopped for a moment under a large pine tree to let the horses rest. Leon seized my hands and made violent love to me. I feel sorry for the poor boy. He has beautiful, dark blue eyes, half hidden by long black lashes. He is twenty-six years old, a year and two months older than myself. He is alone in the world. The poor dear!

April 15th.

I have spent very few evenings with my husband lately. Sometimes Leon and I go to Riga to a concert or a dance. My husband often makes us go out and amuse ourselves. He is overwhelmed with work at the leper hospital, which has recently been enlarged. He has almost no leisure.

Several days ago he asked me whether Leon didn't bore me. I felt guilty. Perhaps I *am* spending too much time with him.

April 28th.

G. has been more reserved than ever for several days. He has had no "madness" for a long time. He is always infinitely kind and tender to me, however. I was slightly ill very recently. He left his work completely and did not leave my bedside during the whole week I was in bed. His dear eyes never left my face.

He never speaks of love, but his silence means more to me than the most eloquent language.

I am his; entirely and eternally his.

To leave him, or to cease to love him, would be absolutely impossible.

His slave! So be it! I have grown accustomed to the thought. Yes, a thousand times—his slave!

April 29th.

He was thoughtful all morning, and his silence oppressed me. This evening, when he returned from the laboratory he was more attentive than I had ever before seen him. He kissed my hands in a most unusual manner. "Listen," he said, "remember to-day well, because, to-day, the rhythm of life has demanded its tribute from me. Life has exacted its ransom. Is it possible that you cannot save me?"

He smiled as he said this. I did not understand what he meant. He smiled again as he kissed my hands a second time.

May 2nd.

Levitsky is madly in love. The poor youngster. He complains of being unable to work, of being nervous, and of being unable to sleep. I am so sorry for him. But what can I do?

May 4th.

To-day G. and I had a talk about Levitsky. It was he who opened the conversation. "Pardon me, Nina, I want to speak to you about our friend, my pupil Levitsky. He is thin. He no longer works. Don't you think he loves you too much?" He laughed good-naturedly as he said this.

I, too, laughed, but I was hurt and disappointed. I don't understand myself. This evening I had a fit of weeping and came to my room without saying goodnight to Garine.

May 15th.

The weather has been glorious for several days. I spend long hours on the beach in silent meditation, listening to the cries of the sea-gulls. They are in continuous, harmonious conversation with the waves. Their existence is one long cadence; their only diversion is love. The word-cries of these creatures are as enigmatic as they are full of rhythm.

Yesterday my husband surprised me here. He crept up to me, and I was astonished at his tenderness. It was more marked than ever.

Am I not his slave? I have yielded all that it is possible for a woman to give—her soul.

Love, a woman's love, is something bigger and better than a man's. It is an incontestable fact that "true" love is the love upon whose altar the soul immolates itself.

Is it a sacrifice? Empty words! No, it is not immolation, it is dedication.

A man's love is different. Whence comes this strange, incomprehensible difference? Is not everything in the world, in life, based upon love? Why is it then that true, absolute love does not exist? Among the myriads of mankind, only a few chosen ones have known this love, and I am one of those. But do I appreciate it? I want to weep all of the time recently. Everything seems like dupery and falsehood to me, and I am not proud of the possession of absolute love.

He remained with me for a long lime. Then turning his head away from me, as though he were displeased about something, he said:

"I was busily at work when I felt your mental torture. You do not believe me? Very well. For you the hour has not yet come to say as I did: 'I no longer believe in you, My God, but I feel your presence.'"

Suddenly he jumped up, picked me up in his arms and carried me home. He kissed me the whole way.

May 30th.

I cannot forget the terrible thing that has happened. I cry out at night, a victim to awful, suffocating nightmares.

I waken my husband and the servant. I have fits of weeping. I can no longer live here. I can no longer bear it. I know this is stupid, but when I think of that horrible mask with bared teeth, my strength fails me.

It happened several days ago on a beautifully bright Sunday morning. I was happy, and the whole world seemed gloriously beautiful; even the cries of the gulls which had recently irritated me.

My husband, unusually gay and talkative, was speaking of forests in glowing terms.

"What do we know of the trees, so silent for us, of their profound and luminous life? They love—for life cannot exist without love. Love is the basis, the reason for life. And yet, for us, the trees are mute and inanimate."

Suddenly we heard cries. In the road, we saw a human being bounding towards us.

Seeing my husband, he threw himself at his feet, and in a lamentable state of excitement, cried out: "Oh, Doctor, save me!" I could not see his face. I drew nearer and must have cried out as I lost consciousness.

The next thing I remember, I was in my room. I begged my husband to tell me what had happened. But he refused to speak and seemed troubled and unhappy.

Yesterday Levitsky told me all about it. It is a most unusual and tragic tale of love.

The man, a rising young attorney—the woman, refined, gracious, and wondrously beautiful—after an exquisite honeymoon lasting two years came the monstrous tragedy. He contracted leprosy. He did not hide his condition. How could he have done so!

Bravely, uncomplainingly, and tearlessly she tried to comfort him, as only one who loves can. But he was disconsolate.

It was necessary for them to go to the Isle of E———. There, in a comfortable little place, they lived near the leper hospital for five years. The illness continued its ravages and his face had long ago become infected; and she—submitted to her fate. Not only did she submit to, but she defied fate. I rebel at the thought of it, I cannot understand it. Is this love? Not only does she continue to live under the same roof with him, but she continues to be . . .

Ugh! A leper's caresses.

I am filled with unspeakable horror. This cannot be love, because love cannot exist in the face of annihilation.

His face was a mask; an inhuman, terrifying mask.

How I hate him! Not only does he impose upon her his horrible caresses, but he is ferociously jealous, thus making her life a martyrdom.

Stupid, stupid woman!

How can any one dare to call this love!

In a frenzy of jealousy he had threatened to kill his wife, then dashed out of the house like a madman, crying out in despair: "Save me! Save her! She is a saint! But I must live!"

This has been going on for years.

When will it end?

I should like to see the poor woman, but I haven't the strength to overcome my fear of the man's horrible face.

June 13th.

The dear boy! He blushes so prettily when my hand happens to touch his. This amuses me a great deal, and I often tease him in order to see his confusion. How awkward he is when he kisses my hand! I try to imagine him in a love scene. I heard his confession the other day, asking him whether he had had many adventures.

"No! What are you thinking of?" said he, in a frightened voice.

Can it be possible that he has not yet had a liaison? How curious and amusing!

G. complains, jokingly of course, that Levitsky mixes up his laboratory cultures and other nasty things. Last Saturday Garine wouldn't let the poor boy eat his dinner in peace. It seems that he is responsible for some terrible disaster. A rabbit is dead on account of it. How I laughed.

June 15th.

Levitsky and I passed the whole day together on the beach. We went in bathing, and I pretended to drown in order to see him dash out to save me. Oh, but it was fun! He has a splendid body and fine, transparent skin. The down on his face is too amusing! He talked continuously about his love. And I—laughed and threatened to tell my husband.

June 17th.

Yesterday we experienced our "madness." Life is worth living for that alone. Everything seems unimportant and superfluous beside the ecstasy. Hours seem like fractions of seconds, and life a passing dream.

What is the power of this strange man?

He is everything to me. I do not count. He means more than all the world to me. I long to spend long hours kissing his dear feet, not even his feet, but his footsteps.

But do I love him? Often his presence oppresses me, and I feel as though there were an immense rock hanging over me, threatening to crush me.

June 23rd.

We are going out to dance. Levitsky is going with us. We have had champagne. My husband is in a playful mood. Our "madness" is lying in wait for us.

The court room awaited Dr. Garine's reply in feverish anxiety. The judge and the jury were visibly disappointed by the testimony. The motive of this frightful drama seemed more obscure, more incomprehensible than ever.

When Garine began to speak the silence was so great that the place seemed to be deserted.

A small detail had been noticed and discussed, especially by the women. It was the excessive, studied fastidiousness and elegance of the murderer's clothing.

"Your Honor, Gentlemen of the Jury," his voice rang out severely, solemnly. "You are united here to-day to judge me of a crime committed in the heat of passion.

"You want to understand the motive for an act as terrible as it was cruel. I will be brief, very brief. Everything leads me to believe that the tragedy of which I am the principal author will remain to most of you, even after I have made all explanations, as strange and as incomprehensible as it is at the present moment.

"A very simple, unimportant incident impressed me many years ago.

"I was working in my room when my attention was attracted by cries in the court-yard.

"A group of janitors, stupid passers-by and inhabitants of our flat had crowded around a woman stretched out upon the snow. I went out, bent over the woman who was already dead, and recognized my aunt.

"Fate had been extraordinarily commonplace.

"For thirty years this woman had waited in poverty and misery for her heritage from her sister. What a life she had led for thirty years! She had been her sister's nurse and had been the victim of her brutal insults. Finally, her torturer died. She inherited the money. Liberated at last, she ran, yes *ran* to get to her own home and fell, stricken at her doorstep.

"An insignificant story! And yet. . . . Since then, I have seen thousands and thousands of sick people pass before me, many of whom were doomed and dying. But, even among those who were most seriously ill, I found some, victims of the rhythm of life, who were held fast by the tentacles of humdrum daily existence.

"The rhythm of life!

"It is possible that you do not hear it?

"Are not you its most servile, most docile, most attentive and most devoted slaves?

"The greater the depth and the extent of life, the more terrible is the power of its rhythm. Yes—terrible. Not every one can free himself."

Garine was silent for a moment, then continued in a dull voice, as though he were talking to himself.

"We men cannot find it again. Most of us are miserable pawns upon the chess-board of life, moved by the sounds of life's barbarism.

"Is not existence a vain, or almost vain, effort forcibly to extract human superiority from daily trivialities? The story of my own life, as you have just heard it, demonstrates this only too well.

"In my hatred for daily trivialities, I worked indefatigably to tear myself away from common, everyday life.

"A longing for harmony and freedom of soul had been born in me.

"I left everything. I fled to the mountains, to the deserts, to tropical forests. For long months I wandered among savage, primitive tribes But in vain!

"The rhythm of life pursued me. It formed a part of my innermost being.

"Vanquished, having lost all hope of evading the bogs of stagnation, I returned.

"I turned to these men, who, it seemed to me, had lost everything. Imagine my rebellion when I found that even these human wrecks, these victims of leprosy, are bound to life just as firmly as those who live across the sea which separates them from the world.

"In analyzing their psychology and their mode of living, I came to understand many things which had escaped my attention up to this time.

"Then suddenly came love; more than love, because that which I experienced is given to few.

"My longing for harmony, my desire for real liberty, must have been so great that it became the life-giving force of my love.

"It would be wrong to call this happiness. No language of mankind could express the delirium of my sentiments. This delirium was the only thing which could free me from my bonds.

"The celestial harmony had been established."

Garine was silent for a moment.

Then he continued in a scarcely perceptible voice, which sounded like the heavy steps of a condemned man.

"Recently, very recently, I noticed that my body had become covered with spots. There could be no doubt. Leprosy! The most cruel manifestation of tuberculous leprosy!

"This discovery awakened me to reality.

"I did not go into frenzy. I did not lose courage—I was on the point of discovering a cure. But the illness progressed rapidly. I could no longer hide it from my wife. Nor did I have the right to do so. Not doubting I would find a cure, everything seemed simple to me. But I had forgotten one thing. Her horror of the illness. Having thought of everything else I had omitted the one essential thing.

"I was happy that evening.

"A wave of passion rose up in me, transmitted itself to my wife, to our home, to the whole world.

"I forgot my illness.

"I rose to mountainous heights, to snowy fields of flowering stars, and, suddenly a cry.

"'Spots! What are they?'

"I, or rather, some one in me calmly replied;

" 'Leprosy!'

"A void, a second, a millionth part of a second separates my soul from that which followed.

"I was carried away by a delirium of savage, bestial ardor.

"Fear of my illness!

"A feeling that I was riding to doom, that I was losing Her, that I was dropping into an abyss, that I was losing 'The Harmony of Life!'

"I was carried away by this wave of delirium in which love and passion are as one. . . .

"I awakened beside the dead body of my wife.

"It was all ended.

"Stern reality took hold of me.

"I dressed, and went to the laboratory to inspect the work.

"You know the rest.

"I judged myself, I inflicted upon myself the verdict of 'Guilty.'"

Garine arose, removed his collar and bared his breast.

It was covered with angry looking, flaming eruptions.

THE OVERCOAT

To understand the importance of "The Overcoat" in the history of Russian literature, one merely needs to know Fyodor Dostoevsky's quote: "We all come out of Gogol's 'Overcoat'." It is, on the surface, a story of a simple crime: the theft of an expensive coat that had been the prized possession of a poor, simple clerk. It can be read at many levels, and often is seen as a form of protest against society. The protagonist's name is meant to show that he is a virtual non-entity, a despised and lowly part of society, with Akaky being clearly derived from the Russian word "kaka," which means excrement.

"The Overcoat" (sometimes translated as "The Cloak") has served as the basis for a significant number of Russian films, as well as a 1952 Italian film; a 1954 American television production for the *Douglas Fairbanks, Jr.* series titled *The Awakening* in which Buster Keaton played the hapless little bureaucrat; a 1997 Greek film; and a 2001 Canadian made-for-television production. It was adapted into a play by the French mime Marcel Marceau in 1951 (which was filmed the same year) and, in 1953, a stage play by Wolf Mankowitz titled *The Bespoke Overcoat*, which in turn was adapted for film two years later, with the setting moved to London.

"The Overcoat" is often listed as having its first appearance in 1842, but it was first published in Russia in 1835 in a story collection titled *St. Petersburg Stories*. It was translated into English by Constance Garnett in 1922.

THE OVERCOAT

n the department of—but it is better not to mention the department. There is nothing more irritable than departments, regiments, courts of justice, and, in a word, every branch of public service. Each individual attached to them nowadays thinks all society insulted in his person. Quite recently a complaint was received from a justice of the peace, in which he plainly demonstrated that all the imperial institutions were going to the dogs, and that the Czar's sacred name was being taken in vain; and in proof he appended to the complaint a romance in which the justice of the peace is made to appear about once every ten lines, and sometimes in a drunken condition. Therefore, in order to avoid all unpleasantness, it will be better to describe the department in question only as a certain department.

So, in a certain department there was a certain official—not a very high one, it must be allowed—short of stature, somewhat pock-marked, red-haired, and short-sighted, with a bald forehead, wrinkled cheeks, and a complexion of the kind known as sanguine. The St. Petersburg climate was responsible for this. As for his official status, he was what is called a perpetual titular councillor, over which, as is well known, some writers make merry, and crack their jokes, obeying the praiseworthy custom of attacking those who cannot bite back.

His family name was Bashmatchkin. This name is evidently derived from "bashmak" (shoe); but when, at what time, and in what manner, is not known. His father and grandfather, and all the Bashmatchkins, always wore boots, which only had new heels two or three times a year. His name was Akakiy Akakievitch. It may strike the reader as rather singular and far-fetched, but he may rest assured that it was by no means far-fetched, and that the circumstances were such that it would have been impossible to give him any other.

THIS IS HOW IT CAME ABOUT

Akakiy Akakievitch was born, if my memory fails me not, in the evening of the 23rd of March. His mother, the wife of a Government official and

a very fine woman, made all due arrangements for having the child bap-
tised. She was lying on the bed opposite the door; on her right stood the
godfather, Ivan Ivanovitch Eroshkin, a most estimable man, who served
as presiding officer of the senate, while the godmother, Anna Semenovna
Byelobrushkova, the wife of an officer of the quarter, and a woman of
rare virtues. They offered the mother her choice of three names, Mokiya,
Sossiya, or that the child should be called after the martyr Khozdazat.
"No," said the good woman, "all those names are poor." In order to please
her they opened the calendar to another place; three more names
appeared, Triphiliy, Dula, and Varakhasiy. "This is a judgment," said the old
woman. "What names! I truly never heard the like. Varada or Varukh
might have been borne, but not Triphiliy and Varakhasiy!" They turned
to another page and found Pavsikakhiy and Vakhtisiy. "Now I see," said
the old woman, "that it is plainly fate. And since such is the case, it will
be better to name him after his father. His father's name was Akakiy, so
let his son's be Akakiy too." In this manner he became Akakiy
Akakievitch. They christened the child, whereat he wept and made a grimace, as though he foresaw that he was to be a titular councillor.

In this manner did it all come about. We have mentioned it in order
that the reader might see for himself that it was a case of necessity, and
that it was utterly impossible to give him any other name. When and
how he entered the department, and who appointed him, no one could
remember. However much the directors and chiefs of all kinds were
changed, he was always to be seen in the same place, the same attitude,
the same occupation; so that it was afterwards affirmed that he had been
born in undress uniform with a bald head. No respect was shown him
in the department. The porter not only did not rise from his seat when
he passed, but never even glanced at him, any more than if a fly had
flown through the reception-room. His superiors treated him in coolly
despotic fashion. Some sub-chief would thrust a paper under his nose
without so much as saying, "Copy," or "Here's a nice interesting affair,"
or anything else agreeable, as is customary amongst well-bred officials.

And he took it, looking only at the paper and not observing who handed it to him, or whether he had the right to do so; simply took it, and set about copying it.

The young officials laughed at and made fun of him, so far as their official wit permitted; told in his presence various stories concocted about him, and about his landlady, an old woman of seventy; declared that she beat him; asked when the wedding was to be; and strewed bits of paper over his head, calling them snow. But Akakiy Akakievitch answered not a word, any more than if there had been no one there besides himself. It even had no effect upon his work: amid all these annoyances he never made a single mistake in a letter. But if the joking became wholly unbearable, as when they jogged his hand and prevented his attending to his work, he would exclaim, "Leave me alone! Why do you insult me?" And there was something strange in the words and the voice in which they were uttered. There was in it something which moved to pity; so much that one young man, a new-comer, who, taking pattern by the others, had permitted himself to make sport of Akakiy, suddenly stopped short, as though all about him had undergone a trans-formation, and presented itself in a different aspect. Some unseen force repelled him from the comrades whose acquaintance he had made, on the supposition that they were well-bred and polite men. Long after-wards, in his gayest moments, there recurred to his mind the little offi-cial with the bald forehead, with his heart-rending words, "Leave me alone! Why do you insult me?" In these moving words, other words resounded—"I am thy brother." And the young man covered his face with his hand; and many a time afterwards, in the course of his life, shud-dered at seeing how much inhumanity there is in man, how much savage coarseness is concealed beneath delicate, refined worldliness, and even, O God! in that man whom the world acknowledges as honourable and noble.

It would be difficult to find another man who lived so entirely for his duties. It is not enough to say that Akakiy laboured with zeal: no, he laboured with love. In his copying, he found a varied and agreeable employment. Enjoyment was written on his face: some letters were even favourites with him; and when he encountered these, he smiled, winked, and worked with his lips, till it seemed as though each letter might be read in his face, as his pen traced it. If his pay had been in proportion to his zeal, he would, perhaps, to his great surprise, have been made even a councillor of state. But he worked, as his companions, the wits, put it, like a horse in a mill.

Moreover, it is impossible to say that no attention was paid to him. One director being a kindly man, and desirous of rewarding him for his long service, ordered him to be given something more important than mere copying. So he was ordered to make a report of an already concluded affair to another department: the duty consisting simply in changing the heading and altering a few words from the first to the third person. This caused him so much toil that he broke into a perspiration, rubbed his forehead, and finally said, "No, give me rather something to copy." After that they let him copy on forever.

Outside this copying, it appeared that nothing existed for him. He gave no thought to his clothes: his undress uniform was not green, but a sort of rusty-meal colour. The collar was low, so that his neck, in spite of the fact that it was not long, seemed inordinately so as it emerged from it, like the necks of those plaster cats which wag their heads, and are carried about upon the heads of scores of image sellers. And something was always sticking to his uniform, either a bit of hay or some trifle. Moreover, he had a peculiar knack, as he walked along the street, of arriving beneath a window just as all sorts of rubbish were being flung out of it: hence he always bore about on his hat scraps of melon rinds and other such articles. Never once in his life did he give heed to what was going on every day in the street; while it is well known that his young brother officials train the range of their glances till they can see when any one's trouser straps come undone upon the opposite sidewalk, which always brings a malicious smile to their faces. But Akakiy

Akakievitch saw in all things the clean, even strokes of his written lines; and only when a horse thrust his nose, from some unknown quarter, over his shoulder, and sent a whole gust of wind down his neck from his nostrils, did he observe that he was not in the middle of a page, but in the middle of the street.

On reaching home, he sat down at once at the table, supped his cabbage soup up quickly, and swallowed a bit of beef with onions, never noticing their taste, and gulping down everything with flies and anything else which the Lord happened to send at the moment. His stomach filled, he rose from the table, and copied papers which he had brought home. If there happened to be none, he took copies for himself, for his own gratification, especially if the document was noteworthy, not on account of its style, but of its being addressed to some distinguished person.

Even at the hour when the grey St. Petersburg sky had quite dispersed, and all the official world had eaten or dined, each as he could, in accordance with the salary he received and his own fancy; when all were resting from the departmental jar of pens, running to and fro from their own and other people's indispensable occupations, and from all the work that an uneasy man makes willingly for himself, rather than what is necessary; when officials hasten to dedicate to pleasure the time which is left to them, one bolder than the rest going to the theatre; another, into the street looking under all the bonnets; another wasting his evening in compliments to some pretty girl, the star of a small official circle; another—and this is the common case of all—visiting his comrades on the fourth or third floor, in two small rooms with an ante-room or kitchen, and some pretensions to fashion, such as a lamp or some other trifle which has cost many a sacrifice of dinner or pleasure trip; in a word, at the hour when all officials disperse among the contracted quarters of their friends, to play whist, as they sip their tea from glasses with a kopek's worth of sugar, smoke long pipes, relate at times some bits of gossip which a Russian man can never, under any circumstances, refrain from, and, when there is nothing else to talk of, repeat eternal anecdotes about the commandant to whom they had sent word that the tails of the horses on the Falconet Monument had been cut off, when all strive to divert themselves, Akakiy Akakievitch indulged in no kind of diversion. No one could ever say that he had seen him at any kind of evening party. Having written to his heart's content, he lay down to sleep, smiling at the thought of the coming day—of what God might send him to copy on the morrow.

Thus flowed on the peaceful life of the man, who, with a salary of four hundred rubles, understood how to be content with his lot; and thus it would have continued to flow on, perhaps, to extreme old age, were it not that there are various ills strewn along the path of life for titular councillors as well as for private, actual, court, and every other species of councillor, even for those who never give any advice or take any themselves.

There exists in St. Petersburg a powerful foe of all who receive a salary of four hundred rubles a year, or thereabouts. This foe is no other than the Northern cold, although it is said to be very healthy. At nine o'clock in the morning, at the very hour when the streets are filled with men bound for the various official departments, it begins to bestow such powerful and piercing nips on all noses impartially that the poor officials really do not know what to do with them. At an hour when the foreheads of even those who occupy exalted positions ache with the cold, and tears start to their eyes, the poor titular councillors are sometimes quite unprotected. Their only salvation lies in traversing as quickly as possible, in their thin little cloaks, five or six streets, and then warming their feet in the porter's room, and so thawing all their talents and qualifications for official service, which had become frozen on the way.

Akakiy Akakievitch had felt for some time that his back and shoulders suffered with peculiar poignancy, in spite of the fact that he tried to traverse the distance with all possible speed. He began finally to wonder whether the fault did not lie in his cloak. He examined it thoroughly at home, and discovered that in two places, namely, on the back and shoulders, it had become thin as gauze: the cloth was worn to such a degree that he could see through it, and the lining had fallen into pieces. You must know that Akakiy Akakievitch's cloak served as an object of ridicule to the officials: they even refused it the noble name of cloak, and called it a cape. In fact, it was of singular make: its collar diminishing year by year, but serving to patch its other parts. The patching did not exhibit great skill on the part of the tailor, and was, in fact, baggy and ugly. Seeing how the matter stood, Akakiy Akakievitch decided that it would be necessary to take the cloak to Petrovitch, the tailor, who lived somewhere on the fourth floor up a dark stair-case, and who, in spite of his having but one eye, and pock-marks all over his face, busied himself with considerable success in repairing the trousers and coats of officials and others; that is to say, when he was sober and not nursing some other scheme in his head.

It is not necessary to say much about this tailor; but, as it is the custom to have the character of each personage in a novel clearly defined, there is no help for it, so here is Petrovitch the tailor. At first he was called only Grigoriy, and was some gentleman's serf; he commenced calling himself Petrovitch from the time when he received his free papers, and further began to drink heavily on all holidays, at first on the great ones, and then on all church festivities without discrimination, wherever a cross stood in the calendar. On this point he was faithful to ancestral custom; and when quarrelling with his wife, he called her a low female and a German. As we have mentioned his wife, it will be necessary to say a word or two about her. Unfortunately, little is known of her beyond the fact that Petrovitch has a wife, who wears a cap and a dress; but cannot lay claim to beauty, at least, no one but the soldiers of the guard even looked under her cap when they met her.

Ascending the staircase which led to Petrovitch's room—which staircase was all soaked with dish-water, and reeked with the smell of spirits which affects the eyes, and is an inevitable adjunct to all dark stairways in St. Petersburg houses—ascending the stairs, Akakiy Akakievitch pondered how much Petrovitch would ask, and mentally resolved not to give more than two rubles. The door was open; for the mistress, in cooking some fish, had raised such a smoke in the kitchen that not even the beetles were visible. Akakiy Akakievitch passed through the kitchen unperceived, even by the housewife, and at length reached a room where he beheld Petrovitch seated on a large unpainted table, with his legs tucked under him like a Turkish pasha. His feet were bare, after the fashion of tailors who sit at work; and the first thing which caught the eye was his thumb, with a deformed nail thick and strong as a turtle's shell. About Petrovitch's neck hung a skein of silk and thread, and upon his knees lay some old garment. He had been trying unsuccessfully for three minutes to thread his needle, and was enraged at the darkness and even at the thread, growling in a low voice, "It won't go through, the barbarian! you pricked me, you rascal!"

Akakiy Akakievitch was vexed at arriving at the precise moment when Petrovitch was angry; he liked to order something of Petrovitch when the latter was a little downhearted, or, as his wife expressed it, "when he had settled himself with brandy, the one-eyed devil!" Under such circumstances, Petrovitch generally came down in his price very readily, and even bowed and returned thanks. Afterwards, to be sure, his wife would come, complaining that her husband was drunk, and so had fixed the price too low; but, if only a ten-kopek piece were added, then the matter was settled. But now it appeared that Petrovitch was in a sober condition, and therefore rough, taciturn, and inclined to demand, Satan only knows what price. Akakiy Akakievitch felt this, and would gladly have beat a retreat; but he was in for it. Petrovitch screwed up his one eye very intently at him, and Akakiy Akakievitch involuntarily said: "How do you do, Petrovitch?"

"I wish you a good morning, sir," said Petrovitch, squinting at Akakiy Akakievitch's hands, to see what sort of booty he had brought.

"Ah! I—to you, Petrovitch, this—" It must be known that Akakiy Akakievitch expressed himself chiefly by prepositions, adverbs, and scraps of phrases which had no meaning whatever. If the matter was a very difficult one, he had a habit of never completing his sentences; so that frequently, having begun a phrase with the words, "This, in fact, is quite—" he forgot to go on, thinking that he had already finished it.

"What is it?" asked Petrovitch, and with his one eye scanned Akakievitch's whole uniform from the collar down to the cuffs, the back, the tails and the button-holes, all of which were well known to him, since they were his own handiwork. Such is the habit of tailors; it is the first thing they do on meeting one.

"But I, here, this—Petrovitch—a cloak, cloth—here you see, everywhere, in different places, it is quite strong—it is a little dusty, and looks old, but it is new, only here in one place it is a little—on the back, and here on one of the shoulders, it is a little worn, yes, here on this shoulder it is a little—do you see? that is all. And a little work—"

Petrovitch took the cloak, spread it out, to begin with, on the table, looked hard at it, shook his head, reached out his hand to the window-sill for his snuff-box, adorned with the portrait of some general, though what general is unknown, for the place where the face should have been had been rubbed through by the finger, and a square bit of paper had been pasted over it. Having taken a pinch of snuff, Petrovitch held up the cloak, and inspected it against the light, and again shook his head once more. After which he again lifted the general-adorned lid with its bit of pasted paper, and having stuffed his nose with snuff, closed and put away the snuff-box, and said finally, "No, it is impossible to mend it; it's a wretched garment!"

Akakiy Akakievitch's heart sank at these words.

"Why is it impossible, Petrovitch?" he said, almost in the pleading voice of a child; "all that ails it is, that it is worn on the shoulders. You must have some pieces—"

"Yes, patches could be found, patches are easily found," said

Petrovitch, "but there's nothing to sew them to. The thing is completely rotten; if you put a needle to it—see, it will give way."

"Let it give way, and you can put on another patch at once."

"But there is nothing to put the patches on to; there's no use in strengthening it; it is too far gone. It's lucky that it's cloth; for, if the wind were to blow, it would fly away."

"Well, strengthen it again. How will this, in fact—"

"No," said Petrovitch decisively, "there is nothing to be done with it. It's a thoroughly bad job. You'd better, when the cold winter weather comes on, make yourself some gaiters out of it, because stockings are not warm. The Germans invented them in order to make more money." Petrovitch loved, on all occasions, to have a fling at the Germans. "But it is plain you must have a new cloak."

At the word "new," all grew dark before Akakiy Akakievitch's eyes, and everything in the room began to whirl round. The only thing he saw clearly was the general with the paper face on the lid of Petrovitch's snuff-box. "A new one?" said he, as if still in a dream: "why, I have no money for that."

"Yes, a new one," said Petrovitch, with barbarous composure.

"Well, if it came to a new one, how would it—?"

"You mean how much would it cost?"

"Yes."

"Well, you would have to lay out a hundred and fifty or more," said Petrovitch, and pursed up his lips significantly. He liked to produce powerful effects, liked to stun utterly and suddenly, and then to glance sideways to see what face the stunned person would put on the matter.

"A hundred and fifty rubles for a cloak!" shrieked poor Akakiy Akakievitch, perhaps for the first time in his life, for his voice had always been distinguished for softness.

"Yes, sir," said Petrovitch, "for any kind of cloak. If you have a marten fur on the collar, or a silk-lined hood, it will mount up to two hundred."

"Petrovitch, please," said Akakiy Akakievitch in a beseeching tone, not hearing, and not trying to hear, Petrovitch's words, and disregarding all his "effects," "some repairs, in order that it may wear yet a little longer."

"No, it would only be a waste of time and money," said Petrovitch; and Akakiy Akakievitch went away after these words, utterly discouraged. But Petrovitch stood for some time after his departure, with significantly compressed lips, and without betaking himself to his work, satisfied that he would not be dropped, and an artistic tailor employed.

Akakiy Akakievitch went out into the street as if in a dream. "Such an affair!" he said to himself: "I did not think it had come to—" and then after a pause, he added, "Well, so it is! see what it has come to at last! and I never imagined that it was so!" Then followed a long silence, after which he exclaimed, "Well, so it is! see what already—nothing unexpected that—it would be nothing—what a strange circumstance!" So saying, instead of going home, he went in exactly the opposite direction without himself suspecting it. On the way, a chimney-sweep bumped up against him, and blackened his shoulder, and a whole hatful of rubbish landed on him from the top of a house which was building. He did not notice it; and only when he ran against a watchman, who, having planted his halberd beside him, was shaking some snuff from his box into his horny hand, did he recover himself a little, and that because the watchman said, "Why are you poking yourself into a man's very face? Haven't you the pavement?" This caused him to look about him, and turn towards home.

There only, he finally began to collect his thoughts, and to survey his position in its clear and actual light, and to argue with himself, sensibly and frankly, as with a reasonable friend with whom one can discuss private and personal matters. "No," said Akakiy Akakievitch, "it is impossible to reason with Petrovitch now; he is that—evidently his wife has been beating him. I'd better go to him on Sunday morning; after Saturday night he will be a little cross-eyed and sleepy, for he will want to get drunk, and his wife won't give him any money; and at such a time, a ten-kopek piece in his hand will—he will become more fit to reason with, and then the cloak, and that—" Thus argued Akakiy Akakievitch with himself, regained his courage, and waited until the first Sunday, when, seeing from afar that Petrovitch's wife had left the house, he went straight to him.

Petrovitch's eye was, indeed, very much askew after Saturday: his head drooped, and he was very sleepy; but for all that, as soon as he knew what it was a question of, it seemed as though Satan jogged his memory. "Impossible," said he: "please to order a new one." Thereupon Akakiy Akakievitch handed over the ten-kopek piece. "Thank you, sir; I will drink your good health," said Petrovitch: "but as for the cloak, don't trouble yourself about it; it is good for nothing. I will make you a capital new one, so let us settle about it now."

Akakiy Akakievitch was still for mending it; but Petrovitch would not hear of it, and said, "I shall certainly have to make you a new one, and you may depend upon it that I shall do my best. It may even be, as the fashion goes, that the collar can be fastened by silver hooks under a flap."

Then Akakiy Akakievitch saw that it was impossible to get along without a new cloak, and his spirit sank utterly. How, in fact, was it to be done? Where was the money to come from? He might, to be sure, depend, in part, upon his present at Christmas; but that money had long been allotted beforehand. He must have some new trousers, and pay a debt of long standing to the shoemaker for putting new tops to his old boots, and he must order three shirts from the seamstress, and a couple of pieces of linen. In short, all his money must be spent; and even if the director should be so kind as to order him to receive forty-five rubles instead of forty, or even fifty, it would be a mere nothing, a mere drop in the ocean towards the funds necessary for a cloak: although he knew that Petrovitch was often wrong-headed enough to blurt out some outrageous price, so that even his own wife could not refrain from exclaiming, "Have you lost your senses, you fool?" At one time he would not work at any price, and now it was quite likely that he had named a higher sum than the cloak would cost.

But although he knew that Petrovitch would undertake to make a cloak for eighty rubles, still, where was he to get the eighty rubles from? He might possibly manage half, yes, half might be procured, but where was the other half to come from? But the reader must first be told where the first half came from. Akakiy Akakievitch had a habit of putting, for every ruble he spent, a groschen into a small box, fastened with a lock and key, and with a slit in the top for the reception of money. At the end of every half-year he counted over the heap of coppers, and changed it for silver. This he had done for a long time, and in the course of years, the sum had mounted up to over forty rubles. Thus he had one half on hand; but where was he to find the other half? where was he to get another forty rubles from? Akakiy Akakievitch thought and thought, and decided that it would be necessary to curtail his ordinary expenses, for the space of one year at least, to dispense with tea in the evening; to burn no candles, and, if there was anything which he must do, to go into his landlady's room, and work by her light. When he went into the street, he must walk as lightly as he could, and as cautiously, upon the stones, almost upon tiptoe, in order not to wear his heels down in too short a time; he must give the laundress as little to wash as possible; and, in order not to wear out his clothes, he must take them off, as soon as he got home, and wear only his cotton dressing-gown, which had been long and carefully saved.

To tell the truth, it was a little hard for him at first to accustom himself to these deprivations; but he got used to them at length, after a fashion, and all went smoothly. He even got used to being hungry in the evening, but he made up for it by treating himself, so to say, in spirit, by bearing ever in mind the idea of his future cloak. From that time forth his existence seemed to become, in some way, fuller, as if he were married, or as if some other man lived in him, as if, in fact, he were not alone, and some pleasant friend had consented to travel along life's path with him, the friend being no other than the cloak, with thick wadding and a strong lining incapable of wearing out. He became more lively, and even his character grew firmer, like that of a man who has made up his mind, and set himself a goal. From his face and gait, doubt and indecision, all hesitating and wavering traits disappeared of themselves. Fire gleamed in his eyes, and occasionally the boldest and most daring ideas flitted through his mind; why not, for instance, have marten fur on the collar? The thought of this almost made him absent-minded. Once, in copying a letter, he nearly made a mistake, so that he exclaimed almost aloud, "Ugh!" and crossed himself. Once, in the course of every month, he had a conference with Petrovitch on the subject of the cloak, where it would be better to buy the cloth, and the colour, and the price. He always returned home satisfied, though troubled, reflecting that the time would come at last when it could all be bought, and then the cloak made.

The affair progressed more briskly than he had expected. Far beyond all his hopes, the director awarded neither forty nor forty-five rubles for Akakiy Akakievitch's share, but sixty. Whether he suspected that Akakiy Akakievitch needed a cloak, or whether it was merely chance, at all events, twenty extra rubles were by this means provided. This circumstance hastened matters. Two or three months more of hunger and Akakiy Akakievitch had accumulated about eighty rubles. His heart, generally so quiet, began to throb. On the first possible day, he went shopping in company with Petrovitch. They bought some very good cloth, and at a reasonable rate too, for they had been considering the matter for six months, and rarely let a month pass without their visiting the shops to inquire prices. Petrovitch himself said that no better cloth could be had. For lining, they selected a cotton stuff, but so firm and thick that Petrovitch declared it to be better than silk, and even prettier and more glossy. They did not buy the marten fur, because it was, in fact, dear, but in its stead, they picked out the very best of cat-skin which could be found in the shop, and which might, indeed, be taken for marten at a distance.

Petrovitch worked at the cloak two whole weeks, for there was a great deal of quilting: otherwise it would have been finished sooner. He charged twelve rubles for the job, it could not possibly have been done for less. It was all sewed with silk, in small, double seams; and Petrovitch went over each seam afterwards with his own teeth, stamping in various patterns.

It was—it is difficult to say precisely on what day, but probably the most glorious one in Akakiy Akakievitch's life, when Petrovitch at length brought home the cloak. He brought it in the morning, before the hour when it was necessary to start for the department. Never did a cloak arrive so exactly in the nick of time; for the severe cold had set in, and it seemed to threaten to increase. Petrovitch brought the cloak himself as befits a good tailor. On his countenance was a significant expression, such as Akakiy Akakievitch had never beheld there. He seemed fully sensible that he had done no small deed, and crossed a gulf separating tailors who only put in linings, and execute repairs, from those who make new things. He took the cloak out of the pocket handkerchief in which he had brought it. The handkerchief was fresh from the laundress, and he put it in his pocket for use. Taking out the cloak, he gazed proudly at it, held it up with both hands, and flung it skilfully over the shoulders of Akakiy Akakievitch. Then he pulled it and fitted it down behind with his hand, and he draped it around Akakiy Akakievitch without buttoning it. Akakiy Akakievitch, like an experienced man, wished to try the sleeves. Petrovitch helped him on with them, and it turned out that the sleeves were satisfactory also. In short, the cloak appeared to be perfect, and most seasonable. Petrovitch did not neglect to observe that it was only because he lived in a narrow street, and had no signboard, and had known Akakiy Akakievitch so long, that he had made it so cheaply; but that if he had been in business on the Nevsky Prospect, he would have charged seventy-five rubles for the making alone. Akakiy Akakievitch did not care to argue this point with Petrovitch. He paid him, thanked him, and set out at once in his new cloak for the department. Petrovitch followed him, and, pausing in the street, gazed long at the cloak in the distance, after which he went to one side expressly to run through a crooked alley, and emerge again into the street beyond to gaze once more upon the cloak from another point, namely, directly in front.

Meantime Akakiy Akakievitch went on in holiday mood. He was conscious every second of the time that he had a new cloak on his shoulders; and several times he laughed with internal satisfaction. In fact, there were two advantages, one was its warmth, the other its beauty. He saw nothing of the road, but suddenly found himself at the department. He took off his cloak in the ante-room, looked it over carefully, and confided it to the especial care of the attendant. It is impossible to say precisely how it was that every one in the department knew at once that Akakiy Akakievitch had a new cloak, and that the "cape" no longer existed. All rushed at the same moment into the ante-room to inspect it. They congratulated him and said pleasant things to him, so that he began at first to smile and then to grow ashamed. When all surrounded him, and said that the new cloak must be "christened," and that he must give a whole evening at least to this, Akakiy Akakievitch lost his head completely, and did not know where he stood, what to answer, or how to get out of it. He stood blushing all over for several minutes, and was on the point of assuring them with great simplicity that it was not a new cloak, that it was so and so, that it was in fact the old "cape."

At length one of the officials, a sub-chief probably, in order to show that he was not at all proud, and on good terms with his inferiors, said, "So be it, only I will give the party instead of Akakiy Akakievitch; I invite you all to tea with me to-night; it happens quite a propos, as it is my name-day." The officials naturally at once offered the sub-chief their congratulations and accepted the invitations with pleasure. Akakiy Akakievitch would have declined, but all declared that it was discourteous, that it was simply a sin and a shame, and that he could not possibly refuse. Besides, the notion became pleasant to him when he recollected that he should thereby have a chance of wearing his new cloak in the evening also.

That whole day was truly a most triumphant festival day for Akakiy Akakievitch. He returned home in the most happy frame of mind, took off his cloak, and hung it carefully on the wall, admiring afresh the cloth and the lining. Then he brought out his old, worn-out cloak, for comparison. He looked at it and laughed, so vast was the difference. And long after dinner he laughed again when the condition of the "cape" recurred to his mind. He dined cheerfully, and after dinner wrote nothing, but took his ease for a while on the bed, until it got dark. Then he dressed himself leisurely, put on his cloak, and stepped out into the street. Where the host lived, unfortunately we cannot say: our memory begins to fail us badly; and the houses and streets in St. Petersburg have become so mixed up in our head that it is very difficult to get anything out of it again in proper form. This much is certain, that the official lived in the best part of the city; and therefore it must have been anything but near to Akakiy Akakievitch's residence. Akakiy Akakievitch was first obliged to traverse a kind of wilderness of deserted, dimly-lighted streets; but in proportion as he approached the official's quarter of the city, the streets became more lively, more populous, and more brilliantly illuminated. Pedestrians began to appear; handsomely dressed ladies were more frequently encountered; the men had otter skin collars to their coats; peasant waggoners, with their grate-like sledges stuck over with brass-headed nails, became rarer; whilst on the other hand, more and more drivers in red velvet caps, lacquered sledges and bear-skin coats began to appear, and carriages with rich hammer-cloths flew swiftly through the streets, their wheels scrunching the snow. Akakiy Akakievitch gazed upon all this as upon a novel sight. He had not been in the streets during the evening for years. He halted out of curiosity before a shop-window to look at a picture representing a handsome woman, who had thrown off her shoe, thereby baring her whole foot in a very pretty way; whilst behind her the head of a man with whiskers and a handsome moustache peeped through the doorway of another room. Akakiy Akakievitch shook his head and laughed, and then went on his way. Why did he laugh? Either because he had met with a thing utterly unknown, but for which every one cherishes, nevertheless, some sort of feeling; or else he thought, like many officials, as follows: "Well, those French! What is to be said? If they do go in anything of that sort, why—" But possibly he did not think at all.

Akakiy Akakievitch at length reached the house in which the sub-chief lodged. The sub-chief lived in fine style: the staircase was lit by a lamp; his apartment being on the second floor. On entering the vestibule, Akakiy Akakievitch beheld a whole row of goloshes on the floor. Among them, in the centre of the room, stood a samovar or tea-urn, humming and emitting clouds of steam. On the walls hung all sorts of coats and cloaks, among which there were even some with beaver collars or velvet facings. Beyond, the buzz of conversation was audible, and became clear and loud when the servant came out with a trayful of empty glasses, cream-jugs, and sugar-bowls. It was evident that the officials had arrived long before, and had already finished their first glass of tea.

Akakiy Akakievitch, having hung up his own cloak, entered the inner room. Before him all at once appeared lights, officials, pipes, and card-tables; and he was bewildered by the sound of rapid conversation rising from all the tables, and the noise of moving chairs. He halted very awkwardly in the middle of the room, wondering what he ought to do. But they had seen him. They received him with a shout, and all thronged at once into the ante-room, and there took another look at his cloak. Akakiy Akakievitch, although somewhat confused, was frank-hearted, and could not refrain from rejoicing when he saw how they praised his cloak. Then, of course, they all dropped him and his cloak, and returned, as was proper, to the tables set out for whist.

All this, the noise, the talk, and the throng of people was rather overwhelming to Akakiy Akakievitch. He simply did not know where he stood, or where to put his hands, his feet, and his whole body. Finally he sat down by the players, looked at the cards, gazed at the face of one and another, and after a while began to gape, and to feel that it was wearisome, the more so as the hour was already long past when he usually went to bed. He wanted to take leave of the host; but they would not let him go, saying that he must not fail to drink a glass of champagne in honour of his new garment. In the course of an hour, supper, consisting of vegetable salad, cold veal, pastry, confectioner's pies, and champagne, was served. They made Akakiy Akakievitch drink two glasses of champagne, after which he felt things grow livelier.

Still, he could not forget that it was twelve o'clock, and that he should have been at home long ago. In order that the host might not think of some excuse for detaining him, he stole out of the room quickly, sought out, in the ante-room, his cloak, which, to his sorrow, he found lying on the floor, brushed it, picked off every speck upon it, put it on his shoulders, and descended the stairs to the street.

In the street all was still bright. Some petty shops, those permanent clubs of servants and all sorts of folk, were open. Others were shut, but, nevertheless, showed a streak of light the whole length of the door-crack, indicating that they were not yet free of company, and that probably some domestics, male and female, were finishing their stories and conversations whilst leaving their masters in complete ignorance as to their whereabouts. Akakiy Akakievitch went on in a happy frame of mind: he even started to run, without knowing why, after some lady, who flew past like a flash of lightning. But he stopped short, and went on very quietly as before, wondering why he had quickened his pace. Soon there spread before him those deserted streets, which are not cheerful in the daytime, to say nothing of the evening. Now they were even more dim and lonely: the lanterns began to grow rarer, oil, evidently, had been less liberally supplied. Then came wooden houses and fences: not a soul anywhere; only the snow sparkled in the streets, and mournfully veiled the low-roofed cabins with their closed shutters. He approached the spot where the street crossed a vast square with houses barely visible on its farther side, a square which seemed a fearful desert.

Afar, a tiny spark glimmered from some watchman's box, which seemed to stand on the edge of the world. Akakiy Akakievitch's cheerfulness diminished at this point in a marked degree. He entered the square, not without an involuntary sensation of fear, as though his heart warned him of some evil. He glanced back and on both sides, it was like a sea about him. "No, it is better not to look," he thought, and went on, closing his eyes. When he opened them, to see whether he was near the end of the square, he suddenly beheld, standing just before his very nose, some bearded individuals of precisely what sort he could not make out. All grew dark before his eyes, and his heart throbbed.

"But, of course, the cloak is mine!" said one of them in a loud voice, seizing hold of his collar. Akakiy Akakievitch was about to shout "watch," when the second man thrust a fist, about the size of a man's head, into his mouth, muttering, "Now scream!"

Akakiy Akakievitch felt them strip off his cloak and give him a push with a knee: he fell headlong upon the snow, and felt no more. In a few minutes he recovered consciousness and rose to his feet; but no one was there. He felt that it was cold in the square, and that his cloak was gone; he began to shout, but his voice did not appear to reach to the outskirts of the square. In despair, but without ceasing to shout, he started at a run across the square, straight towards the watchbox, beside which stood the watchman, leaning on his halberd, and apparently curious to know what kind of a customer was running towards him and shouting. Akakiy Akakievitch ran up to him, and began in a sobbing voice to shout that he was asleep, and attended to nothing, and did not see when a man was robbed. The watchman replied that he had seen two men stop him in the middle of the square, but supposed that they were friends of his; and that, instead of scolding vainly, he had better go to the police on the morrow, so that they might make a search for whoever had stolen the cloak.

Akakiy Akakievitch ran home in complete disorder; his hair, which grew very thinly upon his temples and the back of his head, wholly disordered; his body, arms, and legs covered with snow. The old woman, who was mistress of his lodgings, on hearing a terrible knocking, sprang hastily from her bed, and, with only one shoe on, ran to open the door, pressing the sleeve of her chemise to her bosom out of modesty; but when she had opened it, she fell back on beholding Akakiy Akakievitch in such a state. When he told her about the affair, she clasped her hands, and said that he must go straight to the district chief of police, for his subordinate would turn up his nose, promise well, and drop the matter there. The very best thing to do, therefore, would be to go to the district chief, whom she knew, because Finnish Anna, her former cook, was now nurse at his house. She often saw him passing the house; and he was at church every Sunday, praying, but at the same time gazing cheerfully at everybody; so that he must be a good man, judging from all appearances. Having listened to this opinion, Akakiy Akakievitch betook himself sadly to his room; and how he spent the night there any one who can put himself in another's place may readily imagine.

Early in the morning, he presented himself at the district chief's; but was told that this official was asleep. He went again at ten and was again informed that he was asleep; at eleven, and they said: "The superintendent is not at home;" at dinner time, and the clerks in the ante-room would not admit him on any terms, and insisted upon knowing his business. So that at last, for once in his life, Akakiy Akakievitch felt an inclination to show some spirit, and said curtly that he must see the chief in person; that they ought not to presume to refuse him entrance; that he came from the department of justice, and that when he complained of them, they would see.

The clerks dared make no reply to this, and one of them went to call the chief, who listened to the strange story of the theft of the coat. Instead of directing his attention to the principal points of the matter, he began to question Akakiy Akakievitch: Why was he going home so late? Was he in the habit of doing so, or had he been to some disorderly house? So that Akakiy Akakievitch got thoroughly confused, and left him without knowing whether the affair of his cloak was in proper train or not.

All that day, for the first time in his life, he never went near the department. The next day he made his appearance, very pale, and in his old cape, which had become even more shabby. The news of the robbery of the cloak touched many; although there were some officials present who never lost an opportunity, even such a one as the present, of ridiculing Akakiy Akakievitch. They decided to make a collection for him on the spot, but the officials had already spent a great deal in subscribing for the director's portrait, and for some book, at the suggestion of the head of that division, who was a friend of the author; and so the sum was trifling.

One of them, moved by pity, resolved to help Akakiy Akakievitch with some good advice at least, and told him that he ought not to go to the police, for although it might happen that a police-officer, wishing to win the approval of his superiors, might hunt up the cloak by some means, still his cloak would remain in the possession of the police if he did not offer legal proof that it belonged to him. The best thing for him, therefore, would be to apply to a certain prominent personage; since this prominent personage, by entering into relations with the proper persons, could greatly expedite the matter.

As there was nothing else to be done, Akakiy Akakievitch decided to go to the prominent personage. What was the exact official position of the prominent personage remains unknown to this day. The reader must know that the prominent personage had but recently become a prominent personage, having up to that time been only an insignificant person. Moreover, his present position was not considered prominent in comparison with others still more so. But there is always a circle of people to whom what is insignificant in the eyes of others, is important enough. Moreover, he strove to increase his importance by sundry devices; for instance, he managed to have the inferior officials meet him on the staircase when he entered upon his service; no one was to presume to come directly to him, but the strictest etiquette must be observed; the collegiate recorder must make a report to the government secretary, the government secretary to the titular councillor, or whatever other man was proper, and all business must come before him in this manner. In Holy Russia all is thus contaminated with the love of imitation; every man imitates and copies his superior. They even say that a certain titular councillor, when promoted to the head of some small separate room, immediately partitioned off a private room for himself, called it the audience chamber, and posted at the door a lackey with red collar and braid, who grasped the handle of the door and opened to all comers; though the audience chamber could hardly hold an ordinary writing-table.

The manners and customs of the prominent personage were grand and imposing, but rather exaggerated. The main foundation of his system was strictness. "Strictness, strictness, and always strictness!" he generally said; and at the last word he looked significantly into the face of the person to whom he spoke. But there was no necessity for this, for the half-score of subordinates who formed the entire force of the office were properly afraid; on catching sight of him afar off they left their work and waited, drawn up in line, until he had passed through the room. His ordinary converse with his inferiors smacked of sternness, and consisted chiefly of three phrases: "How dare you?" "Do you know whom you are speaking to?" "Do you realise who stands before you?"

Otherwise he was a very kind-hearted man, good to his comrades, and ready to oblige; but the rank of general threw him completely off his balance. On receiving any one of that rank, he became confused, lost his way, as it were, and never knew what to do. If he chanced to be amongst his equals he was still a very nice kind of man, a very good fellow in many respects, and not stupid; but the very moment that he found himself in the society of people but one rank lower than himself he became silent; and his situation aroused sympathy, the more so as he felt himself that he might have been making an incomparably better use of his time. In his eyes there was sometimes visible a desire to join some interesting conversation or group; but he was kept back by the thought, "Would it not be a very great condescension on his part? Would it not be familiar? and would he not thereby lose his importance?" And in consequence of such reflections he always remained in the same dumb state, uttering from time to time a few monosyllabic sounds, and thereby earning the name of the most wearisome of men.

To this prominent personage Akakiy Akakievitch presented himself, and this at the most unfavourable time for himself though opportune for the prominent personage. The prominent personage was in his cabinet conversing gaily with an old acquaintance and companion of his childhood whom he had not seen for several years and who had just arrived when it was announced to him that a person named Bashmatchkin had come. He asked abruptly, "Who is he?"—"Some official," he was informed. "Ah, he can wait! this is no time for him to call," said the important man.

It must be remarked here that the important man lied outrageously: he had said all he had to say to his friend long before; and the conversation had been interspersed for some time with very long pauses, during which they merely slapped each other on the leg, and said, "You think so, Ivan Abramovitch!" "Just so, Stepan Varlamitch!" Nevertheless, he ordered that the official should be kept waiting, in order to show his friend, a man who had not been in the service for a long time, but had lived at home in the country, how long officials had to wait in his ante-room.

At length, having talked himself completely out, and more than that, having had his fill of pauses, and smoked a cigar in a very comfortable arm-chair with reclining back, he suddenly seemed to recollect, and said to the secretary, who stood by the door with papers of reports, "So it seems that there is a tchinovnik waiting to see me. Tell him that he may come in." On perceiving Akakiy Akakievitch's modest mien and his worn undress uniform, he turned abruptly to him and said, "What do you want?" in a curt hard voice, which he had practised in his room in private, and before the looking-glass, for a whole week before being raised to his present rank.

Akakiy Akakievitch, who was already imbued with a due amount of fear, became somewhat confused: and as well as his tongue would permit, explained, with a rather more frequent addition than usual of the word "that," that his cloak was quite new, and had been stolen in the most inhuman manner; that he had applied to him in order that he might, in some way, by his intermediation—that he might enter into correspondence with the chief of police, and find the cloak.

For some inexplicable reason this conduct seemed familiar to the prominent personage. "What, my dear sir!" he said abruptly, "are you not acquainted with etiquette? Where have you come from? Don't you know how such matters are managed? You should first have entered a complaint about this at the court below: it would have gone to the head of the department, then to the chief of the division, then it would have been handed over to the secretary, and the secretary would have given it to me."

"But, your excellency," said Akakiy Akakievitch, trying to collect his small handful of wits, and conscious at the same time that he was perspiring terribly, "I, your excellency, presumed to trouble you because secretaries—are an untrustworthy race."

"What, what, what!" said the important personage. "Where did you get such courage? Where did you get such ideas? What impudence towards their chiefs and superiors has spread among the young generation!" The prominent personage apparently had not observed that Akakiy Akakievitch was already in the neighbourhood of fifty. If he could be called a young man, it must have been in comparison with some one who was twenty. "Do you know to whom you speak? Do you realise who stands before you? Do you realise it? do you realise it? I ask you!" Then he stamped his foot and raised his voice to such a pitch that it would have frightened even a different man from Akakiy Akakievitch.

Akakiy Akakievitch's senses failed him; he staggered, trembled in

every limb, and, if the porters had not run to support him, would have
fallen to the floor. They carried him out insensible. But the prominent
personage, gratified that the effect should have surpassed his expectations,
and quite intoxicated with the thought that his word could even deprive
a man of his senses, glanced sideways at his friend in order to see how he
looked upon this, and perceived, not without satisfaction, that his friend
was in a most uneasy frame of mind, and even beginning, on his part, to
feel a trifle frightened.

Akakiy Akakievitch could not remember how he descended the
stairs and got into the street. He felt neither his hands nor feet. Never in
his life had he been so rated by any high official, let alone a strange one.
He went staggering on through the snow-storm, which was blowing in
the streets, with his mouth wide open; the wind, in St. Petersburg fashion,
darted upon him from all quarters, and down every cross-street. In a
twinkling it had blown a quinsy into his throat, and he reached home
unable to utter a word. His throat was swollen, and he lay down on his
bed. So powerful is sometimes a good scolding!

The next day a violent fever showed itself. Thanks to the generous
assistance of the St. Petersburg climate, the malady progressed more
rapidly than could have been expected: and when the doctor arrived, he
found, on feeling the sick man's pulse, that there was nothing to be done,
except to prescribe a fomentation, so that the patient might not be left
entirely without the beneficent aid of medicine; but at the same time, he
predicted his end in thirty-six hours. After this he turned to the landlady, and said, "And as for you, don't waste your time on him: order his
pine coffin now, for an oak one will be too expensive for him." Did
Akakiy Akakievitch hear these fatal words? and if he heard them, did
they produce any overwhelming effect upon him? Did he lament the
bitterness of his life?—We know not, for he continued in a delirious
condition. Visions incessantly appeared to him, each stranger than the
other. Now he saw Petrovitch, and ordered him to make a cloak, with
some traps for robbers, who seemed to him to be always under the bed;

and cried every moment to the landlady to pull one of them from under his coverlet. Then he inquired why his old mantle hung before him when he had a new cloak. Next he fancied that he was standing before the prominent person, listening to a thorough setting-down, and saying, "Forgive me, your excellency!" but at last he began to curse, uttering the most horrible words, so that his aged landlady crossed herself, never in her life having heard anything of the kind from him, the more so as those words followed directly after the words "your excellency." Later on he talked utter nonsense, of which nothing could be made: all that was evident being, that his incoherent words and thoughts hovered ever about one thing, his cloak.

At length poor Akakiy Akakievitch breathed his last. They sealed up neither his room nor his effects, because, in the first place, there were no heirs, and, in the second, there was very little to inherit beyond a bundle of goose-quills, a quire of white official paper, three pairs of socks, two or three buttons which had burst off his trousers, and the mantle already known to the reader. To whom all this fell, God knows. I confess that the person who told me this tale took no interest in the matter. They carried Akakiy Akakievitch out and buried him.

And St. Petersburg was left without Akakiy Akakievitch, as though he had never lived there. A being disappeared who was protected by none, dear to none, interesting to none, and who never even attracted to himself the attention of those students of human nature who omit no opportunity of thrusting a pin through a common fly, and examining it under the microscope. A being who bore meekly the jibes of the department, and went to his grave without having done one unusual deed, but to whom, nevertheless, at the close of his life appeared a bright visitant in the form of a cloak, which momentarily cheered his poor life, and upon whom, thereafter, an intolerable misfortune descended, just as it descends upon the mighty of this world!

Several days after his death, the porter was sent from the department to his lodgings, with an order for him to present himself there immediately; the chief commanding it. But the porter had to return unsuccessful, with the answer that he could not come; and to the question, "Why?" replied, "Well, because he is dead! he was buried four days ago." In this manner did they hear of Akakiy Akakievitch's death at the department, and the next day a new official sat in his place, with a handwriting by no means so upright, but more inclined and slanting.

But who could have imagined that this was not really the end of Akakiy Akakievitch, that he was destined to raise a commotion after death, as if in compensation for his utterly insignificant life? But so it happened, and our poor story unexpectedly gains a fantastic ending.

A rumour suddenly spread through St. Petersburg that a dead man had taken to appearing on the Kalinkin Bridge and its vicinity at night in the form of a tchinovnik seeking a stolen cloak, and that, under the pretext of its being the stolen cloak, he dragged, without regard to rank or calling, every one's cloak from his shoulders, be it cat-skin, beaver, fox, bear, sable; in a word, every sort of fur and skin which men adopted for their covering. One of the department officials saw the dead man with his own eyes and immediately recognised in him Akakiy Akakievitch. This, however, inspired him with such terror that he ran off with all his might, and therefore did not scan the dead man closely, but only saw how the latter threatened him from afar with his finger. Constant complaints poured in from all quarters that the backs and shoulders, not only of titular but even of court councillors, were exposed to the danger of a cold on account of the frequent dragging off of their cloaks.

Arrangements were made by the police to catch the corpse, alive or dead, at any cost, and punish him as an example to others in the most severe manner. In this they nearly succeeded; for a watchman, on guard in Kirushkin Alley, caught the corpse by the collar on the very scene of his evil deeds, when attempting to pull off the frieze coat of a retired musician. Having seized him by the collar, he summoned, with a shout, two of his comrades, whom he enjoined to hold him fast while he himself felt for a moment in his boot, in order to draw out his snuff-box and refresh his frozen nose. But the snuff was of a sort which even a corpse could not endure. The watchman having closed his right nostril with his finger, had no sooner succeeded in holding half a handful up to the left than the corpse sneezed so violently that he completely filled the eyes of all three. While they raised their hands to wipe them, the dead man vanished completely, so that they positively did not know whether they had actually had him in their grip at all. Thereafter the watchmen conceived such a terror of dead men that they were afraid even to seize the living, and only screamed from a distance, "Hey, there! go your way!" So the dead tchinovnik began to appear even beyond the Kalinkin Bridge, causing no little terror to all timid people.

But we have totally neglected that certain prominent personage who may really be considered as the cause of the fantastic turn taken by this true history. First of all, justice compels us to say that after the departure of poor, annihilated Akakiy Akakievitch he felt something like remorse. Suffering was unpleasant to him, for his heart was accessible to many good impulses, in spite of the fact that his rank often prevented his showing his true self. As soon as his friend had left his cabinet, he began to think about poor Akakiy Akakievitch. And from that day forth, poor Akakiy Akakievitch, who could not bear up under an official reprimand, recurred to his mind almost every day. The thought troubled him to such an extent that a week later he even resolved to send an official to him, to learn whether he really could assist him; and when it was reported to him that Akakiy Akakievitch had died suddenly of fever, he was startled, hearkened to the reproaches of his conscience, and was out of sorts for the whole day.

Wishing to divert his mind in some way, and drive away the disagreeable impression, he set out that evening for one of his friends' houses, where he found quite a large party assembled. What was better, nearly every one was of the same rank as himself, so that he need not feel in the least constrained. This had a marvellous effect upon his mental state. He grew expansive, made himself agreeable in conversation, in short, he passed a delightful evening. After supper he drank a couple of glasses of champagne—not a bad recipe for cheerfulness, as every one knows. The champagne inclined him to various adventures; and he determined not to return home, but to go and see a certain well-known lady of German extraction, Karolina Ivanovna, a lady, it appears, with whom he was on a very friendly footing.

It must be mentioned that the prominent personage was no longer a young man, but a good husband and respected father of a family. Two sons, one of whom was already in the service, and a good-looking, sixteen-year-old daughter, with a rather retrousse but pretty little nose, came every morning to kiss his hand and say, "Bonjour, papa." His wife, a still fresh and good-looking woman, first gave him her hand to kiss, and then, reversing the procedure, kissed his. But the prominent personage, though perfectly satisfied in his domestic relations, considered it stylish to have a friend in another quarter of the city. This friend was scarcely prettier or younger than his wife; but there are such puzzles in the world, and it is not our place to judge them. So the important personage descended the stairs, stepped into his sledge, said to the coachman, "To Karolina Ivanovna's," and, wrapping himself luxuriously in his warm cloak, found himself in that delightful frame of mind than which a Russian can conceive no better, namely, when you think of nothing yourself, yet when the thoughts creep into your mind of their own accord, each more agreeable than the other, giving you no trouble either to drive them away or seek them. Fully satisfied, he recalled all the gay features of the evening just passed, and all the mots which had made the little circle laugh. Many of them he repeated in a low voice, and found them quite as funny as before; so it is not surprising that he should laugh heartily at them. Occasionally, however, he was interrupted by gusts of wind, which, coming suddenly, God knows whence or why, cut his face, drove masses of snow into it, filled out his cloak-collar like a sail, or suddenly blew it over his head with supernatural force, and thus caused him constant trouble to disentangle himself.

Suddenly the important personage felt some one clutch him firmly by the collar. Turning round, he perceived a man of short stature, in an old, worn uniform, and recognised, not without terror, Akakiy Akakievitch. The official's face was white as snow, and looked just like a corpse's. But the horror of the important personage transcended all bounds when he saw the dead man's mouth open, and, with a terrible odour of the grave, gave vent to the following remarks: "Ah, here you are at last! I have you, that—by the collar! I need your cloak; you took no trouble about mine, but reprimanded me; so now give up your own."

The pallid prominent personage almost died of fright. Brave as he was in the office and in the presence of inferiors generally, and although, at the sight of his manly form and appearance, every one said, "Ugh! how much character he had!" at this crisis, he, like many possessed of an heroic exterior, experienced such terror, that, not without cause, he began to fear an attack of illness. He flung his cloak hastily from his shoulders and shouted to his coachman in an unnatural voice, "Home at full speed!" The coachman, hearing the tone which is generally employed at critical moments and even accompanied by something much more tangible, drew his head down between his shoulders in case of an emergency, flourished his whip, and flew on like an arrow. In a little more than six minutes the prominent personage was at the entrance of his own house. Pale, thoroughly scared, and cloakless, he went home instead of to Karolina Ivanovna's, reached his room somehow or other, and passed the night in the direst distress; so that the next morning over their tea his daughter said, "You are very pale to-day, papa." But papa remained silent, and said not a word to any one of what had happened to him, where he had been, or where he had intended to go.

This occurrence made a deep impression upon him. He even began to say: "How dare you? do you realise who stands before you?" less frequently to the under-officials, and if he did utter the words, it was only after having first learned the bearings of the matter. But the most noteworthy point was, that from that day forward the apparition of the dead tchinovnik ceased to be seen. Evidently the prominent personage's cloak just fitted his shoulders; at all events, no more instances of his dragging cloaks from people's shoulders were heard of. But many active and apprehensive persons could by no means reassure themselves, and asserted that the dead tchinovnik still showed himself in distant parts of the city.

In fact, one watchman in Kolomna saw with his own eyes the apparition come from behind a house. But being rather weak of body, he dared not arrest him, but followed him in the dark, until, at length, the apparition looked round, paused, and inquired, "What do you want?" at the same time showing a fist such as is never seen on living men. The watchman said, "It's of no consequence," and turned back instantly. But the apparition was much too tall, wore huge moustaches, and, directing its steps apparently towards the Obukhoff bridge, disappeared in the darkness of the night.

LEO TOLSTOY

GOD SEES THE TRUTH, BUT WAITS

Count Lev (Leo) Nikolayevich Tolstoy (1828–1910) lost both his parents before he was ten and grew up with German and French tutors. He was a poor student but, coming from a wealthy family, was able to pursue a dissolute life while in his twenties, then joined the army, fighting in the Caucasus and then in the Crimean War. During quiet times, he began to write, selling his first story when he was twenty-four. Tired of his life as a libertine, he married in 1862 and, in an effort at candor, showed his wife his diaries, leading to lifelong distrust and jealousy. They had 13 children, eight of whom survived to maturity. It was in the 1860s and '70s that he produced his greatest work, notably *War and Peace*, published in six volumes (1868-1869) and *Anna Karenina*, published serially in 1873 and then in book form in three volumes (1878). In the late 1870s, he stopped writing fiction and devoted himself to works on his newfound philosophy, which was a combination of Christianity and anarchy, renouncing all forms of violence and power, even against evil or to maintain governmental control. This led to a revolt against capitalism in favor of agrarian communism. When he wrote *What Is Art?* (1897), he preached that all art must be moral in its purpose and conception, dismissing all his work except for two short stories, "God Sees the Truth, but Waits" and "The Prisoner of the Caucasus" (both 1872).

"God Sees the Truth, but Waits" was first published in 1872. It has also been reprinted under the titles "The Long Exile" and "The Man of God." It was made into a short film in 1999.

In the town of Vladimir lived a young merchant named Ivan Dmitrich Aksionov. He had two shops and a house of his own.

Aksionov was a handsome, fair-haired, curly-headed fellow, full of fun, and very fond of singing. When quite a young man he had been given to drink, and was riotous when he had had too much; but after he married he gave up drinking, except now and then.

One summer Aksionov was going to the Nizhny Fair, and as he bade good-bye to his family, his wife said to him, "Ivan Dmitrich, do not start to-day; I have had a bad dream about you."

Aksionov laughed, and said, "You are afraid that when I get to the fair I shall go on a spree."

His wife replied: "I do not know what I am afraid of; all I know is that I had a bad dream. I dreamt you returned from the town, and when you took off your cap I saw that your hair was quite grey."

Aksionov laughed. "That's a lucky sign," said he. "See if I don't sell out all my goods, and bring you some presents from the fair."

So he said good-bye to his family, and drove away.

When he had travelled half-way, he met a merchant whom he knew, and they put up at the same inn for the night. They had some tea together, and then went to bed in adjoining rooms.

It was not Aksionov's habit to sleep late, and, wishing to travel while it was still cool, he aroused his driver before dawn, and told him to put in the horses.

Then he made his way across to the landlord of the inn (who lived in a cottage at the back), paid his bill, and continued his journey.

When he had gone about twenty-five miles, he stopped for the horses to be fed. Aksionov rested awhile in the passage of the inn, then he stepped out into the porch, and, ordering a samovar to be heated, got out his guitar and began to play.

Suddenly a troika drove up with tinkling bells and an official alighted, followed by two soldiers. He came to Aksionov and began to question him, asking him who he was and whence he came. Aksionov answered him fully, and said, "Won't you have some tea with me?" But the official went on cross-questioning him and asking him. "Where did you spend last night? Were you alone, or with a fellow-merchant? Did you see the other merchant this morning? Why did you leave the inn before dawn?"

Aksionov wondered why he was asked all these questions, but he described all that had happened, and then added, "Why do you cross-question me as if I were a thief or a robber? I am travelling on business of my own, and there is no need to question me."

Then the official, calling the soldiers, said, "I am the police-officer of this district, and I question you because the merchant with whom you spent last night has been found with his throat cut. We must search your things."

They entered the house. The soldiers and the police-officer unstrapped Aksionov's luggage and searched it. Suddenly the officer drew a knife out of a bag, crying, "Whose knife is this?"

Aksionov looked, and seeing a blood-stained knife taken from his bag, he was frightened.

"How is it there is blood on this knife?"

Aksionov tried to answer, but could hardly utter a word, and only stammered: "I—don't know—not mine." Then the police-officer said:

"This morning the merchant was found in bed with his throat cut. You are the only person who could have done it. The house was locked from inside, and no one else was there. Here is this blood-stained knife in your bag and your face and manner betray you! Tell me how you killed him, and how much money you stole?"

Aksionov swore he had not done it; that he had not seen the merchant after they had had tea together; that he had no money except eight thousand rubles of his own, and that the knife was not his. But his voice was broken, his face pale, and he trembled with fear as though he were guilty.

The police-officer ordered the soldiers to bind Aksionov and to put him in the cart. As they tied his feet together and flung him into the cart, Aksionov crossed himself and wept. His money and goods were taken from him, and he was sent to the nearest town and imprisoned there. Enquiries as to his character were made in Vladimir. The merchants and other inhabitants of that town said that in former days he used to drink and waste his time, but that he was a good man. Then the trial came on: he was charged with murdering a merchant from Ryazan, and robbing him of twenty thousand rubles.

His wife was in despair, and did not know what to believe. Her children were all quite small; one was a baby at her breast. Taking them all with her, she went to the town where her husband was in jail. At first she was not allowed to see him; but after much begging, she obtained permission from the officials, and was taken to him. When she saw her husband in prison-dress and in chains, shut up with thieves and criminals, she fell down, and did not come to her senses for a long time. Then she drew her children to her, and sat down near him. She told him of things at home, and asked about what had happened to him. He told her all, and she asked, "What can we do now?"

"We must petition the Czar not to let an innocent man perish."

His wife told him that she had sent a petition to the Czar, but it had not been accepted. Aksionov did not reply, but only looked downcast.

Then his wife said, "It was not for nothing I dreamt your hair had turned grey. You remember? You should not have started that day." And passing her fingers through his hair, she said: "Vanya dearest, tell your wife the truth; was it not you who did it?"

"So you, too, suspect me!" said Aksionov, and, hiding his face in his hands, he began to weep. Then a soldier came to say that the wife and children must go away; and Aksionov said good-bye to his family for the last time.

When they were gone, Aksionov recalled what had been said, and when he remembered that his wife also had suspected him, he said to himself, "It seems that only God can know the truth; it is to Him alone we must appeal, and from Him alone expect mercy."

And Aksionov wrote no more petitions; gave up all hope, and only prayed to God.

Aksionov was condemned to be flogged and sent to the mines. So he was flogged with a knot, and when the wounds made by the knot were healed, he was driven to Siberia with other convicts.

For twenty-six years Aksionov lived as a convict in Siberia. His hair turned white as snow, and his beard grew long, thin, and grey. All his mirth went; he stooped; he walked slowly, spoke little, and never laughed, but he often prayed.

In prison Aksionov learnt to make boots, and earned a little money, with which he bought "The Lives of the Saints." He read this book when there was light enough in the prison; and on Sundays in the prison-church he read the lessons and sang in the choir, for his voice was still good.

The prison authorities liked Aksionov for his meekness, and his fellow-prisoners respected him: they called him "Grandfather," and "The Saint." When they wanted to petition the prison authorities about anything, they always made Aksionov their spokesman, and when there were quarrels among the prisoners they came to him to put things right, and to judge the matter.

No news reached Aksionov from his home, and he did not even know if his wife and children were still alive.

One day a fresh gang of convicts came to the prison. In the evening the old prisoners collected round the new ones and asked them what towns or villages they came from, and what they were sentenced for. Among the rest Aksionov sat down near the newcomers, and listened with downcast air to what was said.

One of the new convicts, a tall, strong man of sixty, with a closely-cropped grey beard, was telling the others what he had been arrested for.

"Well, friends," he said, "I only took a horse that was tied to a sledge, and I was arrested and accused of stealing. I said I had only taken it to get home quicker, and had then let it go; besides, the driver was a personal friend of mine. So I said, 'It's all right.' 'No,' said they, 'you stole it.' But how or where I stole it they could not say. I once really did something wrong, and ought by rights to have come here long ago, but that time I was not found out. Now I have been sent here for nothing at all ... Eh, but it's lies I'm telling you; I've been to Siberia before, but I did not stay long."

"Where are you from?" asked some one.

"From Vladimir. My family are of that town. My name is Makar, and they also call me Semyonich."

Aksionov raised his head and said: "Tell me, Semyonich, do you know anything of the merchants Aksionov of Vladimir? Are they still alive?"

"Know them? Of course I do. The Aksionovs are rich, though their father is in Siberia: a sinner like ourselves, it seems! As for you, Gran'dad, how did you come here?"

Aksionov did not like to speak of his misfortune. He only sighed, and said, "For my sins I have been in prison these twenty-six years."

"What sins?" asked Makar Semyonich.

But Aksionov only said, "Well, well—I must have deserved it!" He would have said no more, but his companions told the newcomers how Aksionov came to be in Siberia; how some one had killed a merchant, and had put the knife among Aksionov's things, and Aksionov had been unjustly condemned.

When Makar Semyonich heard this, he looked at Aksionov, slapped his own knee, and exclaimed, "Well, this is wonderful! Really wonderful! But how old you've grown, Gran'dad!"

The others asked him why he was so surprised, and where he had seen Aksionov before; but Makar Semyonich did not reply. He only said: "It's wonderful that we should meet here, lads!"

These words made Aksionov wonder whether this man knew who had killed the merchant; so he said, "Perhaps, Semyonich, you have heard of that affair, or maybe you've seen me before?"

"How could I help hearing? The world's full of rumours. But it's a long time ago, and I've forgotten what I heard."

"Perhaps you heard who killed the merchant?" asked Aksionov.

Makar Semyonich laughed, and replied: "It must have been him in whose bag the knife was found! If some one else hid the knife there, 'He's not a thief till he's caught,' as the saying is. How could any one put a knife into your bag while it was under your head? It would surely have woke you up."

When Aksionov heard these words, he felt sure this was the man who had killed the merchant. He rose and went away. All that night Aksionov lay awake. He felt terribly unhappy, and all sorts of images rose in his mind. There was the image of his wife as she was when he parted from her to go to the fair. He saw her as if she were present; her face and her eyes rose before him; he heard her speak and laugh. Then he saw his children, quite little, as they were at that time: one with a little cloak on, another at his mother's breast. And then he remembered himself as he used to be—young and merry. He remembered how he sat playing the guitar in the porch of the inn where he was arrested, and how free from care he had been. He saw, in his mind, the place where he was flogged, the executioner, and the people standing around; the chains, the convicts, all the twenty-six years of his prison life, and his premature old age. The thought of it all made him so wretched that he was ready to kill himself.

"And it's all that villain's doing!" thought Aksionov. And his anger was so great against Makar Semyonich that he longed for vengeance, even if he himself should perish for it. He kept repeating prayers all night, but could get no peace. During the day he did not go near Makar Semyonich, nor even look at him.

A fortnight passed in this way. Aksionov could not sleep at night, and was so miserable that he did not know what to do.

One night as he was walking about the prison he noticed some earth that came rolling out from under one of the shelves on which the prisoners slept. He stopped to see what it was. Suddenly Makar Semyonich crept out from under the shelf, and looked up at Aksionov with frightened face. Aksionov tried to pass without looking at him, but Makar seized his hand and told him that he had dug a hole under the wall, getting rid of the earth by putting it into his high-boots, and emptying it out every day on the road when the prisoners were driven to their work.

"Just you keep quiet, old man, and you shall get out too. If you blab, they'll flog the life out of me, but I will kill you first."

Aksionov trembled with anger as he looked at his enemy. He drew his hand away, saying, "I have no wish to escape, and you have no need to kill me; you killed me long ago! As to telling of you—I may do so or not, as God shall direct."

Next day, when the convicts were led out to work, the convoy soldiers noticed that one or other of the prisoners emptied some earth out of his boots. The prison was searched and the tunnel found. The Governor came and questioned all the prisoners to find out who had dug the hole. They all denied any knowledge of it. Those who knew would not betray Makar Semyonich, knowing he would be flogged almost to death. At last the Governor turned to Aksionov whom he knew to be a just man, and said:

"You are a truthful old man; tell me, before God, who dug the hole?"

Makar Semyonich stood as if he were quite unconcerned, looking at the Governor and not so much as glancing at Aksionov. Aksionov's lips and hands trembled, and for a long time he could not utter a word. He thought, "Why should I screen him who ruined my life? Let him pay for what I have suffered. But if I tell, they will probably flog the life out of him, and maybe I suspect him wrongly. And, after all, what good would it be to me?"

"Well, old man," repeated the Governor, "tell me the truth: who has been digging under the wall?"

Aksionov glanced at Makar Semyonich, and said, "I cannot say, your honour. It is not God's will that I should tell! Do what you like with me; I am your hands."

However much the Governor tried, Aksionov would say no more, and so the matter had to be left.

That night, when Aksionov was lying on his bed and just beginning to doze, some one came quietly and sat down on his bed. He peered through the darkness and recognised Makar.

"What more do you want of me?" asked Aksionov. "Why have you come here?"

Makar Semyonich was silent. So Aksionov sat up and said, "What do you want? Go away, or I will call the guard!"

Makar Semyonich bent close over Aksionov, and whispered, "Ivan Dmitrich, forgive me!"

"What for?" asked Aksionov.

"It was I who killed the merchant and hid the knife among your things. I meant to kill you too, but I heard a noise outside, so I hid the knife in your bag and escaped out of the window."

Aksionov was silent, and did not know what to say. Makar Semyonich slid off the bed-shelf and knelt upon the ground. "Ivan Dmitrich," said he, "forgive me! For the love of God, forgive me! I will confess that it was I who killed the merchant, and you will be released and can go to your home."

"It is easy for you to talk," said Aksionov, "but I have suffered for you these twenty-six years. Where could I go to now? . . . My wife is dead, and my children have forgotten me. I have nowhere to go . . ."

Makar Semyonich did not rise, but beat his head on the floor. "Ivan Dmitrich, forgive me!" he cried. "When they flogged me with the knot it was not so hard to bear as it is to see you now . . . yet you had pity on me, and did not tell. For Christ's sake forgive me, wretch that I am!" And he began to sob.

When Aksionov heard him sobbing he, too, began to weep. "God will forgive you!" said he. "Maybe I am a hundred times worse than you." And at these words his heart grew light, and the longing for home left him. He no longer had any desire to leave the prison, but only hoped for his last hour to come.

In spite of what Aksionov had said, Makar Semyonich confessed, his guilt. But when the order for his release came, Aksionov was already dead.

LEO TOLSTOY

TOO DEAR

This short story is humorous in execution (a pun, as you will see when you read the story) but also serious in intent, as Tolstoy was vehemently opposed to the notion of capital punishment. It is a retelling of a story by the French writer Guy de Maupassant. It was first published in 1897.

N ear the borders of France and Italy, on the shore of the Mediterranean Sea, lies a tiny little kingdom called Monaco. Many a small
country town can boast more inhabitants than this kingdom, for
there are only about seven thousand of them all told, and if all the land
in the kingdom were divided there would not be an acre for each inhab-
itant. But in this toy kingdom there is a real kinglet; and he has a palace,
and courtiers, and ministers, and a bishop, and generals, and an army.

It is not a large army, only sixty men in all, but still it is an army.
There were also taxes in this kingdom as elsewhere: a tax on tobacco,
and on wine and spirits and a poll-tax. But though the people there
drink and smoke as people do in other countries, there are so few of
them that the King would have been hard put to it to feed his courtiers

and officials and to keep himself, if he had not found a new and special source of revenue. This special revenue comes from a gaming house, where people play roulette. People play, and whether they win or lose the keeper always gets a percentage on the turnover; and out of his profits he pays a large sum to the King. The reason he pays so much is that it is the only such gambling establishment left in Europe. Some of the little German Sovereigns used to keep gaming houses of the same kind, but some years ago they were forbidden to do so. The reason they were stopped was because these gaming houses did so much harm. A man would come and try his luck, then he would risk all he had and lose it, then he would even risk money that did not belong to him and lose that too, and then, in despair, he would drown or shoot himself. So the Germans forbade their rulers to make money in this way; but there was no one to stop the King of Monaco, and he remained with a monopoly of the business.

So now every one who wants to gamble goes to Monaco. Whether they win or lose, the King gains by it. "You can't earn stone palaces by honest labour," as the proverb says; and the Kinglet of Monaco knows it is a dirty business, but what is he to do? He has to live; and to draw a revenue from drink and from tobacco is also not a nice thing. So he lives and reigns, and rakes in the money, and holds his court with all the ceremony of a real king.

He has his coronation, his levees; he rewards, sentences, and pardons, and he also has his reviews, councils, laws, and courts of justice: just like other kings, only all on a smaller scale.

Now it happened a few years ago that a murder was committed in this toy King's domains. The people of that kingdom are peaceable, and such a thing had not happened before. The judges assembled with much ceremony and tried the case in the most judicial manner. There were judges, and prosecutors, and jurymen, and barristers. They argued and judged, and at last they condemned the criminal to have his head cut off as the law directs. So far so good. Next they submitted the sentence to the King. The King read the sentence and confirmed it. "If the fellow must be executed, execute him."

There was only one hitch in the matter; and that was that they had neither a guillotine for cutting heads off, nor an executioner. The Ministers considered the matter, and decided to address an inquiry to the French Government, asking whether the French could not lend them a machine and an expert to cut off the criminal's head; and if so, would the French kindly inform them what the cost would be. The letter was sent. A week later the reply came: a machine and an expert could be supplied, and the cost would be 16,000 francs. This was laid before the King. He thought it over. Sixteen thousand francs! "The wretch is not worth the money," said he. "Can't it be done, somehow, cheaper? Why 16,000 francs is more than two francs a head on the whole population. The people won't stand it, and it may cause a riot!"

So a Council was called to consider what could be done; and it was decided to send a similar inquiry to the King of Italy. The French Government is republican, and has no proper respect for kings; but the King of Italy was a brother monarch, and might be induced to do the thing cheaper. So the letter was written, and a prompt reply was received.

The Italian Government wrote that they would have pleasure in supplying both a machine and an expert; and the whole cost would be 12,000 francs, including travelling expenses. This was cheaper, but still it seemed too much. The rascal was really not worth the money. It would still mean nearly two francs more per head on the taxes. Another Council was called. They discussed and considered how it could be done with less expense. Could not one of the soldiers perhaps be got to do it in a rough and homely fashion? The General was called and was asked: "Can't you find us a soldier who would cut the man's head off? In war they don't mind killing people. In fact, that is what they are trained for." So the General talked it over with the soldiers to see whether one of them would not undertake the job. But none of the soldiers would do it. "No," they said, "we don't know how to do it; it is not a thing we have been taught."

What was to be done? Again the Ministers considered and reconsidered. They assembled a Commission, and a Committee, and a Sub-Committee, and at last they decided that the best thing would be to alter the death sentence to one of imprisonment for life. This would enable the King to show his mercy, and it would come cheaper.

The King agreed to this, and so the matter was arranged. The only hitch now was that there was no suitable prison for a man sentenced for life. There was a small lock-up where people were sometimes kept temporarily, but there was no strong prison fit for permanent use. However, they managed to find a place that would do, and they put the young fellow there and placed a guard over him. The guard had to watch the criminal, and had also to fetch his food from the palace kitchen.

The prisoner remained there month after month till a year had passed. But when a year had passed, the Kinglet, looking over the account of his income and expenditure one day, noticed a new item of expenditure. This was for the keep of the criminal; nor was it a small item either. There was a special guard, and there was also the man's food. It came to more than 600 francs a year. And the worst of it was that the fellow was still young and healthy, and might live for fifty years. When one came to reckon it up, the matter was serious. It would never do. So the King summoned his Ministers and said to them:

"You must find some cheaper way of dealing with this rascal. The present plan is too expensive." And the Ministers met and considered and reconsidered, till one of them said: "Gentlemen, in my opinion we must dismiss the guard." "But then," rejoined another Minister, "the fellow will run away." "Well," said the first speaker, "let him run away, and be hanged to him!" So they reported the result of their deliberations to the Kinglet, and he agreed with them. The guard was dismissed, and they waited to see what would happen. All that happened was that at dinner-time the criminal came out, and, not finding his guard, he went to the King's kitchen to fetch his own dinner. He took what was given him, returned to the prison, shut the door on himself, and stayed inside. Next day the same thing occurred. He went for his food at the proper time; but as for running away, he did not show the least sign of it! What was to be done? They considered the matter again.

"We shall have to tell him straight out," said they "that we do not want to keep him." So the Minister of Justice had him brought before him.

"Why do you not run away?" said the Minister. "There is no guard to keep you. You can go where you like, and the King will not mind."

"I daresay the King would not mind," replied the man, "but I have nowhere to go. What can I do? You have ruined my character by your sentence, and people will turn their backs on me. Besides, I have got out of the way of working. You have treated me badly. It is not fair. In the first place, when once you sentenced me to death you ought to have executed me; but you did not do it. That is one thing. I did not complain about that. Then you sentenced me to imprisonment for life and put a guard to bring me my food; but after a time you took him away again and I had to fetch my own food. Again I did not complain. But now you actually want me to go away! I can't agree to that. You may do as you like, but I won't go away!"

What was to be done? Once more the Council was summoned. What course could they adopt? The man would not go. They reflected and considered. The only way to get rid of him was to offer him a pension. And so they reported to the King. "There is nothing else for it," said they; "we must get rid of him somehow." The sum fixed was 600 francs, and this was announced to the prisoner.

"Well," said he, "I don't mind, so long as you undertake to pay it regularly. On that condition I am willing to go."

So the matter was settled. He received one-third of his annuity in advance, and left the King's dominions. It was only a quarter of an hour by rail; and he emigrated, and settled just across the frontier, where he bought a bit of land, started market-gardening, and now lives comfortably. He always goes at the proper time to draw his pension. Having received it, he goes to the gaming tables, stakes two or three francs, sometimes wins and sometimes loses, and then returns home. He lives peaceably and well.

It is a good thing that he did not commit his crime in a country where they do not grudge expense to cut a man's head off, or to keeping him in prison for life.